Praise for

ANNE KELLEHER

"I found it one of those books which keeps one's eyes glued to the page…an outstandin[illegible]e of work."
—Andre Nort[illegible]ophecy

"…displays vivid imagination."
—*Publishers Weekly*

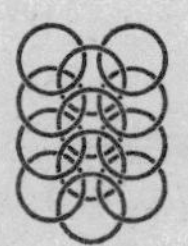

"…engaging and powerful."
—*Voya* on *The Misbegotten King*

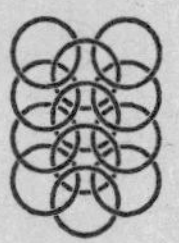

"Fascinating—a most ingenious blend of science fiction and fantasy."
—*New York Times* bestselling author Marion Zimmer Bradley on *Daughter of Prophecy*

SILVER'S EDGE

ANNE KELLEHER

www.LUNA-Books.com

First edition June 2004

SILVER'S EDGE

ISBN 0-373-81114-4

This edition published by arrangement with Harlequin Books S.A.

www.LUNA-Books.com

Printed in U.S.A.

This book is dedicated, with love,
to my son Jamie, my intrepid little adventurer—
may you always believe that tall buildings
are made to be leaped with a single bound.

Glossary of People and Places

Faerie—the sidhe word for their own world. It includes the Wastelands
The Shadowlands—the sidhe word for the mortal world
The Wastelands—that part of Faerie to which the goblins have been banished
Lyonesse—legendary lost land that is said to have lain to the east of Faerie

Brynhyvar—the country that, in the mortal world, overlaps with Faerie
The Otherworld—the mortal name for Faerie
TirNa'lugh—the lands of light; the shining lands—mortal name for Faerie; becoming archaic
The Summerlands—place where mortals go at death

Humbria—mortal country across the Murhevnian Sea to the east of Brynhyvar
Lacquilea—mortal country lying to the south of Brynhyvar

Killcairn—Nessa's village
Killcrag—neighboring village to the south
Killcarrick—lake and the keep

Alemandine—Queen of sidhe
Xerruw—Goblin King
Vinaver—Alemandine's younger twin sister and the rightful Queen
Artimour—Alemandine's half-mortal half brother
Gloriana—mother of Vinaver, Alemandine and Artimour
Timias—Gloriana's chief councilor and the unacknowledged father of Alemandine and Vinaver
Eponea—Mistress of the Queen's Horses
Delphinea—Eponea's daughter

Finuviel—Vinaver's son by the god Herne; rightful King of Faerie
Hudibras—Alemandine's consort
Gorlias, Philomemnon, Berillian—councilors to the Queen
Petri—Delphinea's servant gremlin
Khouri—leader of the gremlin revolt and plot to steal the Caul
Nessa—nineteen-year-old daughter of Dougal, the blacksmith of Killcairn
Dougal—Nessa's father; Essa's husband; stolen into Faerie by Vinaver
Griffin—Dougal's eighteen-year-old apprentice
Donnor, Duke of Gar—overlord of Killcairn and surrounding country; uncle of the mad King and leader of the rebellion against him
Cadwyr, Duke of Allovale—Donnor's nephew and heir
Cecily of Mochmorna—Donnor's wife; heiress to the throne of Brynhyvar
Kian of Garn—Donnor's First Knight
Hoell—mad King of Brynhyvar
Merle—Queen of Brynhyvar; princess of Humbria
Renvahr, Duke of Longborth—brother of Queen Merle; elected Protector of the Realm of Brynhyvar
Granny Wren—wicce woman of Killcairn
Granny Molly—wicce woman of Killcrag
Engus—blacksmith of Killcarrick
Uwen—Kian's second in command

The Hag—immortal who dwells in the rocks and caves below Faerie; the moonstone globe was stolen from her when the Caul was forged
Herne—immortal who dwells within the Faerie forests, from which he rides out on Samhain night, leading the Wild Hunt across the worlds

Great Mother—mortal name for the Hag
The Horned One—mortal name for Herne

ACKNOWLEDGMENTS

Nothing I have ever written
has not owed a great deal to the people
who have to put up with me while I write.
Thanks go to my agent, Jennifer Jackson,
who lit a candle just as the lights were going out;
to Patrice Fitzgerald, Olivia Lawrence,
Robert Becerra and Laura Sebastian-Coleman, who
gave me feedback and wonderful suggestions;
to Anne Sheridan, who proofread the final draft—
any mistakes are mine; to Laura at *The Purple Rose*
and Bobbi at *Maggie Dailey's* for providing tea and
source material; to Loreena McKennitt, Julee Glaub
and Bruce Springsteen, whose music made me
see the OtherWorld; to GTimeJoe, who kept
my head in the clouds; to the folks in the CT
Over 40 chat room on AOL for being so unflaggingly
supportive even when I was at my most cranky;
to the wonderful members of the FMC for
cheerleading; to my darling daughters, Kate,
Meg and Libby, who bore the brunt of dishes,
laundry and trash; and finally, to Donny.
You made it all possible.

PROLOGUE

Then

Down dusty roads the child fled, heart drumming in her thin chest like the gallop of a thousand horses, chased from sleep by hulking hordes of goblins who grabbed at her with gleaming teeth and outstretched claws. She startled awake, the echoes of her dream screams dying in her ears, crying aloud at the sight of the banked grate, where the coals glowed like red eyes in the dark room. A cold wind was howling in the trees, and the window rattled in its frame. A gusty draft stirred the curtains just as something crashed onto the roof above her head. She cried again, louder now, and yanked her thick woolen blanket higher, the rest of her small body stiffening with dread, the whole house, it seemed, shuddering under the impact.

"Nessie? You all right?" Her father's broad face loomed out of the shadows of the doorway, his white nightshirt luminous in the gray light. He came closer, feet bare, the black hair on his chest curling out of the open collar of his nightshirt. A dark haze of beard shadowed his chin. Disheveled and bleary-eyed as he was, the sight of him relaxed her instantly, even as the sound of something scraping against the windowpane made her eyes widen once more.

"Papa, the goblins," she moaned. "They're chasing me—there's one outside my window—"

"Hush, now." His voice was a gravelly rumble as compelling as distant thunder. "That's nothing but the branch I should've had the sense to cut down long before this. The wind brought it down, that's all. There're no goblins outside, not now, not ever."

Cautiously the child peered over the homespun sheet, which was soft with many washings. Her father had spoken, her father who was the rock at the center of her world. Her father was Dougal the village blacksmith and the best armorer for leagues around. Even the mighty Duke of Gar came to Dougal when he wanted a new sword or dagger. "But, Papa," she whispered, "Granny Wren, tonight, at the Gathering, she said the goblins come a-hunting little children—little children is what they like best to eat."

With a stifled hiss of exasperation, the blacksmith crossed the small space to his daughter's bed and knelt on the ragged scrap of rug. "Ah, little one, Granny Wren likes to hear herself talk. It's how she knows she's still alive, I think, for there's no other reason for half the things she says. But come now, didn't you also hear her speak of Bran? Bran

Brownbeard, the greatest smith there ever was, in either Brynhyvar or the OtherWorld, the place called TirNa'lugh?" He paused. Her dark eyes were bright in her rosy little face and she shook her head, falling readily into the spell his whisper wove. "Perhaps you'd already gone to sleep by then? Hmm? Such a tired little girl I carried home tonight." He smiled and smoothed the dark, damp curls off her forehead, his thick slab of a hand bigger than her entire face. "Bran Brownbeard was a mighty mortal man, who with the help of the Queen of the sidhe and her magic, forged the Silver Caul that lies upon the moonstone globe in the great palace in the very heart of the OtherWorld."

"What's a call, Papa?"

"A caul, sweetling. It's like—like a net, or loosely woven blanket, made of purest silver."

"How'd he do that, Papa?"

"He took silver, for silver hurts the goblin, and the sidhe, too, more than anything else—it burns them and that's why a mortal man was needed to do it—and with the sidhe Queen of the OtherWorld, who hates the Goblin King, for he would take her kingdom if he could, together they worked great magic and made a powerful web of finest strands of purest silver. They called it the Silver Caul, and the Queen took it to her palace, and there she placed it over a great green moonstone, and there it lies to this very day, keeping the goblins out of Brynhyvar."

"Why does silver hurt the goblins?"

"I don't know rightly, sweetling. But it's why we wear these—" He fumbled at the neck of his nightshirt and dangled his silver amulet on its leather cord before her.

"That's why we must never take it off?"

"Exactly. The silver protects us."

"But, Papa, if the Silver Caul keeps the goblins out, why must we wear silver, too?"

Because there are worse things than goblins, he nearly replied. It was the race that called themselves the sidhe that were the worst of all, for they seduced mortals with promises of otherworldly delight, leading them to vanish out of sight and time. Your own mother was snared by one of them, he almost said, but he caught himself. They were treading dangerously close to questions for which he must carefully consider the replies. He pushed aside the curtain and peered out into the night. It was coming up to dawn. The low-lying clouds overlay a sky of lighter gray. Time to stir the oats he'd set to cook last night in the great iron kettle nestled in the warm forge, to check for damage left by the now-passing storm, to try to decide what to tell the child if her questions led them to the subject of her mother, and if she were old enough to know even part of the truth. "Not now, sweetheart. I'll tell you the story later. I promise. But 'tis so late, it's early, and I must be about my work. You go back to sleep for a bit, it's too cold to be running about early today." He kissed each one of her grubby little fingers in turn, noticing how pink they were beneath a thin layer of grime, then rose to go. He resolved to remember to drag the bathtub from the shed beside the kitchen before nightfall. Her eyelids were already beginning to droop.

"But, Papa?" Her voice stopped him at the door. "The Silver Caul? That's what keeps the goblins away? For real?"

"There are no goblins in Brynhyvar, Nessa. I promise. So back to sleep with you, now, like a good girl."

"Yes, Papa." She shut her eyes with a sigh.

He ducked his head beneath the uneven frame of the low doorway and paused to look over his shoulder at the little face lying on the pillow. Dearer to him than all he owned, dearer than life, she was. He had lost her mother to the sidhe, and he was determined such a fate should never befall her daughter. Such a headstrong little thing, she could be, so like her mother, curious and engaging. But if she seemed more interested in the fire and the forge, hammer and tongs, than in the tools of more womanly pursuits, so much the better. Better her mind be full of iron, he thought, than the sort of empty-headed nonsense which had contributed to her mother's disappearance.

The child curled on her side, one round cheek pillowed on her open palm, a scrap of threadbare blanket nestled beneath her chin. A line from an ancient lullaby ran through his head. *The might of Bran protects thee, the Faerie Queen shall bless thee, no goblin claw will rend thee.* But he took no comfort in it, for he expected no blessing from that quarter. He would see to it that if ever goblin or sidhe touched so much as a hair of his daughter's head, she would be well-prepared to defend herself.

1

Now

The fat spider leapt lightly along the serrated edges of the stone spikes which rose like a lizard's spine along the high back of the throne of the Goblin King. It scampered across the rough stone, anchored from above by a nearly invisible filament, darting just inches from the leathery maw of Xerruw, the Goblin King, who leaned upon one elbow and watched it with detached interest. So easily he could flick it into oblivion with a snap of his tongue. Its legs waved frantically as it manipulated the gossamer strands, as if it sensed a predator. But, though he watched it with a hungry intent, Xerruw's mind was not bent on food. *Spin, little spider. You have reminded me of the value of a trap.*

A smoky fire burned fitfully in the stone pit in the center of the cavernous hall, and a dull gray light filtered through the arrow slits set within the soaring arches of its central tower. A cold draft whined down from the upper reaches, but Xerruw, if he noticed the chill at all, gave no sign. He sprawled across his massive throne, which had been carved out of a boulder bigger than the huts of men, in that last happy age when the goblins reigned supreme and the sidhe cowered beneath the banks of rivers and glens, hiding in the noon, hunted at night like luminous fish flitting through the dark depths of the primeval forests. Those were the days of glory, he reflected, as he picked his teeth with the fingerbone of a human child.

It was an ancient fingerbone, worn sliver-fine from long years of gnawing—they'd not been fortunate to find a child roaming in these lands for more time than he'd care to remember—but he liked to fancy that it retained a hint of the sweet flavor of young man-meat, enough to envision a time still to come when, free of the fetters of sidhe magic, his kind could hunt both the human herd and the sidhe at will. So he watched the spider, sucking on his bone, while in the niches carved into the rock beneath his seat, three hags muttered among themselves as they crouched restlessly on their nests of lumpy eggs, ceaselessly complaining of the lack of meat.

His gray eyes were nearly closed, and he appeared lost in thought, his attention wholly focused on the spider, but he knew that three of the six guards dicing opposite the hags were cheating on the others, and that the goblins sharpening their weapons closest by the door mumbled mutiny. Let them, he mused, enjoying the worn smoothness of the bone against his teeth. Long years he'd sat, brooding on his throne, biding his time, plotting his strategy, awaiting the very news he'd received yesterday.

For the sidhe Queen was in whelp—the sidhe witch who dared to style herself Queen of all Faerie. It was only a matter of time now, and her power would falter, her magic naturally diminish as the birth approached, giving him at last an opening, a foothold, a chance to once again claim all of Faerie for his own. In the past weeks, he had begun to sense it—a subtle but unmistakable weakening in the complex webs of power which held the border of the Wastelands, where her forces had driven his kind after the last war. And this time, they would attack—not just with blades and spears, arrows and bolts, the weapons of sheer brute force. No, this time he would try something worthy of a sidhe's own cunning. He would succeed where the others of his kind had failed, catching the complacent sidhe off guard when they were most critically vulnerable. Like the spider, he mused. And like the spider, he would weave his own trap and wait.

A chill draft suddenly blasted through the hall, and the hags screeched and cackled, rocking back and forth on their haunches to protect their eggs. The blast of air was accompanied by a thunderous boom—the sound of the inner gates closing. The scouting party had returned. But even as he was about to shift positions and settle more comfortably to await their report, Xerruw bolted upright, for he caught, just beneath the acrid smoke of the fire, a scent, at once coppery and sweet, earthy and sour, threading like a strand of yarn through the smooth texture of the air. He snarled in the direction of the hags, and rose to his feet as Iruk, the Captain of his Goblin Guard, strode in, his fellows jogging behind him, a blur of dull gray limbs and black metal in unison. The guards stopped gaming and sharpening, and looked up, sniffing expectantly. Then the hags caught the scent and their keening cries of pleasure erupted in a hungry harmony. A snarl and another hard glare silenced them, but they licked their lips and stared back at him with eager eyes.

"What is this you bring?" he asked suspiciously, for the unmistakable aroma of man was in the air, and he knew already what lay within the hide-bound burden Iruk bore across his shoulders.

"Great Xerruw." Iruk circled around the fire pit, stopping at the very base of the throne. He glanced at the hags, who squatted over their nests, crooning softly, as though he half expected them to leap at him. He knelt, staggering a little beneath the weight of his burden, then bent his neck and let it roll to the first step of the throne. He pulled away the hide and the still body of a human male sprawled at the base of Xerruw's throne, fresh blood congealing on his skull and at his throat.

Xerruw stared down at the offering. His nostrils quivered and saliva flooded his mouth. But even as a ravenous hunger swelled from the pit of his belly, making it nearly impossible not to rip off the closest limb, misgiving made him raise his head and scan the faces of the guards who stared back at him with unabashed glee. Saliva ran down their jaws, and their maws quivered, nostrils flaring. The last time they'd tasted human meat was countless ages past. It was a testimony to their allegiance to him that they'd returned the carcass intact. One of them was missing.

He looked down at the dead human. It had been a big male, dark and hairy, with burly arms and massive shoulders. Strong on him, beneath the scent of blood and flesh and sweat and urine, hung the smell of smoke and burning metal. His face and beard were damp and he was nearly naked except for linen breeches and the amulet he wore around his neck. In the unsteady light, it shone with a clear, soft gleam. Xerruw's lip curled and his eyes narrowed at the sight. "Silver," he muttered. "This should not be." Silver was anathema to sidhe and to goblin, humankind's only sure defense against goblin teeth and sidhe magic. "I like this not," he said at last, shaking his heavy head. "Where did you find it?"

"By the lake. Upon the farthest shore. He did not know he'd slid across the border. We took him unawares." Iruk dragged one claw through the gelatinous clot on the human's neck, and held it out to Xerruw. The scent of the fresh kill exploded like fire through Xerruw's veins and he licked his lips without thinking.

"Do you not see the silver?" Xerruw gestured down.

Iruk shrugged. "Base metal, most like. We carried him here well-wrapped—there was no problem." He threw the clot at his lord's feet, and gazed up at him expectantly, awaiting some sign of acceptance of the kill. Xerruw squatted down, coiling his tail beneath his haunches, sniffing suspiciously. Iruk was probably right. The amulet must indeed contain a fair portion of base metal. He examined the clothing the human wore. The linen was coarse, the heavily muscled body bore testimony to a lifetime of hard labor. But the hide they'd used to wrap the human in was slightly singed where the amulet had rested, and above it, he could feel a tingle emanating from it, a shimmer in the air. It had potency, enough, then. The amulet must be cast into the deepest part of the lake, where he instinctively knew the dark waters would neutralize its corrosive effect. He pulled his dagger from his sheath and cut the leather cord around the neck. He held the amulet out to Iruk by the cord.

Iruk stepped back with a hiss.

"Throw this in the lake whence it came." He pushed it closer to Iruk's face.

Iruk hissed again as the amulet swung near his jaw, jerking his head well out of reach.

"So maybe this metal is not so base, my Captain?"

"So maybe this is not so much mortal meat, my lord. Shall I throw it in the lake, too?"

"Where is Bukai?"

Their eyes collided in a challenge, as a low growl of impatience rolled through the growing crowd.

"He fell beneath the water. The mortal killed him."

Xerruw snarled, low in his throat, and shook the amulet. "Take it." With a growl, Iruk grabbed it by the cord and dropped it into a pouch he wore at his waist. It made a slight hiss as the troll-hide closed around it. Xerruw smiled grimly. He bent and ripped a single ear off the mortal with a languid wave of his claw, and, holding it high, shook it, then crammed it into his mouth for all to see. He ripped the other ear off and tossed it to Iruk. "Get that thing out of here now," he spat out through the mouthful of flesh and blood and gristle.

Iruk nodded, satisfied, turned on his heel and stalked from the hall.

A cheer erupted from the doorways, where the inhabitants of his castle were creeping forward from their dens, drawn by the seductive scent. The hags exploded into gleeful shrieks, and the rest of the scouting party raised their arms and leapt over the fire pit, tails whipping high, joining the dance. Ogres and goblins bellowed, and more hags rushed from the cellars below to prepare the feast. He reached down, and dragged one long claw through the gelatinous clot, which oozed a metallic-smelling steam, and licked the blood slowly, thoughtfully, while his court capered and pranced around him.

The silver's clear gleam troubled him, the apparent ease with which the human had slipped into Faerie troubled him. He stared down at the hide, where the silver had left a deep mark. Amid the general rejoicing, he felt wary, suspicious. He unfolded his long frame and settled down into his throne, where the spider rested in the middle of a meticulous web. What could account for the presence of silver in Faerie?

The spider scampered higher, as the cacophony rose. Xerruw put the fragile fingerbone in his mouth once more, and crunched down harder than he intended. At once, it snapped into a shower of shards, dissolving into dust on his tongue. He gazed at the stub remaining between his fingertips. There were more goblins now, soldiers from the barracks, hags from the innermost recesses of the keep, capering around the fire pit, leaping high over the flames. Let his people dance. Perhaps this human was a sign—a sign that soon all of Faerie would be his. His mind reeled, as instinct overwhelmed reason. The sweet human scent was sweeping him away into an ecstasy of expectation. He looked around the crowded hall, and forgot the puzzle of the silver amulet, forgot the sidhe witch Queen, forgot everything but the ripe rich aroma that thickened around his head like fog. The bloodlust surged through his veins like a burst dam.

We must grow strong. We must all grow strong. And we will grow strong. He rose to his full height and joined in the rising chorus with a roar. "We will all grow strong on human meat!"

2

"I'm going and you can't stop me." The flicker of the lone lantern caused shadows to quiver across Nessa's face, but the expression in her dark eyes was one of steady purpose.

Griffin closed his own against thumb and forefinger, rubbing away the dry grit of exhaustion. The fat candle within the lantern hissed and spat a gob of tallow. It landed with a sizzle on the dead goblin, which lay between them, slack-faced and limp-limbed, on the straw-strewn dirt of the lean-to next to Farmer Breslin's barn. The stink of singed hair mingled with the putrid odor already rising from the corpse, and Griffin had to swallow hard against a wave of nausea. "It's madness and I can't let you. Your father would kill me—"

"Not if I kill you first." She gave him one hard look, shot from under full brows which arched in a feminine replica of her father's own, then looked down at the corpse, assessed it as dispassionately as she might a lump of ore, then shifted to a more comfortable squat beside the body.

The villagers' decision to place the body in the sty had less to do with proximity or place than concern for the fact that all animals downwind of it within a certain radius whimpered and pulled on their tethers, or pushed against whatever confined them, and it was hoped that the odor might be masked somewhat by the smell emanating from the sty. But the earthy aroma of the pigs was like perfume compared to the reeking miasma which clogged Griffin's nose. He steeled himself against the stench, and leaned over the body, his voice a husky whisper. "What if you can't find him? What if you can't get back? What if everyone thinks you're mad when you return and won't have anything to do with you? Why can't you just wait for the Duke's men?"

In spite of her obvious resolve, Nessa grimaced as she gingerly touched the clammy flesh which hung slack on the goblin's face, and this time, the look she shot him was one of utter disdain. "What do I care what they think? Those old biddies do nothing but whisper about me, but they were all quick to rush to the house tonight, weren't they? Bothersome hens—it was just a chance to poke their noses into the pantry and the kitchen and the bedrooms and make nasty comments about you and me. They don't care about Papa, they care about sticking their faces in other people's troubles—not so they can *do* anything, but so they can talk about it. And the Duke just raised his standard against the King. How much time do you think he'll spare a missing smith?"

"I should think he'll make time for a dead goblin. If he doesn't come himself, you know he'll send some—"

"Maybe, eventually. But by that time, it may be too late. My father could be dead. Or lost forever, like my mother." Her mouth hardened and she reached into the leather sack for the small ax.

"What are you doing, Nessa?" Griffin stared at her in horrified disbelief. These last few hours were like a long bad dream that refused to end. It had started when Jemmy, the herder's boy, had run up from the lake shouting that a goblin lay floating in the water.

The village had reacted as one body, men and women and children, all running pell-mell to the sandy shore, where the thick, hide-clad corpse bumped up against the traps set just at knee depth. The men had waded in, dragging it away from the traps with branches, teasing it ashore. A general gasp had arisen when they'd turned the body over, and the stuff of nightmare and legend lay revealed. Long rows of serrated, jagged teeth in a wide leathery maw, slitted eyes and ears like bat wings, and a hard, leathery hide that ended at each hand in three-inch claws. A jagged wound, curiously singed around the edges, disgorged the contents of its entrails, purplish and glistening with foul-smelling slime.

It was decided that despite the lateness of the hour—the last rays of the sun had long since been swallowed up by shadows—a messenger must be sent to Killcarrick Keep, where it was hoped that the Sheriff, if not the Duke himself, would be in residence. It was during the discussion as to who should go that Nessa had raised her clear voice in one anxious question. "Where's my father?"

But Dougal, who had left the smithy much earlier that afternoon than was his custom, ostensibly to check the very traps that his apprentice, Griffin, had set just that morning, was nowhere to be found. Despite their usual censure, a flock of clucking women descended on Nessa, while the men patted Griffin's back and muttered encouragement. He'd been left standing at the smithy gate, while the tide of women swept past, bearing Nessa inside in a swirl of skirts and a flutter of shawls, watching it all with a growing sense of foreboding. It was common knowledge that Nessa's own mother had been swept into the OtherWorld, carried away by a knight of the sidhe who'd induced her to remove her silver, and Nessa had always been regarded as slightly touched, slightly tainted, as if she had possibly inherited some susceptibility they did not want to share. Dougal's unorthodox method of raising his daughter had drawn harsh criticism, too, for while the goodwives of the village were inclined to be sympathetic to the motherless girl, they strongly disapproved of the freedom he allowed her, the smithing he'd taught her. Each of them had approached the blacksmith about taking the girl under a wing; all of them had been rebuffed. Dougal was above noticing most of it, but these last few years had been hard on Nessa. Griffin had watched her bear it, with the same sort of silence as she watched them argue that there was only a coincidental connection between the goblin and the smith's disappearance, since there was no sign of Dougal's amulet.

But Griffin could well imagine the emotions swirling behind Nessa's shadowed eyes. At nineteen, she was part sister, part rival, part secret love. She adored her father—that had been clear to him from the very beginning, when he'd joined the household as a twelve-year-old apprentice when she was barely ten—and endured the growing distance between herself and the other villagers stoically. In a world without Dougal, Griffin wondered what would become of Nessa. Under Dougal's tutelage, she had gained much proficiency as a smith, and was, to Griffin's mortification, his equal in skill if not in strength. The smithy would of course be hers, someday, on Dougal's death. But was she truly equipped to make her way in the world, he wondered, as he shooed a gaggle of curious giggling girls from her tiny bedroom. She was so different from all the other girls, possessing only what knowledge of housekeeping as Dougal had—what villager would marry her? And how many of Dougal's customers would frequent a female blacksmith? She would need a man to handle the heavier jobs. That thought gave him a grim satisfaction, for he had fallen in love with Nessa years ago. But now was not the time to think of any possible future. Here was an opportunity at last to show how much he cared for her. And so he hung back, hovering, watching, listening, wondering how best to help, turning the possibilities over in his mind.

The day had begun badly, for something was clearly weighing upon Dougal from the moment he got up. At breakfast, Nessa asked her father who the two visitors were late last night, two visitors Griffin hadn't even heard come in. Dougal replied with the same hard look as the one with which she'd just answered Griffin. At Griffin's first opportunity, as he was putting the breakfast dishes to soak, and Nessa was hauling in a sack of coal for the fire, he asked her, "What visitors? When?"

"Last night—long after you were snoring. If you hadn't been so quick abed you'd have heard them, too." She answered him in a quick whisper, for Dougal had said little at breakfast. His eyes were hooded, his mouth grim.

"I hauled ore all day," he protested. "Did you get a look at them? How long were they here?"

"Not long. Papa knew one of them, for I heard him cry 'You!' Then they lowered their voices, and spoke a while but I couldn't hear what they were saying underneath your snores. Then they left—and I heard him working, long into the night."

"What was he mak—" he started to ask, but Dougal bellowed for the coal, and Nessa hefted her burden. There was no further opportunity to ask more, and when Dougal left the smithy, earlier than normal, muttering about the traps, they had watched him uncover a narrow bundle wrapped in cloth from beneath a pile of gear, and looked at each other with questioning eyes. "That's what he was making last night," Griffin had said, as the smith disappeared down the lane in the direction of the lake. "Let's follow him, and see where he goes with that."

"Let's not," said Nessa, smarting under the rough side of her father's tongue, for his mood had been dark all day. Griffin could only imagine what she thought about that now. If only they'd followed, they might have a better idea of Dougal's fate.

As the dinner hour approached, Griffin had laid down his tools, expecting to go down the lane to pick up the evening loaves from the herder's wife, Mara, whom Dougal paid to bake, since Nessa didn't know how. It was yet another reason the goodwives whispered, and a chore Griffin assumed to spare her their sometimes ill-tempered comments. But then Jemmy had come charging down the lane, heralding the news about the goblin, and the bread was forgotten, along with everything else, save Dougal.

As the night lengthened, Griffin stayed on the periphery of the activity, fetching wood and water as required, watching over Nessa from afar. She sat at the rough kitchen table, stone-faced and calm, accepting a knocker-full of hard corn whiskey, tossing it back with such ease even Griffin was astonished. Out of Nessa's hearing, the women argued amongst themselves in lowered voices, alternatively scolding and silencing each other until Griffin wondered how Nessa could sit with such silent dignity. When the last of them had finally departed, it was well after midnight. But instead of going to her bed, she had risen to her feet and rolled her shoulders back in the same stretch with which she approached fire and forge, and reached for the small ax which hung beside the door.

"What are you doing?" he'd asked, puzzled by her obvious purpose. The fire illuminated her tunic. The stains of the day were lost in the play of shadow and the homespun fabric was pinkish in the red light. Her skin was rosy from the fire, color high on her cheekbones, her dark eyes focused with such calm determination, that, as she turned to face him, holding the ax, he was momentarily afraid of her. She looked like the Marrihugh, the warrior goddess, standing there beside the fire, her bare arms round with defined muscle, forearms corded with veins, fingertips still black with soot. Her shoulders were broad, her back was straight. She was not as tall as her father, but she was strong from a girlhood spent hammering molten metal over an anvil. "What are you doing, Nessa?"

"I'm going to find him," she replied, in the same matter-of-fact tone she might've answered a customer.

"At this hour? The woods were searched—where do you mean to look?"

"I'm going into the OtherWorld, into TirNa'lugh. It'll soon be dawn, and that's the best time."

He'd reached across the space that separated them, and grabbed her arm. "Nessie, that's madness."

They were just about the same height and she stared back at him, shaking off his arm. "Where else to look? The goblin appears, my father is missing. What else to think but that they are connected? Why else would my father just go off?"

Griffin stared at her, his mind a mad whirl. "Nessie, please—" How to say gently that Dougal might lay dead beneath the water? Dead within the forest? If Dougal had indeed killed the goblin, wasn't it possible that the goblin had killed him? "Be reasonable. There's nothing to prove he's gone into the OtherWorld. What if he's just lying somewhere—hurt or...even dead?" He whispered the last.

"I won't believe that." She lifted her chin in a challenge, her eyes hard nuggets of iron in her flushed face. He had stared at her as she dropped the ax into a leather sack, buckled her dagger around her waist, and wrapped her cloak over her shoulders. Then she slung the sack over her shoulder. "Not one of them—" she dismissed the whole village with a jerk of her head over her shoulder "—would dream of looking for him in the OtherWorld, and it will take an order from the Duke before anyone else dares." Without another word, she left the house.

He scampered after her, up the hill, in the direction of Farmer Breslin's sty. She had not replied to any other questions, nor even spoken until just now, when they were kneeling on either side of the goblin. He bit his lip, trying to think of something to say that would convince her to stay, but he knew her in this mood. Arguing was useless. She gripped the goblin's matted hair and tugged, but the body had hardened into rigor and the head wouldn't budge. "Then I'll come with you."

She rocked back on her heels, regarding him with surprised gratitude. "I know you'd come with me if I asked you to. According to the stories, if I'm alone I'll have a better chance of getting across the border and into the Other-World."

"And a better chance of getting out if we're together. What if you run into something like this?" He gestured at the goblin.

"It's at dusk the goblins hunt."

"How can you believe the old stories?"

"You mean you can look on this and not?"

He shook his head, mind reeling with frustration and fatigue. "Of course I believe, we all believe now, I suppose. But how do you know the legends are right about everything? What if some of them are wrong? And what if you stumble into a nest of…of these?"

"I can take care of myself." She patted the dagger which lay in the curve of her waist like a lover's hand.

"Nessa, will you listen to me? This is madness. You must

be moonmazed already if you think you can actually get into the OtherWorld and come back, let alone bring your father back, if that's truly where he is. I—I mean, the OtherWorld is a big place. Where do you intend to look?"

"I'm going to the Queen, and I'm showing her the goblin's head. Goblins shouldn't even be able to get into Brynhyvar. Haven't you ever heard of Bran Brownbeard?"

"Of course I have but maybe not every story's true. Don't you think you should at least talk to Granny Wren?"

"Granny Wren?" Her skeptical tone was a perfect echo of Dougal's, an octave or so higher.

"She's a wicce-woman, Nessa, surely you should talk to her before you go—"

"What's corn magic got to do with goblins? There's more to this than either of us understand, Griffin. Those visitors last night—the ones who came in so late? Papa recognized one of them, but the other was a sidhe. I saw the eyes when he drew back his hood, just as Papa ordered me back to bed. You think it's coincidence that one of them comes to the forge late last night, when all decent folk are long abed, and then a dead goblin washes ashore upon our very lake? The same time as Papa disappears? Well, I don't. For all I know, or you know, or anyone else for that matter, this was all part of some trap to snatch him into the OtherWorld. My mother was lost there, and I won't lose him, too." Momentarily her expression melted, as her mouth turned down and her eyes flooded with tears she blinked away hard. She squared her shoulders, mouth set once more in its firm line, and Griffin groaned inwardly. He knew that look. It was the one she habitually wore whenever Dougal set a challenge before them both. "I won't let them have him. I don't have time right now to listen to a wicce-woman repeat some ancient story all of us have heard a thousand times. I'll find Papa and bring him home if it's the last thing I do, I swear." She got to her feet and swung the ax over her shoulder. Her hair tumbled down her arms and she thrust it back impatiently. Her father's insistence that she keep her black curls long was his one recognition of his only child's sex. "Stand back."

Aghast by her casual savagery, Griffin moved back as she brought the ax down, the blade grazing the goblin's slack jaw by a hair. It bit through the flesh and gristle and stopped with a dull thud in the neckbone. She tugged the blade free and raised it once more, heedless of the red slime dripping from it, and in one smooth motion, brought it all the way down again. This time the blade buried itself in the earth, and the head lolled back, rolling slightly to one side on the slight grade. Nessa handed Griffin the ax, picked the head up by the hair and shoved it without flinching into the sack. From somewhere close, a cock crowed experimentally. "I have to hurry."

She slung the sack over her shoulder and picked up the lantern, as he flung the ax aside with disgust. Easier by far to make a new one, than to imagine cleaning off that gore. "What am I to tell everyone?" he whispered.

"The truth, of course. Oh. Here." She set the sack down and felt beneath her tunic for the slender cord which held her silver amulet. She bent her head and worked it over her chin and through the tangled length of her hair. "Take it." She held it out and stamped her foot as the cock crowed again. "I don't have much time."

He caught it as it dropped from her hand, then stumbled after her, his mind roiling with disbelief and desperation. With sure steps she strode up the road, through the silent, sleeping village. The crunch of their feet on the cold gravel was the only sound, their breath curling in long white plumes through the predawn air. Not even a barking dog marked their passing. At the smithy gate, she paused. "No sense in you coming any farther."

He hesitated. What would Dougal want him to do, other than locking her in the root cellar? Nothing seemed viable, but a thought occurred to him. "Wait," he said. He ran into the house, grabbed a round loaf of bread and a hunk of cheese that one of the women had left. He reached for his own pack, a treasured gift from Dougal at last Solstice, and shoved the food inside. He ran back outside and thrust it at her. "Remember, you mustn't eat or drink anything of the OtherWorld."

She favored him with a quick surprised smile, then nodded and slung it on her other shoulder.

"I don't think I should tell anyone the truth, Nessa, about where you've gone. Not unless you don't come back after a day or so, all right? People already—" he hesitated, loathe to hurt her with a reminder of the shadow under which she lived. "Already talk." Their eyes met, and hers were steady, full of sure and certain purpose.

"I guess you're right," she said.

It occurred to Griffin that he might never see her again. He wanted to take her hand, to tell her all the things he rehearsed alone at night. He was not ill-favored, they worked well together, surely the smithy would someday be hers.

They were already a good team. Marriage was not such a ridiculous possibility.

Despite the chill, her face was covered by a fine sheen of sweat, and he thought she had never looked more beautiful. The words felt like a cork in his throat and he felt the moment passing, slipping away as inexorably as the night. He seized her by the shoulders and pressed a hard desperate kiss on her mouth. Her lips were warm and firm and she didn't immediately recoil. Then she pulled away, and he half thought she might hit him. "Just come home," he said by way of apology.

She raised her chin and squared her shoulders. "Count on it."

Then the cock crowed once more. "Hurry," he said, awed and grateful that she had neither slapped him nor wiped away his kiss.

With a nod of farewell, she strode down the road, veering off toward the thick stand of trees which lay between the village and the lake. The lantern bobbed in rhythm to her steps, twinkling like a star.

"Nessa. Don't eat or drink anything!" he called after her, wishing the words were sufficient to change her mind and bring her back. But once Nessa made her mind up to do something, it was always easier to get out of the way.

"Best bank that fire," her voice floated back to him on the wind. "Papa will have *your* head—" The rest was lost, carried off by the freshening breeze, into a half-heard murmur. The lantern flared once more as though she turned to wave, and then it blinked out, swallowed by the trees. He raised his hand, both in blessing and farewell, and saw a dark trickle edging down his palm to his wrist. He had clenched the amulet so hard, his hand bled.

The thick hide sack barely suppressed the reek of goblin flesh. Nessa shoved the heavy bulge on its leather strap behind her, trying not to think of the thing which nestled now on the curve of her rump. She squinted through the trees. The black forest rose around her, the tree trunks silent as sentries beneath the still star-studded sky. White mist swirled in mossy hollows, and a dense odor, musty and faintly sweet, rose from the forest floor and permeated the chilly air. But the scent of morning was on the light breeze which stirred the few leaves that clung to the late-autumn trees, and just now, behind her, where the village lay sleeping in the pre-dawn quiet, she thought she heard another cock crow. She had less time than she'd hoped.

The soft squish of spongy cress beneath her boots assured her that she followed the thin line of the narrow stream that, snaking beneath the trees, led down to the lake. Streams such as this were called Faerie roads, and usually avoided. For the stream itself was nearly invisible, buried by the thick cover of fallen leaves, their edges crisp and sere. The stories said that water was one of the surest conduits between the mortal world and the OtherWorld, the one called TirNa'lugh in the old language. And it was said, it was during the in-between times and in the in-between places, when and where things were no longer one thing, and not yet quite another, that one was most likely to slip into this intersecting reality.

She quickened her pace, breathing hard, and out of force of habit, groped at her throat with one cold hand, forgetting for a moment that she had removed her silver amulet. For the first time in her nineteen years she was without silver. She felt naked and somehow wicked.

Well, it was wicked. Griffin was right. She dismissed his clumsy kiss as a product of anxiety and fatigue. And disbelief that she would do something so irrational. To accidentally fall into TirNa'lugh, victim of a sidhe's spell, was one thing. But to remove one's amulet and to deliberately seek to enter the OtherWorld, was an action so preposterous, Nessa knew of no one who'd attempted it. No one should know better than she the dangers lurking there. Surpassingly beautiful, with voices like music, a sidhe was capable of weaving enchantments so profound that humans willingly gave up home and family to follow their sidhe obsession, trapped out of mortal time, lost to all previously held dear. And, if some hapless mortal did find his or her way back, if he or she had tasted OtherWorldly food or drink, he would refuse all human food, thus, to sicken and finally die. Or, even if he could force himself to take nourishment, he would find that while only a year or two had seemed to pass in the OtherWorld, tens or even hundreds of years would've passed in the mortal world, and everyone ever known was either old or dead, while his own body withered like an autumn leaf. Once it was known that she had deliberately removed her silver and walked into TirNa'lugh, the villagers were likely to add madwoman to their list of gossip. Enough of them believed she was tainted in some way by her mother's actions, even though Nessa had been less than a year old when her mother had been spirited away by some sidhe lord who'd tricked her into removing her silver. Now she existed only as a faceless name in her daughter's memory. Once she had asked her father why he had not sought to rescue her mother, and he had been silent a long time, as if carefully considering his answer. "Well," he'd finally said. "There was you, you see." And in those simple words, Nessa felt the pain of his choice.

Nessa tramped on. She would not lose her father. She steadfastly refused to even consider the possibility that he was dead. He could not be dead. He was all the family she had in the world, and she would not accept the idea of a life without him. Trouble was brewing in the land, civil war and general unrest sparked by a King gone mad and a foreign-born Queen whose large family eyed Brynhyvar with hungry speculation. Dougal had spoken of moving up to Castle Gar, and hinted that their skills might soon be needed on a greater scale than ever before. She would not face the village, the world, and war without him. She would find him or die herself.

The light was growing stronger now, long, silvery-gold shafts that streamed through the mist. She blew out the candle and set the lantern down on the forest floor. She would carry it no farther, for the less encumbered she was, the better. She considered dropping Griffin's pack, but the food was too necessary. With a sigh, she shouldered it once more and set off.

The dawn was nearly over, and with it, her hope of entering the OtherWorld. Ahead, the trees seemed to thin, and through the spindly trunks spears of golden light spiked through the branches, a more intense light than that which seemed to fall about her shoulders. Is it the OtherWorld up ahead? she wondered, as she shifted the sack and gripped the hilt of her dagger. The ground was firmer now, all vestiges of the stream gone, and the thinnest rim of the rising sun just visible above the line of trees. It was nearly morning, nearly day, but the thought of her father ensnared by sidhe magic or goblin claw spurred her on.

She ran faster through the white birch trees, running into the elusive light which seemed to beckon just outside her reach. The spindly leaves shuddered as she passed, until she tripped on a half-hidden root and sprawled flat on her stomach. The goblin head bounced up and down on the earth beside her, and the flap opened and the reek which spilled out made her gag. Bright sun burst above the trees and daylight poured over her. She shut her eyes and banged her fists on the ground in frustration. It was gone. Her chance to find her way into the OtherWorld was over. Sweat broke out on her forehead and hot tears welled up, spilling down her cheeks. She brought one hand to her face, sobbing as she lowered her head to the ground. Griffin was right. She must be mad to have even thought to attempt such a thing. But I won't give up, she vowed. If the Duke's men did not come today, she would try again tomorrow. She sniffed and noticed then that the moss beneath her cheek was soft and thick and smelled almost sweet. Soft and thick as flannel after many washings or the herb known as lamb's ears, and she opened her eyes, pushing up on her elbows to stare down at it, for it was an emerald-green so intense she doubted she could've imagined such a color existed. Wondering, she stroked it, for it felt amazingly smooth against her fingertips, tips that suddenly appeared rough with scars and hard with calluses and very, very dirty. The scent that rose from the moss was fragrant, like sun-warmed earth in spring, and she closed her eyes and breathed in deep.

A sudden hiss made her head snap up.

"Horned Herne, maiden, what do you here?"

The deep voice startled her, so that she scrambled back in a half-crouch, warily straightening, wiping away her tears. The speaker, who stood in the shade of an oak with sprawling branches thick with bright golden leaves, looked unlike anyone she'd ever seen. He was broad of shoulder, the strong cords of his neck just visible above the high linen collar of the shirt he wore beneath a doublet that was made of something that looked even more velvety than the moss. It was nearly the color of the moss, too, and she saw as he emerged from the shadow of the tree that it exactly matched his eyes which slanted above his high, narrow cheekbones. A braid, thick as a woman's, the color of a honeycomb with the sun gleaming through it, hung over his shoulder, like a silky rope that seemed to invite her to stroke it, to wrap it around her neck and arms, just to feel its texture glide across her skin. There was an intricate insignia embroidered on the shoulders and across the chest of his doublet, and she looked at his face, questions forming in her mind. His lips were plump as peaches, red as apples, and his eyes seemed to burn through her, as though he knew exactly what she was thinking. She lowered her eyes as she felt the color rise in her cheeks, noticing that his chest tapered to a narrow waist and hips, how his hose clung like a glove to his muscled thighs and calves. He held a bow, with arrow knocked and ready. She drew a deep breath, and would have answered, when he muttered what sounded like a curse, and beckoned. "To me. Now. Quickly." He raised the bow and she nearly startled back, then realized he aimed at something just beyond her. "Now, maiden!"

She hastened to his side, grabbing for the sack and Griffin's pack, a thousand questions bubbling on her lips. Beside him, she felt herself to be disgustingly dirty, covered in filth and soot and grime, and she wondered how he could stand the smell of her, but he only thrust her behind him, and stood, tensed and ready. The moment hung, suspended, and she wondered if he could hear the pounding of her heart.

The attack took them both by surprise. From the side, a hulking gray shape rushed out of the trees, in a cloud of stench and a rush of leather, a long snout and thick arms which held a giant broadsword of some metal that gleamed with a dark sheen.

But the bowman was quicker. Without flinching, he drew the bow, and the arrow sang across the narrow clearing, landing with a dull thud into the chest of the creature that snarled and lunged even as it collapsed. Nessa stared in horror at the thing that lay in a crumpled heap, its leathery tail still twitching.

Beside her, the sidhe reached over his shoulder for another arrow. "You are just over the border betwixt our worlds, maiden." He spoke in a low whisper as he fitted the arrow into the bow. "I shall see you back across. It isn't safe for you here. We stand too close to the realm of the Goblin King. The wards here must be weaker than we realized."

Nessa gulped. It seemed impossible that such a slender stalk of ash was sufficient to have slain the goblin, but there it quivered in the monster's chest. Swallowing hard, she wrapped her wet palm in the fabric of her tunic, and tried to stop shaking. "I—I don't want to go back. I—I came to see the Queen. To show her this." Without taking her eyes off the still creature in the center of the clearing, she held out the bag.

He frowned as if he wasn't sure he'd understood her. "You've come *deliberately* into Faerie?" He lowered the bow after a quick glance around the clearing. "And what manner of gift is this?" He frowned at the rude leather, and Nessa felt the full measure of his scorn in his look.

"This isn't a gift. It's the—the head of one of—" She paused, gesturing with her chin in the direction of the goblin. "One of them. It was found dead on the lakeshore near my village."

The color drained from his already pale face. "A lake in the Shadowlands? That cannot be."

"This is what we found. Is it not kin to *that?*" She nodded in the direction of the dead creature, and held open the bag. The stench that rose from it was noxious and rank, and made the sidhe grimace in disgust. "And in the same hour that this was found, my father went missing." She stared up at him with mute appeal. She felt the impact of his eyes meeting hers with nearly physical force. "I came to ask her for her help."

"By the Hag, maiden, shut that away." He waved one hand in front of his face. "What's in that other sack?"

"Food." She thought briefly of Griffin, how clumsy and crude he seemed beside the sidhe. He seemed a thousand leagues away. Was it only a few minutes ago that he had thrust it in her hands?

"I see. You even brought provisions—how wise. How long has your father been missing, you say?"

"Since the dinner hour last evening. He was going to the lake when he left the smithy."

"And who killed the goblin?"

"We couldn't tell. There was a long slash in its belly and half its guts had spilled out. But there was no sign of a weapon, or a battle, or my father."

He rubbed his face and gazed around, forehead puckered. "There is a lake that lies that way, yonder, over the border of the Wastelands. You indeed are fortunate that if a lake so like it lies so close in Shadow, you stumbled over on this side, and not on that one."

"What is shadow?" she asked, stabbed by a pinprick of the realization that the possibility which she refused to consider—of a world without Dougal—might, in fact, be far more than a possibility.

"The Shadowlands. The world of mortal men. And maids. You call it Brynhyvar." He turned back to look at her, and their eyes met once more. Her heart stopped in her chest, as he turned the full force of his piercing green gaze on her. A flush was rising in his face and a small pulse beat a quickening tattoo in his neck just above the collar of his tunic. His skin had the texture of velvet and reminded her of the color of cream. A sweet, fresh scent emanated from him, a scent that reminded her of new fallen snow on pine boughs. "So this is the spell you mortals cast," he muttered, more to himself than to her. "Like midsummer wine and winterweed."

Despite a deepening sense of despair, she stared, fascinated by the shades of green swirling in his pupils. Every sense felt inflamed, swollen, and her head was beginning to spin in slow thick circles. She bit down hard on her lip and the taste of her own blood steadied her. She hefted the sack over her shoulder again. She would not lose sight of why she'd risked just this very thing. But she was terribly conscious that her clothes lay rough over her body, crudely made, as if cut by a child's hand compared to his, and that there were wedges of grime beneath her fingernails, that her tangled mane of dark curls hung in lank, sweat-soaked strands about her dirt- and tear-streaked face. But the way he was looking at her made her feel as if he wanted to devour her. She coughed. "I've come to find my father."

He shook his head, as if to clear away the effect of the attraction, and took a step back. "Maiden, if he fell out of Shadow and into the Wasteland beyond—the Goblin Wastes—" He broke off and sighed, as if reluctant to say more. "I cannot give you the help you seek or even take time now to explain the implications of the news you bring. I can, however, take you to one who quite possibly will help you, to the extent that he can, once he hears your story. For it would appear that if indeed a goblin has somehow fallen into the Shadowlands, even a dead goblin, then a greater magic than expected has failed, and the Queen herself must know of this. No one's been expecting this—things could go very badly indeed for all of us if what you say is true. You must come with me." He turned on his heel, still shaking his head, clearly loathe to continue, but anxious to go on.

"But, but wait—" She stumbled after him, hurrying to keep up in boots that suddenly seemed clumsy and stiff, ignoring every injunction every goodwife ever whispered at the end of every tale involving the sidhe. "What about the Silver Caul? Isn't it supposed to keep the goblins out of Brynhyvar? Why isn't it working? Is that the magic you mean has failed?"

He turned and made an impatient gesture. "Hurry, maiden. There will be time enough to explain it all to you in safety." He stretched out his hand and she realized he was wearing gloves of leather so finely wrought they fitted with no more wrinkles than his own skin. "Come. I dare say no more here."

Was this not what she'd come for? It was too late to have second thoughts now, even as the ferocity with which the goblin had attacked sparked the doubt that perhaps Griffin was right and that the OtherWorld was far too dangerous a place for her to be wandering around in alone.

With a quick nod, she let him guide her through the trees, his steps quick and sure, following a narrow trail which threaded through a thick forest of golden oaks and yellow beeches and blazing red maples. They had gone not even half a league when he stopped suddenly and pulled her close to him, one finger pressed hard against her mouth. Her senses exploded as she inhaled a scent at once so vital and pristine it felt as satisfying as food. No wonder mortals withered, rejecting coarser, more substantive nourishment. Without thinking, she leaned into him involuntarily. Their eyes met again and it felt as if her blood had turned to molten metal in her veins. She thought of Griffin's clumsy kiss, and knew this as different as a ripple from a wave. But the sidhe closed his eyes and turned his head. "Maiden," he said, in a whisper so low, she partly read his lips, "make no sound." For one brief moment, they swayed closer, while she wondered idly in some remote corner of her brain, the possible source of his attraction to *her,* for she felt herself to be unbearably dirty and disheveled, her clothes and hair stinking of goblin. And then she heard the low grunt.

A cold wave of fear ran down her back as he lifted a horn off his shoulder and handed it to her, then drew the sword out of its scabbard. The brisk leafy-scented air was suddenly polluted by something that stank of the cesspits, a stink she recognized far too well. He drew a breath and swung his sword up, circling around her. "That track beneath the trees, maiden, will lead you to my fellows. Run hard, and blow the horn. They will be alerted to my need and take you to my Captain. Do you understand? You must run, quickly, maiden, upon my signal." He pointed with the sword at the track, which threaded through the trees. "You must run. And you must not look back." He moved around then, pushing her behind him. Suddenly he shouted, "Go!" as three goblins armed with battle-axes roared out of the trees.

Nessa charged down the trail, the sack with the head thumping against her rump. Thank the Great Mother that her father had seen fit to let her run with the boys of the village, and not confined her to kitchen and courtyard like the rest of the girls. Her boots felt weightless as she sped in the direction her rescuer had indicated and she lifted the horn to her lips, and blew. The horn sounded one pure clear note, and it echoed through the trees, loud and long. Immediately another horn blew in answer, then another, and she raised the horn once more, dropping Griffin's pack off her arm. It slid to the ground, as she blew hard into the horn again. Sudden movement in the trees all around her made her knees quake, and she stumbled in midstride. Forgetting the injunction not to look back, she glanced fearfully over her shoulder, and in that moment, collided with a solid form that gripped her with steady arms. She twisted her face up and around and gasped to see a sidhe, every bit as beautiful as the other, staring down at her. "By Herne's horns," he said, in a voice as richly sweet as honeyed wine, even as he gestured his fellows to continue on in the direction from which Nessa had come, "a mortal maiden, as I live and breathe."

3

It was always the light that Timias noticed first whenever he transversed the fluid borders between the Shadowlands and Faerie. Elusive and fey as the sidhe themselves, it shimmered through the trees, limning the edge of every leaf, pulsating with seductive radiance. More than one mortal had become a captive to the glamour cast by Faerie light, bound for mortal ages by fascination with its constantly shifting play of contrasts more acute than any ever cast by the bleaker sun of Shadow.

Now he strode through the thickest part of the stream, the bottom of his staff encrusted in mud, moving as quickly as his aged bones would allow. In mortal years, he was old beyond reckoning, but he, unlike most sidhe, bore the stamp of it upon his face. For Timias had dared to do what few would even contemplate—he had lived among the mortals, allowing the harsh mortal years to take their toll upon his face. His frame was bent, his face was lined like a walnut, the hair which hung in long silken strands around his shoulders was gray. He had thought, once, that the mortal woman for whom he'd given up one lifetime in the Shadowlands, though not a tenth of that in Faerie, had been worth the price he'd paid. Now he wasn't so certain. For when he'd returned to Faerie, to claim his place among the Councilors to the Queen, he found that Vinaver, that foul abomination, the Queen's twin, had managed to convince several among the lords and ladies of the Council that so long a sojourn as his in the Shadowlands represented some kind of technical resignation and a vocal few had even had the audacity to call for his removal.

In retrospect he should have expected such a move on Vinaver's part. They had been instinctive enemies from the moment of her birth. Timias would never forget how the infant, born aware as all the sidhe, had hissed and spat directly into his face when the midwife had placed her into his unwilling arms. From that moment, Vinaver had worked to do all she could to discredit him with her sister, the Queen.

But Timias had a hereditary right to a seat upon the Council—the most honored right of all in Faerie—and no one had ever heard him surrender it. And so he kept his seat, but it was not as before. For he had been irrevocably changed by his extended time spent among the mortals, and in Faerie, change usually happened so gradually it was hardly discernible at all.

Each day in Faerie was as glorious as the day before it, a long progression of hours that flowed as sluggishly as a lazy river. Few things in the Shadowlands could compare to the stately pace of Faerie time, and nothing within Faerie could equal the breakneck speed with which life progressed in Shadow. It was that, as much as anything that had prompted Timias to stay in the Shadowlands so long. Mortals may not live as long as the sidhe, but their lives were lived more intensely. To one accustomed to the leisurely flow of Faerie time, it was as intoxicating as an inhalation of winter dreamweed.

But if his had been an unexpected return, it was also very timely, in Timias's opinion. For it was immediately clear to him that Alemandine was not the Queen her mother, known as Gloriana the Great, she who'd vanquished the Goblin King and constructed the Silver Caul which kept the deadly silver out of Faerie, had been. Compared to Gloriana, Alemandine was only a pale shadow of the great Queen whose reign had ushered in this Golden Age that had endured for more than a thousand mortal years. Gloriana had birthed her triplets, Alemandine and Vinaver, and her half-mortal son Artimour, without so much as a hiccup in the great webs of power that held the goblin hordes at bay, and Timias was disgusted that it was whispered in some quarters of the Court that Vinaver, who in both coloring and temperament more closely resembled her mother, should have been Queen. Vinaver's hair was like her mother's fiery-copper, her eyes the dark green of mountain firs. Alemandine's hair was white, her skin paler than milk, her eyes like chunks of river ice chipped from the shallows. It was as if Vinaver had somehow sucked up all the pigment out of her twin, as if she would've claimed all the life, all the energy for herself. He disliked her just for that.

But tradition, of course, was on Alemandine's side and so she had taken the throne when the time came at last that Gloriana chose to go into the West. For the first hundred or so comparative mortal years of her reign, Alemandine ruled competently, if with a less sure and certain hand than her mother. The trouble began with her first attempts to call forth her own heir, when the physical strain of her pregnancy seemed greater than it should, and Timias believed that on this short visit to the Shadowlands, he had identified a potential cause that could, with some effort, be ame-liorated. Unfortunately it was difficult to persuade the Council of anything, for Vinaver and her supporters managed to convince the others that he was merely the mad sidhe overcome by his addiction to human passion. It was an image he found difficult to combat. For in Faerie, appearances were everything, and the toll of mortal years had cost him more than he cared to admit.

But Timias, who had been present when the Silver Caul and moonstone globe were created and joined together, understood how closely the Caul and the globe bound the worlds, Shadow and Faerie, together so that events were reflected, repeated and echoed in each other. As long as both remained relatively stable, all was well, petty mortal squabblings over land or gold reflected in the trivial intrigues that permeated the Court. The realization that this relationship also created a largely unacknowledged potential for a spiral into disaster prompted Timias to cross the border into the Shadowlands once more.

What he found made him hasten back as quickly as he could. For the war now breaking out in Brynhyvar, the land lying closest to Faerie of all mortal lands, was one which threatened to spill over its borders and engulf the entire mortal world. The situation there only intensified the growing sense of dread he'd begun to feel when Alemandine's pregnancy was first announced. For while an heir was long overdue, the Goblin King was waiting—waiting for the chance to overcome the bonds of sidhe magic and to overthrow the Queen while she was her most vulnerable. The time of her delivery would be perilous enough—he did not want to consider how full-scale war in Shadow would affect them all, if it coincided with an assault by the Goblin King. The forces of chaos were massing. They must prepare to fight the war on all fronts—including the Shadowlands, if necessary. He glanced up at the piercing blue sky and hurried as fast as he could, hoping that he could catch the Queen in a well-rested mood. For he had noticed that while the Queen might prefer to ignore him, she listened to him more carefully than she oft-times appeared, and that frequently she summoned him to a private audience to discuss the issues he raised. She had always, he wanted to think, regarded him as one of her more trusted Councilors, for he always told her the truth, no matter how unpleasant. It assuaged the remnants of his dignity, and reminded him of the time when he had, indeed, been Gloriana's most trusted Councilor, her closest confidant, more intimate than her unremarkable Consort, whom she'd chosen for his ability to dance and to compose extemporaneous verse.

But even as he strode up the bank to the footpath which

led to the wide gardens surrounding the Palace of the Faerie Queen, he knew what he intended to propose would sound too radical, too incomprehensible to be taken seriously. Blatant and obvious intervention into the affairs of the Shadowlands had never occurred, not even by Gloriana in the Goblin Wars when mortals and sidhe had struck an alliance. Without any precedent, he would have to hope the Queen was in a receptive mood.

He rounded a curve and the trees thinned, opening out onto a broad lawn that swept like a wide green carpet to the white walls of the palace gardens. He looked up as the sun rose above the trees, illuminating the blue and violet pennants which fluttered off the high white turrets. A thousand crystal windowpanes gleamed like rubies, reflecting the red sun as it rose, and on the highest turret, a white silk banner floated on the morning breeze, flashing the Queen's crest, announcing to all who might have cared to inquire that the Queen of all Faerie was in residence within. She was about to leave soon, he knew, and that, too, was cause for concern. Although tradition demanded that each year she retire to her winter retreat on the southern shores, Timias feared the journey would tax her strength unduly. But Alemandine insisted, clinging to the hidebound traditions like a life rope.

He had a trump card to play, he thought, if he dared to bring it up. There was the lesson of the lost land of Lyonesse, which had once lain to the east of Faerie. It had disintegrated into nothingness one day, collapsing in and over and upon itself until it was no more. Now even the memories of its stories were fading, for it was said that the songs of Lyonesse were too painful to bear. But to imply that

Faerie itself stood so close to the verge of ultimate collapse when he was not at all certain that such was actually the case might unduly alarm Alemandine and thus hasten, or even cause the calamity. He needed to convince the majority of the Council to heed his advice, not frighten the Queen, he decided. And to that end, he would seek to use every weapon at his disposal if necessary. But first he would seek to reason with Her Majesty.

So he hastened past the high hedges of tiny blue flowers which opened at his approach, scenting the air with delicate perfume that faded nearly immediately as he passed, trying to think of the correct approach. The lawn ended in a wide gravel path, which opened out onto a broad avenue that encircled a shimmering lake. Ancient willows hugged the shore, branches bending to the water. The sun was nearly above the trees, and the gold light sparkled on the surface. At this hour, both lake and avenue were deserted, but for the gremlin throwing handfuls of yellow meal to the black swans floating regally on the lake.

The gremlin turned his head as Timias passed, fixing him with a hostile stare. Timias met the gremlin's eyes squarely. There were increasing reports of little incidents of rebellion among the gremlins, who, according to the Lorespinners, had been bred of goblin stock to serve the Faerie. The incidents were generally dismissed as the approach of the annual bout of collective madness that occurred among the entire gremlin population at Samhain. The other obvious threat seemed to elude everyone. When Timias had suggested to the Council, that the gremlins, as distant goblin kin, might find it in their best interests to side with the goblins in the coming conflict, and that being in a position to bring about utter ruin, they might be better banished to some well guarded spot until the child was born, he was laughed at openly throughout the Court. But Timias feared the time was coming when the courtiers wouldn't be so amused. He would find that thought amusing himself if the consequences weren't so dire. He picked up his pace, leaning heavily on his oak staff as his aged legs protested.

Once within the palace walls, he didn't pause on his way through the marble corridors, not even stopping to visit his own apartments. He ignored the fantastic mosaics, the silken hangings, the intricate carvings which graced the palace at every turn, a blend of color, scent and texture so harmonious, mortals had been known to gape for days at just the walls. He strode beneath the gilded arches to the Council Chamber, where the guards straightened to attention and saluted as he approached. But at the open door he paused and peered in, ostensibly smoothing his travel-stained garments, assessing as he did so who was in attendance and their likely reaction to his news.

As he expected, the Queen was at her breakfast, attended by her Consort, Prince Hudibras, and those of her Councilors in residence, and to his dismay, he saw that Vinaver sat at the Queen's right hand. Perhaps he'd do better to approach the Queen privately.

The idea that Vinaver, who he had always regarded as some mutant perversion of the magic that created the Caul, was able to enthrall her sister with her wiles sickened him. It had been terrible enough to discover that Gloriana's womb housed two babes—Alemandine and Artimour—fathered separately by a sidhe and a mortal on the same night as the forging of the Caul. But Vinaver's emergence was completely unexpected, completely unforeseen, an aberration of the natural order of Faerie Timias thought best disposed of. He'd suggested drowning the extra infant to the midwife who'd brought her out for his inspection. The infant's eyes clashed with his almost audibly, and he felt the desperate hunger stretching off the wriggling scrap of red flesh like tentacles, seeking any source of nourishment. He shook off the infant's rooting with disgust. "I say drown it," he said again, shocking the midwife into silence as she turned and carried the infant back to her mother's arms, to wait her turn for a tug at her mother's copious teats. Both Vinaver and Artimour were offenses against nature, he'd argued then, arguing tradition, just as he'd argued it when he returned and fought for his Council seat.

He wondered what Vinaver might have been up to in his absence, for any differences between the Queen and her sister that he might have nurtured had obviously been resolved. Vinaver leaned forward with a proprietary hand to caress her sister's forearm as it draped wearily over the cushioned rest of her high-backed chair. Vinaver's back was to him, and Alemandine was turned away, engaged in choosing a muffin from the basket the serving gremlin offered. The creature wore cloth-of-gold, signifying the highest level of service. The hackles rose on the back of his neck. If only he could induce the Queen to at least banish them from her immediate service.

But it was the others who were gathered around the table that made him narrow his eyes. For with the sole exception of the Queen's Consort, Hudibras, they were all Vinaver's closest cronies. Across from Vinaver, on the opposite side of the table, Lord Berillian of the Western Reach sipped from his jewel-encrusted goblet, his attention focused on a dark-haired girl who sat beside him. Timias did not immediately recognize her, but something about her face made him pause, and he realized she was gowned in an old-fashioned gown of Gloriana's era. He realized that they paid him no mind for they were all focused on her and the room was thick with some suppressed tension.

Several vacant seats apart, Lord Philomemnon of the Southern Archipelago, peeled an apple with overly deliberate intent, while at the opposite end, the Queen's Consort, Hudibras, caught another tossed to him by his half brother, Gorlias.

Both Philomemnon and Berillian were Vinaver's closest cronies and cohorts, the voices who'd championed her cause most vigorously in the early days of Alemandine's reign, who'd shouted most loudly for his resignation.

The early-morning sun flooded through the wide windows which lined one wall of the long chamber, and glinted off the polished surface of the inlaid table that dominated the furnishings. Fragrant steam wreathed the air, redolent with the rich feast spread before them on golden serving plates.

The Queen looked uncomfortable and cross, her pale green gown spilling over the edges of her chair, her wings folded up behind her. The swell of her pregnancy was not immediately obvious, but her normally milky complexion was sallow, and dark smudges beneath her upturned eyes testified to restless nights. Her thick hair, white as snow, was bound up in braids, coiled neatly around her head, and topped by a platinum coronet set with pearls. He could retire, he thought, still unnoticed, and approach the Queen privately. But that would only delay the inevitable confrontation. Might as well throw the idea down before them like a gauntlet. He took a deep breath and single step across the threshold.

Only the unknown girl saw him, as she peered over the rim of the goblet she lifted to her mouth, for Philomemnon was absorbed in his apple, and Berillian was eyeing the girl's rounded half-moons of bosom which were emphasized by the old-fashioned cut of her gown with unabashed interest. Timias cleared his throat, ready to speak, when red-faced Hudibras caught the apple he'd been throwing back and forth to his half brother Gorlias and tossed it instead to Timias. He raised his gold goblet just as Timias caught the apple in midair. "Well, well, my dear, see what the sunrise has ushered in today! Good Timias, welcome back from whatever grim hovel you've been hiding in."

Sparing Hudibras no more than a quickly veiled glance of contempt, Timias threw the apple back. He strode immediately to the Queen, and dropped as gently as possible onto a knee swollen with the exertion of his haste. "My Queen." His old man's rasp cut like a discordant note through the melodious hail of mannered greetings which now rose around the table like a chorus. "I bring grave tidings—tidings which shall affect all of us unless we take heed now. For there is war…war in Shadow."

Alemandine raised her long white neck and stared at him,

a play of expression as complex as windblown clouds crossing her thin face. She shifted restlessly on the pale green cushions which lined her chair, and the look which settled upon her face was one of peevish irritability.

Timias steeled himself. If he could manage to at least make her listen long enough to call for him privately, he would count this breakfast a success. Her pregnancy had grown only slightly more pronounced, but it was clearly unbalancing the ornate wings she had cultivated so diligently, which now arced at least a foot above her head. In the morning light, the infinitesimal network of blue and red veins was visible through the translucent flesh. He wondered briefly why no one had discouraged Alemandine from allowing the wings to grow so high, for they clearly now contributed to her discomfort, and heard a little sniff of disapproval from Vinaver. He turned, ready to say more, when Hudibras let out a loud sigh of exasperation and threw another apple back to Gorlias. "So what of it, Timias? The mortals are always sparring back and forth amongst each other—half the time I don't know why we ever bothered to protect them from the goblins, they kill each other with as much glee. Come, let us introduce you to a newcomer to our Court—this is the Lady Delphinea, the daughter of our Horse-mistress, Eponea of the High Mountains. Sit, break your fast with us and tell us of your travels. You must be starving after a week or more of naught but mortal slop."

A few chuckles went around the table, and Timias could not help but spare a moment to peer more closely into the dainty, delicate face of the girl who sat poised on the edge of her seat. She was young, he could see that, barely ready to make an appearance at Court, and he wondered briefly why her mother, Eponea, had not accompanied her. But there was something about the chit's face—something that tugged at his awareness, even as he turned away from the arch faces and concentrated only on the Queen. For all he cared, they might have been alone. He looked directly into Alemandine's pale green eyes. "Events in the Shadowlands are moving toward a great war—a war which will sweep across borders and which will create repercussions that we are ill-equipped right now to bear. You must hear me out, Alemandine, I beg you."

Not once in all her years on the throne had he ever so addressed her and the Queen stared at him, her pale eyes wide in her angular face. For the first time he saw the real fear hiding behind the petulance. Alemandine was afraid. She faced the greatest challenge of her life, and she was afraid. For a long moment he stared back, sympathy wreathing his ancient features. She desperately needed to assert control over the Council, but as long as they resisted acknowledging the breadth of the challenge that lay before them, she was too torn between the unfamiliar demands of her pregnancy and the constrictions of her fear. What would shock the rest of them out of their complacency? Must he invoke the forbidden name of Lyonesse in order to make them understand the enormity of what they faced?

But Lord Berillian was speaking, the movements of his bejeweled hands sending colored prisms across the Queen's face as he plucked the grapes off the dark purple bunch lying across his plate. The fat locks of chestnut curls lay coiled on his shoulders, the precise shade of his intricately embroidered doublet. "Indeed," he spoke between bites of grape. "So what if a new war has broken out in Shadow? What is war within Shadow to us? Have we not our own—" he paused and glanced at Alemandine, and then around the table with a look that seemed charged with some meaning Timias could not read "—our own delicate situation on our hands?"

Alemandine lifted one eyebrow, clearly expecting him to answer, and Timias turned to face the rest. At least she hadn't had him escorted from the room. This was his chance. He forced himself to speak slowly, deliberately, hoping to make an impression with the weight of his words. "War in Shadow can only undermine our already precarious stability. The greater the unbalance there, the greater the unbalance here. And the greater the unbalance, the more we shall all feel the strain. The Caul does more than hold the silver at bay. The Caul binds our worlds together. What is felt in Shadow is felt here—what is felt here is felt in Shadow."

Hudibras snorted. "You croak like a crow, Timias. Why not just go about in black and have done with it? We'll all be warned of doom just by looking at you and you can spare us all your speeches."

"I beg your pardon, my lord," put in Delphinea suddenly, her pale cheeks flushing pink. "I think if Lord Timias speaks forcefully it is from his concern for the welfare of your Queen and child, and for the continuation of Faerie as we know it."

Startled, Timias met her eyes and saw that they, unlike those of nearly every other sidhe he'd ever known in all his long life, were a clear and startling sapphire blue. *She is not yet one of Vinaver's,* he thought suddenly, grateful for the unexpected support. *She's not in their pocket yet.* And he wondered once again what had brought her to the Court, though maybe not so prematurely as he'd first supposed. "Thank you, my lady." He bowed in Delphinea's direction. "We all know that it is not a matter of if the Goblin King will attack, but when. It is in our best interests to ensure that there is peace in the Shadowlands while we face this inevitable foe."

"Well, what do you think we can do about it?" Hudibras asked, his angular face flushing red. "Mortals are best left to decide the outcome of their squabbles for themselves. We of Faerie have never intervened." At that Philomemnon looked at Hudibras and laughed openly and Vinaver rolled her long eyes to the ceiling. "Not officially, I mean."

Timias turned back to the Queen, his expression changing from disgust to resolve. "Your Majesty. I have long studied the affairs of Shadow to understand the impact they make upon our world—"

"This we know, my lord." Her voice was querulous, and she hid her impatience poorly. Timias sighed inwardly. He had hoped that Alemandine would be sufficiently rested first thing in the morning to willingly entertain such discussion, but now he saw that the demands of her pregnancy had intensified to the extent that such opportunities were becoming unpredictable, if they yet existed. They had better yet exist, he thought suddenly, once more overwhelmed with concern for this fragile creature who bore such a great weight. She was nothing like her mother, but she had ruled perfectly adequately for nearly one hundred and fifty mortal years. Why now did he compare her so unfavorably to her mother? Because, a small voice muttered deep in the back of his mind, she wields the power unevenly, and thus she is vulnerable in ways her mother never was.

"Why should we invest even the time to speak of it, when clearly it would divert us from our concerns?"

He leaned upon the table, his gray robes falling around him, the long locks of his gray hair hanging over his shoulders like a cloak. "Your Majesty. This is no diversion. The welfare, not just of your child, but of all of Faerie hangs in the balance. This is not merely one of their usual disputes, Your Majesty. You must believe me when I tell you that this is a most serious war—with the potential to engulf the whole of Shadow, not merely the country that lies nearest our borders, the one mortals call Brynhyvar."

At that, Philomemnon sat forward, arching his own brow. "Then tell us, Timias, how is this war different?"

"The King of Brynhyvar is mad—there's some talk it's because of one of us, but I haven't found anything to substantiate that, thank the Hag. It surfaced shortly after the young Prince died last winter. At any rate, his Queen is a foreigner, and her relatives see an opportunity to take over Brynhyvar. But the Duke of Gar has raised his standard against the King, and now, war not only overshadows Brynhyvar, but all its neighbors as well, even to the Farthest Reaches, for the web of blood ties, trade agreements, and strategic alliances stretches across the entire world."

"And how, exactly, do you propose we intervene?"

"A decisive battle on Gar's side would win the war before it had a chance to spread. But Gar's forces are spread out, and the troops which the Queen has summoned from her native land are a professional army capable of decimating the current rebels, unless, you see, Gar calls in alliances from other countries, and thus the war will escalate."

"Surely you are not proposing we send our own soldiers?" Berillian was incredulous.

"I am proposing we send Lord Artimour as an emissary to the Duke of Gar, along with perhaps one of our own hosts—"

The table actually shook as those around it exploded with guffaws. "Surely you jest, Timias," put in Vinaver, leaning on her hand. Her mouth curved up in a languid smile, as though she tolerated the ranting of a dotard. "Since when have you ever had time for Artimour? And now, now that Finuviel, by the Queen's grace, has seen fit to answer her call to assume command of the defenses of Faerie—why, Finuviel depends upon Artimour as he does upon no other—Arti-mour has become his most trusted second. Even now, Finu-viel leads a hosting of our finest knights to the Western March, where Artimour holds the line. And to send such a force into Shadow is unheard of and I'm surprised, good Timias, to think you of all of us would even suggest such a thing. What are we of Faerie but our traditions?" Those were his own words, spoken in this very chamber, now flung back at him. The wings she had grown in deference to Alemandine's fashion quivered.

Timias flushed as Alemandine raised her goblet. "Our brother is needed where he is. The border there grows more tenuous every day—is that not what the reports tell us, good Timias?"

"I do not doubt what the reports tell us, my lady. And I do not dispute that Artimour is a brave and worthy captain, and that his presence is a great help to Prince Finuviel on the border. But among the mortals, his father is revered and loved and stories of him are told around every hearth in every dwelling no matter how rude. Gar would listen, if we offered him enough forces to make the difference. I have every reason to believe he would accept our help if properly presented."

"And you would risk our own—"

"There is no risk. We cannot be killed by mortal weapons—wounded perhaps, but as you well know, nothing short of total beheading will kill us. A quick victory will stabilize the Shadowlands. One battle, and the entire problem could be settled."

"But there's silver there, Timias. Our knights could be killed by that, or have you forgotten the stuff exists?" Hudibras shook his head.

"And what guarantee of victory is there, Timias? Forgive me, my old friend," said Philomemnon, "and I do not hesitate to call you that, for though your years in the Shadowlands have aged you, long we have dwelt in the same region, you and I. I understand your concern, and I, unlike some others—" here, he paused and looked at Hudibras and Gorlias "—well appreciate the effect the Shadow-world has ever had on ours, much as many of us would prefer to deny it. But there's no surety your strategy would work. For one thing, mortals are marvelously unpredict-able, not to mention wholly illogical. One thing I've learned, in my admittedly limited experience of them—" and here he sighed and a bemused smile flitted across his face, like the flutter of a butterfly's wings "—is that the only possible way to predict what they are likely to do is to decide what I would do in a given situation and then assume they will do the opposite." He inclined his head with a little flourish, and another chuckle, louder this time, perhaps even a bit forced, went around the table, and Timias shot each Councilor in turn an assessing look. There was an undercurrent he could not quite understand, but Philomemnon was continuing, "Better our energies remain concentrated here."

To what purpose, wondered Timias, as his gaze fell on the back of Vinaver's head, where her thick copper braids hung massed in jeweled caul. What mischief had the witch planned in his absence?

"And what's in it for us, Timias?" put in Gorlias, interrupting Timias's train of thought. "It's not as if we could expect their help against the goblins—except as bait." This time the laughter was longer.

Timias shook his head, suddenly weary with frustration. "Laugh at me if you must, Gorlias. I tell you all, if the war in Shadow expands across the entire mortal world, we will disappear—like the lost land of Lyonesse." There. He'd said it. He straightened and folded his arms across his chest.

An awkward silence fell across the table while the courtiers exchanged shocked glances and Delphinea shifted uncomfortably in her seat. This time she avoided his eyes. Alemandine rubbed her temples as if her head ached. Vinaver snorted. "If this is all the tidings you bring my sister, Lord Timias, you might consider a stint on the perimeter, yourself. A few weeks and you might begin to understand what we face. If you hadn't been off indulging yourself in Shadow, you'd have been here to hear Finuviel speak of the situation himself. We have not the troops to spare to such a dangerous distraction." Her green eyes flashed in a manner so reminiscent of her mother that Timias took a step back. Vinaver raised her head and her wings quivered.

No one could accuse her of not being utterly loyal to her sister, thought Timias.

But now she was rising, bending like a copper lily over Alemandine, her skirts rustling with a soothing swish. "Come, sister, soon we'll be away from all this. Allow me to make you a posset. 'Twill soothe your head and we'll talk about what to pack." Glaring in Timias's direction, she rose, edging him aside with her skirts, drawing Alemandine to her feet. "You foolish, blind old man. Come, dear sister." With gentle murmurs, she drew Alemandine from her chair, allowing the Queen's head to droop against her shoulder, as she led the Queen away. The breeze raised by the trembling of their wings swirled past Timias's cheek like a voiceless reproach.

"I hope you're satisfied, Timias." Hudibras bit savagely into the apple.

"I shall not be satisfied, my lord Consort, until everyone at this table, within this entire realm, understands the gravity of the situation we face." He looked over his shoulder and lowered his voice. "Our Queen is no Gloriana. We all know it—Alemandine herself knows it. She needs more from us than a nod of approval. Alemandine needs our help, our guidance—"

"Diverting our own forces to the Shadowlands when we know we will need them here is scarcely the way to do it, Timias." Philomemnon folded his arms over his chest and shook his head.

Timias tightened his grip on his staff, drawing himself up, wondering how to impress upon them the reality of the threat. But then he caught the Lady Delphinea's look once more. Her expression did not change, but she raised one eyebrow infinitesimally. He swallowed the words, and shrugged. Something about her appearance nagged at his awareness. Perhaps an opportunity to speak to her privately might be arranged. If he could persuade her, there might be a way Philomemnon and Berillian could be brought to his side. And there were others. A majority of the Council would outweigh the voices of Vinaver, Hudibras and Gorlias and help convince the Queen he was right. Better to let it go now. So he spread his hands and only said, "Think on it. But think not long. Events in Shadow proceed apace. Already it may be affecting Alemandine. If we linger too long, our decision may well be made for us. Remember Lyonesse." He bowed to each of them, turned on his heel, and walked slowly from the room, leaving them sitting in a flood of silent light, gasping audibly that he should have once again invoked the forbidden name.

The news that a mortal maiden, carrying a goblin's head in a sack, had arrived at the outpost awakened Artimour and brought him blinking, upright, barely two hours after his head had first touched the pillow just before dawn. "A goblin's head?" he repeated, as Dariel, his body squire, moved about the room, shaking out fresh underlinen, opening a shutter to let in enough light for him to dress. "Are you sure it's a goblin's head?"

"There's no mistake about that, my lord. I was in the kitchens when they brought her in—you could smell it coming half a league off."

"And how'd she find her way here?" Artimour dragged himself out of bed, and splashed cold water from the pitcher on the table into a basin and onto his face. He looked up to take the towel Dariel proffered.

"The scouting party you sent out after that last raid, my lord. They found her just as she crossed over the border."

"They've all come back?"

"No, my lord." Dariel handed him hose and underlinen and did not meet his eyes. "The captain of the watch sent them out again. There are three of the company missing."

"Missing." He sank down onto the edge of the bed. The word punched through the fog of his exhaustion like a fist. Something had happened last night, something had shifted, changed. He could smell it, like a flake of pepper just under his nose; feel it, like a tiny piece of gravel in his boot. There was a difference in the goblins last night—they had attacked with a ferocity he had not experienced before. He wondered bitterly how far away Finuviel—Finuviel, his nephew and his junior and his newly appointed Commander—was with the much needed reinforcements. The thought of Finuviel automatically made him even more bitter, for it was difficult to accept that the much less-experienced, much younger sidhe had been rewarded with the title of High Commander of the Queen's Guard, which meant that he was now Artimour's commander-in-chief and while he had not yet begun to meddle with Artimour's carefully constructed plan of defense for the outer wards, there was no doubt at all in Artimour's mind that once Finuviel arrived, he would begin to question everything that Artimour had done up to now. *The line was holding,* he thought. *But something's changed, something's different, and will Finuviel listen and understand?* Or would he simply assume that Artimour's half-mortal blood interfered with his competency, as the Queen and her Council so obviously did?

But Dariel was continuing, relaying the mortal woman's story, "—and what's more, my lord, she's insisting she intends to show it to the Queen."

"Great Herne, that might kill her." He accepted the shirt Dariel held out, pushing away all thoughts of resentment and Finuviel. He had to deal with this latest crisis with a clear head. "The Queen, I mean. Not the mortal." He shoved his arms into the sleeves of his shirt. Before last night, they might have laughed. Now not even the ghost of a smile bent either of their mouths. "Any word from—" he hesitated, loathe to speak the name of the rival who'd supplanted his command "—Finuviel?"

"A dispatch came in for you shortly after dawn. I had thought it better not to disturb you."

"I appreciate that, Dariel." And he did appreciate it, for there'd been very little rest for anyone lately. And after last night, he doubted there would be more until Finuviel arrived with the reinforcements. And once Finuviel arrived, who could say what changes he'd insist on? The mortal was right in one respect—the Queen and her Council might not need to see the goblin's head to believe it, but they had to be made aware that a goblin had somehow crossed the border into the Shadowlands. For such a happenstance could only mean one thing. The magic of the Caul—the Silver Caul of lore and legend and song—forged by his mortal father and imbued by his mother Gloriana with her sidhe magic, had somehow—momentarily at least—failed. It was the only thing that could upset him more than the possibility of losing three more of his troops after last night. If only Finuviel were here—it might be amusing to watch him struggle with this unexpected development.

But Finuviel was not. Artimour plucked the doublet from Dariel's hand and whipped it on, then sat down on the edge of the bed, and reached for a boot, thinking fast. Perhaps there was a way to turn this unexpected calamity to his advantage. "Bring the mortal to the library, then have my horse saddled and pack my saddle roll. The Queen must be told of this as quickly as possible." Tidings such as this should be brought directly to the Queen and her Council. It would also provide him an opportunity to discover how his replacement had been engineered. He paused in tugging his first boot on. "You're sure it's a goblin's head?"

Dariel looked up from handing over the second boot. "You'll smell it on the mortal yourself, my lord."

Artimour allowed Dariel to tug and brush and pat until he stepped away, satisfied. "I'll see the mortal now. And something to break my fast—I can't remember if I ate dinner last night or not."

"You had no time to finish it, my lord." Dariel handed him a parchment packet, and with a quick bow, was gone.

Artimour stalked down the hall to the library he shared with the other officers and sank into the deep cushions of the chair behind his desk. On the one hand, he was sickened by the potential loss of three more soldiers, soldiers they could not afford to lose, men who'd become friends in the long days of their preparations. And on the other, a mortal maiden come to show the Queen the head of a goblin found lying dead in Shadow could only mean that against all expectation, all assumptions, the Caul's power had failed—or fluctuated, perhaps, like the webs of magic that bound the borders. But how was that even possible? he wondered. The magic of the Caul was supposed to be a special blending of mortal and sidhe energies. It was not linked to the reigning Queen in the same way as the magical wards containing the goblins, and thus, was not expected to be affected by Alemandine's pregnancy. But how else to explain how a goblin could have fallen into Shadow? It struck him odd that the task of bringing the goblin's head here—a wholly unexpected stroke of logical behavior coming from mortals he would not have foreseen—should have fallen to a mere girl-child. Were there not warriors worthy of the task? Born under the shadow of mortal taint, he had always distanced himself from anything having to do with humans. And yet, even to him, this action seemed extraordinary, the last thing one might expect from a mortal.

He ripped open the parchment packet. It was from Finuviel advising him to expect the reinforcements in ten days. Ten days? He put the parchment down and rubbed his eyes. Ten days meant something different today than it had before last night, before he'd witnessed his first true death. Ordinarily the sidhe did not die. They boarded ships and went into the West, when their time in Faerie grew wearisome. That is, unless they were slain by either goblin or silver. It was not something he had ever seen until last night, and it had shaken him profoundly, shocked him to his very core. The goblins that had roared across the boundary last night were different, he thought, his mind replaying the events with such crystalline clarity it felt as if he relived them anew. Their hides were tougher, their claws longer and thicker, and they fought with a ferocity he'd never seen before. The web was strained nearly to the breaking point and though ultimately it had held, and they'd successfully driven off the goblins, it had cost him a knight. He had seen Lothalian's eyes flash green as his essence, his soul, his self was consumed on the spot before them all by a greedy goblin who grinned as he raised the lifeless corpse to his slavering maw. "No!" Artimour had heard himself roar, and with a mighty sweep of his broadsword, he'd beheaded the goblin where he stood. But there was no saving Lothalian.

And now, possibly three more lost to Faerie forever? Winter was coming soon, when the landscape grayed, and the goblins' natural color gave them an added advantage. He felt a grim and growing certainty that something worse than was predicted lay in store. He scanned the dispatch again. Finuviel had sent it three days previously. They were still seven days out. Riding hard, and alone, he could intercept them probably within two, maybe make it to Court in three. Or he could go directly to Court, and send another messenger to intercept Finuviel.

He'd hear for himself the mortal's story, and then be off.

As if on cue, the door opened, and Dariel stood aside to let the mortal woman pass. Artimour looked up, scrutinizing the first mortal he'd ever seen with an interest far more intense than he would have cared to admit. Dariel followed her into the room, carrying on an inlaid serving tray a basket of bread, fresh from the ovens, a pot of warm yellow cheese, and a pitcher of foaming milk beside two crystal goblets. The squire set the tray on a corner of his desk. He poured the milk into the goblets.

"Thank you, Dariel. You can leave us." He motioned the squire to shut the door, and stared at the girl who stood before his desk, with raised chin and squared shoulders, proud as any princess, and grubbier than the meanest garden gremlin that had ever worked in the Palace gardens. Long, black curls tangled around her face, haphazardly tied back with a rough ribbon of indeterminate color. Her simple tunic was made of undyed homespun. The front of the tunic was stained with soot and sweat and suspicious smears that stank of goblin. It fell just below her exposed knees, revealing bare legs covered by the slightest shadow of fine dark hair. Her boots were made of leather so crudely cut and sewn he wondered how she could walk in them. She wore a cloak that had as much style as if she'd pinned a tent around her broad shoulders, and a belt barely worthy of the name, a rude scrap of leather buckled around her thick waist. Her face was just as dirty as her hands, which were black to the nails. Her cheeks were streaked with grime, but it was her eyes, her eyes that burned like two dark coals, that arrested him. There was such mettle, such passion in those eyes that something deep inside him responded immediately. His sidhe half recognized it as the potent lure of the mortal, the magnetism that sucked his kind into a vortex of need for the rush of raw energy said to emanate like a tangible thing from every human. He drew a deep breath as those dark eyes seared his skin. He could feel desperation rising from her pores like a hot mist.

But even as part of him responded, another part recoiled, disgusted by the dirt that seemed embedded into her skin, by the sharp odor of stale sweat, by the lank strands of greasy hair. No wonder his mother's people regarded his father's as something to be toyed with, or, better yet, avoided altogether. No wonder Timias was mocked and scorned for being mortal-mooned, as they called it. It looked as if these creatures lived little better than their own animals.

Suddenly Artimour was angry, angrier than he could ever remember being. It appalled him to think that three of his comrades—creatures of grace and light and beauty all—might have died for such an appallingly filthy clod of mortal flesh that had the audacity to live and breathe and stand before him as though her dirty little life might be worth even half one of theirs. "They tell me three scouts are missing." He spoke quietly, evenly, but the accusation was clear. "At dawn, the goblins should have returned to their lairs, weakened by the rising sun. But your human scent drew them on, and into the patrol who should have been safe in their barracks. But for you."

She cast down her eyes, her hands laced together like a lump in her lap. "I did not mean to make trouble or cause you grief."

He pressed his lips together. What in mortal experience

could compare to the death of a sidhe at the hand of a goblin? He thought about what he knew of mortals. They were born, they dashed through their helter-skelter lives, breeding faster than rats, and then died, burned out like cinders, their bodies turned to ash. In between, they tempted hapless sidhe foolish enough to bother with them. "Cause me grief?" He shook his head, spitting out the words like cherry pits. "You've no idea what you've caused or what's been lost." He looked away, overcome by scorn and disgust and the weight of the potential loss of not just one comrade to the true death, but four.

When she spoke, her words shocked him speechless. "You're part mortal, aren't you?"

He gripped the arms of his chair, stunned into forgetting his grief, for he had always been reassured by everyone how remarkable it was he bore no human stamp upon his face. If anything, from the time he could remember, everyone went to extravagant lengths to agree that his eyes were like Vinaver's, his seat upon a horse like Gloriana's, his dance step, Alemandine's. And since Finuviel was born, his hair and skin color were compared most favorably to those of his cousin, as the sidhe referred to every kin relationship which was not parent and child, or consort and mate. "Maiden," he nearly choked. "How did you know?"

"You aren't like the others—not exactly." But her attention had already drifted, her eyes ranging around the room, from ceiling to floor, lingering over the wall-hangings, the scrolls and the weapons. She looked at the food and he saw her throat work as she swallowed.

In what way? he wanted to demand, but her attention was

riveted on the intricate patterns in the carpet. Judging by her clothing and the state of her person, the outpost must appear as sumptuous as a palace. He gestured to the food. "Are you hungry?"

She shook her head slowly. "I dare not—don't you know? To eat or drink of the food of the OtherWorld—it's dangerous to us—there's an enchantment in the food—" She broke off, her attention caught by some aspect of the weapons hanging on the long walls above the bookshelves. "I brought some food with me, but I dropped it in the forest when the goblin was chasing me."

"I see." Better get on with it, then, he thought. At least she had a compelling reason to go back to her own world quickly. The sooner she returned to her world, the sooner he could be on his way. "They tell me you wish to see our Queen."

Without leave, she sank down onto the edge of the chair in front of his desk. He heard the soft rasp of her rough fingertips caressing the supple leather on the arms, as once more she fixed him with that piercing look, which rendered him wholly incapable of reprimanding her. "I need to see the Queen. I need her help. My father's missing. And we—the people of my village—we found the goblin floating dead in the lake. The sidhe who found me here told me there is a similar lake in this world. I believe my father killed the goblin and fell somehow into Faerie. I've come to find him."

Artimour placed the tips of his fingers together carefully. If her father had foundered into the Wastelands he was as good as dead. But she was looking at him with such mute appeal, such naked need, his own heart twisted in his chest and he knew he had to convince her to leave. Her very presence was too unsettling, too distracting, too intoxicating. And the way this one looked at him with her pleading eyes that burned like tiny twin flames in her sweat-streaked face and her desperate need to find her father—this one was rousing memories and feelings and questions he'd thought long buried and forgotten.

Where's my father? he had asked his mother, one evening when Gloriana had favored his nursery with a visit, for he had just learned that such things existed and that most had one. And she had laughed, softly, touching his cheek with a caress as light as a rose petal. "Don't worry about your father, child," she answered. "He's gone to a place you can never go." Why has he gone there? he'd asked. "He has returned to his people, who need him," she replied. But why did he leave me? He was desperately curious as to the identity of the faceless person few ever spoke of. "Because," his mother answered gently, "you belong to me." And that was the end of the only conversation he could remember having with his mother concerning his father. Even the Lorespinners generally considered the mortal's contribution to the making of the Silver Caul scarcely worthy of mention, let alone detail.

He rubbed at his head as if erasing the memory, pushing all the questions he'd ever had about his father back into the dark place to which they'd long ago been consigned. The last thing he needed was this girl, who stared at him as if she expected him to conjure her father out of the air. But her very presence signified a potential problem so large it made his head ache to consider it. "What's your name, maiden?"

"My name is Nessa. My father is Dougal, the finest blacksmith in all of Gar."

His head jerked up. He looked at her more closely, observing the deep slices of grime beneath her fingernails, the scars and calluses beneath the charcoal-stained skin. "Your father's a blacksmith?"

"Yes. He was."

Again he sat back, stunned, even as that one slip of her tongue told him that the girl who could spot the mortal stamp upon his features was not blind to the possibility of her father's fate. He stared at her, every question he'd ever had about his own father rising to his lips, for the fact his father had been a smith was the only other piece of information Artimour had about him. A wild, insane thought leapt to his mind from what could only be his mortal half—that Dougal and Nessa were somehow related to his own father. He could smell the scorch of burning metal in her clothes and in the wild tangle of her hair. He hesitated, torn between the urgency to address the situation and the sudden desire to ply her with questions.

But he saw clearly that the consequences of a failure of the Caul's magic were so dire, they made even his rancor at being shunted aside seem petty. He had to get to the Queen as quickly as possible, not to confront, but to warn. So he drew a deep breath and let it out in a long sigh. "My name is Artimour, Maid Nessa. I am the second-in-command here, under Prince Finuviel." What else was there to say? He should send her on her way, but something held him back, something wanted to keep her talking. A few minutes more wouldn't hurt. "Tell me how you came to find the goblin."

He leaned forward over the desk, observing every minuscule detail of her appearance. Surely his father hadn't smelled quite that—that ripe? Distress poured off her like a tide, dragging him back to the present, making him disregard the odor.

"My father left the smithy just before dusk last night—earlier than usual, but he—he—had gone to check the traps at the lake." She paused, and looked at him, as if considering what to say.

"Go on."

"He'd been gone just a short time, when some of the children came running back from the lake saying there was a dead goblin floating in the water. And so we all—everyone who could walk—dropped what we were doing and followed the children back. And there it was, floating in the water, among the traps we set to catch the lakefish. But my father was missing. We looked, everywhere we could think of, but there was no sign of him. Only the goblin."

"And so who decided to cut off its head?"

"I did."

"How did you know to do that?"

"Do what?"

"Cut off its head. We—the Faerie and the goblins that inhabit this realm—cannot be slain by mortal weapons, but by beheading. If your father really did kill that goblin, unless he used the goblin's own weapon against it, it would've revived ere the sun had set on another day. Did you not know that?"

"There hasn't been a goblin in our parts for over a thousand years, they say. I'm sure there's a few things we've forgotten twixt then and now." She leaned forward, fists clenched. "I lost my mother here. I will not lose my father, too. I know about the Silver Caul. I thought the Queen would listen to me if I brought the goblin's head. Why didn't the Caul work?"

He shook his head, silent, uncertain how to answer. It was difficult to think at all, because the stink coming off her was enough to turn his stomach. At last he decided to tell her as much of the truth as he believed she would understand. "I don't know. The Caul was forged in another age—under another Queen. The present Queen carries an heir at last, and thus this is a dangerous time in Faerie, for her magic, which normally sustains the land, is diverted to another source, and the wards that contain the goblins within the Wastelands are strained. This we expected and have, to the extent we can, prepared for. But the Caul was made of greater magic. We did not think that it would fail. And if it has—" Artimour stopped. The possibility that the Caul would fail had never even been considered, and no contingency had even been bandied. The idea of a mortal world vulnerable to the goblins was not what made him shudder. The Caul's failure meant Faerie lay open to silver. "You've achieved your purpose, maiden, for I myself will bear this message to Her Majesty. Even now, my saddled horse awaits. You can re—"

"But—" she leaned forward, and once more he felt the scorch of her stare "—I didn't come here just to tell the Queen about the goblin. I'm here to find my father. I won't go back until I find him."

Her obstinacy was like a brick wall. He couldn't take her

to Court—that in and of itself would cause such an uproar, he would never hear the end of it. It would most assuredly end all his hopes of regaining his command. What could he say to convince her? He cast about. She cared passionately about her father. Maybe there were others for whom she cared just as deeply. "What about the others—the other people—"

"What others?"

He spread his hands. "The others—the other people in your village? Don't you care about them?"

"Not the way I care about him," she shot back. She leaned forward and for a moment he thought she would leap over the table. "You don't understand. The other people in the village, in our district, they all know about my mother. They all know about me. They think I'm tainted somehow. My father raised me to be a blacksmith just like him, and they think that's odd, too. So no, there aren't any others. I have no one else in the world. He's my whole life. I am not going back without him. Dead or alive." She raised her chin and he groaned inwardly, even as something deep inside him recognized a kinship with her.

He knew what it felt like to stand on the margins of all that is acceptable and accepted. But he had to make her understand that this crisis was greater than even her need to find her father. So he leaned across the desk and met the fire in her eyes with as much calm assurance as he could muster. "I see that your father means a great deal to you, maiden. But there are more lives than his at stake. You must go back and warn the mortals of your village. If the magic of the Caul has indeed broken in some way, the people living nearest that lake are in utter danger. And time runs differently in our two worlds. You've spent but a few hours here by my calculation, but a few days or more could've run in Shadow. Guards must be set about the lake, armed with weapons tipped in silver. For if even one goblin somehow fell into Shadow, living or dead, it is possible that more will find a way there. And they most likely won't be dead."

He watched the realization of the truth in his words dawn across her features and war with her own desire. "But my father—"

"Was he wearing silver?"

"Of course. Everyone does. No one ever takes it off—though I did, so I could get in."

"Then it's still extremely unlikely that he's here, maiden. A magic as great as the Caul cannot simply fail all at once. Even the magic here within the wards that hold the border—a much different sort from that which made the Caul and not as strong—it fluctuates, but does not fail." At least, he thought, he hoped great Herne would see that it wouldn't.

"But if a fluctuation in the—the Caul's magic has let a goblin into Shadow, is it not possible that despite the fact my father was wearing his amulet, the silver wasn't enough to keep him out?" She pressed on relentlessly, arguing with a determination the most exacting Lorespinner might envy.

The force of her logic, fueled by the intensity of emotion, was inescapable. Much as he would prefer to deny it. He sighed and shifted in his chair, crossing and uncrossing his legs. "You force me to agree. Such a possibility—that at the moment the goblin fell into Shadow, a mortal slipped into Faerie—does exist. So I will order the scouts who escort you back into the Shadowlands to search for him, once they see you safe across, and alert all the patrols from now on to search as well. And if your father has not fallen into the Wastelands, I'm sure we'll find him. But much as you wish to stay and search for your father, I tell you, your people are in danger. You must make them understand they must act to protect themselves immediately. Samhain is approaching in Faerie, the time when the veils between our worlds are thinnest. If the Caul is failing in some way, the goblins may break through on Samhain, and nothing here will hold them back. Whatever defenses you can mount will have to come from your side. Surely your father would not want you to leave your people so vulnerable?"

To his relief, Nessa sat back. She lowered her eyes. Thank Herne he'd found a way to get through to her. A last-minute check with the captain of the guard—an inquiry into the fate of the scouts—and he could be off. Then she raised her chin, and straightened her back, and this time, when her gaze collided with his, he saw a renewed fire that made him groan inwardly. "There's something else you ought to know."

He cocked his head. "Say on, then."

"No. I won't tell you, unless you promise to help me."

"Help you how? I've already promised to help you, maiden. My troops are in utter jeopardy out there—and I have duties and responsibilities—"

"Is it not your duty then to hear what I say? I've done you a service by coming here—I've risked much—you've said it yourself. Now you know about a problem you wouldn't have known otherwise."

He slumped back in the chair, assessing her eager face, her shrewd eyes, and resisted the urge to wipe his brow. "I shall instruct my soldiers to search for him, maiden."

"Then I'll leave and not tell you what else I know."

"What else you know about what? Maiden, these are troubling, difficult, dangerous times we live in. I don't have time to play games with you."

She folded her lips and turned her head away. Exasperation boiled through him. No wonder the sidhe were warned to avoid mortals. This up-and-down rush of feeling was dizzying, disorienting. He slapped his hand down on the desk. "What is it that you want?"

"I'll go back and warn my people, so you can go to the Queen and take this news to her. But I want to come back. And when I come back, I want you to help me."

Deny her, shouted the voice of what he knew to be common sense. But something made him hesitate, and think, for just a moment, of what up to now had been unthinkable. The mortal was most likely dead. The odds were great that by the time he'd returned here from the Court, the mortal's body would've been found—either here, by one of the patrols, or in Shadow. It may even have been found already. How likely was it he would have to actually help her search? It was a reason to visit the Shadowlands—a reason to visit a smithy—possibly even to see a mortal smith at work. One quick glimpse, he thought, a turn of the glass or two was surely all that was required to fill the void with some image of the father he'd never known. And the girl—she might be filthy, but she had acted bravely, and while she was clearly motivated only by a desire to save her father, she had undeniably performed a great service. How otherwise might they have known that the power of the Caul had failed to keep a goblin out of Shadow? She deserved some reward.

So he leaned forward and spoke softly, quietly. He had to be careful. There was far more at stake than either of their fathers. "If you go back, just as you say, and warn your people, and promise to wait for me to come for you, I'll help you search for your father, after I see the Queen. But you must be patient—remember that time does run differently and I must get leave from my commanding officer. But I give you my word that I will come myself, if you give me yours you won't come back on your own and you tell me everything you know."

"Agreed." Her eyes filled with tears, but she spoke with a simple dignity befitting Alemandine herself.

She was not at all what he had been led to expect. He wondered suddenly what sort of human her father was, to have raised a daughter of such determined character, and who her mother was. She'd been lost in Faerie, the girl had said. Did that mean she was still here? But there was no time for idle speculation. "Well, then?"

"Last night, two visitors came late to the forge. They spoke a while to my father, then left. But he was up half the night hammering away at something, and the last we saw him, he was carrying whatever it was toward the lake."

"And what has this to do with the goblin or the Caul?"

"One of the visitors was a sidhe, for in the firelight, I saw his eyes—they gleamed the way all of theirs do."

And mine don't? he wanted to ask.

She jerked her head slightly toward the door, and continued. "I saw how his skin shone. I understood why some call them the Shining Ones."

Them? he nearly shouted. It offended him to his very core that she excluded him from the people he thought of as his own. But this new piece of information was as tantalizing as a little puzzle piece, one of those that could fit nearly anywhere. It teased his brain, tempting him to gnaw at it like a hound over a bone. With effort he dismissed it. He rose to his feet, resolving to think on it while he rode. "We must both be off."

But her next words made him reel. "Was it your father who was mortal?" she whispered.

He fumbled for the gloves he usually wore tucked inside his belt, and when they weren't there, he flexed his hands, wondering what she would say if he told her the truth. "My father—" He paused. Her father was the center of her world. His was nothing more than the name of a minor character in a holiday masque. Nothing he could say now would make sense to her, and to say more would only delay them from their purpose. "My father is of no concern to anyone anymore." She looked at him as if he'd slapped her, but he was too unsettled to feel anything like remorse. There was part of him that whispered how easy it would be to follow her over the border, to peek, as it were, into his father's world. She could even show him a smithy. But another part of him hoped the blacksmith's body would be found with little further ado as quickly as possible, and suddenly he wanted to be away from this dark-eyed mortal who saw so much. This was the part that would prevent him from following her into the Shadowlands. He tugged his doublet into place, and scooped a hunk of cheese out of the pot with the crusty heel of the bread. It was warm and tangy and rich in a way he instinctively knew nothing of Shadow could match. He chewed and swallowed and gestured to the door. "Come with me, maiden. We must get you across the border ere the shadows lengthen over Faerie. It's at dusk the goblins hunt."

Timias was not terribly surprised when a face materialized in his mirror just as he had finished adjusting the drape of fresh sandalwood-scented robes more comfortably around his shoulders. He was, however, quite horrified to see the wrinkled features of a house-gremlin coalesce within the glass. The small figure stepped out of the glass and bowed. Silently it proffered a wax-sealed parchment.

Out of habit, Timias took it, broke the seal and scanned it. Amazingly, it was from the Lady Delphinea, but the fact that a gremlin had stepped through the mirror appalled him. Such magic was only the purview of the sidhe. The idea that a gremlin had unlimited access to the network of mirrors throughout the entire Palace made his blood cold, and he wondered who would have thought to teach one such a thing. He would have to speak to Delphinea at once.

He looked at the gremlin, brow raised. "Who told you to come through the mirror?"

The gremlin bowed, its impassive face not changing. The gremlins had long ago been forbidden to speak, since their voices were so harshly discordant. Instead they communicated with the sidhe by means of gestures, involving both hands and tail. With eyes downcast, the gremlin answered:

The Lady Delphinea bid me come to you through the mirror, great lord. Her matter is of great urgency.

"I understand that," replied Timias, deeply disturbed. "But who taught you such a thing? Who allowed you admittance?"

The Lady Delphinea, great lord. One day when the Queen was in great distress. It's been said I saved her life.

Timias raised one eyebrow as he felt a deep foreboding. Delphinea's understanding of the gremlins and their nature was obviously deplorably lacking, but what truly troubled him was the fact that this rank newcomer to Court, this young girl who scarcely looked as if she belonged away from her mother, not only knew the mirror magic but understood it well enough to teach it to a gremlin. He would have to speak to her about it. But there was no help for it now. The damage was already done. This one knew the mirror magic. Soon they all would, if they didn't already. Steps would have to be taken to protect the Queen. "Would the lady receive me now?"

She bid me tell you she will come to you at your convenience, great lord.

There was nothing wrong with the gremlin's attitude. He spoke with sufficient humility, not a hint of aggression or bad temper. But it galled Timias nonetheless to think that Delphinea may have unwittingly exposed the Queen to attack. He said nothing to the gremlin, of course. "Fetch your mistress, then." He gathered his robes and turned away, unable to watch it step back through the glass.

He fumed until a gentle cough behind him made him turn in time to see Delphinea step out of the frame in a rustle of heavy satin skirts. Her gown was the color of midnight skies, and tiny diamonds twinkled in the dark folds like stars. She had not been at Court long enough to have been infected by the fashion for growing wings, and indeed, the old-fashioned style of her gown precluded them, for a great lacy ruff rose from the back of the gown, framing her wide-eyed face and graceful neck in a style he had not seen since Gloriana first established the Court of Faerie. He wondered if the gown itself was meant to serve as a message of some sort, for Delphinea looked as if she'd stepped out of one of the tapestried panels which depicted the beginning of Gloriana's glorious reign. And he wondered why Eponea had not come herself. But as lovely as the girl was, he could not control his annoyance. "My dear Lady Delphinea, you are a delight to look upon but I did not expect the pleasure of your company quite so soon. And, while it may be rude of me to be so direct with you, my lady, whatever possessed you to teach that detestable creature the mirror magic?"

She paused in the very act of settling her skirts and raised her startling eyes to his. She met his gaze with a directness that bordered on insolence, and he felt a twinge of discomfort. What was it about this young girl-sidhe that was at once so compelling and so unsettling? Her words shocked him even more. "Petri is not at all detestable, my lord. He is a good and faithful servant to me, and his quick action saved the Queen much distress."

"I see." He measured her up and down and decided that her honesty was not so much born of courage as an utter lack of artifice. She would speak her mind, until she learned the value of holding her tongue, a lesson she would learn soon enough at the cutting hands of the Court. And then it occurred to him that she resembled someone—someone not immediately obvious. He frowned, trying to remember what her mother looked like.

The frown intimidated her and he saw that his assessment was correct. She was not so much insolent as she was innocent. Her mother had not taught her to lie at all. "Forgive me, Lord Timias, it was not my intention to intrude on you." She stumbled over her words as she turned to look over her shoulder, into the mirror's polished surface. So she'd been at Court long enough to know she could've been followed.

He softened his gaze and extended his hand. "It's no intrusion, my lady. But you must understand a gremlin is the last thing I expected to see stepping out of my mirror." He frowned a little. "Is everything all right?"

She reached up and drew the thick velvet curtains over the mirror. The network of mirrors within the castle meant that it was possible for the unscrupulous, the bored, and the curious to eavesdrop in any room a mirror hung, although to linger more than a minute or two was to risk the danger of becoming visible. Thus all mirrors were curtained. It was possible however, for a careful listener to overhear. He drew her through another door, into the antechamber of his suite, where all the walls were lined with long windows that overlooked his tiny gardens. He shut the door to his dressing room firmly. "Now you may speak freely, lady."

"My mother told me to seek you out, Lord Timias. The others don't want to listen to me, but she said your loyalty to Faerie was unquestionable."

He bowed, reading as much as he was able in the fast play

of emotions which swept across her face. She was too young, too unschooled in the ways of the Court to dissemble. And she was frightened. He could see that clearly. "I wish more on the Queen's Council shared your sentiments, my lady."

"Ah—the Council." She shook her head and walked to stand beside a window, gazing out into the garden below, small hands clasped before her. They were lost in the magnificence of the gown. A green marble fountain splashed merrily in the bright autumn sun, and tiny gold finches twittered among dark purple sage and golden snapdragons. "It's all so beautiful, my lord. But since I've been here, I think I'm the only one who sees how fragile it is—how easily it could all be broken and brought down into ruin."

She turned and once again he was startled by the uniqueness of her beauty. Her hair was glossy and so black the highlights were blue. They matched her eyes, which were the color of the sapphires embroidered into the frilly frame around her sober face. "I believe there is something terribly wrong, my lord. Something terribly wrong within the land—within the fabric of Faerie itself. That's what brought me to Court. My mother sent me here. Alemandine did not summon me."

Her words shocked him speechless for a moment. No one ever came to the Court unless at the express invitation of the Queen. To simply arrive without an invitation was a breach of such long-standing protocol no one but the Lore-spinners remembered its origins. "What are you talking about, my lady?"

"The reason I came to Court. You know I've never been here before?" She paused, as if putting her thoughts in order, then continued. "The Queen has not summoned a Council and no Convening has been called—for all are occupied with their own defenses and the raising up of their hosts. But I had to come—even my mother agreed—" She broke off, clearly too upset to continue.

"What is it, my lady?" Her distress unnerved him, distracted him from remembering something much more important that continued to evade him.

"The cattle are dying." She said the words slowly, deliberately and he frowned. The great herds of milk-white cattle which roamed the hills and pastures of her mother's mountain province provided the ultimate source from which so many Faerie delights were concocted. The herd had roamed for as long as anyone could remember over the rolling meadows, sheltered by the high mountain peaks, fed by the lush green acres of thyme and clover, and watered by the clear streams which ran down from the heights. The care and tending of this herd had passed in an unbroken line from mother to daughter for as long as anyone could remember. "The first time it happened—a few springs ago—our people came to my mother and asked her to come and see the body of a calf they'd found in one of the pastures. This calf—" She shuddered and turned her face away, as though from the memory. "It did not die a natural death, for I had never seen anything like it. The body was marked all over by a pox that oozed some greenish, foul-smelling pus. It was as if something ate it from the inside out. Then it didn't happen again for a while, and we hoped that perhaps it was simply some odd incident. But then, just before Alemandine's pregnancy was announced, last Midsummer Eve, there was a spate of such bodies and not just within the cattle herds. Birds, fish, the great cats that roam the highest peaks—we found these and more. One stream was fouled by the bodies, so thick did they lie. And then, my mother's foals began to die. I came here for Alemandine's help, never suspecting to find her so—so weakened."

Timias stared into her face, which was no less lovely for the worry that creased her forehead. "And you've no idea of the cause?"

"Well..." She turned back to the window and crossed her arms, as though bracing herself. "I do. But everyone—including my mother—considers it so outlandish, no one will listen."

"A position I've found myself in more than once recently, my lady, as you saw this morning." Timias bent toward her, gesturing with one hand in the general direction of the Council room. "You just heard me advocate the leading of a Faerie host into the Shadowlands, and you were kind enough to encourage the others to listen to me. How could I not do likewise?"

The half smile that quirked across her lips was displaced immediately by a look of such gravity, Timias leaned forward as if to offer comfort. But Delphinea only spoke with that same simplicity that this time chilled his bones. "I think it's the Caul—the Caul made of silver that's poisoning the land, the cattle—" She broke off. "I think the Caul must be removed."

Despite his resolve to listen to her with as fair a hearing as she had given him, he shook his head vehemently. "Lady, surely not. I was there when the Caul was forged—every precaution was taken, only the mortal handled it—"

"But think of it, my lord—" She raised her chin, refusing to back down. "All these turning years, it's lain, untouched, unlooked at—no one goes near it—and there it just sits on that green globe. The most poisonous thing in all of Faerie. What if—what if it's the Caul that's poisoning the land? If it's the Caul that's weakening Alemandine? Is that not possible?"

Timias backed away, her words tumbling in his mind as a new vision occurred to him—one so monstrous it defied comprehension. Could it be that the Caul—deemed so necessary, so perfect a solution to the problem of both silver and goblin—was in reality slowly leaching poison into the fabric of Faerie over the years? Alemandine had indeed appeared sickly, even to his untrained eye. The Queen was bound to the land more intimately than the Caul to the Globe. Could it be that her growing weakness was due to the very thing they thought protected them all? Could it be that they had erred? He shook his head. It was difficult to even wrap his mind around the idea. It was too terrible to consider, but he was forced to confront the possibility of truth in Delphinea's words. He sank down onto a chair, and even as the plush cushioning relieved the ache in his back, he felt the enormity of the potential problem as a physical pang in his chest. He must simply find a way to prove Delphinea wrong. For the first time he actually feared he might not make it into the West. If he weren't careful, a true death might yet claim him.

For Delphinea was continuing, pressing her point on with a passion almost mortal in intensity. "I know you based the making of the Caul in that most elementary of magic—the law of Similiars. But the amount used in such undertakings is critical—the amount that determines whether it heals or kills—"

"Do not lecture me, my lady!" He raised one gnarled hand to his forehead, feeling every one of his thirteen hundred mortal years. They stared at each other in a shocked silence, and then he said: "Forgive me, my lady. I should not have spoken to you in that tone. The tension of the times affects us all. Soon we will all be squabbling like mortals."

"My lord Timias," she replied, her eyes dark with pity. "I don't mean to imply you and Gloriana and the mortal deliberately did wrong. It was made with the best of intentions—surely that's why the Caul's magic has prevailed for so long. But what if too much silver was used in its making? This was something no one ever tried before—how could you or anyone else have been sure what was too much?"

Timias stared up at her. Backlit by the window, she stood poised before him like a harbinger of doom made more terrible by its beauty. "Have you told anyone this?"

"I've tried. They think it's nonsense. I can't get into the Caul Chamber alone, but I can't convince any of the lords or the knights to come with me. Even that sot Berillian—he fawns all over my bosom in a manner most unseemly, but can't bestir himself to help me open the doors."

He rubbed his head. In Faerie, where the progression of years was experienced as a never-ending circle rather than a linear march into some indeterminate future, shifting accepted thought was as difficult as shifting the calendar in the mortal world. The sidhe understood that what was materialized around them was an expression of their collective thought. An idea such as the Caul, which had worked for mortal centuries, would not easily be abandoned. "And is that what you suggest we should do, my lady?"

She smiled, and knelt at his feet, covering his spotted hands with her own like new-milked cream. "My mother said I should come to you. All I ask is that you come with me—we can go through the mirrors and no one need see us. How could it hurt to look? Maybe these are only the fancies everyone says they are. After all, when was the last time the doors were even opened?"

He shook his head, gazing past her face at some spot outside the window. She was right about one thing. There could be no harm in looking at the Caul. The spell which held the doors of the Caul Chamber was a relatively easy one to overcome—it required a simultaneous touch of the combined polarity of male and female energy. "To my knowledge—never. For once it was done, it has never seemed that there was a need—" He broke off and took a deep breath. "That's not to say that no one has ever gone to look."

She gave him a reproving look and he was forced to admit to himself she was correct about that. Once done, the sidhe would not return to it, because they would not expect it to change. It was the fundamental difference between the mortals and the sidhe. It would simply not occur to anyone in Faerie to enter the Caul Chamber. He lowered his eyes to the bubbling fountain, where the finches hopped from rim to ground to shrub, reminding him of the courtiers who leapt so lightly through the days, as if the gravest danger they'd faced in ages was not at hand.

He remembered the night the Caul was forged, the ring of the hammer as it slammed down on the soft metal, fixing it with that raw energy that had crackled through the air like bolts of lightning. What if that energy had not been sufficient to bind forever the relentless poison of the silver? He turned to face her and held out his hand. "Come. You must lead me, lady—'tis an age or more since I have used the mirror magic."

With a look of gratitude, she took his hand and he led her to stand before another mirror. He placed one hand on her shoulder, the other clutched his staff. For a moment they stood poised, reflected in the polished surface of the glass, and Timias felt his heart contract when he stared at the perfect beauty of her face. It was the color of her eyes, he decided, that gave her appearance such a compelling quality, one that was as fascinating as it was apparent. Or was it? he mused, murmuring aloud to cover for his moment of hesitation, "When I look at you, my lady, I see how foolish I am to waste any time at all in Shadow."

Despite the cast of worry in her dark blue eyes, a delicate pink stained her cheeks, and her lips quirked up in a fleeting smile. "I'm glad you came back when you did, my lord Timias." Despite the guileless innocence of her reply, he felt a fleeting throb of warning. There was more to this girl-sidhe than met the eye. Far more. She pressed his hand against her shoulder, then stepped into the glass. Together they walked through the weirdly refracted world behind the mirrors, through twisting corridors and winding staircases lit by intermittent shards of splintered light, until at last they stood behind the mirror which hung opposite the chamber deep within the very heart of the palace.

As she attempted to step through glass, for the first time that Timias had ever experienced, the surface of the mirror seemed to impede her progress, as though it were covered in some sticky, translucent film. She backed away, fine strands of some sticky white fiber clinging to her hand. "What is this?" she murmured.

She pushed through the film with more determination and it gave way with a slight puff. She forced her way through it. As they stepped into the vestibule, they looked back and Timias saw the surface of the mirror was covered with a fine sheen of what he recognized at once as dust. "What is this stuff?" she whispered, more to herself than to him.

Dust, he realized. But did she even know the word? Dust did not exist in Faerie. "It's dust," he said aloud.

"Dust," she echoed, shaking out her skirts. "It's all over the place." But there was no more time to wonder about its presence, for she gripped his hand, and pointed at the floor. It was covered with the same sheen of fine white dust as the mirror. And clearly, just as their outlines were visible in the dust of the mirror, the outline of a single set of footsteps led from the set of doors in the left wall, directly to the high bronze doors opposite the mirror.

"Someone else has been here. Not that long ago." Her voice was flat in the stillness.

"And we cannot ask the guards on the other side of that door, can we?"

"Why would something that cannot be touched need a guard?" Her lips quirked up for a moment in a satirical little smile.

The footsteps led directly to the door, and both Delphinea and Timias were careful not to disturb them. "I wonder who it was."

"A single person alone could not open the door."

Whoever had come in had paused before the door, then reversed himself, and exited the vestibule through the set of doors in the right wall. Whoever it was had not wanted to leave by the same way he'd entered.

"Could these be your footsteps, Delphinea?"

"No. I've only looked through the mirror. I didn't even know about that—that dust."

All around them, Timias had a sense of enormous age, as if something heavy beat through the atmosphere, like the throb of a great drum, more felt than heard. He had fled this chamber, thinking then he would never come back, shuddering in the wake of the magic they had raised. Now nothing of that awful midnight echoed in the chamber. A vague sense of dread descended on him. This was one place he had never hoped to revisit.

Delphinea placed one palm flat on the right hand side of the golden panel set on each of the bronze double doors. The metal glowed and hummed at her touch, and the great hinges groaned, as if rousing themselves from an age asleep. Timias placed his left palm on the left panel, and gripped Delphinea's left hand with his right. The doors themselves shivered, and with a harsh screech, the great doors swung inward, to reveal a small chamber where the ceiling soared fifty feet or more, all the way to a round window of faceted glass, where the morning sun streamed down in long prisms of color. The colors formed a shifting pattern that shimmered in long shafts all around the moonstone, which stood on a simple pillar of white marble in the middle of the room. Timias clutched at the door, and Delphinea stifled a cry. "Timias, whoever it was got in." The single set of footsteps led directly to the marble pillar.

In the bright light, the moonstone shone a pale, milky green, its surface polished to a high shine. It sat upon its marble base, seemingly as pure and pristine as the night it had been placed there, bare and round and naked as the rump of a newborn child. The Silver Caul was gone.

4

The low moans of the wounded and the dying rose and fell from the floor of the great hall of Castle Gar, the sullen light of flickering fires and fretful rushlights glowing red on blood-crusted bandages and pain-ravaged faces. A small army of women roamed between the crowded rows, their skirts rustling over the blanketed forms, voices low, as they offered water, changed bandages, spooned gruel, and oversaw the removal of the dead to the stables, which had been hastily set up as a temporary morgue.

Donnor, Duke of Gar, standing on the balcony which in happier times served as a musicians' gallery, folded his arms across his chest and his lips into a thin, tight line as he surveyed the scene below. Despite the unseasonable late-autumn heat, low fires burned in the great hearths along the walls, numerous iron pots steaming on tripods over the banked flames. The stench of mud and sweat, blood and fear, was thick in the heavy, humid air, but there was no escaping it. More wounded crowded the corridors leading into the hall, and even more of the less wretched, those who'd escaped the battle with only minor injuries, such as a severed finger, were being tended out in the courtyard. Thank the Great Mother that the blasted rain had ended at last. The carnage on the battlefield was far worse than this, if such a thing were possible, and the heavy rain made the retrieval of the dead impossible.

An image of his last glance at the battlefield as his captains had urged his retreat flashed before his eyes: the dead in contorted heaps of arms and legs and torsos; discarded spears and swords and broken arrows sticking up at crazy angles like twisted, tortured trees out of a nightmare forest; the red flare of fires; white smoke, which stung his arid eyes, drifting like ghosts above the corpses, even as lightning forked across the sky, thunder rolled down the valley, and the enemy poured across the hills like the sudden onslaught of rain that enabled his own escape.

Neither side could claim victory, but time was of the essence. If the warchiefs of the North did not respond to his call for assistance immediately, his cause could very quickly be crushed beneath the weight of the foreign army the Queen Consort was surely summoning from her homeland of Humbria across the Morhevnian Sea. He had sent a messenger north nearly three weeks ago, and so far, there had been no reply from any quarter. But the usual late-autumn storms in the higher mountain passes may have delayed both the messenger and any response, he tried to reassure himself.

Out of habit, he cursed the ill-fated day that he and the other members of the King's Council had granted approval to Hoell's marriage to Merle, the young princess of Humbria. He remembered the eager, earnest look on the younger man's face as he pled with the Councilors to allow him to marry Merle. A match to seal an alliance, a friendship between the two nations forever, Hoell had argued. The princess was young, healthy, and being from a family of seven brothers and six sisters, surely fertile. And Hoell himself—approaching thirty and free of fits for nearly ten years—surely it was past time he married and produced his own heir? Not that he was in a hurry to disinherit his dear kinsman, Donnor. He'd added that last so charmingly, so disarmingly that Donnor and the other members of the Council—old men all—looked at each other and in the young King's words felt the tug of their own faded vigor. How could they deny the King the chance to father his own legitimate heir, after all? And so, beguiled by their own deepest regrets, fears, and wishes, they failed to see the trap they'd fallen in. The shrugs and nods had gone around the table, from Councilor to Councilor, from old man to old man. *We were seduced by our memories, not convinced by fact*, Donnor thought bitterly.

But a seed of foreboding had been sown that day in the back of Donnor's mind—a nameless fear he steadfastly, and in retrospect foolishly, ignored through all the days of Hoell's official engagement. As the wedding approached, misgiving repeatedly raised its face and danced an ugly jig;

each time a cousin, a younger sister, a nephew-by-marriage of the new Queen was granted some post or title at the Court. But for a year after the wedding, nothing of consequence happened; Hoell seemed content and the newlyweds held court in a style that reflected the new Queen's Humbrian preferences. The new courtiers made no secret of the fact that they thought the customs of Brynhyvar rude and uncouth if not downright barbaric compared to their own, and Hoell, eager to please his bride, allowed their influence to grow to the point where even the chiefs of the Outermost March spoke openly at the Beltane Gathering that foreigners were taking over the Court.

Donnor retired to Gar and hoped the new King's infatuation would run its natural course. Then, within a few months of the marriage's first anniversary, three of the Council members either died or reached an age where it was impossible for them to continue in their duties. They were replaced, as was customary, by three members of the same clans, although of these, two were recently married to Humbrian wives, and held Humbrian titles, and the other was a cousin of the Queen's, a member of the clan in question only by virtue of the fact that he had married into it.

Cadwyr, Duke of Allovale, Donnor's nephew and heir, demanded that they raise their standards then. But Donnor insisted on waiting, torn by loyalty to the oaths he had sworn both to Hoell and to his father.

And then, on the second anniversary of the marriage, just as it was announced that the Queen was pregnant, the youngest brother of the Queen, Renvahr, the sixth in line to the throne of Humbria, was named the Duke of Longborth, one of a series of titles normally reserved for the heir to the throne of Brynhyvar, a title that should have been bestowed on Donnor himself long before this.

Almost immediately it was clear that Donnor's reluctance may have cost them the rebellion. For in the same year that Hoell's baby son died of a lung infection, Hoell's fits returned, leaving him docile, innocent as a child, and utterly unfit to rule.

Too late Donnor recognized the strategy of the King of Humbria—overburdened with children, he ranged far and wide, brazenly gobbling as many thrones and titles as possible through strategic marriages and their resulting alliances. The Duke of Longborth's appointment as Protector of the Realm in his own stead was the final slap to his honor. For he, Donnor, both by blood and marriage, was the rightful heir to the throne of Brynhyvar—not the foreign upstart Renvahr, whose only claim was his relationship to the Queen Consort and a title he had no business receiving. It should have been Donnor's place to rule the country while the King was incapacitated, rampant rumor blaming the fit on a chance encounter with one of the Shining Ones.

Privately Donnor disbelieved the theory. There was madness in Hoell's family—but dynastic necessity demanded his brother marry the lovely Elissade. Lovely she was, but dangerous, too, a woman given to fits of anger so fierce she was finally locked away in a tower for her own good. She died by leaping out the window in the midst of a fit, dashing her brains on the paving below. Fortunately Hoell had not inherited his mother's rages. Instead he became meek as a newborn lamb, easy to care for, but wholly unable to deal with the fractious, brawling chiefs and lords who comprised the nobility of Brynhyvar, let alone the insinuations of his foreign bride and her relatives.

Another image flashed through Donnor's mind: the bewildered look in the King's sad, slack eyes when Donnor had thrown down the ritual gauntlet on the floor beside Hoell's chair at the head of the Council table, where Hoell sat, a forlorn figurehead, King in name only. Queen Merle shrieked a curse in her native tongue, her black eyes blazing like jet in her white face. The other Councilors, all foreigners like Renvahr and the Queen now, gasped as one body.

But Hoell only picked up the glove, and stroked the much-creased leather. "You dropped this, Uncle," the King said, a hesitant smile lifting the full, soft mouth as plump and red as a woman's. Donnor closed his eyes, remembering the pain of betrayal that lanced through his chest.

Renvahr rose to his feet, hand fumbling for the hilt of his sword, while the two Councilors sitting on either side of him struggled to hold him back. "You want war, Gar?" he shouted. "Then, by the goddess, you shall have it!" Renvahr's eyes had flicked over to Cadwyr, where he stood beside the door, waiting to follow Donnor out of the room. "And what about you, Allovale?" he'd barked. "Will you betray your blood?"

"You are no blood of mine, Renvahr," had been Cadwyr's terse reply. They had stalked out of the Council chamber together, shoulder to shoulder, the only two native-born members left, for not even Renvahr had dared to remove them. Yet. Donnor allowed himself one last look at Hoell's face, and felt another stab of guilt that he should so betray his brother's son, even as the Queen screamed obscenities, Renvahr cried for order, and Hoell dissolved into a slow stream of tears.

Below, a low, keening wail erupted from one of the women as she recognized a father, a brother, a lover, or a son, and Donnor braced his shoulders against the nameless woman's grief. A familiar form crossed his line of sight—the slim, blond shape of Cecily, his Duchess—as she hurried to the grieving woman's side. Was she even five-and-twenty yet, he wondered? Surely she'd been no more than sixteen when her parents had agreed to the match. It was a wildly advantageous marriage for him, for it linked two rival septs of the Clan Garannon, but it did not prevent tongues across the breadth and length of Brynhyvar from whispering about the forty-year difference in their ages. But he'd learned long ago that such a plum ripened only rarely, and he hastened to seize it while he could. In all the eight years she'd been his wife, she'd failed him in only one respect—she had never carried a living child to term. Now the front of her apron and her gown was stained with blood and dirt and worse, while worry creased her forehead and sleeplessness smudged dark shadows beneath her eyes. She looked nothing like the innocent girl she'd been when they'd danced at their wedding. How happy he'd been that day, how sure that at last, he'd found his heart's own yearning. How much he'd looked forward to settling down into the rosy glow of the late afternoon of his life, beget an heir, or two or more. A sadness, a regret swept over him at how differently it had all worked out.

If only they'd had a child, he thought. Surely things would be far different, if only they'd had a child.

With a sudden screech, a black shape plunged from a ledge high above and as Donnor startled back, a raven swept low over the hall. It wheeled and dipped over the long rows of wounded, gave a shrill caw and flew out an open window. There was a general stir throughout the hall, and Donnor shuddered involuntarily. There was no mistaking that omen, for the raven was a harbinger of the Marrihugh, the warrior goddess. He could almost feel her striding across the land in her crow-feathered boots, crying out for foreign blood. But how many of his own men must die? he wondered, as he watched the stretcher-bearers carry away the corpse, while Cecily folded the grieving woman in her arms, rocking her gently as if she held a child. How many more must die, he wondered, before her thirst was slaked?

He noticed that Cecily looked up, following the raven's flight, as she hugged the woman close. Then his eye was caught by the familiar gleam of hair so pale it was nearly white, and he saw that Kian, the First Knight of his household, and thus the captain of his personal guard, had slipped into the hall, and was making his way across the crowded floor to Cecily. From this height, he could not see Kian's expression, but Donnor had no doubt of the eager light burning in Kian's eyes. Since Beltane, Donnor saw it every time his captain looked into his Duchess's face.

In only a few quick steps, Kian was beside her, the thick strands of his long hair clinging damply to the green and blue plaid he wore flung over one shoulder. Donnor stared, rooted in place by a hard anger made even hotter by shame. It had been a year—no, closer to two, really—since he had last shared Cecily's bed. After the last hope of an heir had bled itself away, he had excused himself, murmuring that he could not bear to hear her weep over yet another unborn babe.

But that was not the real reason. If he went not to her bed, it was because he could not, and if ever Cecily bore a child, he would have to know it was not his. As her husband, he would be bound to acknowledge the child or cry her out for adultery, and see her burned at the stake. As Kian bent over her, his mouth close to her ear, Donnor broke free of the spell, turned on his heel, and fled, unable to watch any longer.

Cecily heard the crow's harsh cry, and looked up from the desperate clutch of Rowena's arms. Beside her, she could feel the comforting bulk of old Mag, chief still-wife, who could always be counted upon as much for a broad shoulder and an open ear as a soothing brew in times of trouble and distress. So many dead, she thought, as Rowena's warm, wet weight pressed against her neck. She had known the moment she had seen the long procession of wounded carted through the gates that the slaughter begun on the battlefield wasn't over. As the stretcher-bearers lifted the corpse, she whispered the ancient words to speed the newly-dead to the Summerlands, and hugged Rowena closer:

"These three things I bid thee keep—
The memory of merry days and quiet nights
Of quiet days and merry nights,

Honor unstained by word or deed
And all the love I bear for thee."

Rowena's thin shoulders shook with sobs as the body was borne away. "He was my whole heart," she choked, while old Mag crooned a gentle hush.

Cecily glanced up at the balcony, where Donnor still stood, staring fixedly at the door as if he could will the messenger to arrive. She wondered if he even saw the men dying here below. She could not imagine weeping so hard for Donnor, if it were his body on the bier. Would she feel anything but a nebulous sense of regret, if the old lion, as most of the inhabitants of the castle lovingly referred to their Duke, were to die? As she rocked Rowena back and forth, she imagined herself a widow, and recognized it felt as odd to imagine herself a widow as it did to remind herself that she was Donnor's wife. Lately she'd been plagued more and more by the constant vague feeling that there was something else she should be doing, some other role she was meant to play. Whatever it was, it continued to escape her.

Easy for him to stand above, removed, and watch, she thought, suddenly angry, leaving her to deal with this river of death; leaving Kian to deal with what defenses they could muster until the clan chiefs answered Donnor's summons. She sighed to herself as she thought of Kian—at just past thirty, he was tall and strong and courageous, well-liked by all for the uplander's courtesy he extended to even the meanest of the castle scullions. Although he had been a member of Donnor's house for at least three years now, their duties kept them separate and apart much of the time and she had never even noticed him except in briefest passing. It was only this past Beltane their eyes had met and she had noticed a look in his she attributed to the nature of the rite, a look that had made her knees weak as a wave of longing and desire swept over and through her. That night, after the feast, as was her right, she had turned to him to lead her out into the forest. She closed her eyes against the memory of how gently he had kissed her before they were swept up by the goddess and the god into a maelstrom of passion that left her wondrously replete as a foggy sun rose over the low hills, and changed, changed completely. As the last shadows faded to gray, he had covered her body with his once more, and tenderly, tiredly, made love with her a final time—all sense of god or goddess long vanished. That was when I fell in love with him, she thought, and tears sprang into her eyes as loss and need closed like a fist around her heart and for a moment she shared Rowena's grief utterly. But the marriage contract was exacting, explicit, and under the current circumstances, divorce was not to be thought of. But since that Beltane night, neither she, nor Kian, nor Donnor had been the same.

"My lady Duchess?"

Kian's low voice startled her, so that she pulled away entirely from Rowena's stranglehold grasp, and stared up, feeling that he must have appeared in response to her thoughts. His dark brows were knit over his intense dark eyes, his mouth drawn down and grim. As he leaned down to speak into her ear, his hair, the color of sun-bleached seashells, brushed against her cheek. It was damp from the rain, and on his blue and green plaid, tiny droplets of water gleamed like pink-tinted pearls in the reddish light. "If you will, my lady, I need a word with you at once."

Cecily took another step back. In Kian's presence she felt herself young, and ripe and ready as a peach to fall into his hand—the opposite of everything Donnor made her feel. But she heard a new timbre in Kian's voice that she had never heard before—an urgency that bordered on fear. She saw him glance above, and following his eyes, saw that Donnor no longer stood like a sentinel at the watch. "What's wrong?"

Kian shook his head, his mouth barely moving. "I—I cannot say here. Please, come with me, my lady."

Their eyes met, and while her spine stiffened against her body's involuntary response to his closeness, she realized that there was nothing of the lover in the man who stood beside her, tense as a stallion poised to bolt. With a brief murmur to Mag, and a final squeeze on Rowena's shoulder, she allowed Kian to lead her to a seldom-used retiring room off to one side of the hall, now stocked with barrels and baskets of every description and size, in which were piled high everything from candles and the season's first apples to bandages and twine. "What is it? What's wrong?" She wiped her hands on her apron, and watched, puzzled as he led her into the center of the room, then shut the door behind them. He filched an apple from a large basket beside the hearth and turned to face her. His expression was as grim as she had ever seen it, but it was colored by that new element, an element that looked very much like fear and tinged by doubt and disbelief. He looked, she decided, like a man who'd seen a ghost. Or a sidhe.

He hesitated, clearly gathering his thoughts. "In truth, I scarce know how to begin. I would have showed it to you before I had it burned, but I would not inflict such a curse upon your memory." He ran the apple under his nose. "Faugh—the stink of it is still on me, and I've washed my hands three times." He threw the apple into the empty hearth, where it landed with a bounce and a roll.

Show me what? she wanted to interrupt, but he went on, his words tumbling over themselves like stones falling downhill. "It was just past three—" she startled at his words, realizing that the day was much farther advanced than she had realized "—just past three, just as I had come to stand my turn upon the watch—you know that every able-bodied man over fourteen is taking a turn?"

When she nodded, he continued. "Within the first hour, two men came in. The first was from Tuirnach of Pentland. Donnor's own messenger hadn't arrived yet, not by the time this messenger left, which was only two days ago, which is troubling enough in and of itself, but it's the second one that has unsettled me, to the point where I stand before you now like a moon-mazed calf." He paused and shook his head as if to clear it. When he spoke again, his voice was so low, she had to strain to hear it in the quiet room. "The second messenger—though he's no more a messenger than I am a cook—came from a little village, in the uplands, just above Killcarrick Keep. Donnor knows it—it's the village where Dougal lives—Dougal the smith who forged the sword Donnor wears in battle. You know the smith I mean?"

She nodded mutely, listening intently, trying to discern the source of his disquiet.

"Donnor's messenger isn't the only one missing. For Dougal himself is missing—he disappeared four or five nights ago."

"What happened?"

"I don't know what happened. I do know that the piece of carcass this man showed me was part of nothing ever spawned in this world." His eyes sought hers and held them, as if gauging her reaction. "For you see, in the same hour that it was realized Dougal the smith was missing, the villagers found a goblin—a dead goblin, thank the goddess—floating in Killcarrick Lake." He took a deep breath and in the gloomy light that filtered through the translucent sheets of yellowish horn which filmed the windows, she saw that he absolutely believed the truth of what he said. "I saw it—smelled it—touched it—" He shut his eyes and grimaced. "I told my squire to burn it behind the midden, lest the stench of it alone cause a panic."

Cecily's mind raced. A thousand years or more had passed since the days of Bran Brownbeard, and the only time one heard talk of goblins was in the legends told around the winter fires, in the histories chanted through the annual cycle of ritual and ceremony. "But—but that isn't—that's not possible."

Kian gave a soft snort of derision. "Believe me, if what that man had in that sack wasn't goblin flesh, I don't know what would be. The claws—they were exactly as the old tales describe, and the way it reeked—" He shuddered. "There's no doubt in my mind at all. But beside the problem it presents all its own—which is how a goblin got here in the first place—there's the effect it could—it will—have on the outcome of our rebellion. For after yesterday, we hang on by not much more than a few threads here. The Humbrians are loading up their warships even as we speak. If the men desert our cause to return to protect their homes from goblins, we shall not stand."

For a long moment, she was silent. "But—but," Cecily began, frowning. "If this is true, at the news of a goblin in Brynhyvar, the druids will step in—surely there will be a halt to the hostilities—the druids will insist—"

"Indeed, and the Humbrian army will continue to grow on the other side of the water and we will not be able to mobilize or maneuver while the druids wrangle amongst themselves." He looked at her, and she knew he expected her to understand the greater meaning contained in his words, beyond the obvious. "If that happens, Donnor will be forced to call in old alliances across the Sea and beyond the mountains. And the war will spread across our borders, like a fire raging out of control."

"Why have you come to me?" Her voice quivered, for his presence unsettled her. She clasped her hands before her, to steady them. Too easily he stirred up feelings she thought firmly suppressed. And why did he always make her feel as if there was something about her that he knew and she did not, as if he could see some aspect of herself she could not? In the hazy light, his pale hair glowed with a pearly luminescence and not for the first time, she thought he looked like a lord of the Shining Ones.

"Where's Donnor?" he asked abruptly.

"Gone to rest at last, I imagine. He was up on the balcony until just now—hoping some word would come, I think. He will be glad to hear from Tuirnach at least."

"I sent the messenger to eat—he's ridden without stopping through two nights to reach us as quickly as he did."

She took a single step closer, and fancied she could see the beating of his heart through the thin linen shirt. "You didn't answer me."

His dark eyes bored into hers, and the room was so quiet, she could hear her pulse pounding in her ears. In two quick steps he was beside her, and for a moment, she thought he might sweep her up into his arms. But he only spoke in a whisper that seared her to the bone. "I come to you, my lady, because I remember who you are, even if you choose not to."

She stared up at him, taken aback. "If I ever forget that I am the wife of the Duke of Gar, I am always reminded soon enough." Tears welled in her eyes. "Kian, I wish we could leave all this behind us. This is Donnor's war—Cadwyr's war—it doesn't have to be ours. We could go somewhere, anywhere—south, perhaps, to Lacquilea—leave this whole dangerous mess—" she broke off, as sobs of frustration and fatigue choked her.

"Ah, Cecily." With a sigh, he pulled her into the circle of his arms, cradling her head against his rain-damp chest. She relaxed against him, savoring the blend of horses and damp wool beneath the acrid tang of his sweat-stained linen. He pressed his cheek against the top of her head, and she heard him draw a deep breath. When he spoke, his voice was low with regret. "You know we cannot do that. Would you have us be outlaws, exiles, unwelcome at every hearth? We must just be patient a little while longer, until—"

"Until what?" she asked, as the tears spilled down her cheeks and she twined her fingers in the rough wool of his plaid. His dagger's leather hilt dug into her waist, but she pressed closer uncaring. "Until our cause is lost?"

"Hush now, don't say that. We will prevail. It's just the northern chiefs are somewhat slow to rouse themselves—"

She pulled back and met his gaze with a stubborn chin. "Don't pretend to me, Kian. I see the look on your face—on Donnor's. I see the number lying here and I see how many didn't come back at all. And now you say they've found a goblin of all things. What difference does it make if we stay or go?"

"You have but to say the word, lady, and ten thousand men of Garannon and Garleugh both would march beneath a standard of your raising. It is *you* should reign in Brynhyvar, not that old lion run to fat. And Cadwyr crowds close behind—think you the throne will pass to you, should Donnor fall?"

"Cadwyr is loyal to Donnor," she choked out.

"Aye, to Donnor for he is Donnor's heir, but what if Donnor falls in battle? I do not trust Cadwyr—his eyes are slippery and he unpockets his smile at will. And Donnor will not listen to me. Oh, he trusts me to preserve his life, for he knows I shall stand upon my word. But ever since Beltane, he hates me, Cecily, and all I say to him falls on deaf ears."

She lowered her eyes against the pain she read in Kian's face. They had not, either of them, in fact betrayed the vows they had sworn to Donnor. Beltane was sacred—it was not unheard of for husbands and wives to choose others—although it was usually by preagreement.

But the goddess was on me, she thought, I could not help myself. There was no dishonor, no shame in what they had done. Honor was all, but the goddess and the god must be answered as well. And honor was cold comfort on winter nights, and honor was a lonely partner when memory made the blood run hot. With effort she ignored the recollection of his hands on her breasts, and asked, "So, you want me to go to Donnor...?"

"No." The force with which he answered took her aback. "Cadwyr, curse him, was right. We should have thrown down the gauntlet long ere this. But we did not, and thus we must play the hand we've dealt ourselves. The carcass is burned and I've ordered the man who brought it not to speak of it, and thank the goddess he seems to understand the reason not to cause a general panic. But I promised I'd go back with him—back to the village where they found the goblin and organize a search for the smith and possibly the messenger, and make sure nothing else is amiss. And I will see to the gathering of the clans myself. I'll take a small troop with me—a couple dozen or so. They can fan out across the upcountry, while I attend to this other business."

"But—but, Kian—" She understood that there was something he seemed to be asking her, but she failed to comprehend what it could be. "Why do you come to *me?* 'Tis Donnor's place to bid you stay or go."

He took her hand and caught it up between both of his, and she curled her fingers around his involuntarily. "Can you not see? Donnor is old, and already defeated. He sees the mistakes he's made—indeed that's all he sees. He will not outlive this war, I see it in his eyes. And unless you are content to live in a land ruled by Cadwyr, *you* are the one with the best claim to the throne of Brynhyvar. *You* I would follow into the deepest dungeon of the Goblin King himself. Cadwyr I would sooner leave upon a dung heap."

She made a soft sound of derision and smiled ruefully. "Well, my gallant champion, you are an army of exactly one."

"You're wrong, Cecily. You were not trained in sword-craft, and you cannot throw a spear, but you could rule this realm. Too soon your parents sold you out to Donnor. You have a claim in your own right. Donnor is failing—Donnor will fall. And when he does, I do not want to see Cadwyr step into his place, but Cadwyr will take it the moment he has the opportunity, unless another choice clearly presents itself."

Wonderingly she searched his face. "You truly believe this."

"Of course I believe it. I will not bend my knee to Cad-wyr. I ride out within the hour. Tell Donnor I have gone north to rally the clans. But say nothing of the goblin—at least not yet, and not until we have more information and nothing—nothing at all of any of this—to Cadwyr. He should not be here for another day or two, at least. Donnor sent him into the east to raise up Far Nearing." He raised his hand and for a moment, she thought he might kiss her, but he only tucked an errant blond strand behind her ear. "I will go to the chiefs, and I shall raise up an army—in *your* name, not Donnor's. And when I return, my lady, I'll bring you an army that marches beneath *your* colors, not Gar's. 'Twill remind everyone, including Cadwyr, that there are certain choices yet to be made—and while he may be Donnor's heir, he will only be King by the consent of us all."

He bowed and would have swept out of the room, but she held out her hand, and spoke. "Kian—"

He reached for her then, and crushed her to his chest, his arms wrapping around her, holding her close. He bent his head and spoke quietly but harshly, his words hotter than his breath. "Do not think because I do not touch you I don't want you. I burn for you, Cecily, night and day—" He took her hand and crushed it against the rigid bulge at his groin. She moaned a little and swayed on her feet. "But we cannot let this love we have between us divert us from the greater purpose, and I cannot let this lust keep me from what I know I must do." He turned his head and his mouth found hers.

The world spun, and she shut her eyes, surrendering to the insistent pressure of his lips. He lifted her hand up, entwining his fingers with hers in a desperate fist. Then he set her back on her feet, and lifted his head. "Stay well, my lady."

For a long moment after he had gone, she stood motionless, feeling the blood pound in every vein, her mind racing. He was right, of course. If they took off, across the sea, or south, beyond the Marraghmourn Mountains, they would indeed be exiles in every sense of the word—for while Kian's sword would be welcomed into the service of any foreign lord, the hearths and halls of their own country would be forever barred. It was more than anyone had any right to ask. There was wisdom, too, in saying nothing about the goblin—for it may indeed yet turn into nothing, she thought. Some strange fluke, some odd coincidence. An omen, perhaps, but scarcely a good one. With a puckered frown, she opened the door, and thought she saw, slipping up the staircase behind the dais at the far end of the hall, two tall shapes, both cloaked in plain black. The hood slipped off the first's head, as he turned around to speak to his companion. He drew it quickly over his head, but not before Cecily saw the unmistakable gleam of Cadwyr of Allovale's bright gold hair. But how could that be, she thought. Kian had just said that Cadwyr was in the east, to rally the lords of Far Nearing. She hurried closer, trying to make sure, for if Kian's hair glowed like the full moon, Cadwyr's shone like the noon sun. They were as different as night and day, too, she thought, as she squinted in the semidark. The second figure, who appeared leaner than the first, followed close behind, and the black cloak he wore blended so perfectly into the shadows, he seemed to vanish. She blinked, and he *did* vanish, and all she saw was the one, moving up the stairs with Cadwyr's familiar swagger, two and three steps at a time. As she stepped on the first stair, he reached the top of the staircase, then rounded the corner and disappeared out of sight. By the time she set foot on the first landing herself, she could see that the corridor in both directions was deserted.

Images of Cadwyr, Kian and goblins roiled in her mind as she walked up the steps. She disliked Cadwyr—had always thought him overforward, and aggressive, but he had always seemed devoted to Donnor. After all, in the absence of a son, Cadwyr was Donnor's heir. She paused in midstep, catching the wooden banister for balance, as a monstrous thought occurred to her. Cadwyr was Donnor's heir. Cadwyr had been one of the loudest voices insisting on the rebellion—insisting Donnor lead the rebellion—but Donnor was an old man, well over sixty. If the old warrior did not survive to rule, who would be surprised? She went up the steps much more slowly, pondering. Kian had not meant to imply the possibility of treachery, or had he? At the top, she paused and looked both ways down the corridor. The heavy door of Donnor's Council chamber was closed. On a whim, she pushed the door. It swung open without a sound to reveal a chamber empty but for the long table littered with maps in the fading afternoon gloom.

At the other end of the corridor, the door to the antechamber of Donnor's bedroom was closed. Could she have been mistaken, she wondered? The two figures—nothing but a trick of the shadows and an imagination overwrought by Kian?

She bit her lip, uncertain, then straightened. Kian was right about one thing. Her claim to the throne of Brynhyvar was as good, if not better than Donnor's alone. She strode purposefully to the door and knocked. She heard quick, heavy footfalls, and then Donnor himself opened the door. He looked very surprised to see her. "My lady Duchess?"

"I came to see if there was anything you required, my lord," she said, using the only excuse she could think of.

He narrowed his eyes, and she noticed the deep pits smudged beneath them, the furrowed wrinkles in his grizzled brow. "No. No, my lady, nothing."

She tried to see over his shoulder, into the room beyond. "Someone told me that my lord of Allovale has arrived?"

He started at the name and his face flushed an ugly red. "Cadwyr? No, of course not."

He glanced down and she knew, in that moment, that he

was lying, that Cadwyr had somehow come into the castle, unannounced and unnoticed, in a manner so unlike him, that coupled with Kian's insinuations, made her immediately suspicious. What possible reason could there be for Donnor to lie to her about Cadwyr's arrival? But she only backed away, and dipped a bob of a curtsy. "I see. I must've misheard. Forgive me, my lord, for the intrusion. If there's nothing else you require—"

"Disturb me only if a messenger comes." He shut the door firmly even as she backed away.

Why would Donnor lie? She wandered in the direction of the staircase. It was possible for someone to enter the hall from the back entrance, the one which led from the kitchen yard. But was it possible for anyone as well known as the Duke of Allovale to enter the castle without being recognized? *I ride within the hour.* Kian's voice echoed in her mind. Kian would know if such a thing were possible, and certainly Kian should know what she'd seen just now, before he left. She raised her skirts and scampered down the staircase. At the bottom, she stopped the first guard she saw. "Go to Lord Kian at once," she said, crisply, feeling oddly, wholly sure of herself. "Tell him I must speak with him before he leaves—I shall await him in my retiring room."

She watched with satisfaction as the guard bowed and went to do her bidding. Perhaps this war was not just Donnor's war after all.

5

"Slide the bolt," Cadwyr said from the shadows, as Donnor turned away from the door. "What'd she want? I thought you said she never comes here."

The insolence with which Cadwyr referred to Cecily made Donnor frown. Angry as the sight of Cecily and Kian together made him, it burned in his stomach to lie to her. He was already taken off guard that Cadwyr should suddenly appear, just as afternoon was fading into dusk, unannounced and accompanied by only one companion—a companion who was standing still and silent beside the empty hearth, his black hood pulled low over his face. Donnor folded his arms across his chest and pinned Cadwyr with his most piercing stare. "So what's this about, Cadwyr? Why have you come sneaking into my house like a thief in the night?"

Cadwyr grinned, showing even white teeth in a face many

thought handsome, and glanced at the other. His nostrils flared, and Donnor narrowed his eyes. The younger man's face was flushed, the color high in his broad cheekbones. There was a furtive quality about the way he hunched on the stool, in the way he clasped his hands together on the unpolished surface of the table and spoke in a hoarse voice so low it was nearly a whisper. "I've brought someone I want you to meet, Uncle." He glanced once more at his companion, then licked his lips. He turned back to Donnor, eyes dancing in his sweat-streaked face with some suppressed emotion Donnor could not read. He looked at the stranger, standing so motionless and quiet beside Cadwyr, his black cloak falling around his tall, lean frame as fluid as a shadow. "Who are you?" Donnor barked. "Show yourself, man."

The stranger bowed. "As you wish, my lord of Gar."

Cadwyr made a sound that might have been a chuckle as Donnor hissed in reaction to that unmistakable cadence. The stranger raised black-gloved hands and pushed the deep cowl off his face, and for the space of a heartbeat, Donnor stood mesmerized. Coal-black curls fell in lush waves to the sidhe's shoulders, framing a fine-boned face the palest shade of gold, in which green eyes glittered like emeralds in the wavering flame. A scent, sweet as summer meadows and clear water, rose from the folds of his garments. Then the implications of the presence of a sidhe in his own bedchamber broke the spell and he stepped back, staring in disbelief. "Cadwyr—by all that's holy and all that isn't—what have you done?"

Cadwyr coughed. "Uncle…Donnor, Duke of Gar, may I present the Lord Finuviel, Prince of the Sidhe."

Donnor gasped. The creature before him glowed like a

candle in the low-ceilinged room, which suddenly seemed far too small for all three of them. "Great Mother," he breathed. "I can't believe you've done this." Heedless of the sidhe, he gripped Cadwyr by the upper arm and half-lifted, half-dragged him into the inner chamber, where his bed and a few chests beneath the windows were the only furnishings. He slammed the door shut, then rounded on Cadwyr. "Whatever are you thinking? If this is known, every poor wretch down there who isn't dying of his wounds will die of terror. What about Far Nearing? Have you forgotten what we're in the midst of here? What madness is this?" He tried to keep his voice to a low hiss, for from the open courtyard far below, the voices of the guards floated up in disembodied snatches, signaling the changing of the watch. He ran a hand over his balding head, forcing himself to remain calm. "First that disaster of a battle and now this. What in the name of the Great Mother are you thinking?"

Cadwyr glanced at the door, then looked back at Donnor, a wolfish smile on his face, bright hair gleaming like the morning sun. He reached out and gripped Donnor's forearm, his eyes excited in the uncertain light. "That battle was no disaster, for they suffered losses as heavy as we did, if not heavier. But that's of no matter now, Uncle, for I bring us hope—no, even better. I bring us victory—victory assured and certain."

"Victory?" The word felt like gravel in Donnor's throat. There was a damp flush on Cadwyr's face and his lips were full, swollen, as if he'd just swallowed wine. He looked drunk or worse, thought Donnor, like a boy in his first rut. Donnor narrowed his eyes and shook free of Cadwyr's eager grip. "Control yourself, man. That sidhe has you all unsettled." He drew a deep breath to calm his own beating heart. "Now tell me, if you can, why you've brought this creature under my roof when it could be the ruin of everything before it's scarcely begun?"

"Uncle." Cadwyr's voice quivered with suppressed excitement. "I am not moonmazed, I swear it. Finuviel has offered us victory; indeed, he hands it to us on a plate. We have a chance to strike decisively at the Queen before the main body of the Humbrian army reaches our shores. If we can crush them now—now while they believe we wait for the clans to rally—we can drive the Pretender and the Queen into the sea before the rest of the scum ever reaches our shore."

Donnor hesitated, for the strategy that Cadwyr outlined was ideal. Indeed, it was why he so desperately awaited word that the chiefs had answered his call. But the idea that help could come from the sidhe—the Shining Ones who treated mortals as playthings at best—was so preposterous his mind refused to consider even the possibility. He snorted at the sheer absurdity. "And you believe him? No good ever comes of anything *they* meddle in for they delight in making fools of us and worse. Have you forgotten that some say *they're* to blame for Hoell's fits? And don't you recall my own great-grandsire? He was trapped in TirNa'lugh more than a hundred years and when they finally let him go he was a wreck of a man. What's this one promised *you?*"

"He's promised *us* an army of the sidhe. Archers, foot and horse of his own house who can't be slain by mortal weapon—"

"Save those of silver," finished Donnor sourly. "And what's he want of *you?*"

Cadwyr flushed a dark red and he drew back as though stung, but he lifted his head and met Donnor's eyes with a brazen assurance. "Nothing that will matter to either of us. But I'll let him explain. You'll see." A high thin wail curled through the open window as a lone piper called the changing of the watch, and Cadwyr jerked his head in the direction of the door. "Come, Uncle, the Prince is here. 'Tis rude to keep him waiting."

With a dark look, Donnor shouldered past Cadwyr, flung the door wide and strode back into the antechamber, where Finuviel waited beside the empty hearth. In the light of the single candle, he cast an enormous shadow against the dark bricks. "Why've you come here?" Donnor asked without preamble.

There was a brief pause while Cadwyr and Finuviel exchanged a look Donnor didn't understand. Then the sidhe began to speak, and Donnor was forced to concentrate, lest he lose the thread of meaning in the seductive rise and fall of the sidhe's speech. "I understand you mortals are at war amongst yourselves because you seek to wrest the throne of your country from the mad King who reigns over it, and from the foreign Councilors and the foreign Queen who rule in his stead." As musical and as lilting as the voice was, it was yet entirely and completely masculine. Donnor blinked, trapped for a moment in the full thrall of that compelling stare, so vividly green in the candlelight, as Finuviel continued. "And just as you have need of my help to drive the foreign infection from your soil, I have need of yours."

Repelled, but utterly fascinated, Donnor found himself wondering if Finuviel's skin really were as velvety as it appeared, if the curls that spilled over his hood and brushed against his smooth-shaven chin were truly as soft as spun silk.

Abruptly Donnor straightened, even warier than before. "And what do the affairs of your kind have to do with us?"

Finuviel had grace enough to shrug. "Not a thing that need concern you, my lord Duke." Once again his eyes locked with Donnor's. They glittered with an alien light, so cold, so foreign, that despite the superficial perfection of his manner, his look sent a chill down Donnor's spine.

"Then what kind of help do you look for from us?"

Cadwyr leaned forward, as if he feared Donnor would insult the sidhe. "My lord—"

"Hush, Cadwyr." With a flick of his hand, Donnor silenced Cadwyr and turned back to confront Finuviel. "Let him answer." The idea that there was something within their ken a sidhe needed enough to bargain for was even more unbelievable than Cadwyr's sudden arrival in Finuviel's company. For all the old stories—especially the ones about the great-grandsire who'd been seduced by the Queen of the Sidhe herself—emphasized that the sidhe treated humankind as playthings, and at best, in something of the same way as Donnor might a favored hound. He met the sidhe's eyes and this time steeled himself against the beguiling charm. "Well?"

Finuviel's gaze shifted to Cadwyr, who shrugged and answered. "He only wants a dagger, Donnor. I told you 'twas nothing we couldn't provide easily. He only wants a dagger—a dagger made of silver."

"Made of silver? What for?"

"That's none of your concern, mortal." Finuviel's voice was so cold, Donnor swore the temperature in the stifling room dropped noticeably.

But Donnor was the veteran of more battles than together he and Cadwyr had years and he would not be intimidated. "You agree this is an unusual request, my lord sidhe. For a silver dagger must be commissioned—it's not that we have such things lying stored. How soon must we produce this? And why would you be wanting or needing such a thing? Is not the touch of silver poison to all your kind?"

"The hilt will be of leather and bone," burst in Cadwyr. "The blade itself won't hurt him so long as he doesn't touch it. And what does it matter to us how he means to use it? And as for where to find it, we go tomorrow night to get it."

"Where?"

"I went to your favorite smith, Donnor. Dougal—the smith who forged your own sword."

At that Donnor felt as though the air had been punched from his lungs, and he sagged as though he'd been struck. For a moment, he said nothing, as he gathered his scattered, racing thoughts. He wondered if perhaps exhaustion had finally brought on some sort of waking dream state. But the stench of his own sweat and the ache in his muscles assured him that he was indeed wide awake. "You went to Dougal?" he said at last. "Dougal of Killcairn?"

"And why not? Is he not most skilled? And there's some story of how he was taken into Faerie—"

"It was his wife, not him," Donnor muttered.

"That's not the story I've heard."

"What matter the story? What story did you tell him? What did he say when he saw a sidhe at his own door?" Donnor sat back, incredulous at Cadwyr's daring. He could not imagine how Dougal had reacted, but something Cadwyr said must've convinced him to do such a thing. That or what Cadwyr had offered to pay. Or what Cadwyr had threatened to do. Suddenly a cold finger of fear traced itself down his back. What else would Cadwyr dare?

"I told him we needed such a dagger to win the throne of Brynhyvar. What else would I tell him but the truth? For that is the truth, Uncle. Think of it—a host of the sidhe—with such a force we need not wait for the northern chiefs to bestir themselves, nor crowd upon the walls, searching the horizon for signs of allies. We need not beg for favor or parley away that which is not even ours yet to parley. We need not rely on the strength of new friendships bandaged over old sores. With a company of the sidhe we can draw the foreign scum through the Ardagh Pass and drive them into the sea. Just think of it, Uncle." Cadwyr shook Donnor's forearm. "Think of it. Renvahr and the Queen can never prevail if we have troops that can't be killed—"

"Can't be killed?" repeated Donnor softly, and suddenly, understood the nature of the bargain. "But who do you want to be killing, my lord sidhe? Because that's it, isn't it? That's what's brought you to us. There's someone of your kind that you want to kill, and you need a silver weapon to do it, and you want to do it very very badly." He paused to gauge their reaction. Cadwyr only shrugged, but Finuviel met his eyes with a silent, grudging acknowledgment. "And if we hand over this dagger, if we give you this thing you should not even wish to possess—who's to say what repercussions there'll be? What happens next?" Cadwyr looked momentarily confused, but Finuviel only stared back with a look that made the hackles rise on the back of Donnor's neck. But he persisted. "If you succeed in this killing, all well and fine, perhaps. But what happens if you fail? Who might come looking for the maker of that dagger? Or the one who made the bargain in the first place?" He looked at Cadwyr. "Have you considered that?"

In the flickering light of the stubby candle, Cadwyr flushed again, and the cords in his throat tightened, but before he could answer, Donnor looked back at Finuviel. "Well?"

The sidhe stiffened. His eyes looked back at Donnor with a biting gleam that chilled him to the marrow of his bones, and when Finuviel spoke, it was with an edge as sharp as any dagger. "Such things are not your concern, mortal. But believe me when I tell you that the fate of my world hangs as much in the balance as does that of yours. If I fail in what I must do, there won't be anyone or anything left to come looking."

There was the ring of truth in the quiet words, and this time, when their eyes met, Donnor saw something familiar looking back. Startled, he recognized a common bond with the sidhe, impossible as that might seem. And then he remembered all the ancient warnings—that they entrapped their mortal victims, not just by a seduction of their senses, but more insidious means as well. After all, those unlucky mortals who removed their silver and followed the sidhe into the OtherWorld believed they did so freely.

He shook off the feeling of kinship, of connection and closed his eyes. Finuviel could not simply take the dagger. He needed it enough to bargain for it, but there was no warranty so far that would guarantee he would actually provide the troops he'd promised. "And when you hand over this dagger—this dagger you've had my own smith forge—what assurance do we have he'll come through with these troops, Cadwyr?"

The long silence thickened with each passing second. The air felt heavy and charged, and drops of sweat trickled down his neck. Finally Cadwyr cleared his throat. "That's a fair question, Uncle. But you can rest assured that Finuviel has given me a satisfactory guarantee—a guarantee that warrants any of the sidhe would honor the bargain."

Donnor narrowed his eyes. "Don't riddle me like a druid, Cadwyr. What're you talking about? How can you be sure he'll honor his part?"

Cadwyr exchanged another glance with Finuviel, who shrugged with a graceful lift of his shoulders. He patted the front of his doublet, then slipped his hand inside. "I have it here, Uncle." He removed a small leather bag of light tan hide. Donnor wrinkled his nose at the strong and subtly disagreeable odor that rose from it. "Hold out your hand, Uncle, since you insist." His eyes glittered with a mischievous gleam as though he alone were privy to some delicious secret.

Donnor glanced from Finuviel to Cadwyr, and held out his hand.

Cadwyr upended the bag and a fine silver stream poured out like a waterfall onto the leathery surface of Donnor's palm. In the dim candlelight, it lay shining like a puddle of water in starlight. "Great Mother," Donnor whispered. With a shaking forefinger, he spread it out, and saw that it was a web constructed of gossamer strands of silver mesh so fine it was obvious that no mortal hand alone had wrought it. "This—this cannot—" He raised his head and stared at each in turn with horror. "Tell me this is not the Silver Caul of Bran Brownbeard—"

"So long as we hold *that,* Uncle, we need have no fear that Lord Finuviel will not hold to his word."

Finuviel bowed. "Such a weighty promise demands a weighty guarantee."

The Caul lay light as a feather in the palm of Donnor's hand, as fragile and as deceptively innocent as any chain which might grace Cecily's neck. "What doom have you brought upon us, Cadwyr?" he muttered, shaking his head slowly. "What doom have you brought upon us all?"

The room seemed to shrink and the air grew heavy, so heavy Donnor thought he could see it, hot and tangible, stifling as a cloak. Or a shroud. On his hand the silver gleamed silent as a star.

"The sooner I bring my knights to you, the sooner I shall return the Caul." The sidhe's voice carried a gentle pressure, as soft and as insistent as a caress.

Donnor looked up. Once more their eyes locked, and Donnor felt the siren lure of the offered promise contained in that compelling gaze. This was it, he thought, the answer to every plea he placed before the goddess, a chance for victory both swift and certain.

Cadwyr spoke and his words hung in the silence. "This

is not our doom, Uncle, but our salvation. Wouldn't we be fools not to seize this chance Fortune's seen fit to serve us?"

Victory, Donnor thought, seeing in his mind's eye the enemy's final rout, the roar of his warriors, the triumphant skirl of the pipes. So easy and so close. By this time next month perhaps. The whole nightmare scene in the hall below consigned to fading memory, erased by the tide of jubilation for the victory accomplished so quickly and so well.

Cadwyr was an excellent tactician, whatever else might be said of him. He understood how to turn the natural terrain to his advantage, and his mention of the Ardagh Pass sparked a plan in Donnor's mind—a plan so easily achievable with Finuviel's help he could nearly smell the victory feast. He had but to acquiesce, to hand back the Caul and turn a blind eye to Cadwyr's involvement with this sidhe and whatever plots he wove in TirNa'lugh. He could imagine himself acclaimed King of Brynhyvar, being led to the queenstone, mounting it for the ritual mating with the land, descending to a Cecily smiling and radiant. He almost smelled the boggy mist rising from the fields of spongy peat in the foggy autumn dawn. He opened his eyes into Finuviel's and knew himself seduced.

He drew a deep breath and held out his hand, gesturing for Cadwyr to take the Caul back, for the skin of his palm prickled where it lay, as though it were formed of a thousand tiny pins. "You tamper with things that shouldn't be tampered with. I wish you'd come to me before you made this bargain, Cadwyr." His back itched and he remembered that at some point in this endless day, he had intended to bathe. The stubby candle was sputtering now, and what little light filtered from the open bedroom door had long since faded into a dark well of shadow.

Cadwyr said nothing as he poured the Caul back into the pouch, knotted it and slipped it back inside his vest. There was a sharp rap at the door. "Who is it?" Donnor shouted, startled by the unexpected knock.

"I come from Tuirnach of Pentland, my lord."

Donnor shut his eyes in response to the muffled reply. "Thank the goddess," he murmured. "At last." He strode over to the door, slid the bolt back, and opened it a crack, squinting into the rushlit corridor as if just awakened. The man—or boy—who stood before the door wore Pentland's familiar colors. He was not much more than a lad, thought Donnor, a stripling chosen for how lightly he'd sit upon a horse. There was scarce a haze of beard upon his youth-smooth face. "Wait a moment," Donnor said. He shut the door, took a deep breath and turned back to face Cadwyr and his unorthodox companion.

The room was empty, but for the swirling shadow of smoke spiraling from the dying candle. It blended into the shadows around the perimeter of the room. He blinked, ran a hand over his head and rubbed his eyes with a thumb and forefinger. "Cadwyr?" he whispered.

The only answer was the low whistle of a cool breeze down the chimney. The temperature had dropped considerably since the rain had ended and gooseflesh rose on his arms and tickled the back of his neck. He threw open the bedroom door, but even as it slammed into the wall with a dull thud, he knew before he peered within that the room was as unoccupied as the antechamber. He shuddered, flirted momentarily with the explanation that the visit had been a fluke, a dream, a manifestation of exhaustion and anxiety. But a hide-bound message packet lay on the table, a packet that bore his own seal in red wax. He picked it up, broke the seal and opened it. It was his message to the chiefs of Far Nearing. Too busy with his own plots, Cadwyr had never gone to Far Nearing. Wooden at the realization that he had been so deceived, Donnor opened the door and beckoned the waiting messenger through it.

But even as he sat, listening with half an ear to Tuirnach's reassuring message of sworn loyalty, a sickening dread writhed to new life, a fear that events had been set in motion that went far beyond the physical boundaries of Brynhyvar. Cadwyr—his nephew and his heir—had deceived him. What game was Cadwyr playing? How dare he disregard Donnor's express command? What desperation had led him to tangle with the sidhe? There was a wild and unpredictable streak in Cadwyr that made him increasingly wary of the younger man. Cadwyr might be his heir, but perhaps he was not the best candidate to rule the contentious country.

The seldom-stirred memory of his great-grandfather rose before his eyes, his great-grandfather, Donn, who'd disappeared into TirNa'lugh before his son, Donnor's grandfather, was even born. He'd returned long after the child—who'd lived to be an old, old man, himself—was dead, and had lingered on a few more years, a wizened, shriveled shell, whose eyes leaked slow tears as if he perpetually mourned the loss of the son he'd never known. *There's only one thing that keeps us safe from them, lad.* Donnor remembered the old man's rasp, the dark eyes that burned in the wrinkled face, as if lit by some inner fire. *The Silver Caul of Bran Brownbeard, bless him. As long as you wear your silver you'll be safe. Never take it off, no matter what they promise.*

He fumbled automatically for the silver chain he wore around his neck, fingering the heavy amulet. *I have mine here,* he'd said, remembering the sound of his own childish treble. I have mine here, he thought, rubbing the thick disk between his thumb and forefinger. Though what was the good of it now? It had not kept him safe. For what his great-grandfather had neglected to tell him was that when the sidhe wanted something badly enough of mortals, no amount of silver could stop them from taking it.

The messenger's cough brought Donnor out of his reverie and he realized that the lad had stopped speaking, and was waiting for some response. He swallowed hard, and ran his hand over his bald head. War was a business best left to younger men. He cursed the dark day of Hoell's marriage and forced himself to think like the warrior he was supposed to be, not like the old man he felt.

If there was to be a battle fought within the next fortnight, there was not enough time for Tuirnach's men to be of any help. And better, anyway, to keep as many mortal warriors as possible out of it. There'd be less explaining to do—the bards would have more margin to spin a tale the fewer mortal witnesses there were. He would not call Tuirnach to the Ardagh Pass.

But his words felt heavy in his mouth, heavy as stones upon his tongue, and he wondered as he spoke why he felt as though he pronounced a death sentence. "Go back to Tuirnach," he said at last, "and tell him to await us at Killcarrick Keep."

"I'm sure it was Cadwyr. As sure as I am that it's *you* who stands before me. On my mother, I swear." Cecily lifted her chin and met Kian's eyes with a stubborn insistence.

The setting sun suffused the whole room with a rosy-pink glow. The last of the rain clouds were rapidly disappearing into the purplish twilight, for a fresh, clear wind was in the west. It blew through the long row of open windows in the casement above her window seat, a welcome change from the unseasonable heat. In the dressing room, just off the antechamber, she could hear her maid, Eofe, humming in short snatches between her breath as she brushed out Cecily's winter dresses with long bunches of rosemary and lavender. It was not the usual time of day for such an activity, but this way, there could be no question that their behavior was above reproach.

Now Kian looked at her with dismay, the threads at the ends of his plaid fluttering in the fitful breeze. "If you're that sure, I suppose I must believe you. But—" He shook his head. "There's no reason I can think of why Cadwyr would come to Donnor in secret, unless, perhaps with some very bad news—"

"What if it's to kill him?"

"Kill him?" Kian stared down at her.

"Isn't that what you were hinting at before? That Cadwyr could kill Donnor—in order to take the throne?"

Dismay deepened to disbelief in his dark eyes and he shook his head so hard that the feather he wore in one braid fluttered. "No, Cecily, you mistook me—I never meant to imply that even Cadwyr would stoop so low, to so dishonor himself."

"But it's possible, isn't it? You said yourself not a turn of the glass ago that Donnor was old, defeated? What if Cadwyr sees the same thing? Might he not consider it his duty to remove Donnor if he believes that the rebellion would fail otherwise? I tell you I saw him sneaking up those back stairs, and I swear to you, on my unborn children, that—"

He dropped his eyes, but not before she saw that his expression had changed from one of disbelief to one of capitulation. He held up his hands, as if to stop her. "I do believe you, Cecily, when you say you saw Cadwyr. I just don't believe he'd choose this hour of the day to kill Donnor." He gestured to the dressing room, where Eofe's high thin soprano wailed a mournful lament. "There're people everywhere. Donnor's about to be disturbed at any moment by Tuirnach's messenger. The chances that Cadwyr could get away with such a thing is highly unlikely, and as for Cadwyr himself, well, I don't like him, but curse him, he's no fool. And did you say you thought you saw a second man with him?"

She shook her head. "I said I thought I saw a second man. But I'm quite sure that was just a trick of the shadows."

He took a single step toward her and her heart gave a soft throb. "Now it's true that I cannot imagine why Cadwyr would come sneaking into this castle at dusk—certainly he's never gone sneaking into so much as a cattle byre in his life. But if it's true that he has, whether alone or in the company of some mysterious other, it seems to me that the only thing to do until he shows his hand, is to watch carefully." He broke off. "Do you by any chance possess a silver corselet, or silver bracelets, mayhap?"

She nodded. "Of course. Why?"

He shrugged. "It just occurred to me while I was dressing, that it would not be a bad thing to increase the amount of silver you wear about your person, considering all that's happened. I like not the thought of such claws as I saw today on your fair flesh."

"Kian, take me with you." The words burst out before she could call them back, and she looked at him in startled wonder. But it was the truth, she realized. It was the thing she wanted most desperately. "I'll be safe with you. We can raise the army together."

He gave her a long, sad look and tucked an errant strand behind her ear in that same gentle gesture as before. She felt a physical pang in response. "You know we cannot." He paused. "Listen to me, Cecily. If there's even a chance that Cadwyr might be plotting against Donnor, don't you think you should be here to watch and see what he does? After all, even if Cadwyr did sneak into the castle, I think it will not be so easy for him to sneak out. There're too many who will know him as you did—by his walk, by his hair." He drew one rough finger down the line of her cheek and she swallowed hard and choked back a sob. "We must finish this, Cecily," he whispered. "It doesn't matter why this has come to us. It only matters that it has."

In the dressing room, the singing had ceased.

She folded her arms across her chest and looked outside, where the gloomy day had given way to a crimson sunset.

In the valley below the castle, she could see silvery pines reddish in the sun's last long rays. Directly across her line of vision, torches flared on the walls and in the watchtowers, and the orange shadows of the yellow flames flickered across Kian's face. The air was colder than it had been all week, with a sharp tang that hinted at the coming winter.

The truth he'd spoken felt like a chain hanging over her shoulders. She glanced down at the thick gold wedding ring Donnor had placed upon her finger nearly eight years ago—the one visible link in the chain that held her captive here. That reminded her of something else.

She crossed to the small chest on the floor beneath the window seat that held her jewels. She knelt and, wrestling it from its hiding place, she withdrew from it a thick silver chain. She held it up, spread wide and let it catch the rosy light, so that it shimmered like a living thing between her fingers. "Please, take this. Wear it. It may keep you safe."

He looked surprised, then touched. "Then I will have no fear of goblin claws for truly, lady, there's enough silver in that necklace to protect every man who rides with me."

"Then may it be so." Tears filled her eyes, as he bent his head. She slipped it over his smooth braids, and pressed a kiss on his forehead.

He slowly straightened, then pulled his folded gloves from his belt. He paused before he put them on. "Some day, Cecily, some day I promise you, we shall ride out across the land together. I count you already my Queen and someday you will be the Queen of the land. I see it as surely as I see the sunset over the walls of Gar. But it's not yet time. Let me go and do what must be done, and you must stay and be the eyes and ears that watch Cadwyr." He stopped and allowed his gaze to rest on hers. "Besides, you're safe here, safer here than anywhere else, even with me. If you're the hope of Brynhyvar, I must keep you safe as possible. And Gar is well defended—it will not fall easily, and the Pretender will think twice about attacking it, especially with the possibility of so many allies advancing." Their eyes met again, and this time, she felt old, tired, lost. He had called her his Queen, but the only time she felt like a Queen was when she was with him.

And in his absence, she would play her old role. Stay home, tend the wounded. Pour the wine, keep the mead and the whiskey flowing, sing when asked. There was no point in keeping him any longer. He had that look that men wore when they were impatient to be off. She gave a deep sigh. "How far will you go tonight?"

"I expect to reach the Daraghduin by midnight. We'll rest there and cross the river in the morning. If we ride hard, we can be at Killcarrick by dusk, and then, if all goes well, part company at dawn the day after. I'll go to Dougal's village with five or six—the rest will fan out and raise the chiefs."

"And when should I tell Donnor you'll return?"

"A week. You'll hear from me within a sennight, anyway." Again he hesitated. "I don't know what we'll find up there."

She resisted the urge to throw her arms around his neck. The humming had started up again, and this time she caught enough of the tune to recognize it. *The knight and his lady did ride out across the plain so wide-o*. No one could accuse Eofe of not having a sense of humor. She smiled in spite of the situation. "Keep the chain close. And stay well, my knight."

"And you, my lady." He bowed, and after a quick kiss that burned the skin of her palm, he was gone with a sweep of his cloak, leaving her murmuring an incantation for his protection. *"By the setting of the sun, see him safe when midnight comes."* As his quick footsteps faded behind the thick oak door, she repeated the charm three times, visualizing a clear, moonlit road, an uneventful journey, and his timely arrival at the keep beside the river. She breathed a heavy sigh and turned to see Eofe standing in the doorway, hands clasped over her gray gown, watching with concern in her deep-set eyes. Cecily forced another smile, trying to ignore the foreboding in her heart. "Tomorrow," she said, nodding at the chests beneath her window seat, "I thought we might look through my jewelry, Eofe."

"That might be a very good idea, my lady."

Their eyes met in silent communion, and Cecily knew her maid had overheard enough.

6

The door closed behind them so seamlessly, so soundlessly, Nessa turned to look at it as Artimour led her down the wide flagstoned corridor. She scurried after him, the hard soles of her boots making a loud clatter that echoed off the smooth white walls. He strode a few paces ahead of her; his own dark brown leather boots, which fitted him like a second skin, making no noise at all.

He moved with the silent grace of a mountain cat, and she followed as quietly behind him as she could. She knew that she disturbed him in a different way from the others. He was angry for the disappearance of three of his men, and that was perfectly understandable. What captain would not be upset by such a loss? But it was the way he'd recoiled from her, the way his lip had curled when he'd looked her over, the way his nostrils had flared and he'd leaned farther back in his chair, as if her very smell was offensive, that was so very different from the way the other sidhe responded. It was exactly how she would've imagined any mortal lord would've reacted to her. That's how she'd known, she realized. If the sidhe part of him was in any way attracted to her, it was painfully clear that his mortal half was repulsed.

He seemed angry about the fact she'd recognized that mortal blood, too. She wondered who his father might've been—if his father might even be the great Bran Brownbeard himself. He could be the son of her childhood hero. The thought nearly brought her to a standstill and she stood a moment, gaping after him. His hair was a rich dark brown, reddish where the light fell on it. Was it possible? She had to hurry after him, wondering if there were others like him—if her own mother had borne another child. Could she have a half brother or sister here in the OtherWorld? Such a possibility had never occurred to her before, and there were certainly no stories told of children born of such unions. She wondered what it was like for him, growing up here in the OtherWorld and if he'd ever had contact with his mortal father. Questions bubbled up as if from a spring, threatening to spill over. But his handsome face was closed and grim, and she contented herself with staring at the surroundings, as he led her through halls that bespoke a degree of comfort and luxury unknown anywhere in the entire mortal world, as far as Nessa knew. Even the King of Humbria across the sea, and the Emperor of Lacquilea, far to the south, could not boast such beauty in their palaces, let alone a remote border outpost, which is what Artimour had referred to it as. They rounded a corner and entered a huge high-ceilinged hall. It made her think of the forest, for the intricate oak arches that supported the ceiling glowed like golden branches in the morning sun, which slanted through the mullioned windows set high and long on all four sides of the great chamber.

The windows were festooned with airy hangings of blue and white and purple, embroidered in fantastic designs that glowed as if woven of an incandescent thread. At this hour the hall was empty, long trestle tables neatly stacked against the long walls, benches piled neatly beneath. She looked up, eyes drawn to a flash of color between the wooden roof supports, and gaped at the painted purple grapes, so lifelike in appearance that she thought she could see the vines swaying in the cool breeze. "It's not an illusion," he said abruptly.

Startled, she asked, "What's not?"

"The grapes. They're moving. They grow, too. A few years ago we finally had to prune them back. Sometimes you can even eat one or two."

Their eyes met, and she suddenly understood that the difference in color and texture and sound was due to the difference in the entire structure of the reality that was the OtherWorld. It was possible that things were different here, in some way she had never imagined. She met his eyes, and in the muddy-green depths, she saw something other than cold reserve—something that told her she was like nothing he'd ever known. It was a combination of curiosity, and longing, and something else, something that took her so completely aback, she was certain it was only a trick of the light. Could it be need? But he turned away, before she could take a second look. "Come."

She had to scamper to keep up with him, feeling herself as lumbering and ungainly as a cow wandered in from the byre. Desire burned in her belly every time she looked at him. Could he possibly feel it, too? Griffin was considered by everyone to be a nice-looking lad, but Artimour made her palms wet and her knees weak. That he might look at her with anything more than disgust made her pulses pound. He had promised to come and help her. Maybe he wouldn't find her quite so repulsive if she bathed. He strode on ahead so quickly she thought he wanted to forget she followed. Would he keep his promise? If she was right about what she thought she'd glimpsed in his eyes, he would. And she was beginning to understand how her mother must've felt.

Once outside, he paused at the top of the steps which led down to the courtyard, and squinted up at the sun. It was high in the sky now, well above the trees. The sky was a clear, cloudless blue, a blazing brilliant color that shimmered. It was as if everything in the OtherWorld were alive, for everything glowed with a transcendent essence like a candle flame behind a parchment shade. She understood suddenly, why the sidhe referred to the mortal world as the Shadowlands.

"It's close to noon," he said. "It may be difficult to get across the border now, but it's the safest time of day."

"It's at dusk the goblins hunt." She spoke his words which echoed through her mind, and for the first time, he smiled at her, a genuine smile that lit the depths of his eyes with a hazel light. She was aware of a bone-deep exhaustion, but that smile was like an infusion of pure energy, so intoxicating, she felt jolted awake. Flustered, she looked over at the far side of the courtyard, sidhe soldiers drilled in long double rows, engaged in such intricate fighting techniques with their swords and daggers, it seemed that they danced. But she was acutely aware of Artimour beside her.

"Come," he said again, releasing her from the spell.

She looked up, dazed and dizzy, and saw that the squire who'd escorted her to Artimour approached, leading a great black horse saddled and ready. She turned to Artimour, with a quizzical look.

"I'll see you back across myself," he answered her unspoken question. "'Twill not overburden me much. The saddle is broad enough for two, over a short distance, at least."

So he meant to ensure she kept her word. It had not even crossed her mind to try to stay behind, for the idea of Griffin at the mercy of a goblin hunting party had convinced her quickly. She looked from Artimour to the ornate leather saddle buffed to a high shine. Across the animal's rump, a leather pack lay rolled and strapped. The saddle looked big and comfortable, but for the two of them to share it, it would necessitate contact both intimate and prolonged. She found, to her utter mortification, she could not raise her gaze off the ground. Her cheeks grew warm, as he turned to her, brow raised, hand out. "Unless it will distress you to ride with me?"

To her horror, she knew she blushed deeper, but she raised her chin even as the color flamed across her face. "No."

He beckoned and she saw his nostrils flare. So he was not so immune from whatever effect she had upon the sidhe. Or maybe it was just the way she smelled. "Then come." He lifted her up and onto the big stallion as effortlessly as if she were a child. He swung up behind her, and spoke as he settled himself behind her. "It may be difficult in the full sun to navigate the border. But I have a good idea of where you came across."

With a word and a gesture, the massive gates swung open. As the great horse moved forward, Nessa's bare legs dangled awkwardly in front of his. He held the reins in one easy hand, and she noticed that his hands were, like her father's, broad and covered in a fine shadow of dark hair, but so clean she wanted to hide her own. She tried to hold herself upright, but the sun's glow was hot on her face and, lulled by the motion of the horse's steady jog, and the sweet scent that rose from his body, she began to slip into a hazy half-sleep.

She was so tired. It had been nearly a whole day since she'd last seen her father and she'd slept for not so much of five minutes of it. Her head nodded in time with the horse's motion, and fell back of its own accord into the hollow of Artimour's chest, and he was as solid to lean against as her favorite spot just above the shore of the lake, where the grassy dunes gave way to tiny-leafed thyme.

Her eyes slid closed, and she thought she might be dreaming. They rode beneath an avenue of golden oaks and scarlet maples, of yellow beeches punctuated by stands of solemn dark green pines. The air was filled with leaves that drifted down off the branches like golden snow. The sunlight was an incandescent glow, the air thick with the resin and water scent of the pines, of the waxy scent of the falling leaves. A breeze tickled her tangled curls as delicately as her father's fingers when he coaxed her back to sleep.

Behind her, Artimour rode easily, his body keeping fluid rhythm with the horse, so that he felt as solid as a tree trunk, as pliant as a pillow. She was acutely conscious of the places their bodies touched. At first he held himself stiffly, rigidly, but gradually, he, too, relaxed, and their bodies conformed to each other's, so that she felt as if she drowsed on her own low bed tucked beneath the eaves. Her heartbeat slowed, lengthened into long, pounding throbs, and time seemed to stretch itself out, so that she was intensely aware of each moment as it ticked through her veins. Another odor engulfed her—the mingled musky aroma of the man and the horse. Her breathing deepened, pulling at the air as greedily as a baby sucking milk. She closed her eyes against the dappled light, and listened to the muffled clip of the horse's hooves on the packed pine path.

She thought of her mother, swept up and away by a lord of the sidhe. Surely he'd had the same effect on her mother as Artimour had on her, so that she did not mind where he rode on his great black horse, so long as this dream continued. Was this what her mother had felt, as she was carried deeper and deeper into Faerie, farther away from the baby and the husband waiting for her in the humble mortal cottage beside the forge? A longing as old as she could remember swept over and through her, and she felt once more the desperate despair of an infant bereft. *How could you leave me?* she thought, addressing the faceless, voiceless void of the mother of her imagination, a thought she'd had countless times before. But this time an answer came in the fragrant rush of Faerie air, in the muted whisper of the Faerie forest, in the solid presence against her back. *Can you not see now, daughter?* The answer was a sigh upon the wind, echoing through her dream. For the first time in her life, Nessa felt some connection to the mother she could not remember. Like a blanket, like a cradle, she felt suspended and surrounded by something tangible. The steady rhythm of the horse's gait lulled her further, until she bolted upright, remembering that her father might be in the grip of just such a similar enchantment.

She fought off the lassitude that threatened to make her forget where she was and where she was going, and clung to her resolve like a life rope. She would go back, warn her people, and then perhaps, while she waited for Artimour to return, she might see if there were some way to discover who the two mysterious visitors had been. For it occurred to her, that it was possible, an outside chance, perhaps, but one worth considering nonetheless that perhaps Dougal's disappearance was not at all related to the goblin's appearance. He had recognized one of his visitors, she remembered. Who could it have been? Suddenly she was eager to get back to the village as quickly as possible. She turned to look at Artimour, over her shoulder. "Where are we going?" she asked.

"As close to your point of entry as I was able to ascertain from my knights," he answered, eyes fastened on some point up straight ahead. His mouth was tight and he would not meet her eyes. She wondered if the missing three had been found. But the rigid set of his shoulders did not invite conversation and she did not dare to ask. It would only pick at a wound too raw and new.

They turned to the left, following the line of a stream that tumbled through the wood. The trees grew thick all around them, and Nessa wondered how he could be so sure of where he was going. Several times Artimour guided the horse close to the middle of the stream and they crossed to the opposite side. They continued in this fashion for about a hundred yards or more, when he reined the horse to a halt. The sunlight filtered through the high branches, penetrating the forest canopy in long golden shafts. She looked back at him over her shoulder in time to see him frown.

"What's wrong?" she asked. The horse pawed at the ground, and shook its head as if pushing something away.

"There's something—something different here. I can feel the border—it's running right through this stream—but something's bound it. It's sealed here, almost as if there were a caul on the other side, holding the border closed."

"In my world?" She looked around, trying to peer more closely at the invisible air, as if she might catch a glimpse of this elusive mysterious border, but all she saw was the flash and twinkle of the sunlight on the water as it rushed through banks of lush green cress. "You can see this border?"

"It's more a feeling or a sense than a sight. But this thing—" he broke off and stared moodily around. "Tell me again, where and how did you enter?"

"I followed a stream like this."

"All right. This one runs into the river. Where did that one lead?"

"Into the lake. It's not really a stream all the time. It dries up most summers, but this year we've had a lot of rain."

"So it runs into a lake there," he mused. He put out his hand, and held it up, as if feeling for something, something invisible, in the air. "It's here—I can feel it—but, it's as if something's holding it closed." He frowned again.

Hesitantly she put out her own hand, but felt nothing. The air felt empty. She moved it side to side, slowly, imitating his movements, trying to feel something, anything. But the air was empty. "It doesn't feel any different to me," she said.

"Of course it doesn't." He sounded cross. He swung off the saddle, and dropped to the ground, striding ahead a dozen paces, hand held out to the side, following the stream, crossing to the opposite side and back again. Perhaps twenty paces from where she sat upon the horse, he turned back, and stood, feet on either side of the stream, hands on his hips. "I just don't understand," he said shaking his head. He seemed to be talking more to himself than to her. "What is this strange new thing?"

"What is it?" she called. "What's wrong?" Beneath her, the horse took a few steps and Nessa looked down dubiously at the reins lying slack across the bridle. The idea occurred to her that the sidhe horse might bolt, but it only shook itself and whinnied, as though calling for its master. Her stomach rumbled alarmingly, but Artimour appeared not to have heard.

He shook his head again. "Whatever it is, it's like a seal—but from the mortal side. I've never felt anything like this before." He raised his head and looked at her directly. "It seems you have brought me yet another piece of information in this most intricate puzzle. I am triply in your debt, maiden." He shrugged. "Well, it's clear that this won't work. We must find another portal." He walked back to the horse, and gripped the pommel. In one easy motion, he was mounted, and she settled back against him. The sun-warmed velvet of his doublet brushed against the bare skin of her arm, reminding her of the texture of melting butter. Her mouth watered and she wished she had not dropped Griffin's pack. She would have to see that she replaced it somehow—it was one of his most treasured possessions, she thought, just as her eyes slid closed.

When next she looked up, they had halted upon the shore of a river. To one side, a waterfall gushed from a higher ledge and a pool foamed as the banks broadened out and then shrank. The angle of the sun was such that the opposite shore was reflected in the surface, an upside-down duplicate of the dark line of pines. "Here," said Artimour, as she blinked in the bright sunshine, and looked around. "This is the broadest portal I know, for miles around. It is near the place you entered, maiden, but it will not be exactly the same. Will you be all right? The people in these parts, they'll help you?"

"I'll find my way home," Nessa answered. She knew the byways and the villages around the lake like the back of her hand. But his muddy eyes were searching hers and she realized with a shock that he was concerned for her, that he had understood on some deep level when she told him why her father meant so much to her. And she realized she could trust him to keep his word.

He dismounted, then held out his arms, and helped her off the broad back of the stallion. Her thighs were unexpectedly stiff, and she straightened with an effort, tying back her hair more securely. "Can you swim?"

"Of course I can swim," she replied. "Everyone can swim."

"No, maiden, not everyone," he said. Was there really a flicker of amusement in his eyes? Or was it contempt? "The bodies of those who drown in Shadow occasionally wash up upon our shores."

"My father knows how to swim. He didn't drown."

"I did not mean to imply otherwise." Something that might have been amusement flickered in his eyes and then was gone. He paused as if he considered saying something and then stopped, as though he'd changed his mind. She wondered if he were about to ask her something about Dougal. But he only gestured at the opposite shore with a broad sweep of his hand. "When you reach the opposite shore, you'll be back in Shadow, though exactly where I cannot say." His words were clipped and she got the distinct impression he wanted her gone.

"You'll promise you'll come to Killcairn? You swear?"

He drew himself up and looked down his narrow nose at her. "There is a three-fold debt between us, maiden. I have no choice, if I would not be dishonored." He pulled a ruby ring set in gold off his finger and reached for her hand. He slipped it down one finger. "In token of my bond. May I burn in the belly of the Hag if I do not keep my word." He bowed. She remembered Griffin's clumsy leave-taking and she wondered what it would be like if this man—this half-sidhe, half-mortal with eyes as impenetrable as the surface of the lake on a summer afternoon—were to press a kiss upon her mouth. He was staring at her with equal intensity, and it crossed her mind that he was going to tell her that he would follow her into Brynhyvar right there. Then a heron, perched upon a rock, cried out. It dove with sure precision into the foaming pool beneath the waterfall. Artimour pressed her hands together between his, and raising them, kissed her rough knuckle right beside the ring. "Keep it close."

She looked down at the ring. An oval stone the color of blood glowed in the center of an intricate setting. It looked as odd on her hand as her grimy hands clasped in his soft-tooled leather gloves. She glanced past their entwined hands, and noticed her boots which, beside his, looked even thicker and heavier than they felt. She would never be able to swim in them. With a sigh, she unfastened the brooch which held her cloak, and removed it from the fabric. It was only a simple circle of polished steel, with an opposing clasp fastened by a coil of twisted bronze, but her father had made it for her. Handing him her cloak, she used the pin to kilt up her tunic as high as she dared. She tugged at it, making sure it was secure. It would never do to lose it in the water. She bent, and awkwardly pulled off her boots, and gazed at them with regret. They were her favorite pair and no more easily replaced. The cobbler who'd made them had long since moved on to other districts and they'd not seen him in well over two years. But she would never be able to swim in them. Still not resigned to their loss, she bent and unlaced them. Then a thought occurred to her. From her knees on the sand, she looked up. "In Brynhyvar when such a vow is made, it is customary to exchange tokens."

"Well," answered Artimour, again looking as if that was

the last thing he expected her to say, "under the circumstances, I hardly can expect you—"

She stood up and held out her boots. "These are my favorite work boots. I'd like them back, when you come for your ring."

He looked first startled, then taken aback. But then he smiled, this time with grudging respect. "A most unusual token, maiden, but then, perhaps it's fitting. I'll bring your cloak as well." He bowed and tucked her boots under one arm, and indicated the water with the other. "The reflection is strongest at this hour. As the sun passes, the shadow fades."

She turned to face the riverbank, uncertain suddenly, for it seemed she stood upon a crossroads. She was going back to the world she knew, but in that moment she had a premonition that what she would return to would be a place utterly different from the one she had left. She squared her shoulders and lifted her chin, made sure her pin was secured to her tunic and strode barefoot across the gravelly sand and into the water with the same resolve as that with which she beheaded the goblin. The river bottom was lined with round, smooth stones, fitted as neatly together as a cobbled road—a road to TirNa'lugh and back is how the stories described it. When the water reached her waist, she dove in, stroking with hard, sure strokes, through the cold, clean water, trying to quell the nagging fear that threatened to overcome her with doubt: *what if I can't get back?* So many strange things were happening, she had the eerie feeling that nothing was the same as it was. What if the Caul had somehow stopped working? What would protect them from the goblins?

She pushed such thoughts away, consciously forcing herself to breathe in time with her strokes, aware of the caress of the water against her body, inevitably, effortlessly, washing away the sweat and the blood and the grime and the stink of the goblin. All she could smell now was the flow of the water, bubbling around her, flushing through the tangle of her tunic and her hair. The linen swished and swayed, the belt hard against her belly. She kicked and felt stones beneath her toes. Another strong stroke and she stumbled upright, into a foggy mist that rose off the surface of the lake.

She shouldered through the water, gathered up her tunic and wrung it out as best she could as she reached the pebbled shore. Water streamed off her hair, the sodden tunic clung to her like a second skin. Shoeless, amuletless, without so much as a cloak or a coin to her name, she thought she had never been so naked since she was born. The air was limpid and still and it felt unseasonably warm for the time of year, but the stillness and the subdued light made her think that it was morning. Early morning.

She frowned into the mist as she walked onto the beach, following the line of a path that led up from a long dock she did not recognize. But the coracles tied to it were of familiar shape and design, and she knew, as she stepped on the brown pine-needled path, that she was once again in the mortal world. The silence was profound, puzzling. If a village of that many coracles lay so close, there should be some sound of human life. She rounded a curve. Before her lay the cluster of cottages that she recognized at once as Killcrag, a village about an hour's walk on a sunny afternoon from Killcairn. She breathed a sigh of relief. She was not so very far from home at all. She might even find a cottager to give her a ride. Her appearance she would explain by saying she'd been looking for her father. *In the lake?* mocked her common sense, as water dripped off her shoulders and trailed down her legs. *First just find someone. Anyone. And then maybe a dry tunic. And breakfast,* she thought as her stomach rumbled alarmingly.

There was an eerie stillness lying over all. This was the hour, if she were correct about the time, that the village should be rousing itself to life. Dogs should be barking, children whining as they stumbled through the first round of morning chores. The scent of oats and new-stirred fires should be in the air, the goodwives calling greetings. But the village was deserted.

She walked up to the first house, and pushed the door open. She knew before she stepped across the threshold that the hearth would be cold, for no smoke rose from its clay chimney. A half-burned log lay within the hearth, hinting that the fire might have been hastily extinguished.

There was a loaf of bread lying on the table. Saliva flooded her mouth, and she ripped it in half. It was still doughy in the center, as if it had been pulled from the oven half-baked. But the ends were edible, and she crammed them in her mouth, munching heavily on the chewy brown bread. They had left in a hurry, she guessed, for there was porridge congealing in a pot. But they'd had time to take most of what they owned, she saw, for the numerous hooks hanging from the walls and the rafters were mostly empty, save for a string of onions beside the chimney, a tattered shawl behind the door. She grabbed at the shawl, and used it to mop the worst of the water from her hair. Still chewing, she unpinned her tunic, shook out as much water as she could upon the hearthstone, then kilted it up again, so the sodden fabric wouldn't cling to her legs.

She peered into the sleeping room behind the kitchen. Even the mattresses were gone. She looked behind the door. There was a shirt hanging from a wooden hook. It was much too small—a child's. There was no way it would fit. She shivered and wrapped the shawl closer. Thank the Great Mother that the weather was so unseasonably warm.

From house to house, she scavenged, finding a hard hunk of cheese in one, a dry tunic at last in another, a pair of rough sandals that were better than bare feet for the long walk home. Even the animals were gone, save for a few stray chickens, left to cluck and scratch in the mud in the center of the village. Mud, she wondered. When had it rained?

A chicken wandered up to her, fixed her with a dark beady eye and clucked and shook its head, though if in explanation or as a demand for one, she wasn't quite sure. "I don't know, chicken," she murmured aloud. "Where did everyone go?"

The logical place was to the castle at Killcarrick—the seat of the Sheriff who governed this district of the Duke's holdings. But what would have forced them to leave? She hoped it was only the threat of war and not something worse. Although she knew she should make for Killcarrick, where she would be safest from whatever had caused the village to evacuate, Killcairn was just up the road. She had to go home. Even if everyone had left Killcairn, Griffin wouldn't leave without her. She was overcome with the feeling that more than a day had passed. But better not to read too much into it, until she knew more. For all she knew, the messenger could have arrived in the village an hour or so after she'd left. In which case, Griffin would definitely be waiting for her.

She could reach home fastest by taking one of the coracles, but Nessa was leery of going back out on the lake. It was obvious that the OtherWorld and Brynhyvar intersected in waters that were somehow commingled. Given a choice she would walk.

She looked down at her bare toes in the sandals and regretted the loss of her boots. She adjusted the faded plaid she'd found neatly folded on a bed, and wondered if the owner regretted leaving it behind. Well, to her benefit, it was, for there was a clammy damp in the air that made her glad of the thick plaid.

At the last house on the lane she paused. It was the house of the wicce-woman of Killcrag, a woman not as old by half as Granny Wren, perhaps closer to her father's age. Granny Molly was her name. Nessa had seen her from time to time, but it was at last Beltane, when the villagers from miles around gathered at the clan stone circle at Killcarrick, that she and the woman had exchanged a few words—not many, but enough to make her wonder every once in a while.

It was before the ritual, Nessa remembered. They had just arrived, in fact, pitching their camp as the spring sun lowered to the western hills. She had come picking young herbs, Nessa remembered, coming up the hill with her basket on her arm and her face flushed with exertion or maybe, since it was Beltane after all, something else. She had raised her chin at Dougal's greeting, and Nessa had known at once that Granny Molly intended to claim him for the night. 'Twas an honor the taciturn blacksmith would have to endure for months of good-natured ribbing. But Dougal's face had darkened at the sight of the woman, and the words they exchanged were brief, barely short of rude, and Nessa could tell by the set of the smith's shoulders he had no intention of allowing her to extend such an invitation.

Molly noticed Nessa, standing by the wagon, watching, and smiled, her full red lips curving in a wide arc. The men said that Molly had a well-ripened look, and in that moment, Nessa understood exactly what they meant. Molly was like a rose at the height of its bloom, fully open, ripe and lush, a few of the outermost petals might be missing, a few edges cracked and browned at the tips, but still a lovely flower. If Dougal had no interest, Molly would have no trouble finding another to take her into the forest. But Nessa had looked at her father curiously, wondering as she did every year why Beltane of all holidays should put him in such a dark mood. Her father was regarded by many as a good-looking man, but he had always shunned female companionship. Beltane was a different story, of course. If you were called by the god, you answered the summons. But Dougal deliberately shut his ears and turned his back on any possible call from the god.

But the wicce-woman had looked at Nessa more closely, as if she'd recognized her, then turned back to Dougal. "A Beltane child, is she?"

Dougal's head had jerked up, as if he'd been slapped, and his face had darkened like a thundercloud. "Whatever do you mean, woman?"

She gave Nessa another measuring look. "When's your birthday, girl?"

"Eleven days past the balance day of spring," Nessa blurted. It had passed just a few weeks ago.

"Ah—not possible at all, I suppose. But you have the look of it." She glanced back at Dougal, her head cocked. "She has the look about her, is all. I meant no insult, sir. A blessed Beltane to you and yourn." She'd gone back down the hill singing, leaving Nessa wondering why on earth he'd reacted so strongly. For just a moment, she wondered if it could possibly be true, but counting back, she dismissed the idea at once. Unless she'd lain nearly a year in her mother's womb. But why did the question make Dougal so angry? Anyone she'd ever known who'd conceived a baby close to the festival was always proud of it. Privately, she doubted most of the claims, for children conceived on Beltane were said to have special abilities, and every supposed Beltane child she'd ever met was as ordinary as a boot. But why get so angry about it? she wondered. It was clear the woman had meant no offense. Most—if not all—would have considered it a compliment.

As Molly's song faded down the hillside, Nessa had turned to Dougal. "What exactly do the wicce-women do?"

He'd only shaken his head, and his answer, as always, was maddeningly vague. "They work that corn magic—you know that silly superstition. Though it does no harm, I suppose and surely gives a grand excuse for a holiday. Go talk to Granny Wren if you want to know more." He waved his hand dismissively. "I've no time for such nonsense."

"I think we should all find time for nonsense tonight," interrupted Griffin, who was coming up from the well with two full buckets. And they had snickered, and Dougal had pretended to stomp away in disgust, and in Griffin's eyes, she saw an unmistakable hope that when the time came, she would extend her hand to him. But something held her back, and that year, like all the previous years, she did not go to the Beltane woods.

It was not the first time she'd asked the question. It was not the first time he'd said to talk to Granny Wren. But she was afraid of Granny Wren, afraid of the shrunken frame, the curved spine, the long white braids and wrinkled face. She had a large, liver-colored birthmark on one cheek that covered nearly the whole half of her face, giving it the appearance of a light and dark half. But if it was her look that repulsed Nessa, it was her eyes that scared her, for Granny Wren's dark eyes seemed to smolder with some hidden flame, as if a fire burned within her skull.

And while Dougal told her to go to the old woman, he would not have been pleased if she'd actually done so. He made it clear by action more than word that he preferred her to focus her attention on the daily business of the forge.

But now and then she wondered. She had even thought, once or twice, of seeking out Molly. Somehow she'd known that that would have pleased her father even less. But it wouldn't hurt to have a peek now.

She pushed the door open, and saw that Molly, unlike the rest of the villagers, had been forced to leave behind a fair amount of goods—mostly drying herbs hanging in fragrant bunches, skeins of cord in different colors and small baskets filled with dozens of different pebbles of varying colors and sizes. Woven crosses of reeds and sheaves were stacked together. Corn dollies, she thought, used to make the corn grow. But how, she wondered. What exactly was it that they did to make the corn grow, to make the fields and cattle fertile? But Molly's house held no answers, only tantalizing accouterments.

Nessa left the wicce-woman's house, and started on the road, taking stock of her salvaged possessions. She had the cheese, a couple onions and a waterskin. In one house an upturned jug of mead had yielded a few last drops and now it burned in her veins, giving her a strength she'd never thought she'd find. She had the plaid and a dry tunic. She regretted the loss of her boots. But the sidhe ring Artimour had given her in token gleamed upon her hand, the stone blood-red in the hazy morning light. It seemed like a dream now, that she should have stood upon that opposite shore, and left her boots in exchange. She cast a last look at the village over her shoulder, and rounded the final corner that took her out of sight. She had a rusty knife in her belt, but she was conscious that the skin around her throat was bare. No one had left their amulets behind.

She walked on and gradually, her senses seemed to grow preternaturally acute. An eerie feeling descended on her and, just as she had in the OtherWorld, she felt as if she'd slipped into a dream. Only this time she did not feel so safe, so secure, as when she was borne on the back of the sidhe horse, bolstered by Artimour. This dream had the aspect of a nightmare. The hackles rose on the back of her neck, but she fought the uneasy feeling down as vigorously as she had the dreamy compliance. Of course it felt like she knew this place, she scolded herself, as the mist swirled around her knees. She knew this road like she knew her own name. If it seemed familiar it was because it was. Of course it felt like she'd been here before.

But the feeling was more than that, she knew, try as she might to deny it. It was the flat slap of her sandals, the way the mist floated just above her knees. It was the heavy, limpid air that seemed to suffocate her. On the other side of the stand of pines, she could hear the lake water lap against the beach with the sound of a suckling infant. A bullfrog croaked experimentally and was still. Not even a bird called, she thought.

She forced herself to stay calm, to stride down the road, although the weight of the pack and the weight of the plaid made the sweat trickle down her neck and down her sides. But she forgot she was exhausted.

The empty village troubled her, the empty road troubled her. At this hour of the day, there should be foot-traffic, a few wagons, a cart or two, herds of cattle, sheep and goats being driven to pasture. But the rutted roads were deserted. Ahead she saw what looked like a piece of crumpled fabric lying by the roadside. She narrowed her eyes as she came closer, then bent and picked it up. It was a child's rag doll, dusty from the road, but tattered and faded with the marks of much loving. She turned it over and dropped it, shocked. The entire other side was stiff with dried blood.

"Great Mother," she muttered aloud. She swallowed hard against a sudden wave of nausea. Was she too late? The doll made it harder to cling to the hope of an orderly evacuation due to the Duke's rebellion. She adjusted the pack and looked around. The air was thick and heavy, and she understood what had her so unnerved. It wasn't just the absence of a breeze. There was absolutely no movement, anywhere. Not a squirrel or rabbit, or bird of any kind was in sight. The only animals she'd seen at all were the few forlorn chickens. It was as if everything that could, had left, leaving only the green things behind.

She was about to set off down the road with renewed determination when, from the underbrush, she heard a sound. Her head snapped up. Automatically she sniffed, searching for some hint of that all too familiar stench. *Protect me, Great Mother*. Was it really the same muffled snort she'd heard before? She drew a deep, silent, careful breath, even as she gripped the rusty knife's handle tightly and withdrew it from her belt. The hair on the back of her neck rose. She stood stock-still, listening, breathing as quietly as possible, feeling helplessly exposed in the middle of the open road. She glanced up at the sky. A pale disk of sun appeared through the cloud cover; with any luck at all it might burn off the mist. The seconds ticked away, until all she heard was the pounding of her heart. She twisted the knife, and the ruby flashed red in a sudden shaft of sun. Suddenly she felt comforted. Artimour had said it himself. *It's at dusk the goblins hunt.* She repeated that aloud. "It's at dusk the goblins hunt." She set off down the road at a quicker pace, the knife still clutched in her hand.

By the time she'd reached the outskirts of Killcairn, she knew that it, like Killcrag, was deserted. But it was quickly very clear that there had been no orderly evacuation here. Her neighbors had fled.

Her first hint were the cows on the green hillsides, with distended udders, plaintively mooing. They were desperate for a milking, she realized, as she walked past the stone fenced fields, and came down at last into the silent village. In the middle of the road, a black boot rested on its side, apparently abandoned. As she approached, she peered at it closely, for the surface appeared to be moving. In the same moment that the sickening sweet stench of rotting meat filled her nose, a buzzing cloud of flies rose from what she immediately realized was not a boot at all. It was a foot, bound in a sandal much like the one she was wearing. Nausea overcame her, and she stumbled to the side of the road, retching, her stomach heaving. She vomited her doughy breakfast, then rinsed her mouth with a warm swig from the waterskin.

There was no doubt any longer that the worst had happened. It may have been the result of the Duke's rebellion, of course, but something told her that wasn't the case. She had returned too late. She edged past the houses, staring in dismay. The people of her village had been like lambs at the slaughter, or worse—fruit ripe for the picking. It was clear they had fled, fled in the wake of something awful and ugly—something that left behind pools of congealed blood in the uneven ruts of the road, from which clouds of flies rose as she passed.

Doors and shutters yawned wide, but she stolidly walked down the middle of the dusty street, trying not to see the blackened hands and feet and heads lying scattered all around. This was what Artimour had warned her of. However long she'd stayed in the OtherWorld, it was too long.

She was too late. Bile burned the back of her throat and her stomach heaved again, but mercifully she'd nothing left to vomit. Her chest ached as if a heavy weight pressed on it.

Worst of all, there were no whole bodies, just parts, lying like discarded scraps of meat. Which is exactly what they were, she thought woodenly. All of them—everyone she knew. Meat.

Her vision darkened and narrowed and she forced herself to put one foot ahead of the other. Everyone she knew—not just her father. Griffin. Granny Wren. Everyone. Gone.

Twice more she retched by the side of the road, overcome by the horror of what she saw, until her stomach ached. Had anyone at all escaped? she wondered. The condition of the corpses told her that at least two days or more had passed since this catastrophe. She felt a deep pang of guilt. It seemed impossible to think that Griffin was dead, that all the people she'd known since she could remember might be gone. Artimour had been right. Without the magic of the Caul, the people of her village had been as vulnerable as newborn babies.

She walked on, and heard, carried on the wind, a low humming noise that she couldn't quite place. The flies, she thought, shuddering. She hurried on, conscious of the rising, then falling croon. It seemed too deliberate, somehow. It was coming from the direction of the lake. But she didn't want to stop there now. She passed the herder's house, and the lane that led to Farmer Breslin's barn. The door to Granny Wren's was wide open as were all the others, the contents of her baskets scattered. On impulse, she peered inside, bracing herself against what she might see. She gazed around the wicce-woman's snug little hearth. The shutters were bolted, benches stacked up against them, ropes of garlic laced around the shutters and the frames. And then a piece of thatch fell from the roof to the floor in front of her feet, and she looked up, to see that part of the roof had been pulled away. Items were ripped off the walls, baskets and clay pots lay upturned on the floor. But there was no blood. Perhaps the old wicce-woman had escaped. She thought of Griffin and a deeper pang went through her.

Perhaps some escaped, she thought, as she shut the door and strode quickly up the lane, toward the smithy. She pushed open the familiar gate and rushed up to the house. Halting in the open doorway, she took stock. The air was foul with that now too familiar reek and there was no longer any question in her mind that goblins, and no human army, had raided the village. Tools and implements were lying smashed and plundered, the forge itself tipped over. She looked around for some sort of clue, something that would tell her how long ago this had happened. Something other than the remains.

The sun was just turning in the sky, she thought, when I swam across the river. So—maybe six hours? Seven? But here—it was obvious that at least three or four or maybe even more days had gone by. The only ones who could tell her weren't here. She gingerly stepped across the threshold of the smithy, tears welling. The odor was growing stronger. She looked over the destruction, then gasped.

On the wall, next to the door that led to the kitchen, a goblin arm hung from an ax—an ax that gleamed in the afternoon light with an unmistakable glimmer. It was coated with silver, she saw, as she reached for it, wrinkling her nose as the goblin arm fell with a splatter of foul fluids to the floor. She turned around and looked at the scene again, from the vantage point of the kitchen, and realized that someone, presumably Griffin, had been in the very act of making such a silver-coated weapon, for there the charcoal was tipped across the floor, the bellows askew, the tongs and hammers scattered, an anvil lying on its side and a mess of congealed silver on the floor. Hope surged through her. If he'd had silver weapons ready, surely the greater the chance that he'd escaped. She bent closer, searching through the jumble, gathering up silver coins. He must've raided Dougal's stash beneath his bed. Well, who would blame him? she thought. Not even Dougal would consider it stealing under such circumstances. And if he'd saved his own life, or that of another—

Someone must've gotten away, she realized with a start. Someone must've alerted at least Killcrag. She set her pack down beside the cold hearth, and found a tattered hide behind the kitchen. Wrapping the goblin arm securely, she threw it down the midden.

Then she righted the long table, and picked up the benches, and as she did so, noticed something wrapped in parchment. She picked it up and unwrapped an amulet. The parchment had three symbols scratched upon it: house, mountain, to connote a large house, and lake. Killcarrick. The amulet was Griffin's. So he had taken hers. She sank back on her heels, wondering exactly what it signified. On one level, it was a gesture both simple and profound. Normally an exchange of amulets signified the deepening of a couple's intentions toward each other. Had he meant it in that way? she wondered. Perhaps there was more meaning in his kiss than just overwrought emotion. The vision of a possible future flashed before her—one where she and Griffin married, shared the work of the forge. It was attractive, it was comforting, and it was flat in some way she did not have time to consider. But so far it looked as if his life had been spared. And if Griffin had gotten away, so perhaps had more of the others.

He had known that she would come back here. She should probably turn right around and go back the way she'd come—toward Killcarrick and safety. After all, what was to guarantee the goblins wouldn't be back? Here she was vulnerable, alone. But here was where Artimour would come to look. At least she had an amulet, a silver-edged ax and silver coins. She was better armed than most right now, and if Killcarrick was a two days' walk away, at least that's where Griffin was. But should she go? Would it be better to wait for Artimour?

She unpinned the plaid, and mounted the steps which wound up to her room under the eaves. Everything was just as she had left it—her pillow just as she had fluffed it, her blue blanket neatly folded at the foot. *The last time I folded this blanket,* she thought, *my father was alive and dickering with a customer who was insisting he needed a job done that very morning. I heard them arguing as I put it there. And Griffin was singing in the backyard.* A wave of weary grief swept over her. The low bed beckoned, dust motes dancing in the hazy light that streamed in through the horn-paned window. An hour or so to sleep wouldn't hurt—couldn't hurt. If the goblins hunted at night, surely it was safest to sleep during the day. But it was stuffy in the little room. She knelt on her bed and unlatched the casement, opening the windows wide to catch whatever wind might be blowing.

A breeze blew in from the lake, and again, she caught a snatch of that strange low humming. What was that noise? It was coming from outside, a low, thrumming croon like the buzzing of a thousand beehives, something as much felt as heard. She knew she would never be able to rest until she located the source of the sound.

She reached under her bed and took out her second pair of boots, the ones she wore to Gatherings and other times she wasn't working. She laced them on, wriggling her toes, and climbed back down the ladder. Picking up the silver ax, Nessa stepped outside, listening intently. The light breeze was coming up from the lake, carrying with it that curious thrumming. She paused on the threshold, then shut the door firmly behind her.

Thunderheads were massing over the trees, the air without the breeze was oppressive, and she knew there would be a storm by evening. Evening, she thought. She wouldn't think about how vulnerable she might be come nightfall. The sound was definitely coming from the direction of the lake. She swallowed hard, steeled herself, then hurried down to the lake. In the sandy road, she saw deep footprints, splayed and huge, of the monsters' feet, and implements, scattered and twisted almost beyond recogni- tion—a hoe here, a pitchfork there, a shovel torn apart. These were the weapons the villagers had tried to use. In deep gouges, she saw scraps of blood-soaked clothing, torn pieces of leather, an infant's bloodied swaddling. Flies buzzed audibly, and she covered her nose and her mouth with one hand against the stench. Her skin crawled and she considered going back. But she'd have no rest until she knew what that sound was, and so she went on, following it all the way down to the lake.

The trees thinned out and the lane ended in a broad sandy sprawl. She gagged against her palm at the sight that greeted her on the beach. Long dark gouges in the sand—that was where they'd dragged the bodies, she realized. Here and there footsteps ended abruptly in deep depressions. Some of them had tried to run, she thought. The crooning rose once more in intensity and she whipped her head around, searching up and down the beach. The sound, she thought. Where was it coming from?

She walked gingerly down to the water's edge, refusing to look into the water, or even too carefully at what might be lying beside it, and looked first right, then left. There was a small figure huddled beneath a rocky outcropping, a small figure that seemed to sway back and forth with the rhythm of the water lapping on the sand. As Nessa looked closer, she gasped as she recognized who it was.

Granny Wren sat facing the lake, leaning against a rock, her legs splayed wide and open in the posture of a woman in childbirth. The lake water lapped at her ankles and at the base of her thighs. Between her hands she held a rope, in which were three large knots. She was the source of the chanting, but as Nessa came closer, she saw that the old woman's face was gray and drawn, her mouth slack, her eyes closed. "Granny Wren," she whispered. "Are you…are you all right?" She touched Granny Wren on her shoulder, and to her horror, the old woman collapsed onto her side, her knees falling together into a fetal position, her face slack jawed upon the sand. "Sweet Mother," Nessa breathed. "Now what?"

She pushed the ax securely into her belt, and half lifted, half dragged the old woman away from the water's edge. Her feet were blue and the puckered flesh was white and waterlogged. How long had she been sitting there? The rope hung slack in her hands, and Nessa reached down for it.

"*Nooooo.*" The word was a long low moan. "Mustn't—mustn't—" The old woman took a gasping breath.

"All right, Granny, I won't take it," Nessa said, looking around desperately for something, anything, to put around the woman's frail shoulders. "Come, we've got to get off this beach—"

Mercifully the old woman didn't contradict her. She slumped into a faint, and was scarcely the weight of a half-hod of coal as Nessa hoisted her and carried her up the path to the smithy. But the rope remained clutched in her talon-like hands. As Nessa laid her down on Griffin's cot, the old woman opened her eyes. "A fine young lad, he was," she nodded as if satisfied. "A fine young lad."

Who, Nessa wanted to ask, wondering if she could by any chance mean Griffin, but something held her tongue. "Granny Wren," she said, as she covered the old woman up with Griffin's blanket, and sank to her knees beside the pillow, "what's happened here? Please—can't you tell me? Has everyone gone to Killcarrick?"

The old woman's eyes were bright in her skull-like face. "'Twill only hold till Samhain. But not a thing 'twixt here and the Summerlands 'twill hold them back come Samhain eve."

"Samhain?" Nessa bent closer. "Granny, what about Samhain? What happens on Samhain?"

"The doors," she whispered. The word was a long, drawn-out sigh. "The doors." She drew another deep breath, and fell fast asleep. Beneath the blanket, her thin chest rose and fell, fragile as a bird's, the air rustling in her throat.

Nessa sank back onto the floor, gathering her knees up beneath her chin. Great Mother. Now what? What could the old woman have meant? What would hold till Samhain? She remembered how Artimour had not been able to get her across the border—the border closest to Killcairn. *It's as if something's holding it closed—closed from the mortal side.* Could it have been Granny Wren who closed it?

She yawned mightily and a wave of weariness swept over and through her, dragging her head to slump against the bedside. How long had it been since she'd slept? Her eyelids felt heavy, her head as heavy as rock. It must be safe, she reasoned, as sleep overtook her. Whatever magic Granny had worked must've worked to the extent that no goblin had come to seize her, even while she was perched on the water's edge like a piece of bait, hung out on the skewer. But what about now? Was the key in the knotted rope she clutched so close to her breast, even in sleep? Nessa sighed, resting her head on the edge of Griffin's bed. She was tired, so tired, so utterly bone weary. There was no sense in even attempting to go anywhere else. The sun was high in the sky—a few hours' rest would not harm her. Could not harm her, for she could not go anywhere.

Her stomach growled experimentally, reminding her it had been some time since she'd eaten her fill in Killcrag. But the stench of rotting corpses, the goblin stink was too strong in her nose, and she was much too tired to find something to eat. The heavy humid air settled around her like a blanket, and her head fell deeper into the mattress beside Granny Wren's slight body as her own eyes slid shut.

"Blacksmith!" Heavy knocking roused Nessa from her drowse. She opened her eyes reluctantly, as the knocking sounded again. She raised her head. The room was in near total darkness, though she could hear rain pounding on the kitchen's low roof. In a sudden flash of lightning, she saw that Granny Wren slept on, softly snoring. At least the woman was still alive. The heavy knocking came again. "Blacksmith!"

A peal of thunder rumbled down the valley, echoing across the lake. Just as she'd expected, the day's humidity had culminated in a thunderstorm. Another burst of lightning illuminated the cottage. "All right," she answered. "I'm coming." She got to her feet, shaking off exhaustion. She'd fallen asleep where she sat. Although she'd no idea how long she'd huddled against the bed, she was stiff and cramped and felt as if she'd slept in that position for hours. She stumbled into the main room of the smithy, and felt above the mantel for the tinder and flint, then lit a stub of a candle. What felt like a gale wind was blowing through the cold room. She opened the door a crack, ever wary. In the reddish glow of the stubby candle, she saw two tall hooded figures, age indeterminate, though clearly male from their build. "Who're you and what d'you want?"

"Where's Dougal?" The shorter man's voice was as rough as the wooden planks of the door, and he spoke quickly, as he pulled the hood off his head to reveal bright blond hair and a square-jawed face. He glanced over his shoulder into the wet night, as though he feared someone might overhear.

"He's not here." She stared up suspiciously, wishing she'd remembered to grab the ax when she'd sprung to her feet.

"Where is he?"

"He's not here," she repeated. "Who're you and what do you want?"

Another peal of thunder rumbled through the valley. "I'm Cadwyr, Duke of Allovale." He flashed a jeweled medallion from around his neck. "You're his daughter, aren't you? If he's not here he would've left something for me. Do you know where it is?"

She shook her head. "I don't know anything about it. I have no idea whether he did or not."

For a moment she thought he might barge through the door. But he only smiled, a thin-lipped smile that uncurled across his lips like a narrow ribbon. "May we come in out of the weather, lass?"

His use of the endearment made her wary. But common hospitality demanded she give shelter on such a night. She drew back and opened the door. "You're the ones who were here the other night."

But he didn't answer her directly, only looked over his shoulder and motioned for his companion to follow him into the forge. "Can you tell me what in the name of the good god happened here?"

"It was goblins," she said evenly, watching his reaction

closely. "Somehow goblins got into the village. They came in from the lake, somehow."

But his reaction took her totally by surprise. For he did not question her at all, only rounded on his companion. "We must work quickly before the entire country panics."

He wasn't surprised, she thought. He wasn't surprised that the village had apparently been attacked by goblins, and what was worse, he didn't particularly seem to care. She remembered that her father had clearly recognized at least one of these visitors. When had Cadwyr ever come to the forge? A chill ran through her and suddenly she was afraid for some reason she could not name. She backed away and stood just beside the forge, arms crossed over her breasts, eyeing them both impassively.

Cadwyr looked at her. "We're not here to hurt you. We just came to get what your father made for us."

"Why would you think he'd say anything about it to her?" At the first word, Nessa's head jerked up. Her instinct was right. Cadwyr had been accompanied by a sidhe, for there was no mistaking the lilt of the OtherWorld in that voice. These were indeed the two who'd been here last night—well, whatever night it had been. And then another thought occurred to her. What if Cadwyr wasn't the one her father had recognized? What if it were the sidhe instead? The tone of his outburst had sounded shocked and horrified, as surely no mortal visitor, even one late at night, could rouse in the usually taciturn blacksmith. What if it were both? What possible connection could there be between her father and these two?

Lightning flashed once more, and to steady herself, Nessa

picked up another candle. She lit it from the other, and stuck them both on the table in a cracked piece of pottery. "We don't know what happened to my father. He disappeared the same night they found a dead goblin in the lake."

"When was this? How long has Dougal been missing?"

"Since the day after you were last here." She raised her chin and met his eyes. There was no need to mention to this very dangerous looking nobleman that she had ventured into the OtherWorld and had lost track of time. In another sudden burst of lightning, she saw the look the men exchanged. Thunder rolled down the lake valley.

Cadwyr slung his sodden cloak off his shoulders, revealing a face that some might call handsome. To Nessa, he looked as weather-beaten as his voice beneath the bright blond hair coiled close in soldier's braids. He picked up a hammer and swung it experimentally. "I've heard your father speak of you, lass. He says you're an amazon, that you've a skill with a hammer few men twice your age can equal. Is that true?" Again he flashed that white-toothed smile that made her shiver. He picked up a silver coin and spun it on the tabletop.

She moved behind the forge and picked up the nearest hammer. "What is it you need?"

He looked at her, and the smile widened. "Have you any other silver?"

She nodded at the stack of coins on the table. "Why? What for?"

"We need a dagger, little amazon. A dagger made of silver. Can you do that?"

She lifted her chin. She refused to feel threatened by their presence, even though every instinct she possessed told her these men were dangerous. "Why do you want a silver dagger?"

Cadwyr moved closer and the room seemed to shrink. "Can you do that for us? Or not?"

"Why do you want such a thing?" Nessa braced herself as if she were about to swing the hammer. She glanced over at the sidhe. "You going to kill him?"

"I'll give you the same answer I gave your father, little amazon. With this dagger we buy the throne of Brynhyvar. Is that a good enough reason for you?"

There was something in his eyes that glittered in the candlelight, something cold and hard that made her realize that while she might be armed with an ax, she was yet a nineteen-year-old maid, and he was a battle-hardened warrior in full prime. For the first time in her life, she felt completely and utterly vulnerable, for his eyes were stripping her naked, even while he continued to smile. She swallowed hard. "I've never worked with silver. I'm not sure it can be done."

"You're frightening her, Cadwyr, stop it," said the sidhe from the shadows. He looked at Nessa. "Bind it with iron. Hard iron." He swept the cloak off his face and his features were revealed, his thin face chalk-white, his ears faintly pointed beneath his flowing black hair. His green eyes glowed in the reddish light, deep with age beyond imagining, at stark odds to a face that belonged to a man no more than five-and-twenty.

Nessa inhaled sharply. A shiver ran up her spine. This was what her father had made that night, she realized. This was what he had taken down to the lake. This was what he was carrying when he disappeared. But Cadwyr was looking at her as if he refused to accept no for an answer. She picked up her apron and tied the leather strings around her waist and around her neck. "I'll see what I can do."

"Do what you can," said the sidhe. And then no one spoke again for a long time.

All through the night, she worked, pounding the metals into one narrow bar, shaping it in a scant half dozen heatings. The forge rang with the sound of her hammer, and the walls shook with the force of the blows, even as the storm outside subsided into an occasional distant rumble. Sweat ran down her face, until finally she tied a rag around her head. The moisture trickled down her neck and between her breasts and her shoulders gleamed, muscles rippling beneath her grimy skin. The stench of sweat and hot metal blended into an acrid odor which stung the nostrils and made all eyes water in the smoky light.

At last she laid her hammer down and rolled her shoulders back in a final stretch. All three were dirty from the fire and the forge. The dagger lay on the forge, less than nine inches long, with a narrow groove that ran the length of the entire blade, just an inch wide where the blade joined the hilt. It had a simple crosspiece for a hand guard. The hilt was barely six inches, counterweighted to balance the blade. The metal shimmered in the gray light, slim and deadly and silent as an assassin. Nessa looked up at the sidhe, who with flared nostrils, was staring at it with a lover's intensity. Somewhere close by, a cock crowed once, paused, then crowed again. "It must be sharp," Cadwyr said.

Silently, she turned to the whetstone, and the wheel

sparked and sang as she held the blade to it, carefully coaxing the metal to a razor-edged precision. At last she placed it once more in front of him.

Cadwyr turned to the sidhe, who had neither spoken unless necessary, nor revealed his name. "Pick it up." The sidhe hesitated and Cadwyr laughed. "Oh, go on. There's no silver in the hilt. What use will you have for it, if you're afraid to wield it?"

With a look of disdain, the sidhe reached for the dagger. As his gloved hands closed over the hilt, Nessa spoke once more. "I can't promise that blade will hold fast in a fight. It could snap in two pieces at the first—"

"It won't matter," said Cadwyr. "It only need strike one blow."

"One blow," murmured the sidhe. He pushed open the door and stepped into the yard, as a rush of cool morning air, scented with rain, filled the smithy. He swung the dagger in a vicious arc. He handled it as easily as if it were weightless, but Nessa noticed he stood well away from the blade, as though the merest touch of it would wound him.

"Well?" asked Cadwyr, watching from the door.

Nessa slumped beside the forge, her hand slack upon her hammer, exhaustion plain in the sag of her shoulders, the droop of her head. But her eyes were alert and all that long night, her wary expression had never faltered.

"It's well enough."

"Bring it here. We'll see if it has the edge you need," answered Cadwyr. He pulled out a piece of white fabric from his doublet, an embroidered piece of silk so fine it seemed to float. Nessa wondered that a man like Cadwyr should have need to carry a thing so finely wrought. He held out his hand for the dagger, then callously sliced through the fragile wisp. As half of it floated to the floor, he grinned at the sidhe. "What do you think?"

The sidhe nodded, satisfied. "'Twill serve. Now we must be off. We're late already."

Behind Nessa, Granny Wren gave a low moan, and Cadwyr peered behind Nessa. "Who've you got there, little amazon?"

"'Tis the wicce-woman."

"You've earned our thanks, little amazon." He placed three gold coins on the table, then picked up their cloaks and slung them over his shoulder.

They were heavy medallions of gold, stamped with the Duke's seal, worth, doubtlessly, a fortune. But utterly unspendable. "I don't want your gold," Nessa said in a sudden rush.

He looked back at her, surprised. "Then what?"

Nessa gestured over her shoulder. "Granny Wren and I. See us to Killcarrick." There was no way the little wicce-woman would survive here alone with her. And there was no way she could wait here. Time moved so slowly in the OtherWorld, surely she had time to find out if Griffin was all right. "We won't survive here if the goblins come back."

To leave them was tantamount to murder, and the life of a wicce-woman and a free tradesman's daughter was not insignificant. Cadwyr exchanged another look with the sidhe. "I'm not going that way, little amazon. But I'll come back for you, and take you there on my return." He indicated the gold. "'Tis sufficient to pay your head-prices if I don't come back in time." He strode out, and Nessa gasped, realizing that he meant to abandon them.

She rushed after them, grasping the bridle of Cadwyr's horse. "Please…you can't… What if the goblins return?"

"There're greater doings afoot, little amazon, than your two lives warrant."

Disbelief that he could leave them both, that so cavalierly could he dismiss their lives, and one of them a life she had gone to some trouble to save, gave way to a rage such as she'd never felt before. If she'd been holding a hammer she would've thrown it at his head. "Curse you to the Summerlands, Cadwyr of Allovale," she spat.

His face darkened and momentarily, he looked as if he might strike. Then his eyes fell on the great red ruby in Artimour's ring, and he caught her wrist in a hard grip. "What's this you wear, little amazon? A ring of the sidhe I'll be bound. From where did you get this?"

Don't trust him. Every instinct screamed that Cadwyr was not to be trusted as she yanked her wrist out of his grip. She thought furiously. "My father gave it to me. He had it from the sidhe who took my mother."

Cadwyr looked at his companion, who only shrugged. Nessa threw the sidhe a desperate look, but he only leaned over and touched Cadwyr's arm. "Leave her. We must be away."

"Until I return, little amazon." With a wave, he tugged at the reins and the horses jogged slowly up the muddy lane.

Nessa watched them go, her heart sinking into a leaden lake of despair, even while she was grateful he'd let the matter of the ring drop. Somehow, she had not thought it wise to let him know that one of the sidhe—albeit a half-mortal sidhe—had promised to help look for her father. Or that she had been able to cross the border into the Other-World and return in the first place.

She dropped down onto the stone stoop, squatting in the threshold as tears of anger and frustration, fear and desperation bubbled up out of a deep, aching well of exhaustion. She couldn't leave Granny Wren, but the two of them couldn't stay here. If Granny Wren didn't come to herself soon, surely she would die. She needed a druid—and the only druids Nessa knew of were all at Killcarrick. She rubbed her grimy hands across her face. Her whole body hurt, her hands and head and back all throbbed as if she'd been beaten. She felt as old as Granny Wren. From the back of the house, she could hear the old woman snoring in the morning stillness. At least they'd both survived the night. She leaned her head against the doorway, and fell immediately asleep.

It was thus the Duke's men found her, much later in the morning.

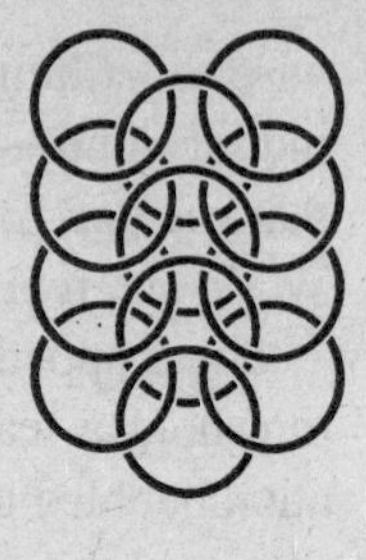

7

"Horned Herne and the Hag, it's gone, my lord." Delphinea's horrified whisper echoed up and around the curving, colonnaded walls and cascaded down from the roof in a swirl of dusty spirals. She felt a wrench in the pit of her belly, the same nausea that twisted in her gut each time word was brought that something else had fallen prey to the mysterious rot. But this was so totally unexpected she felt as if the air had been punched from her lungs. She had been braced to see something—anything—but the absence of the Caul itself. "Someone's taken the Caul."

"But—but—how in the name of Herne is it possible…?" Beside her, Timias clutched at the door and shuddered, his robes shivering on his old man's shoulders like broken wings.

"Someone's been here before us. And not that long ago, judging by the footprints."

"But who would have done this terrible thing?" With effort, he pulled himself up, leaning heavily on his staff with a white-knuckled grip.

Delphinea turned to look at him. His reaction to Petri's use of the mirror magic had disturbed her, but right now he only seemed very old and very frail and hardly a threat to anyone at all. "Are you all right, my lord?"

He shook his head, eyes darting around the room, as though expecting to see the Caul, somewhere, anywhere, within the chamber. "In truth, my lady, I can't say for certain, for I find I can't believe what my eyes tell me I see. To think that I have lived to see such a day." He closed his eyes and spoke in a low murmur. "Forgive me, Gloriana, I have not kept your charge." He sighed, opened his eyes and shook his head again. "To think that in addition to all that we face, now we should deal with this catastrophe." He leaned upon the staff with both hands. "I fear we shall not prevail, Delphinea, for surely this is beyond bearing."

"Do you suppose it's possible that someone took it, because they realized the same possibility I did? They realized it could be a poison…"

"Poison? There's nothing here that proves that the Caul is poison."

His voice was hard-edged and surly, but his eyes were wide and fixed and Delphinea understood that it was fear that made him angry. He was terrified, she realized, shocked and terrified, that what they all took for granted should so simply disappear. So she said nothing, though it seemed clear enough to her that the Caul had caused some breakdown in the atmosphere surrounding it. She only reached up, and touched the nearest door hinge with one fingertip. She turned, hand outstretched. "Look at this orange residue. I've never seen such a thing before. Do you have any idea what it is, my lord?"

He nodded, mouth slowly turning down into a bitter grimace. "The mortal word for it is rust."

"When has there ever been rust—or dust—in Faerie?" She did not wait for an answer. She gathered her skirts, stepping carefully around the first set of footprints. The room seemed otherwise unchanged, and she cautiously approached the green globe resting on the pure white pillar, circling it warily, surveying it from all angles. At perhaps a quarter turn to the left of the door, she paused, frowned, and bent closer.

At the top of the pillar, a thin brown line, like an old scar, snaked its way to the bottom. It started where the green globe rested on its golden base, and looked as if someone had drawn a dagger from top to bottom. Such a flaw within the otherwise perfectly pristine marble would never have been acceptable in a magic of such great undertaking. She bent to take a closer look, and saw that from this fracture, this seam, tiny brown pearls of moisture seeped. They ran down the surface in long, sporadic rivulets, staining the pure white like a trail left by muddy raindrops. Or tears. Or the calves, covered in sores which wept yellow-green pus, as they rotted from the inside out. A chill of revulsion ran through her. "Before you refuse to consider that it's poison, my lord, I think you should look at this."

He, too, was careful to avoid the first set of footprints. For what seemed like a long time, he stared at the seeping seam, and when he finally spoke, his voice was flat, without inflection, as though part of him was forced to acknowledge what the other part refused to accept. "Even if someone removed the Caul with the intention of somehow stopping possible contamination, the Caul cannot be simply destroyed or discarded. It must be UnMade as deliberately and with as much intent as when it was Made. There would be no point in attempting to do it in secret. Magic such as would be required would call attention to itself. And it isn't possible to work it alone. To raise the energy necessary would require the participation—at least on some level—of every sidhe in Faerie. Which would require the agreement, and Herne knows how close we are to that happy hour." He drew a deep breath, brows knit in a deep crease, mouth drawn down and grim. "So the question remains, not just who, but why? Why now remove the Caul—when circumstances are so dire?" He stroked his chin.

"Surely the contamination is obvious. You can see it there for yourself." Delphinea could scarcely contain her frustration. Much as he preferred to see himself as different from the other Councilors, Timias was just as single-minded as they when it came to certain things. Like the Caul. "How can you see it as anything but certain? This rot runs all the way through the bodies of my dead calves, to our sickly Queen, to the rust on the hinges and dust on the floors—that is the depth to which this rot has run, my lord."

"Which it may well be, my lady, but I will wager my life and all that's mine that whoever took the Caul off this globe was not immediately concerned with the long-term effect of the Caul on Faerie." He bent, and touched the moisture with one fingertip. He grimaced as it touched his skin, but he did not wipe it away. Instead he stared at it for a long moment. Finally he looked up. "It stings."

It was as much of an agreement as she could expect. So she only replied, "We should go to the Queen."

He struggled to his feet, knees creaking audibly. "Now, you've heard no mention of the Caul among the Court? Nothing's been said of it—not in passing, not in rumor, not by—"

"No one on the Council was interested, and no one else would listen. The Caul isn't considered part of this current situation, as everyone delicately insists on calling it."

"I agree we must go to Alemandine at once. But I think we must be very clear about our purpose. There are two problems here—one is long term and can only be corrected in the long term. But the other is very short term. And given the current situation, it is that short term problem that must be addressed immediately."

Delphinea frowned. "I'm not sure I understand."

"As an immediate result of the Caul's removal, the goblins are now free to hunt, virtually at will, within Shadow. The mortals are unprepared to face the horde—and human meat will increase the goblins' growth and breeding. So we will be faced in the very near future with a goblin army more fearsome than anything we've been anticipating. On human meat, their hide will thicken, their claws grow longer, their senses more acute. This is not something we want to deal with." He gathered his robes, took a single step away from the pillar, then paused. "Presumably the person who took the Caul knew this, and doesn't care. Either because they're confident they will prevail, or for some other reason I cannot fathom."

"I don't understand, my lord. I spend my time raising cattle, not formulating strategy. What are you talking about?"

"I'm talking about the reason someone would remove the Caul. The first effect is to wreak utter chaos and havoc within the mortal world, but that didn't stop whoever it was. Obviously they don't care about mortals—or how big and strong the goblins get. So it's the second effect that must be the reason—" Here he paused and looked straight into Delphinea's eyes. "Someone intends to bring silver into Faerie. More silver. More silver than the Caul will let pass through. And so it has to be removed—"

"But why would anyone want to do that? To bring silver in is to invite utter disaster."

"The gremlins." Timias spun around with unexpected agility. "I warned Alemandine. I tried to tell her they must be watched—and you taught one of them the mirror-magic." His eyes blazed and Delphinea drew herself up and met his stern look.

"Whoever took the Caul didn't come through the mirrors, you see that for yourself. The footsteps are clear enough. But why do you think the gremlins would take the Caul?"

"To kill the Queen, of course. To bring a silver weapon of some sort—probably a knife, a dagger, into Faerie. They will use it to kill her, and then...what would they care whether or not the goblins hunted men? Or sidhe, either—there's no love lost there for any of us, believe me."

Delphinea stared at Timias, her mind a jumbled swirl. What he said made sense, unfortunately. While the removal of the Caul and its ultimate destruction or transformation into some other object might be to the greater good of all, it could not be accomplished overnight or without the help of many. And in the short term, the Caul still performed its functions—better to face weaker goblins without the incipient threat of silver. And Timias had argued that the gremlins, bred of goblin stock, might well be ripe to throw off the fetters perceived inflicted by the sidhe. It was true there had been increasing surliness among some of the gremlins, but Delphinea heard everyone at the Court attribute that to the approach of Samhain—a most unsettled time for the gremlins, who grew gradually more aggressive as the great holiday approached. The madness culminated on Samhain night, when the gremlins were traditionally rounded up and confined to a specially fitted dormitory, where their howls and screams could be muted, at least, and their madness allowed to run its course in relative safety. There were always one or two found disintegrated the next day. It was generally acknowledged to be a distasteful business but a small price to pay, nonetheless, for the incipient satisfaction of being served by miniature replicas of their archest enemy.

Delphinea thought of Petri, the little gremlin who served her meals and oversaw the running of her simple household here at Court. He had never expressed any sort of discontent. But then, she'd never heard him express anything. The gremlins' high-pitched shriek was considered discordant, and they had long ago been forbidden to speak unless commanded in a sidhe's presence. It limited their range of expression considerably, but to compensate, they'd developed a complex system of hand and tail signals. It was essentially a silent means of communication the sidhe, lacking tails, could not completely share, a means of communication that therefore lent itself to plotting. She looked down at the footprints. They were fairly close together, she saw, closer than the single strides of either her or Timias. The steps of a shorter person. Or a gremlin.

"Come, my lady. We must go at once to the Queen. Lead the way—"

But the mirror was not so cooperative, and finally Delphinea realized it was futile. "Perhaps it's the dust, but I can't get through the glass."

"Then we'll take the longer route, my lady, through the corridors. And hope Her Majesty is in a receptive mood."

They chose the set of double doors through which the thief had entered the vestibule. As the doors swung open, Delphinea paused and glanced over her shoulder. From this vantage point, she noticed a subtle discrepancy in the footprints. "My lord, look," she pointed down. "A single person—gremlin or sidhe—didn't take the Caul. There were two people, two people who were careful to interchange their footsteps so that it only looks like one set."

"Two different size feet." Timias nodded. "Well. And we must assume one was male, and the other female."

"But could gremlins have even opened the door?"

He gripped her arm, and the look he gave her was one of bleak despair. "We have to hope that they did, my lady. For if not, then we have to believe that at least two of our own have betrayed not just our Queen, but all of us who dwell in both Faerie and the Shadowlands."

A preternatural silence settled over the palace of the Queen of Faerie, a silence as profound as the moon-dark sky, a silence that was belied by the sounds of revelry that floated up from the Great Hall, where the Court kept the obligatory feast at the express order of the Queen. The Queen herself was absent. In her darkened bedchamber at the very center of the palace, Alemandine slept, the hard, deliberate sleep of escape.

Alone in the round turret room at the top of one of the highest towers, Delphinea listened to the thin, piping music as it floated intermittently upward, a rift of melody here, a snatch of lively chorus there. On the other side of the glass, the silver stars spiraled across the night sky like diamonds across black velvet. She had changed her court gown for a white robe embroidered all over with periwinkles and cornflowers. Her feet were bare. She curled her toes in the tufted silk cushions of rich red, and wondered how all could still seem so much the same when everything had changed. It seemed impossible to believe that something so powerful had simply disappeared, plucked away as if it had never been at all. The crystal windowpanes, the thick silk, the deep purple wine within the crystal goblet standing on the inlaid tray, all still seemed as solid and substantial as ever. But was it?

As she had made her way through the corridors and galleries, through the halls and up the winding stairs, one single word continued to echo through her mind, over and over, the word that she'd heard for the first time that morning, spoken by Timias. Lyonesse. Like the sibilant hiss of a malevolent snake, the word hovered, lingered in the air, wreathing the faces of the Councilors with some nameless, unnamed dread.

She shivered. For the thousandth time that day, Delphinea wished her mother had accompanied her to Court. Surely her mother would've had far more counsel to give Alemandine. Surely her mother could answer the hundreds of questions that were constantly on Delphinea's lips, questions that changed continually with every encounter she'd had with all the unwritten, unspoken rules of etiquette and custom that reigned supreme within the Court. Manner was all, tradition was everything. It wasn't what one did so much as how one did it. But Delphinea did not understand why it mattered that certain colors were only worn on certain days. Even ordinary conversation was nuanced and she did not understand, for example, why how one inquired after another's health was more important than the fact that one did. She felt no closer to the answers to any of her questions here in the dazzling Palace than she had wandering the high mountain pastures among her mother's herds.

For the distressed herds were not the only reason she had come. With a little sigh, she dragged a woolen shawl around her shoulders and tucked her knees under her chin. She wrapped her arms around her legs, trying not to think about the part she had not told Timias. Nor anyone else, including her mother.

She had hoped that here, in the glittering Palace, among the shining Court, she would find someone who could explain to her the reason for the troubling visions that were beginning to plague her sleep more and more. She had gleaned enough to know that the mortal word for such visions was dreams, but that there was no such word in the sidhe-language, for the sidhe did not dream.

Except for Delphinea. She had not been surprised when the first word came from the higher pastures that the dead calf had been found. She had seen it in a flash of color and image and sound that had wrenched her out of a deep sleep, leaving her gasping and drenched in sweat. That was the first. Lately, there had been more and more. That was the beginning of her bond with the little gremlin, she mused. Petri had heard her sobbing, one night, when her sleep had been broken by a kaleidoscope of terrors. And while she didn't tell him exactly what the trouble was, he had seemed to know just what to do. But a serving gremlin could scarcely help her understand why she dreamed. Or what. But so far, she had not yet met anyone, including Timias, she trusted enough to tell. And now, even Eponea's original charge must take second place to this new and dire turn of events. The troubling thought flitted through her head that there was some other reason her mother had not come to Court herself—some other reason she was deliberately concealing from Delphinea. But she dismissed the thought, confident it was only a consequence of the stress of the day.

Surely it was the longest day Delphinea could remember, the longest day of her life. She tried to imagine what advice her mother would offer her and failed miserably. What was there to do about the missing Caul, but find it as quickly as possible? But who even knew where to begin to look?

Timias and she had gone at once, of course, to Alemandine, interrupting her as she sat drinking one of Vinaver's endless possets. At the news that the Caul was missing—vanished, disappeared, stolen—the Queen's face had drained of what little color it had, and she had looked frighteningly, eerily translucent, as though her very substance was little more than ice. She had glanced immediately at her sister, and the look she had given her was pure—pure what, wondered Delphinea. Pure malice? Pure hatred? Vinaver's patience with her sister was exemplary. What could explain the moment of loathing in Alemandine's eyes?

But if Vinaver noticed her sister's fleeting expression, she did not react to it at all. She only watched silently, her face composed and unreadable as she sat in the shadow of Alemandine's chair, perched on a stool. Only the tremor of her wings betrayed the intensity of her attention. But something troubled Delphinea about the entire exchange, something that eluded her exactly as she reviewed the entire day in her mind.

She closed her eyes, brushing her long hair, trying to define the undercurrents she had sensed as the Councilors had assembled within the room. Something was off, something different, not quite what it should have been. It wasn't just that moment when she'd seen the expression in the Queen's eyes as she looked at her sister. Vinaver had acquiesced on every point Timias raised—agreeing that the borders must indeed be reinforced, that the gremlins be dismissed from the Queen's immediate service, that special dispatches should be sent to Artimour and Finuviel, apprising them of the situation.

It was Lord Berillian who'd suggested that the disappearance of the Caul be kept quiet, shared only with the Council and those, such as Artimour and Finuviel, who had reason to know. Vinaver had gone along with that, too, and the meeting terminated abruptly with Vinaver's insistence that Alemandine must rest.

Which was exactly how the Queen's devoted sister should behave, Delphinea mused, as she listened to the tinkle of laughter filtering up from the lower reaches of the palace, to the snatches of flutes punctuated by bursts of applause that drifted on the breeze. The ivory and crystal towers were tinged purple in the deepening twilight, the light of countless candles flickering in crystal windows.

Hudibras and Gorlias, Berillian and Philomemnon, even Timias, had all joined the evening's feast, spurred on by Alemandine's decree that it was imperative the revelry continue unabated. All would be as it always was, ever more perfectly executed. But Delphinea had neither stomach nor heart for such meaningless merriment. And so she sat, alone in her high turret room, leaving the little gremlin, Petri, to deal with the endless onslaught of admirers and supplicants who sent wave after wave of sweetly scented notes, cunning verses, elaborate posies, and other tokens even more ornate to her door. Tucked away in her corner, she could hear the tinkle of the caller's bell, the murmur of mellifluous voices, punctuated by silence as the gremlin gestured his responses. She picked up her ivory hairbrush, and dragged it through her long dark hair, wondering what it was that disturbed her about Vinaver.

And then she remembered. It had happened in the beginning, when they had first come in, interrupting the Queen in the drinking of her posset. Vinaver had listened to the news of the Caul's disappearance, and when she raised her head, Delphinea happened to see Vinaver's expression as she looked at Timias. It was hatred she saw there, far more obvious than the malice she thought she'd seen in the Queen's expression. And that's what it was, Delphinea realized. There'd been hatred in Vinaver's look, but not shock. Anger, but not surprise.

She thought about the others, each in turn. Of them all, Hudibras and Gorlias had reacted the most strongly. But Berillian had seemed more…impatient. Yes, impatient was the word that came to mind. Philomemnon was conspicuously silent, speaking up only when a vote was required. Was it possible they weren't surprised because they already knew the Caul was missing? Timias's words as they left the Caul Chamber echoed in her mind. *Better to hope it was gremlins, or accept that at least two of their own kind had turned against the throne.* Was it possible that at least three of them—Vinaver, Philomemnon and Berillian—had indeed turned against the throne? Her fingers faltered and she nearly dropped the hairbrush.

"Do I disturb you, my lady?"

Her fingers faltered, and she nearly dropped the brush at the sound of Vinaver's voice. Delphinea jumped and gasped. Vinaver stood in the doorway, unannounced, almost as if she'd come in response to Delphinea's thoughts. She must have come through the mirror, for Petri would never have allowed her to be so taken unaware.

Vinaver had changed from her ornate flame-colored court

gown, and now wore one of simple dark green wool, absent all ornamentation. Her hair was pulled back beneath a black velvet snood. Her wings were folded so close and tightly together they were scarcely noticeable.

Delphinea shook herself a little. Vinaver was the last person she expected to see this evening. She rose to her feet. "My lady Vinaver?"

"I see I've surprised you, my lady. I hope I don't disturb you as well?"

"Not at all, my lady." Delphinea gestured to the broad window seat in the turret. "Will you join me? The view is most pleasant from here."

"Thank you." Vinaver crossed the small space with the perfect, mincing steps so diligently cultivated by every dame and lady, which, when properly executed, produced the illusion the walker floated above the ground. She seated herself carefully, settled her wings and looked out the window. "You speak too modestly, my lady. The view is more than merely pleasant. It is magnificent."

Delphinea regarded Vinaver curiously. Although Vinaver's status within the strict hierarchy of the Court was questionable, Delphinea was the most junior of all the Council members, only admitted in her mother's stead. A request for an audience should have come in an obliquely worded note that was really an encoded command. Suddenly it occurred to Delphinea that Vinaver was dressed as if she were about to leave on a journey. According to her mother, both Vinaver and Artimour, the Queen's half-siblings, occupied vague positions at the Court. Artimour, as a half-mortal, was considered something of a curiosity, but it was Vinaver, the twin sister of the Queen, something that had never existed before in Faerie, that was considered the most extraordinary of all. Siblings were rare—Gorlias and Hudibras were the sons of two different fathers—but a twin birth had never happened before. Nothing upset the sidhe more than an unexpected event, nothing so unsettled them as an unresolved point of etiquette. Vinaver's unpredictable behavior was doubtless due to her unanticipated appearance.

Eponea had taken great pains to explain to her how Vinaver was regarded by some as an abomination, and by others as something more of a nuisance, since she had no readily definable place. Everyone, however, agreed that Vinaver should have left the Court as soon as Alemandine was crowned. But Vinaver had steadfastly refused. Eventually the sisters struck a sort of bargain—from Samhain to Bel-tane, Vinaver joined the Court. From Beltane to Samhain, she was banished—forced to spend the summer months away. But the demands of Alemandine's pregnancy had superseded the agreement—when Vinaver had offered to come to Court immediately after the pregnancy was announced, Alemandine had eagerly agreed.

And then her mother spoke briefly of Finuviel—Finuviel, known even in their remote part of Faerie as Vinaver's handsome son; fathered, she claimed by Great Herne himself one Beltane. Her mother dismissed this as a pathetic attempt on Vinaver's part to assert some special status. But it was universally acknowledged by one and all—even her mother, who paused long enough to give Delphinea a measured look—that Finuviel was loved by one and all from the moment of his birth. Thus, he was always free to come and go and to join the Court as he pleased. He was away now, leading an army to help stem the growing goblin threat. And Delphinea was glad, for there was something in the name, something that reverberated in her bones, something that told her she'd heard his name in her dreams.

Alemandine—like every other female at the Court—never made a secret of the fact that she adored her nephew, and it was widely held that jealousy accounted for Alemandine's animosity toward her twin. But Delphinea remembered the look in Alemandine's eyes when she looked at Vinaver. It was more than simple jealousy. And not for the first time, in all the short time since she'd been admitted to the Queen's Council in her mother's name, she wondered about the complex nature of the relationship between Alemandine and her sister, and the son they seemed to share in some odd way. So she clasped her hands together on her lap and resolved to play the game as well as she could. "How does the Queen?"

"Resting at last." Vinaver paused. "Your dedication to Her Majesty is both noted and appreciated, my lady."

"It is my pleasure to serve." Delphinea waited. This mannered exchange could go on for a turn of the glass or more, and she wondered how long Vinaver needed to state her real purpose. "Will you have wine, my lady?"

But Vinaver surprised her. She ignored the question—a serious breach of etiquette in and of itself—and said instead something so extraordinary Delphinea dared not respond for fear she had almost certainly misunderstood: "You're right about the Caul. It's poison, and it must be destroyed."

Delphinea could only stare. In the wavering light of the

gardenia-scented candles, Vinaver's face appeared fixed and grim and Delphinea realized to her complete astonishment that Vinaver was completely serious. "But why didn't you agree, when I spoke of this in the Council—"

Vinaver laughed, a short, harsh bark that held no hint of mirth at all. "Surely, my dear, you understand I sit at the Council table on sufferance. I have no real voice there—"

"But I heard you speak…"

"Surely you're not so naive as to think I actually have a vote? Oh, I can say anything I wish. My sister prefers that I do speak, in fact, for it spares her the effort. But I have no real power." Her long green eyes glittered. "I've learned to choose my friends very carefully. And I've learned too well that those who would be my friends usually have reasons of their own. So when a stripling such as you, dressed in her mother's clothes, appears in her mother's stead—well, let me just ask you this. How much does your mother's life mean to you?"

"What about my mother's life?" whispered Delphinea, for in the strange green light that burned in Vinaver's eyes, she read a threat to everything she held most dear. She understood why Timias disliked her, why Eponea called her a deviation without a real place. There was something about Vinaver that frightened Delphinea, upset her as if the floor beneath her feet had suddenly tilted and might crumble away without warning.

Vinaver sat back. "Can you mean you haven't realized? Your mother's dying. The silver in the Caul has seeped into Faerie, poisoning the land and all that are bound to it. Like your precious cattle. Like your mother's horses. Like your mother. Why else did she send a sapling green girl like you, here, of all places? Unchaperoned and unprepared?"

"My mother's not dying." Delphinea frowned, but the ghost of doubt raised its face and danced a short jig. Was it possible that giddy with the prospect of her sojourn at Court, she had somehow missed it? Was it possible that the intuitive feeling she'd been plagued by was true and that there was indeed some other, more disturbing, reason to explain Eponea's decision to send her daughter in her stead? "She told me to go to Timias—"

"Stubborn fool, blind fool." Vinaver bit her lip as if she would say more, but shut her mouth tight. She turned away a moment, and when she turned back, she spoke more kindly, but her long eyes glittered dark green in the candlelight. "Oh, but she is dying, little one. For you have it exactly right. The Caul is poison, and all that are bound to the land are affected by it."

"But there's nothing wrong with my moth—"

"Are you sure? Are you certain? Have you received any sort of communication from her at all since you've arrived at Court?"

"No." It was Delphinea's turn to bite her lip, to stare blindly out the window into the dark night.

"You see, my dear Delphinea, that's why I'm here. I wanted to know what the life of she who brought you to birth means to you."

Far more deeply troubled than she wanted to admit to Vinaver, Delphinea looked back at her with dismay. "How can you be so sure of this, my lady?"

At that Vinaver shook her head. "I'm not ready to tell you

how I know certain things. Only think of it. It makes sense, doesn't it?"

As the immensity of the implications of what Vinaver said dawned on her, Delphinea whispered, "Does that mean the Queen is dying, too?"

Vinaver looked down and away, clearly considering how to answer, and Delphinea struggled to read the complex play of emotions which duelled across Vinaver's thin face. Finally she shrugged and answered, "Yes. The Queen is dying."

"And if the Caul is found, and destroyed, all will be as it once was?"

"No." Vinaver's eyes held hers. "Everything will be changed. But it is the only way to preserve Faerie at all. For if the Caul is not destroyed, your mother, indeed all of us, will die the true death, and all of Faerie will pass into nothingness—just like Lyonesse."

Lyonesse. A ghostly chill shivered down her spine, the word itself at once lovely and dangerous. Delphinea racked her brain, trying to remember how her mother had appeared in the days and weeks before her departure. It was true that in retrospect her mother had seemed pale, tired, possessed of an uncharacteristic languor. But Delphinea had assumed it was worry and fear for the herds, hardly sickness unto death. She looked back up at Vinaver. "Assuming I believe you, my lady, what can be done?"

"You know what must be done, my dear. The Caul must be destroyed, then Made again."

"And what if we can't find it? What happens then?"

Vinaver rose to her feet and paced to the opposite side

of the round turret, and gazed out, to the eastern horizon, where the dark was unbroken by even the dimmest star. "Then all is lost. We are lost, and we shall pass beyond time and memory like the land of Lyonesse—and even those who try to escape into the West will find it all for naught. And it may already be too late. The final disintegration is almost complete. There's already talk of ships, you know. But that won't save them and there's very little time as it is."

"Very little time for what?"

Vinaver hesitated, clearly struggling. "Every day that passes—every sun that sets—our hold on Faerie grows weaker, the magic that makes us what we are and this world what it is diminishes. We have a chance, but there's much to be done before the Caul can be destroyed."

"Like what?"

Vinaver did not answer immediately. "Many things. Many things I cannot speak of yet. But you'll have a part—I can see that, now. I was foolish to have missed it before."

"What part?" Delphinea stared at Vinaver suspiciously. There was something in this strange, wild-eyed sidhe that frightened her. It was the force of her will, Delphinea realized, that burned like a living flame in the depths of those hard green eyes.

"I think it will become obvious. Such things usually do."

Alarmed, Delphinea tried to make sense of Vinaver's words. "What if we can't find the Caul?"

"I already told you. Like the lost land of Lyonesse, all of this—" she waved one long white hand to the wide sweep of the windows "—all of this will be gone, out of time and all remembering."

"What is this Lyonesse? Why does no one speak of it?"

Vinaver smiled. "You've never heard of it, but you knew at once when you heard the name it portended something terrible, didn't you? That's the effect of its name on all of our race. Lyonesse was the land that lay east of Faerie—and it is said a fairer land by far. In fact that's why they say its memories have been allowed to fade into forgetting, for to hear of its greatness and its glory is to have to live with the pain of the knowledge that such beauty has passed away forever."

"And this will happen, if the Caul is not destroyed?"

"If it is not UnMade and then Made again."

"I don't think you came here tonight to tell me I was right about the Caul," Delphinea said suddenly. The round turret room suddenly felt close, the lattice panes looked like a hedge hemming her in. "Why did you come here? What do you want of me, really, my lady?"

"I came to tell you to stay away from Timias. He's no friend to anyone in Faerie, and once he realizes who you are, your life will be in danger."

Delphinea's jaw dropped and she drew herself up, regarding Vinaver with a wary eye. She should have known she was risking Vinaver's wrath when she'd sent Petri to Timias in the first place. "Timias was only kind enough to come with me to the Caul Chamber. Everyone else ignored me."

"I would not have ignored you. But you didn't come to me, did you?"

"There are those who say you don't belong at Court." Delphinea refused to be intimidated. After all, she was the daughter of an ancient and noble House, and her place in the Court and within the ranks of the sidhe was both assured and ordained.

It was Vinaver's turn to look startled. Then she smiled, a little grudgingly. "Point scored, my dear. And yet, so much trouble could've been avoided if you'd only come to me, instead of Timias."

At that Delphinea paused. What did Vinaver mean by that? What could've been avoided? The discovery that the Caul was missing? "But my mother said his loyalty to the Queen is without peer. Surely no one is more—"

"Perhaps not. But to what and to whom should we be loyal, and where exactly do our duties to each other and the Queen and the land truly lie? This is where everyone makes the same mistake. Have you ever really thought about what that means? Have you ever considered they might not always be the same?"

Delphinea rocked back on the cushions, confused and leery. Vinaver was clearly testing her, probing her for something she wasn't quite sure she understood. "I'm not sure I understand you, my lady. Surely you don't mean Timias would betray…and as for me? Why do you say my life is in danger?"

"Timias has already betrayed us all." She looked as if she might say more, but she only folded her long white hands in her dark green lap. "And as for you—your mother had no way of knowing, of course, for she would never have sent you to Court otherwise."

"No way of knowing what?"

Vinaver gestured to the golden hand mirror lying on the table beside Delphinea. "Look in that, and tell me what you see."

Delphinea shook her head. "Please don't toy with me, my lady. I may be young, I may be out of place here, but I am not stupid. I know what I see in the mirror. Why don't you tell me what you see?"

Vinaver leaned forward, and touched Delphinea's cheek with the back of her hand. "I see my son. I see Finuviel."

Finuviel. The name prickled across her skin, rippled down her spine. Delphinea felt the gooseflesh rise down her arms and back. She picked up the mirror and stared into it, seeing only her own familiar features. "What do you mean, my lady? Finuviel is your son—"

"Tell me what his name means to you—quickly, now, before it goes away."

Delphinea could only stare at Vinaver. The name did mean something to her, she could not deny that, nor the unbidden images it conjured up, images she recognized from her dreams. But she couldn't trust Vinaver.

And Vinaver seemed to understand, for she sat back and folded her hands in her lap. "When I look into your face, Delphinea, I see the confirmation that all I have done, and all I am doing is right—that the path I have chosen is yet the right one." She broke off and stared at Delphinea, and in Vinaver's eyes flared that same wild light that had so unnerved her before. "Tonight I shall content myself with that. But you must believe me that I am not the only one who thinks Timias is a witless fool better left to play in Shadow. It is not without good reason he believes the gremlins took the Caul—" And again she broke off, as if she inadvertently said too much. "You must understand that Timias helped Make the Caul. He was the one who stood on the other side of Gloriana as the mortal smith wielded the silver. He will never have a hand in its destruction. Can you understand that?" The look in Vinaver's eyes stoppered the hundred questions bubbling up to Delphinea's lips.

"But surely if the Caul is poison—"

"You don't understand, do you? The magic in the Caul is a blend of mortal and sidhe, male and female, silver and moonstone. Timias is that male principle. He gave of himself—he bound himself into the fabric of the Caul and as long as it endures so does he. No need for him to go into the West. Ever. My mother chose to go for her own reasons." She looked at Delphinea. "Now. Do you understand?"

Stunned by the whole conversation, Delphinea could only nod mutely.

"Good." Vinaver turned her proud head to the window and gazed out, as if somewhere on the horizon, she could find some inspiration. "Perhaps you should come with me now."

"Go?" Delphinea echoed in alarm. "Go where?"

"I must ride out this night—Her Majesty requires specific herbs, which must be gathered under a certain moon. I think it would be safer for you to come with me."

Delphinea shook her head. "My lady, my mother sent me here. I shall only leave when I have solved the problem of the dying herds, or my mother summons me."

"You have solved the problem, don't you realize that?"

Delphinea raised her chin. "I don't think I should leave."

For a long moment, Vinaver was silent, as if she weighed possibilities, considered actions and words. Then she rose to her feet. "Forgive me, Delphinea. Knowledge purchased at a price higher than you can imagine is not easily shared. If you won't come with me now, at least be wary of Timias. He's far more dangerous to Faerie, to all of us, and to you, than you can possibly understand right now."

"Then explain it to me." Delphinea bit her lip to hide her frustration, then shrank back as Vinaver suddenly advanced, and cupped her chin in one cold hand.

"You wear your part in this upon your face, and I am not the only one who will notice. If you want to stay alive long enough to play it, stay away from Timias and trust me until I return."

"But—" Delphinea paused. "Do you mean you know where the Caul is?"

Vinaver smiled, an enigmatic smile that held no answers, and her eyes contained only a sort of bright-eyed amusement, as if she regarded Delphinea as a new player in a very complicated game. Her expression sent a chill down Delphinea's back. "No, my dear. I have no idea where it is at the moment." Pliant as a willow, she dipped a little bow. "Forgive me again for the intrusion, my lady."

"That's all?"

"Fear not. All your questions will be answered sooner than you think. Look for me on Samhain night." Without another word, and an inscrutable smile, she slipped away as gracefully as a bird taking flight, leaving Delphinea listening to the faint strains of ghostly music. Ghostly music, indeed. How many nights more would the whole enchantment hold? Samhain was approaching—Hudibras and Gorlias had argued vociferously that they must find the Caul by then. But who knew even where to begin to look?

She wished she might've asked Vinaver more questions. A strong resemblance between two unrelated male and female sidhe was considered a rare sign that the potential to work great magic existed between the couple. What designs did Vinaver have for her son that she believed Delphinea might have a part to play? Delphinea had never considered that the dreams might have something to do with a mate—such a thing seemed too mundane, too predictable for the dreams, which were odd, unsettling and strange. Just like Vinaver. Another chill went through her as she realized that Vinaver roused the same feelings as the dreams. *Look for me on Samhain.* Vinaver's words echoed through her mind. Without the Caul, what would happen at Samhain, when all the doors between all the worlds swung open? What would happen when the gremlins went mad?

She thought back to earlier that evening, when she'd made her way from the Queen's apartments to this, her tower suite. The courtiers dipped their fans in greeting, bowing their elaborate curtsies in deference to her rank as she passed, as determinedly oblivious as ever. What would they think if she told each of them what she had seen? Would any of them stand still long enough to listen? Music, sweet as the tinkle of water, filtered through the air, and she could imagine the scent of roasting beef and warm bread dripping with honey and butter wafting thick in the high-ceilinged feasting halls.

It had not tempted her to join the throng. She had made

her way silently through the bright glowing halls, where thousands upon thousands of beeswax candles twinkled like stars, illuminating the company. She remembered watching the gremlins sidle through the company, serving, pouring, slicing. But had she really seen one deliberately allow a door to slam in a lady's face, and had not another jostled the arm of a lord as he raised his goblet to drink so that the scarlet wine spilled down the snowy velvet of his doublet? Was it her imagination or were their expressions markedly sullen? It could be the usual Samhain madness, she thought, as she resumed brushing her hair. Couldn't it? Timias was so certain it was the gremlins.

She put the brush down, and turned to the window, gathering her knees up under her chin. Once more, Delphinea wished her mother were in the next room, not halfway across the land. Part of her wanted to saddle a horse, order an escort, and ride home as quickly as possible, if only to ascertain that Vinaver was wrong about her mother. *Maybe she should have gone with Vinaver. Maybe she should go home. But Mother sent me here.* Here was where duty compelled her to stay, no matter how much she might miss or be concerned about her mother. Here was where her mother would expect her to stay.

It was later, much later, when the lamps had burned low, that Petri slipped almost silently into the room, bearing a tray with a sweetly scented posset. He bowed, placed it on the table beside her, and then, instead of leaving her alone to attend to the turning down of her bed, clasped his small paws before his chest in the position of supplication.

She looked at him, bemused. "What is it, Petri?"

May I ask a question, great lady?

She nodded, and touched his small head with a quick caress. "We've become friends, you and I, Petri. You know you may ask anything." He took a great breath, and glanced around, as if he suspected a pack of courtiers would materialize out of the walls. His whole frame seemed to quiver with some suppressed excitement, and she cocked her head, puzzled. What could so arouse this interest? "Say on, Petri. Ask what you will."

I have not the gestures to make the question, great lady.

"Then speak, if you must."

It will not give offense?

"No." She waited, curious.

He was silent, still. Then he drew himself up, made a low, gargling noise in his throat, as if to clear it, drew a deep breath and began to speak in a piercing shriek that made chills run down her spine. It took all her self-control not to cover her ears. "Is it true you mean to help in the UnMaking of the Silver Caul?"

"You heard the Lady Vinaver in here, just now?"

He nodded, looking comically, pathetically eager.

"These are unsettled times, Petri. The Queen—like the very land itself—is sick." Maybe she was sick, as well, she thought suddenly. Maybe that was the reason for her sleeping visions, for the dreams. "I believe the Caul is the reason and—" She broke off, wondering why the gremlin should care enough to ask. "Why? What does the UnMaking of the Caul have to do with you?"

He turned away, shaking his head. *Forgive me, great lady, I have overstepped myself.*

"Wait, Petri." Delphinea regarded the little gremlin closely. Some emotion she could not read flickered across his usually expressionless face, his whole body was taut with tension. "Why do you care about the Caul?"

He shook his head. *It is of no importance, great lady. Forgive my forwardness.*

"Petri, I want to understand. I believe the Caul should be destroyed. But why does that concern you so? I can see that it does—it's no use denying it. Can't you tell me?"

There was a long silence. Finally he shook his head. *It is better that I do not say.*

Delphinea bit her lip. "Then will you tell me something else?"

He looked startled, surprised. *If it is in my power to tell you.*

"Why do your people go mad on Samhain?"

He looked distressed. *I would rather not answer that question, great lady.*

"Well, I would rather not be burdened with the UnMaking of the Caul, but it doesn't appear as if any of us will have much choice in the matter, does it? Come, Petri, I answered you."

With a sigh, he gestured slowly, *It is said among my people it is then we smell the land of our begetting.*

She frowned, uncertain, despite his slow movements, what exactly he meant. "The land of your begetting? What do you mean, Petri? Your people were begotten in Faerie."

That is the story your Lorespinners tell, great lady.

"But that is not the truth? Where is the land of your begetting? Are you—are you of Lyonesse?"

I know not that word, great lady. I only know that this is not something that should be spoken of to one such as you.

"But, Petri, if I can understand why it happens, perhaps something can be done to stop it."

He dropped his eyes and turned his head, even as his hands and tail twitched. *There is only one way to stop it.*

"To stop the Samhain madness? What is it? What must be done? I taught you how to move through the mirrors, didn't I? You know I want to help you."

You won't believe me.

"How will you know until you tell me?"

There are no gestures to say what must be said.

"Then speak."

Defeated, he drew another breath and glanced around the room once more. Then he leaned forward and his labored whisper was like the cry of a strangled nightingale. "The story told by the Lorespinners of the sidhe is not the truth. We are not bred of goblin stock at all. We are not even of Faerie. We are the race the mortals call pixies or brownies or sprites—the earth elementals who inhabited the glens and cairns and hollows of the Shadowlands."

Stunned, she sat back, the brush slack in her hand, and despite the grating sound of his speech, she had to know more. "How in the world do you know this? What makes you think this is true?"

"These are memories that have come to us, great lady. In the beginning, when we were first bound into these forms, our memories were similarly ensorcelled. But as the years have passed, the spells wore thin, and thus, some of us began to remember. At first we called them dreams, wishes, and we did not realize they were not at all images of what we wished for, but of how we once lived, of what we once were. But as more time passed, and more of us remembered, we realized these were not dreams. They are the true rememberings of the life we lived in Brynhyvar before the Making of the Caul."

"Then—then how did you come to be in Faerie? And why do you look like small versions of goblins?"

"This is the shape in which we were bound, my lady, when first we were brought to this captivity."

"But how did you even come to be here? Who brought you here? Who bound you here?"

There was another long silence. He took a deep breath, and his mouth worked. When he finally managed to speak, his voice was like the softest scrape of fingernails over chalk. "We were handed over by the mortals, given to the sidhe."

"But why? For what purpose?"

"In payment for the Caul. 'Twas in the Making of the Caul we were thus bound within these forms."

Shocked into silence, Delphinea stared at the little gremlin. She looked into his eyes. Not the goblins' hard reptilian stare, these were soft and dark and brown as new-turned spring-time earth. "Horned Herne," she whispered. The shadows seemed to thicken all around her, the night sky darkened. What exactly was it that Timias and Gloriana had done? Was this what Vinaver meant when she said that Timias was no friend to anyone in Faerie? It was impossible to think that the courtly sidhe, so mannered and so faultlessly kind to her, could have had a hand in such an oppression. He must have some sort of knowledge of it, she mused. He was the only sidhe left in Faerie from that time—all the others had long gone into the West. And he was so certain no love was lost between the gremlins and the sidhe. Nor mortals, either. Now she understood why he thought the gremlins had reason to take the Caul. And if the Caul were ever UnMade, Delphinea realized, the bindings on the gremlins would be unbound as well. No wonder Petri was so excited. But the little gremlin still hadn't answered her original question. "But why at Samhain, do you all go mad?"

"The doors swing widest then—it's then we smell the earth."

"The earth? You mean the Shadowlands? Brynhyvar?"

"I mean the dirt, the ground, the soil in which everything that is, is rooted." His light brown eyes burned with a sudden hunger.

"But there's earth—dirt—in all the gardens. Surely 'tis the same?"

"It's not at all the same, my lady." He choked, and she had to bend closer to hear him.

"How so?"

He was silent, small leathery head bowed, hands clasped behind his back, resting on the stump of his tail. He gave a deep sigh and squeaked, "Well, for one thing, it doesn't stick." He looked at her with such bleak despair, her own heart clenched. To her shock, she saw his eyes were brimming with tears. He bowed his head and gestured. *I must be about my duties and can speak of this no more.*

She gestured him a thanks and watched him leave, scampering away with an air of escape. *Doesn't stick.* The words echoed in her mind long after Petri had trimmed the wicks and turned the bed down. She thought of the dust, viscous and sticky, clinging like a spider's web to her hands and face and garments. What power did the stuff of Shadow hold, that made it so adhesive? Before she climbed into bed at last, she stood a while longer, staring out the turret window to a world that felt weightless as a bubble compared to the sturdier stuff of Shadow. Far below, she saw a lone rider on horseback emerge from the shadows of the Palace and disappear into the night.

No dreams troubled her sleep that night. In the morning she learned that Vinaver had indeed gone to gather herbs for a special posset to be made for Alemandine's health and that a gremlin named Khouri, a scullion in the Palace kitchens, was missing.

8

The long shadow fell straight across the forge, and Griffin looked up from wiping his brow with the dirty rag he kept tucked in his belt for just that purpose. In the late afternoon light, the backlit figure clearly wore a homespun tunic and a simple plaid shawl, a dark riot of curls about her shoulders. His heart leapt, and a broad smile stretched across his face. Nessa, he nearly cried aloud.

But the figure stepped farther into the high-raftered forge, out of the glare of the doorway, and he saw gray threading through the dark hair, a bright blue kirtle such as Nessa would wear only under duress, and that it was only Granny Molly, the wicce-woman of Killcrag.

His face fell and her wide lips quirked, as though she understood she'd been mistaken for someone else. He glanced around the forge, but the smith and his two apprentices were occupied.

"There someone you're hoping to see, lad?" She spoke with a gentle, teasing tone, the sort of voice his mother used to coax something from his father.

Griffin flushed, stuffed the rag into his belt and tried to come up with something to explain his enthusiasm. "I was hoping the Duke's men had returned from Killcairn." He'd had a hard time keeping his mind on his work all day, which, for a blacksmith, was never a good thing. But he couldn't help himself from wondering what Kian would find when he reached Killcairn, and from hoping that despite all the odds against it, Nessa had managed to get safely out of Faerie. But what if she found a horde of goblins waiting for her, such as had descended on the village the very night after she left?

Molly's answer was even, matter-of-fact. "They rode out of here looking like men who knew how to get to wherever they wanted to go. I wouldn't be surprised if they were back today. Or tomorrow, depending on what they find there." Her dark eyes met Griffin's.

"You mean, they may have to travel more slowly with Granny Wren?"

Molly only nodded. It was better not to speculate too closely on what Kian and the other knights would find. It was better just to hope.

He cleared his throat. The others were glancing at them now, a glimpse here over the shoulder, a brief look there. He was acutely conscious of Molly. He wondered how he could have mistaken her for Nessa. They had the same general build, he decided, but Molly was all ripe curves beneath her homespun kirtle that fell to just below her knees. She was not at all young—old enough to be a granny, he supposed. But there was nothing of the wizened crone about her at all. Old enough to be his mother, she must be, but she was as out of place in that hot sooty forge as a swan among crows. Or maybe swan wasn't the right image for her, he thought. Something about her put him more in mind of a cow: round, substantial and nourishing. "Is there something you wanted of me, Granny Molly?"

From the other side of the room, out of the corner of his eye, he saw Engus, Killcarrick's master smith, an affable man, less taciturn by nature than Dougal by far, but, like Dougal, with no time at all for corn magic except as an excuse for a holiday, wink at him, and Griffin, to his horror, felt himself blush.

If Molly saw this bit of byplay, she ignored it. "I thought we might walk a bit, you and I. There's been some talk among the children and I thought you might want to talk to someone about the other night."

To his complete mortification, he felt himself redden to the roots of his hair.

But she only smiled at him, with a bland smile that held no promise of anything but a kind word, a sympathetic ear. The expression in her eyes reminded him of his mother's. With a little pang, he realized he had not thought so much of his mother as he had in these last days, when the devastation of Killcairn aroused memories of the fire that destroyed his father's smithy and burned all within.

"Master Engus, have you need of me right now?"

The burly blacksmith turned, and spoke to Griffin, but his eyes fell square on Granny Molly. "No, lad." His blue eyes danced in his weathered face. "'Tis not my place to bid you come or go. You've worked hard here all day—you go on now, if you wish." He indicated the small pile of silver-coated weapons. "We've run out of silver as it is. And the Sheriff's treasurer will not give the order to melt down any more of the Duke's coin."

Griffin exchanged a quick glance with Molly, who shrugged. "He answers ultimately to the Duke, you know. Maybe he's afraid he'll have a hard time explaining what's happened to half his wealth if you melt it all down."

"If he'd seen what I have, he'd think it money well spent." Griffin ripped the cords of the leather apron off his neck and threw it across the workbench. "Thank you, Master Engus. I'll be back to help set the forge to rights."

As he turned to follow Molly out into the courtyard's clear sunshine, Engus spoke again. "You might ask the granny to have a look at that hand of yourn, Griffin. It's not healing clean." Molly glanced back and Engus gave her a knowing nod. "A smith needs both hands sound."

Molly only beckoned. "Come with me, Griffin."

She led him out into the open air. Last night's storm had left large puddles in the cobblestoned courtyard. It was crowded with refugees lined up at the kitchens, an endless stream of open mouths and empty bowls. The harried inhabitants of the keep were doing their best to cope with the swell of refugees, who burrowed down into the vastnesses of Killcarrick as if they wished the rocks themselves would swallow them.

And who could blame them? As if swept by a giant broom, every person living between Killcairn and the keep had packed up and hastened to the castle. The only thing that bothered him was that in the wake of the goblin attack, no one mentioned Nessa, no one spared a thought for the missing girl and her father.

"Let me see that hand." Granny Molly had paused just beside the gate which led to the outer ward of the keep, where the long lines of male refugees of fighting age who'd been handed weapons and inducted into the Duke's service, practiced in ragged rhythm. The only thing that spared Griffin from their ranks was his identification as a blacksmith. He stuck his hand out, palm up. The cut from Nessa's amulet wasn't wide but it was deep. It was in the thickly callused part of his palm just below the fingers, and except for the fact it refused to close completely, he didn't find it particularly bothersome or even painful at all. But it continued to seep blood, and Engus had noticed it the first morning he'd walked into the smithy.

Gently, she untied the dirty rag that had served him as a bandage and, with a puckered frown, probed the reddened flesh around the puncture with a soft touch. "It's deep. Come with me. I have some salve I managed to bring from Killcrag. 'Twill keep it clean. And I have some clean linen, too. Engus is right. You should have this bandage changed. Come."

Too tired to protest, too preoccupied by imagining what the Duke's men may have discovered in Killcairn, he allowed her to lead him through the throng, through the outer wards where the shepherds and farmers and herders learned to throw a spear and parry a swordthrust, through the guard-towers of the outer gates, into the sprawling tent-city that had sprung up just outside the main walls. She led him past the long multicolored rows of tents constructed of blankets and canvases and even ancient strips of carpet of every size and description. From a distance, he imagined the entire periphery of the castle must look as if it were blanketed by a crazy-quilt strung together by ropes and tentpoles.

He followed Molly closely, ignoring the faces that peered up at them as they passed, trying not to think of all the faces he would never see again, the faces his last memories of would forever be marked by agony and terror. All that long day, he remembered, that first long, long day after the sun had risen on the headless goblin and an absent Nessa, a grim certainty that the twilight would bring something terrible had plagued him, driving him finally, as the shadows of the trees reached out over the lake, coloring the depths black in the late afternoon, to retrieve the chest Dougal kept beneath his bed, the chest of gold and silver coins that represented the entire sum of the blacksmith's wealth.

With a heavy heart, and the sure knowledge that apprentices found to have stolen from their masters faced the loss of at least one ear and the fine of three times the equivalent of whatever was stolen, he'd melted down the silver coins and gathered whatever implements that might serve as a weapon he could find—kitchen knives, hammers, axes, a pitchfork, and a rake. Guilt plagued him as he heated the silver into liquid, as he dipped the first of the three knives, the first of two axes. And then he heard the first screams.

Set up on a hill, the smithy was far enough away from

the lake that Griffin had time to grab the silvered weapons and run out, into a deepening dusk, where nightmares with teeth and claws whipped their long leathery tails around all who scattered, tripping them as they tried to run. It was the wicce-woman who'd saved all of those who'd managed to crowd within her cottage, for the goblins couldn't cross her threshold or breach her windows, all through that endless night. But Granny Wren had forgotten the roof. They were trying to pull it off when the dawn finally drove them back across the borders into the OtherWorld.

He stumbled after Granny Molly, unseeing, lost in the memory of what the old woman had said when she turned to him, when they'd finally heard the goblins driven off by the blessed sunrise. "I need your help, lad." It was the sort of help she'd needed of him then as much as any other memory that left him shaken to his core.

"Sit." Granny Molly's little push on his chest broke the thrall of memory.

He looked around. Somehow they had ended up on a slight rise in what looked like an apple orchard, overlooking the river. A rough sort of lean-to was positioned beneath the spreading branches of the tree, a structure that compared with the tents that served as everyone else's shelter, appeared remarkably solid for something so hastily constructed. He shoved the memory of what he'd seen and done away and let her push him down on a little three-legged stool beside a hide and leather bound trunk. She said nothing as she poured a little water into an earthen basin and sprinkled some sort of powder in it. She took his hand, carefully turned the palm face up and rested it in her lap.

The cloth beneath his hand was rough, and patched, but through it he could feel the firm round muscle of her thighs beneath. She dabbed the wound with the water, making little tsk-tsking sounds between her lips. "You've got to rest this a bit. It's got to close up. If it goes bad deep inside, you could lose the use of the hand."

She smiled gently, reached for a pot and, uncorking it, scooped out a greenish salve that smelled strongly of pine and lavender with a little spoon of hollowed bone. She rubbed it gently all around the wound, then bandaged it with a long strip of clean linen that smelled like laundry fresh off the line. "There you are," she said, sitting back, placing his hand gently on his own thigh. "Rest it a bit and it'll be good as new."

He fumbled with the bandage, suddenly tongue-tied and shy.

"I've been wanting to talk to you, Griffin, and find out how you are." Her voice was soft, her eyes kind. "Some of the survivors from Killcairn told me what you did. You did a great thing, you know. You saved our lives."

"It isn't that," he said suddenly. "I only did what Granny Wren said needed doing."

"But participation in a rite is never something done lightly, or quickly, or without great care. It's never done without great preparation. What you did could not have been an easy thing."

He did not dare look up. "Not at first it wasn't." He looked at her, but her expression didn't change. She was waiting for him to continue. "But something happened—something happened when I kissed her." He paused. "I didn't expect that."

"What happened?" Molly probed with delicate skill.

"When I kissed her...I don't know how it happened. She—she just—just changed. And that made it—" He searched for the word. "Possible."

"What do you mean? How did she change?" She was leaning forward, her head cocked. She looked as though much depended on his answer.

He was silent, thinking how to put into words an experience he could barely comprehend, let alone describe. But Molly was waiting for his answer, and he did not think she was going to let him leave without one. "Kissing her wasn't really what I wanted to do," he admitted, feeling sheepish. "Granny Wren is very old, meaning no disrespect to her, you understand? But—but she said it was necessary and so I did—and when I did, I felt—I felt the way her mouth felt—it changed—it felt different, and then I opened my eyes. And I saw she wasn't—wasn't old anymore." *And I imagined she was Nessa.* But he couldn't possibly say that.

The illusion had lasted all the way through the experience, through the slow sweet richness of their sex, through her belly swelling up like a pregnant woman's at full-term, to him propping her up against the great rock which rose up from the shore like the round mounds and heavy pillars of a woman's buttocks, the knotted rope between her teeth.

"Go!" she'd whispered, teeth clenched around the rope, her blue-veined breasts splayed on either side of the rising swell of her enormous belly, her skin as rosy as a maiden's, nipples brown and stiffly erect, as if already straining toward an infant's mouth. Her belly convulsed in a great heave and she cried out, sweat breaking out all over her forehead.

"Go!" she snarled. She nearly dropped the rope out of her mouth as she balanced back on her fists, her thighs spread wide, ankles drawn up beneath her, as if she would birth whatever thing she held within directly into the lake water itself.

Naked, confused, he'd stumbled off the beach, lurching up the forest path to retrieve his clothes by the cairn she'd insisted he build, somehow throwing on enough to make himself decent. He'd gone back to the wicce-woman's house, gathered up the survivors—sixteen out of nearly two hundred—and fled to Killcarrick, leaving Granny Wren there beside the lake, taking only enough time to hide the amulet and the note for Nessa. But that's what she had told him he must do.

A breeze whispered through the apple boughs above his head, and the scent of apples filled his nostrils and he realized that while most of the fruit had been harvested, a few windfalls were scattered at their feet.

Molly was smiling, a grim, satisfied smile that did not quite reach her eyes.

"That's a good thing, then? That she changed?"

"Yes. That's a very good thing. Granny Wren is a wicce-woman of great power. Thank the goddess. I doubt a lesser granny could've done it." She gathered the edges of the shawl together as the breeze blew chillier. "It means the magic you made was successful—the god and goddess were with you. But no magic—no corn magic, anyway—can withstand Samhain." She took a deep breath, and her eyes swept over the lake, to the river which snaked around the outcropping that was Killcarrick. "We're surrounded here on three sides by running water." She nodded. "We may have a chance here."

"A chance?" Griffin leaned forward.

"To survive. If the goblins come on Samhain, as I fear they will."

"Why will they come again at Samhain? Why not before?" It was his very insistence that had led the Sheriff to grudgingly agree that some silver must be melted down.

"I suppose it's possible, perhaps. But at Samhain, all the doors between the worlds swing open—all the boundaries and the borders blur. If the goblins have found a way past the magic that holds them bound in the OtherWorld, I fear that at Samhain, those bonds will be especially weak. The old stories, of the time before the Caul, say that at Samhain the goblins hunted far and wide and no village or croft was safe, and only those lucky enough to gather in the keeps and the castles survived. But here—" she gestured to the river "—here we're three sides surrounded by running water. They can't cross running water—at least, not so easily." She wrapped her arms around herself and shivered, looking around. "Something's at work all around us, Griffin. I can feel it."

Her dark eyes fell on him and he, too, felt chilled. There were men who said that the wicce-women, mostly known as healers and midwives, the keepers of the corn magic, could be had for a silver coin. It was a ridiculous thing to say about Granny Wren, but looking at Molly, he could believe it. Each of them were somehow wedded to the land in some mysterious secret rite that none ever shared, but involved stone circles, corn sheaves, and fallow fields. And a man. He had some inkling of how it all worked now. If it were true that the wicce-women did take men in exchange for silver, he suddenly knew there was far more involved than a simple exchange of coin.

"So how'd you get that cut?"

"This—this one?" he started at her abrupt change of topic. "I—I cut myself—on a—on a knife."

She touched his forearm lightly, as if she would gentle an uneasy horse or hound. "I don't mean to pry, Griffin. If you don't want to speak of all you've seen, it's all right. I only wanted to find out how you were. It seemed only right," she said, and in that moment, he knew she knew he lied.

He shook his head, then leaned back against the trunk, feeling supported by the solidity of its bulk. "How I am," he echoed, seeing once more Jem the herder's boy carried off before his eyes, slung screaming over the shoulder of a goblin who casually ripped out the boy's throat, gashing so deep into his neck that the boy's head had bounced off into the road like unwanted offal, eyes still living and aware, mouth still screaming soundlessly. "I've seen terrible things," he said at last. "And I'm afraid I will see things more terrible still."

"We owe you our lives," she said, and in her expression he read both compassion and an acknowledgment that he was right. "It's not sunk into the rest of them yet, but it will. And even here—insisting they coat some of the weapons with silver—the Duke's First Knight was impressed with that, as well. You've a good head on your shoulders, young man. Everyone is afraid of what's to come. And if they aren't, they should be."

He dipped his head awkwardly, uncomfortable with praise, uncomfortable at taking credit for something he wasn't sure was true. *Not a good enough head on my shoulders to be able to stop Nessa,* he thought. He closed his eyes. A vision of her face in the lantern-light, before she'd headed down the road rose before him. Where was she now? he wondered. Had she managed to find her way back? Did she find his note, his amulet? Would she take offense to his taking hers and leaving his for her? It might seem like a bold move, scarcely justified, but the goblin attack had made him resolve to declare his feelings for her as soon as he saw her. Which might be tonight. Or tomorrow. His pulse pounded just a little bit faster. He still wasn't sure exactly what he would say to her.

"Griffin, you looked terribly glad to see me just now, when I came to the forge. Who were you hoping I was? Dougal's girl?"

Mutely, he nodded. His own personal danger from the goblins was nothing compared to Nessa's.

"The children told me she went to look for her father. Where'd she go?"

He was conscious of the weight of Nessa's amulet against his bare chest, warm as his own flesh, comforting as the pressure of her hand. "She went away—she went off."

"Off where? Where's she gone, Griffin?"

He dropped his eyes, unwilling to meet her gaze. There was something about Molly that again reminded him uncomfortably of his mother, and he looked away, over the water, that today lay like a silver mirror under the cloudless blue sky. Last night's storm had cleared away the humidity, and the air was colder today, more seasonable. Should he tell Molly? he wondered. All he'd told the people of Killcairn was that she'd gone off looking for Dougal. But loyalty to Nessa warred with his own need to tell someone—anyone—and this woman with the broad face and the kind eyes—a wicce-woman, after all—well, she had some knowledge of such matters, didn't she? But he hadn't been able to tell Granny Wren, either. "She's gone off," he said, feeling trapped.

"But where?" Molly was watching his face closely. "Griffin, you must tell me what you know."

He took a deep breath. It had been the longest five days of his life. He hadn't been so worried since Nessa had the spotted sickness. He clenched his hands together into one hard fist. "She's gone into the OtherWorld," he said, meeting her eyes with something like defiance. "She's gone into TirNa'lugh."

But to his surprise, Granny Molly only sat back, rearranging her shawl more comfortably around her ample curves. "Gone to TirNa'lugh, you say. To look for her father?"

Miserably, he nodded.

"But what made her think to look there? The goblin that washed ashore?"

"No." He shook his head. "Well, that was part of it."

"What's the all of it, Griffin? Nessa might be in terrible danger—"

"You don't have to tell me that!" he cried. "I tried to warn her, tried to talk her out of it, tried to go with her—"

"What do you mean, tried to go with her?"

He shrugged. "I tried to follow her. I told her she

shouldn't go alone. So when she left, I waited, and then I followed her into the woods. But I couldn't follow her into the OtherWorld. One minute she was there, just ahead of me, and then the next she wasn't. It happened just as the sun came over the trees—there was a flash and she walked into the light and then she wasn't there anymore."

"I see." Molly sat back, looked down, brow knit, as if what he'd told her meant something more to Molly than it did to him.

"She was afraid Dougal had gotten himself involved with something to do with the sidhe."

"Concerning her mother?" Molly's sharp look pinned him against the tree as surely as if she'd stuck him with a dagger.

Griffin shook his head. "I don't think so." He looked her squarely in the eyes. "Two visitors came to the forge, the night before he disappeared, and Nessa said that one of them was a sidhe."

"A sidhe? What made her think so?"

"She said she saw the eyes."

At that, Molly shifted and inhaled sharply. "And did you see this sidhe, as well?"

"I was asleep. Nessa said that Dougal was up late that night—making something Nessa thinks he took with him when he went down to the lake. Just before they found the goblin." He looked down at his injured hand. "She left her amulet with me. I think that's why I couldn't get into the OtherWorld. I forgot to take my silver off."

"Yes," Molly nodded. "So she went into the OtherWorld to look for Dougal. Any idea where she intended to look?"

"She wasn't really planning on looking herself, I think.

She hoped to get the Queen to help her. That's why she chopped off the goblin's head. She said the Caul should never have let the goblin in and she wanted to show the Queen that the magic had somehow failed. So she chopped off its head and took it with her in a sack."

"By the Great Mother," Molly breathed. "For someone not Beltane-born, she has all the signs."

Griffin cocked his head. "You said that before about Nessa—that she'd the mark of a Beltane child about her. What did you mean?"

"It's a sense—a knowing, an awareness. They can feel the OtherWorld—and the OtherWorld feels them. I'll explain more—but tell me, when did she go?"

"She crossed in the dawn after Dougal went missing."

"She wasted no time, did she?"

"I begged her to wait for the Duke's men." His voice was hoarse over the lump that rose in the back of his throat, and his eyes clouded with tears.

Molly drew a deep breath, reached over and grasped his arm. "It's hard to love someone so much, isn't it?"

A tear spilled down his cheek and he wiped it away with the back of the bandage. "Yes," was all he managed.

She gave him a long moment to compose himself. Then she asked, "You've been with Dougal long?"

"Since I was twelve. I've but another year to serve."

"And then what?"

Griffin shrugged. "I guess I dared to hope there might be a future for me there. With Dougal. And Nessa."

Molly nodded. "'Twouldn't be a bad life at all, would it now?"

"No," he said, remembering long winter evenings spent cracking nuts, telling jokes and stories around the hearth, summer nights spent relaxing by the lake, or in the wide yard of the smithy, drinking Dougal's own clover mead. Dougal had treated him like a son, taking him into the family in a way he had not expected.

"Where are you from, lad?"

"Up Pentland way. My father had a smithy—burned to the ground one night—all were lost. That was the night I'd chosen to sneak out into the woods. I came home at dawn to find the house and everyone in it gone to ashes. Everyone thought I was dead too. But when I showed up, they asked around, put out the word and Dougal took me in."

"A good arrangement."

"It was—it is." He corrected himself with insistence.

"You know Dougal well then?"

"As well as possible I suppose. He keeps to himself—he's a good man but he doesn't talk much. Nessa teases him he brought me into the house not so much to work for him but to talk to her. He can go days without saying a word, I think."

Molly said nothing, only tucked her knees under her chin. In the shadowy light, she looked not much older than Nessa. She was the youngest wicce-woman he had ever seen and he wondered, suddenly, how exactly one became a wicce-woman. Then she asked, "Do you know where he's from?"

"From somewhere beyond Ardagh," Griffin said. "Why?"

"Curiosity as much as anything," she said. "The blacksmith doesn't say much, as you know. And there're lots of stories told about him, you see. Some say it wasn't Nessa's mother that got taken by the sidhe. Some say it was him."

"Oh, no." Griffin shook his head. "No, that's not it at all. It was Nessa's mother, sure enough."

Molly shrugged and tossed her curls back over her shoulder in that girlish gesture. "When the Duke's men return, you must be sure to tell them all this. I like this not. There's some working afoot here—some great doing of which we—"

"Griffin!" The shout interrupted Molly in midsentence. "Griffin! Griffin of Killcairn!"

Griffin scrambled to his feet. "You think that's them? Maybe they're here." He dusted off his clothes, smeared his hands down the front of his tunic and took off at a run down the hill, through the drillyard crowded with refugees, and skidded to a stop just inside the inner ward. A group of men—armed men in some unfamiliar plaid—were sitting on horseback in the center of the courtyard.

They turned to look at him as he ran up. Engus stood in front of his forge, his face gleaming with sweat, his bullish head lowered as if for battle, arms crossed across his massive chest. No less a person than the Sheriff stood beside him, obviously entreating him with a parchment scroll from which dangled ribbons and seals. "I'll go but only under duress, Lord Sheriff, and I want a hearing at the Court of Gar, when this is all over, for it sticks in my throat to leave this keep with only boys—"

"The boys are wanted as well," interrupted one of the riders, the one Griffin presumed to be the leader. "Every man with blacksmithing skills are wanted—"

"And the Duke's got none of his own?" broke in Engus. "I like this not, my lord. There's the smell of something dirty in this—"

"Enough," cried the Sheriff. "I have the order here, signed and sealed. 'Tis not my choice, or yours, either, Engus. The Duke calls, you go. We'll make do without you here somehow."

Molly gripped his arm, but Griffin shook her off, pushing through the crowd. "What's wrong?" he asked, breathing hard, sweat breaking out on his brow. "What is it? What's needed?"

"You're the smith from Killcairn?"

"I'm his apprentice."

"Good enough. You're to come with us. The Duke needs all the able-bodied smiths he can find."

"What?" Griffin gasped. He looked at Engus, who shook his head and spat over his shoulder. "Go? Go where? I don't want to go—"

"'Tis not a question of what you want, boy," replied the rider. "'Tis the need of the Duke of your clan. Will you decline to answer?"

"But—" Griffin turned to Granny Molly, who'd run up just behind him. "They say I must go with them."

"What for, sir?" Molly raised her chin, and opened her shawl, displaying the lush curves of her bosom.

Predictably, the man glanced down and answered her breasts with a leer and a lick of his lips. "He's needed for the war, goodwife. We're rounding up the smiths."

"On whose order?" Molly asked.

"On the order of the Duke." Abruptly he wheeled his horse, and indicated a long wagon that Engus's apprentices were slowly scrambling into, a few weeping sweethearts and mothers clutching at them with desperate hands. "Gather up your things, now."

"But—" Griffin stood paralyzed, unable to comprehend. "I don't want to go."

"It doesn't matter, lad." The Sheriff dangled the parchment, seals and ribbons and all, in front of him. "The Duke's sent out a call for smiths and armorers—you're bound to answer."

"Griffin, you've no choice." Molly shook his arm. "Go along with you now. I'll tell Nessa where you've gone when she gets here—help her send word to you that she's all right. I promise."

The warrior's face was darkening fast. "Get a move on, boy. There's a war to be fought while you stand dithering with your mam."

"She's not—"

"Your light of love then," he said. "Get ready or we take you as you stand."

"Go now, Griffin, get your things," Molly said. "But, sir, where are you taking him? Where are you going?"

"To Ardagh. The Duke would pay a call on Mad King Hoell and he wants to make sure he's got enough gifts to go around, if you take my meaning."

Molly gave Griffin another little shove. "Go on."

He felt as if his limbs had turned to iron, as if his mind had turned to ash. Blindly he allowed Molly to pull him into the long room behind the forge, where he'd bunked with Engus's apprentices. She looked around for the few possessions he'd saved from Killcairn, and stuffed them into a linen sack. On the way back outside, she picked up a silver-coated ax and a silver-coated knife and put them both inside as well. "Here. You take these as well. Don't let them know you've got them, unless you have to." He only gripped the sack with a desperate fist. She gave him a hard stare and lightly slapped his cheek. "Times like these we do what we must, Griffin. You're thinking about yourself—not Nessa. You've a skill that's needed—a skill most don't have. You must go. She'd go, wouldn't she?"

I wouldn't mind if we could go together. But he couldn't find the voice for that agonized thought. He stumbled into the courtyard, where a strong hand gripped his upper arm and heaved him up and into the wagon. He fell into a great heap among the other apprentices, an unruly tangle of arms and legs that pushed and shoved him upright. The driver flapped the reins and the wagon heaved and bounced over the uneven cobbles. The warriors gathered seamlessly into formation and as one body, streamed past the lumbering wagon with its mostly glum cargo. Engus continued to fume softly under his breath.

Griffin wrapped his arms around his sack and sank down against the back board, scarcely aware of the cries of farewell for the others, the families and friends who crowded around the wagon, reaching for one last kiss, one last handclasp. Only Molly waved farewell to him, and he had no heart to raise his arm and wave back. The wagon trundled past the outer gates. As it cleared the tent-city, Griffin raised his head. *I can feel her,* he thought. *I know she's coming. And I'm leaving. I won't be here when she comes and she's coming, she's coming soon. What if I never see her again? I could wait for her. We could go together.*

A sense of desperation overtook him and, as the wagon cleared the last row of tents, he grabbed his sack and leapt, landing on his knees in the mud. He scrambled to his feet and took off, ignoring the driver's shouts. As one mass, the horsemen wheeled, but he didn't look back, even as the thunder of their hooves overtook him. He ran as fast as he could across the wide green meadow, heading for the dark line of trees just a few hundred yards away, a tantalizing sanctuary just out of reach. He could climb a tree—wait for the horsemen to give up the search.

He was nearly at the trees when a club behind his legs brought him to his knees and he fell forward, dropping his pack. The ax spilled out, blade flashing. He collapsed onto his chest as a spear butt thudded into his back, punching the wind from his lungs. He gasped, tried to struggle to his hands and knees and was pushed back down. He flopped on the ground like a hooked fish. The ax blade gleamed, unmistakably silver in the bright autumn sun. The warriors crowded around him, prodding him with the tips of their spears—spears which he saw were coated silver. "Look, he's already got himself a silver ax," one hooted.

"Then he's prepared for where he's going," said the leader with a chuckle. "For surely he'll spend more time putting more silver on more axes than he's ever done in his life."

High above Ardagh, the hawks dipped earthward, lazily riding the afternoon air. From the window seat of her solar in the round tower room, Queen Merle watched the black birds circle, a worn pack of scrying cards loosely held between her hands. Up to now, she'd hesitated to consult them. She had not expected the initial victory to come at so high a cost in men, horses, and supplies and it occurred to her that a look at the cards was required. Still she hesitated. Experience had shown her more than once how difficult it was to read the cards for oneself. Too easily one saw what one wished to see, not the true picture the cards portrayed.

And so she sat, watching the hawks, gazing out over one of the most unparalleled views in the known world. Cradled on a promontory of rock that extended out like an open hand over the vast falls of the Daraghduin River as it thundered into the great pool of the Goddess's Cauldron, Ardagh Castle, seat of the High Kings of Brynhyvar, perched above the water that foamed and boiled at the base of its walls before it fell away into two separate rivers, Baeve and Ishluin, the daughters of the goddess. These two rivers flowed like arteries down into the broad meadows of the Brynnish lowlands, connecting the country with the Morhevnian Sea on the east, and the ocean on the west. The thickly forested hills of the Ardagh uplands rose around her, overnight a burst of flame and crimson, orange and saffron, the darker lines of evergreens spiking like sentries at the crests. She watched one of the black hawks wheel and dive, talons extended, falling with a shriek upon some hapless victim below. Merle shuddered. Winter was closing in around them—summer's last gasp had dissipated in weeks of violent storms that had left poor Hoell clinging to her in bed, sobbing like a frightened child. There was enough of the man left in him to accomplish her purpose, though. She smiled, briefly touched her belly. *Root deep, little seedling. Root deep.* Winter would force the clans—Gar and Allovale, Pentland and Darharagh, traitors and oathbreakers all—back into their lice-ridden warrens, even if it kept her father's armies stranded on the other side of the sea. Here, safe in Ardagh, virtually impregnable keep that it was, she would nurture the infant within, and hopefully, coax the King out from whatever inner recesses of Hoell into which he'd fled. That would be the best answer to the rebels—a king, competent to rule once more. But a prince—an heir—would not be far behind. She would indeed bear another son, she knew with sudden certainty. A prince for Brynhyvar.

The King rolled around at her feet on the thick carpet she'd brought to this barbaric place upon her marriage, cavorting with the litter of hound puppies his once most-favored bitch had whelped just last month. He laughed aloud, sounding so happy, so carefree and young, she only felt a deep sadness. She shuffled the cards restlessly, remembering how readily she had loved him such a short time ago.

He had been so easy to love, especially in the beginning, when he had come courting her, spurning her two older sisters—insisting against custom on her hand, refusing both of theirs. She had gone to her father and begged him to allow Hoell to marry her. She was his youngest daughter, the spoiled baby princess of the realm. He could ultimately deny her nothing, and though her older sisters had slapped and spit on her the day her engagement to Hoell was announced, she'd only laughed and thought it all worth it.

They were the ones laughing now. For it had all changed. One day, she and Hoell had been the perfect princess and her King, cooing over the cradle of their baby son. And the next it all slipped away like the breath of their child in the night. So suddenly. So quickly. So unexpectedly. The death of their infant son had completely undone him.

With a deep breath, she shuffled the cards once more, and turned three over in rapid succession. *"Matra mea,"* she whispered. The Tower. The Wheel. The Star. Surely this was so clear there could be no mistaking the meaning at all. She laid the rest of the cards down on their dark square of silk, clasped her hands briefly over her belly, then turned over a fourth card. The Page of Water. She smiled, and glanced over her shoulder at Hoell. Not a bad image for the life now forming in the deep cauldron of her womb.

Hoell was on bent elbows now, crouched on the hearth rug, wagging his hips like a puppy its tail. He looked, she thought, for all the world like a happy three-year-old—a happy three-year-old with the face of a thirty-three-year-old man. She sighed.

How quickly she'd decided she loved him. When they met, it was like a bell had tolled somewhere deep within her and when she looked into his eyes—so deep and kind, as soft a brown as the silk velvet of her latest ball gown—she had known she'd met her destiny. All the months leading up to their wedding seemed to bear it out. Her father was pleased to have a direct access to the mostly unexploited silver mines, the great virgin forests of Brynhyvar, and Hoell was happy to do anything to please her, anything to make her happy. It continued after their marriage and it was noted far and wide that no man was more tender or solicitous of his wife when she carried his child than Hoell. He created this very nest of comfort and luxury for her and the coming child, importing anything she'd asked for from as far away as Lacquilea. The child's birth had moved him to tears. The child's death had destroyed him.

She closed her eyes against the aching pain of the double loss. In less than one day she had lost both her husband and her son. Just as the Tower card depicted, her entire world had shattered at its core. But she would not go down, dissolving into either surrender or madness. She would not lose everything else she had, too. Especially now that she could see there was a chance to recoup it all. She stared down at the cards. Fortune's Wheel lay silent, leading on to the promise of the Star. If it were her destiny to uphold the King through the darkest days of his madness, so be it. Perhaps the birth of the new baby would bring him out of it. It was not so vain a hope. Hoell adored the son they'd lost. She touched the Star, the Page of Water, with the tip of one finger, the hint of a smile playing at her lips.

Then the door opened and her brother, Renvahr, Duke of Longborth and the Protector of the Realm, walked into the room, just as Hoell, along with all the other puppies, sat up and yipped.

Renvahr paused just inside the door. Like her, he was dark-haired and dark-eyed, but olive-skinned like their Lacquilean mother, while she was fairer, like their father. He was dressed against the autumn chill in burgundy hose and doublet of Humbrian cut, a style far more elaborately tailored than the simple plaids and trews the Brynnish wore. The doublet was absent all ornament but for ornate black embroidery, a sophisticated counterpoint to the sleek, tailored design. He spoke directly to his sister, over Hoell's bobbing head. "I see His Majesty's feeling well today, and enjoying himself, as usual."

She could see that Renvahr was in a mood to be vexing.

She steeled herself against the sting of his sarcasm. "Hoell does well enough," she said. "I've been reading the cards, Renvahr, come, look and see what they say. The signs are good—we're fated to succeed." With a broad sweep, she indicated the four upturned cards.

He shook his head, his lip curled. "I can't believe you put faith in this nonsense, Merle."

She narrowed her eyes. "Don't you dare dismiss me, Renvahr. I'm not the only one who reads cards—Father himself regularly consults his Oracle. It's plain, I tell you. The Tower—cataclysmic change, sudden and unexpected. But this is Fortune's Wheel—reversed—which means it turns, and look—the Star." She patted her belly with one hand and gripped his forearm with the other. "Renvahr, I bear another child."

A shadow of disgust flickered across his face. "By the King? How's that even possible?"

She withdrew her hand. "He likes to sleep in my bed. Nightmares—storms—loud noises—they may frighten him like a child, but he takes his comfort like a man." And if the truth be told, she liked Hoell in her bed, too. In the dark it was easier to pretend that he was still the gentle prince come to woo her out of dreams.

Renvahr snorted. "Better you than me, sister. So what else do your cards tell you?"

She shot him a dark glance from beneath her heavy brows. "That which supports—" She picked up the deck and dealt out three cards, smiling when she saw them. "The King of Earth, the Queen of Water. The Fool." She shrugged. "Well, that's obvious. Father. Me. And Hoell." There was one more card to draw. She turned it over and frowned. Willing Sacrifice. It depicted the Fool, turned upside down and bound to a hangman's tree. He hung there, face void of expression but an enigmatic smile above eyes like dark pools.

"What's that one mean?"

"Someone's going to have to make a lot of sacrifices," she snapped.

Renvahr rolled his eyes. "That's more a statement of the obvious than an earth-shattering prediction, given the current situation. And next?"

"That which opposes—" She lay down three more cards. The Page of Earth. The Queen of Air. The Sun Child. A chill went down her back, and she sensed she was seeing a part of a pattern, teasing, indistinct. It was like looking through her father's kaleidoscope at a fragment of a great tapestry. Like the three cards she'd drawn in support of the matter, these three, too, were upright, therefore almost certainly these were people, not inner aspects of herself. She considered the possibilities, turning them over and over in her mind. She had expected Kings and Knights of Air and Fire. But a page, and a queen? And the Sun Child—the Star bursting into fruition—could it be her own child turned against them? No—surely, that could not be.

She slowly laid the fourth card down. There he was, after all. She hadn't been completely wrong. The King of Fire—standing on his fiery throne with arms crossed, red-gold hair ablaze, a golden sun blazing in the top half of the card to signify the power of noon. She could almost feel the energy emanating from it like a living pulse. This was her true enemy. The King of Fire opposed to her Queen of Water—well, water douses fire. Their ultimate victory was indeed predicted.

She looked at the card of Willing Sacrifice bound to his tree, and bit her lip. Did he look at her with Hoell's eyes? No—surely it could not be. Hoell couldn't die. Not if they were to succeed.

"Well, who are these people?" asked Renvahr. He stroked his little black mustache, nudging away a puppy that strayed too close to his boot.

"I don't know," she said. "This King—Gar, most like, though it puts me more in mind of Allovale for some reason. And the page—a young man or a young woman, perhaps. The Queen's an older woman—my age or older. And this one—the Sun Child. I've no idea. But it doesn't matter, don't you see? Water destroys Fire—we are assured of winning. These others are just details." Flashes, possibilities swirled through her head and she knew she was reaching too hard for an answer. Better to let it go. Let it rest. If it truly were a part of the pattern, it would reveal itself. Eventually. Hopefully in time to be of use.

He snorted and nudged the persistent puppy away more firmly. "In truth, Merle, that makes as much sense as a pile of puppy shit. Speaking of which—?" He nodded pointedly at the King.

To her utter horror, Hoell crouched beneath the long table that dominated one side of the room, watching a puppy squat with breathless fascination. With a little shriek, she strode to the door. "You," she cried, to the attendants loitering in the antechamber. "Come and clean this mess up and take these wretched puppies away. He's had enough of them for one day."

Silently, she retired to the window seat, where Renvahr sat watching with one raised brow. Servants—Humbrian all—rushed to do her bidding, housemen to scoop away the puppies, maids to clean the mess. The King watched in a sort of disbelieving horror as his toys were carried away in a cacophony of squeals and yelps. He scooted over to Merle, and clutched her gown in both hands. She resisted the urge to pat his head. "Enough for today, my lord. 'Tis nearly time for dinner." He nodded agreeably, and contented himself with tracing patterns in the wood grain of the floor. Merle looked back at Renvahr with a sigh. "This isn't difficult just for you."

Renvahr drew a deep breath. He paced over to the fireplace, put his hand on the mantel carved in the sleek new Humbrian style, then ran the other through his hair. "I know you don't want to hear this, Merle, but perhaps it's time we gave thought to ending this whole sad enterprise, and go back to Humbria where we belong. Father'll allow Hoell to live out his life in peace, I'm sure—you can retire with him to wherever you like. If you want more children, well—" He shook his head at Hoell who rubbed his cheek in slow circles on her green velvet gown. "I'm sure that can be arranged, too."

If he had doused her with ice water, she could not have been more shocked. "What are you saying? What are you talking about?" she whispered.

"I'm saying I'm getting tired of this damned country. It's always either about to rain, raining, or just rained. These people are—are hardly half a step away from savages. They've no art, no music worth hearing, no literature worth reading and no poetry worth reciting. The butter, the cheese, and the milk are rancid most of the time, and so's the meat and we're too far off the spice routes to get anything to make it palatable. The only thing that is palatable is the whiskey and the mead. What they don't burn they eat raw. You sit up here in your solar and you insulate yourself by surrounding yourself with everything that looks like Humbria because it is from Humbria and you have no more to do with that land on the other side of that window than you might a tapestry you'd hang upon the wall. I'm sick of dealing with these people. They're fractious as children—unruly, ill-behaved double-dealing children at best. They'd stab you for the right price of a cow. I know you always found him charming—" Here he indicated Hoell with a jerk of his chin. "Still must, I suppose." He folded his arms and looked away.

"You're saying we just give up. You're saying we just pack up and go back and what? Pretend that it never happened?" For an excruciating moment, a vision of what her life would be like if she were to return to Humbria, the cast-off Queen, married to a deposed madman. She would never bear the humiliation. Her sisters alone would make her life a living pit of shame, and Renvahr would have no use at all for her. He'd go on about his merry way careless as a clam. She drew herself up and spoke quietly, forcefully. "Hoell is the anointed King of this land, it is not for us to simply take him away. He rules by right—"

"He rules by acclaim. They elect their monarchs here—

it gives them a chance to beat their chests and wave their spears and prove who's got the biggest."

She made a little face. "I don't think I like it when you're crude."

"Forgive me, sister. I've no wish to upset your suddenly so tender sensibilities. It's not something the Brynnish are particularly known for."

"Hoell was elected to rule for life."

"He wasn't mad when they elected him. No country should bear the burden of a mad king, and this one in particular can not afford it. You've got to accept it."

"I shall not," she spat back. "I am his anointed Queen and I carry his heir. If he is not anointed King, and I am not anointed Queen, then perhaps Father's anointing means nothing, either. Be careful what point you argue, Renvahr, for may I further remind you, Father supports this. Father thinks this is a very good idea, and you surely stand to gain from it. You already have. I think Father would want me to be able to rely on your cooperation, don't you?"

His face darkened, and he spoke with tight lips, his voice careful and controlled. "I wonder what will happen, baby sister, when you're no longer able to play the little princess card?"

She glanced across the room where a parchment map, the most detailed in all of Brynhyvar lay pinned to the long table, under a clear sheet of glass that had cost nearly a bull's weight in gold to import. The map had been drawn by the King of Humbria's own cartographers, who had made a detailed journey through the country just before the wedding. There was another just like it, in the map room of the Humbrian King. It would enable her father and his generals to guide the war from across the Sea. Even if Renvahr, the coward, decamped, she was not alone. "That's not your concern, dear brother." She slapped another card down. The heart of the matter. Somehow she wasn't surprised. The World. The figure danced in the center of a garland of roses. *I'm right. That will be me.* Matra mea, *the cards are clear. On the life of my unborn child, I swear I shall dance.*

She reached down to draw another card, just as there was a knock at the door. Startled, she dropped the entire pack, and the cards scattered over Hoell like colored rain. He crowed with delight, and reached up to catch them. Merle called, "Enter."

A black-clad attendant, garbed in the style of the current Humbrian court, entered, accompanied by a grizzled messenger wearing a weather-beaten plaid. Hoell sat up, and crossed his legs, the scrying cards spread out before him. The attendant's eyes flicked over the King momentarily before he spoke in the sophisticated court dialect known as High Humbrian. "A scout from the uplands, Your Majesty, my lord." He bowed, turned on his heel, and left.

The scout glanced uneasily at the King, who smiled back, blissfully unaware of his subject's discomfort.

"Greetings, sir scout," said Merle. Her Brynnish was accented, but Hoell had always complimented her on how well she spoke. "What news?"

His first sentence was unintelligible. She blinked. He was looking at the King, then turned to her and spoke more slowly. "The uplanders are massing at Killcarrick, it looks like." He nodded to the map on the table. "May I, my lady?"

"Of course."

They crowded around the table, leaving Hoell sitting on the floor, examining each card carefully, one by one. The scout glanced once more at the King, then looked quickly down at the map. He coughed. "Here." He indicated the long lake of Killcarrick, lying like a finger in the hollows of the eastern highlands, the river Daraghduin running through it. He punctuated his nearly unfathomable speech with gestures on the map. "The keep is here—at the juncture where the river runs out of the lake. I myself saw the Pentsmen on the move and I heard that there's movement in the clans of Allovale and Darharagh in the same direction. They're at least a month from mustering any force of any consequence. And by the time they do, with any luck, the winter will keep them bottled up above Gar."

Merle shot a triumphant look at Renvahr across the table. "There, brother, do you see? We've but a need for a week of fair weather and Father's armies will mass upon these shores and crush these rebels for us."

Renvahr drew a deep breath and crossed his arms over his chest. "If only you could command the weather to our cause, sister."

She refused to take the bait. Instead she addressed the scout. "See to yourself, now, if you will, sir. There's food in the kitchens and a bed for you in the billets."

With a quick bow, the scout tugged at his forelock. "With all due respect, Your Majesty, I'll be returning to my company." He gave Renvahr a little bow. "If you'll excuse me, my lord? Your Majesty?" He hesitated as if he thought he should bow to Hoell, thought better of it and left the room with the look of one escaping.

Merle folded her lips in a thin line and waited for Renvahr to say something sarcastic. Instead, across the room, next to the window seat, Hoell held the Fool card against his chest, a sweet smile on his childlike face. The Fool was dressed in brightly colored motley of blue and yellow, a red dog nipped at his knees. "Look," he said. "This one likes dogs. Like me."

"You know," said Renvahr, stroking his chin, "I'm not so sure, my dear mad brother, if Brynhyvar has a Fool for a King—or a Queen."

At least he had the grace to look ashamed before she slapped him.

There was mist and there was pain. Like the hottest coals burning in the depths of a forge, like metal heated to the melting point, the pain boiled through the very marrow of his bones, seared his blood and pounded like hammers on anvils of his flesh. On the edges of his awareness the mist hovered, an ever-present companion, teasing as the promise of rain on Beltane, light as the touch of Nessa's hand on his cheek, gossamer as his memories of Nessa's mother, Essa, and for whom she had been named—not Essa. Those were the words which had run through his mind, even as he slipped and slid through slick mud, splashing through ankle-deep puddles, shoulders hunched against the icy rain that pelted his face with merciless fury, no kindness to spare for the infant he cradled to his heart. The cruelty of the rain fed his rage at the cold-hearted sidhe, even as it inflamed his need to protect the squalling red scrap. Her cries spurred him on, so that he ran, ran as if the Black Hag of the Mountain herself were after them, muttering the words that were to become his daughter's name: Not Essa, not ever.

Now he clung to each snippet of reality like a drowning man to a log. In feverish dreams, he saw shapes and forms coalesce out of the mist: sometimes Nessa—round-faced and rosy, toddling around the forge with some determined purpose; sometimes Griffin—serious and shy, earnest and eager as the orphaned pup he was; sometimes the contorted maw of the goblin as he'd plunged the silver blade deep into its belly and jerked up, ripping through layers of gristle and gore. Sometimes he heard the screams of Donnor's dying messenger, yanked headfirst beneath the surface of the water, legs kicking helplessly, body thrashing like a netted fish, through the sibilant hiss of the goblins' tails as they whistled through the air like whips.

And there were other faces and other voices: Finuviel's, the last face he'd ever thought to see again on this side of the border, his hated, hateful eyes gleaming green fire in the light of the hearth, his voice like the sigh of the wind in the pines on a warm summer night; Cadwyr's, boastful and proud, so full of swagger and show. And sometimes, through the mist, like the whisper of his own long-stifled longings, he heard the ghostly voice of his lost love, singing so sweetly he sank willingly into the still dark pool of sleep, murmuring her name as he fell—sweet, sweet Essa.

In some more rational corner of his brain, he knew he raved, he knew he dreamed. He knew the visions and the mist were effects of the pain. He even suspected he had somehow fallen into the OtherWorld, despite the silver blade, his silver amulet.

But the pain was like a river, and the mist was like a shroud, and the two receded at the same time only rarely. He opened his eyes. He was lying against the trunk of a huge tree, an oak he was quite certain did not exist in Brynhyvar. He was staring up through the branches at a cerulean sky that pulsated, as if the light moved through it, like water over sunlit sand. Oak leaves, gold as coins in Brynhyvar, gleamed as if infused by the light, undersides a shimmering play of violet shadows. Sweat oozed from his pores in slow thick drops, as if his body gave up its moisture only grudgingly. His mouth was a dry hole, his tongue a wilted flap of skin, his eyelids thin as parchment and as dry.

But he clutched the unfinished silver blade against his chest as desperately as if it were the infant Nessa. In the rarefied air of the OtherWorld, he could feel the energy emanating off the metal like a living thing. He closed his eyes as an iron fist of pain clamped around the goblin bite on his upper arm, throbbing down his arm and up into his chest. A wave of nausea swept up and through him, and the mist clouded his vision once more, rosy with a starburst of pain, gray with the promise of imminent peace. He slumped back against the rough bark, and closed his eyes. Cradled by the roots of the great tree, he gave himself back to the mist.

When he heard his name the first time, he thought it only another echo of a memory. But then he heard his name again, this time as clear as the peal of a new-minted bell, penetrating the mist like a dagger cutting through cobwebs, calling him up and out of its enveloping embrace. "Dougal? Dougal the blacksmith?"

This time the voice spoke so loudly he felt it in the putrefying mess that boiled like a furnace in his upper arm. He opened his eyes and saw that another face had materialized out of the mist, a face that was somehow far more substantial than anything he'd conjured so far, a face that peered down at him with slanting, wide-set green eyes, feral as a cat's across a distance of time and reality so wide he had hoped it would never be breached again. "Vinaver," he whispered, the edges of his tongue razor-sharp inside his leathery mouth.

"Hello, husband." Her lips bent up in what on a sidhe passed as a smile, and the bright orange and gold glints in her eyes spiraled so that he had to close his eyes against the nausea which flopped over in his belly like a dying fish. Then the dark red mist mercifully rose up all around him, folding him back into the blanket of oblivion.

9

"Blacksmith?"

"Is that the blacksmith?"

"It's not the blacksmith—it's a woman."

"His wife, most like—"

Nessa opened her eyes to jumbled voices and the glare of the bright noon sun, in front of which passed the dark shapes of riders on horseback. She squinted, raised her hand to shield her eyes, and thought for one sleep-clouded moment that Cadwyr had relented and come back. Then she realized that there were five or six mounted warriors crowding into the smithy yard, their horses churning the wet dirt to mud. *Someone's bound to lose a shoe in that muck,* she thought, just as she recognized the unmistakable pattern of the blue and gold and green plaid they wore. She sat up straight, heart leaping, voice hoarse from sleep. "Are you—have you come from Killcarrick?"

"We come from Gar, but aye, we rode through Killcarrick." The rider of a pale yellow gelding nosed forward, his fair braids spilling over his chest and the bright strip of fabric he wore over one shoulder. Like them all, he was fully armed as if for battle, with a broadsword strapped across his back, a short battle ax across his saddle, a short sword at his side, two long daggers strapped to one boot. Nessa dragged herself to her feet, swiping back her bedraggled hair, wiping her hands on the sides of her filthy tunic, as the rider continued, "I'm Kian, First Knight of Gar. Who're you?"

She cleared her throat. "I'm Nessa. My father's Dougal, the Duke's fav—"

"Then you're the one the lad said to look for—" A reed-thin redhead on a roan mare nudged his way to the first speaker's side. "You remember the one I mean, chief—the one who tipped the spears with silver. What was his name?"

"Griffin?" Nessa took a step closer, scarcely daring to believe what she heard. "You've seen Griffin? He's safe?"

"Aye, he's at Killcarrick with the rest of them who managed to escape," answered Kian. "He said you'd gone off to look for your father. But he didn't say where."

She ignored the unspoken question, but the redhead leaned in his saddle, assessing her with unabashed interest. "You find any sign of him, lass?"

She raised her chin, and crossed her arms over her breasts. She cared no more for his eyes on her than she had for Cadwyr's. But despite his formidable array of weapons, this one looked not much older than Griffin and wasn't so much built like a reed as a scarecrow, she decided, all long gangly bones covered in no more meat than a day-old calf's. His face was covered in tufts of scruffy red beard, giving him an almost comical appearance. "No," she answered, biting back a giggle. "I didn't. Were you sent to help me look?" She was conscious of the weight of Artimour's ring on her finger. Her promise to him included nothing about preventing others from searching for Dougal in the OtherWorld.

It was the first, Kian, who answered her as he swung out of his saddle and lashed the reins around the hitching post. "We've come to look for survivors, and bury the dead. We've come to see for ourselves what happened here. But we've no time to linger." He glanced around the smithy, taking in the door half pulled off its hinges, the claw marks in the half-timbered walls. In the bright sun, the ruined village lay shattered as the broken shards of pottery that crunched beneath his feet. He started, looked down, checked his boot, and Nessa knew he'd thought he'd stepped on bone. "You see what did this?"

"No. I wasn't here. I was…off." She pushed her lank hair from her face. "Looking for my father."

He gave her a sharp look, as if he sensed there was something she was hiding from him. "Well, you were lucky, maiden." He put his hands on his hips, and looked around. "Very lucky indeed." He paused, then turned back to his men. "All right. Maddig, Tuavhal, Ciariag, fan out. We'll gather up the remains that we can find, then bury the lot in a common grave that Uwen and I will dig."

The redhead leapt off his saddle with the flourish of an acrobat. "I'm Uwen." He flashed a gap-toothed smile in

Nessa's direction. He'd be missing several more teeth soon, she thought, if he didn't stop grinning at her like a fool. She watched Kian give the orders.

Clearly Griffin had kept it secret where she'd been. Maybe she should heed his wisdom. After all, if the villagers thought her tainted, what would these grim-faced warriors think? Following Kian's lead, the others dismounted. They gathered around Kian, speaking little, expressions already hardened against what they would encounter, gesturing over their shoulders, pointing up and down the road, across to the lake. She wondered if she should tell him about Cadwyr. From the depths of the smithy, a low keening wail, thin as a strand of hair, fragile as a bird's bone, mournful as a sigh, arose. It made the gooseflesh ripple down her arms and up her back. It lingered in the air, hovered almost tangibly, then faded.

"What in the name of the Great Mother's that?" Kian whispered, turning to look at Nessa, hand on the hilt of his short sword, even as the others reached for assorted weapons.

Nessa started, holding out her hand. "That's Granny Wren—the wicce-woman—she's in some kind of trance, or sleep. She'll do you no harm."

"The lad said to look for her, too." Uwen nudged Kian. "Remember? He told us there was some rite she did. It was supposed to hold the goblins back, remember?"

Kian took a deep breath and looked at Uwen squarely. "What need have I to remember anything, when I've got you to remind me of it all?" He looked at the other men. "Look around for shovels. I'm sure there's a lot of—"

"Wait," interrupted Nessa. "I've got shovels." She picked her way through the mud and opened the door of the shed that stood on one side of the yard. She handed out two shovels of different sizes. "Here—look in here if you wish. There're more. Sometimes customers don't come back." The men looked at her with surprise and gratitude as she handed out shovels of various sizes. She thrust one of the largest into Uwen's hands. "If you're Uwen, you'll need this." Kian turned away but not before she saw him grin. "There's a wheelbarrow 'round back." The other three tugged at their forelocks respectfully, then trudged off down the lane.

Kian nodded at Uwen. "Best get to digging. Where's the burial yard, lass?"

"It's up the hill," she answered. "The men—your men—they might have to make a lot of trips. It's a steep hill to climb. Maybe another spot… There's high ground near the crossroads at the bottom of the lane. Perhaps that would be better?"

Uwen nudged Kian. "Crossroads, chief. That's what the wicce-woman said. Remember?" Kian's only answer was a stifled hiss. "I'll scout it out, chief." Uwen winked at her. "I'll be right back."

Kian waited until he'd disappeared down the lane, then turned to Nessa, still shaking his head, though in amusement or exasperation, she couldn't be sure. "Perhaps you'd better show me this wicce-woman."

She led him through the shambles of the forge. She'd set up just enough last night to make the dagger. He glanced from side to side, taking it all in. She wondered if he knew

Cadwyr, decided that he must know Cadwyr, and if he knew about the silver dagger. Did he know about Cadwyr's affiliation with the sidhe? He seemed too levelheaded to traffic with sidhe. But as the Duke's First Knight, shouldn't he know? Perhaps it would ease his mind to know that the dagger had been made.

As she stepped aside to let him peer into the small room where Granny Wren lay curled on Griffin's cot, she considered whether she should tell this tall warrior about the visitors last night. He stared down at the fragile woman curled up like a corpse on her side, naked beneath a gray blanket. Her breathing was once more slow and steady, and Nessa thought somewhat less labored than last night. The mournful keen had stopped but Granny Wren clutched the red cord so close to her mouth, it seemed she sucked on it. "What's the rope for?" Kian asked, his big frame nearly filling the doorway, so that Nessa had to peer around him to see where he pointed.

"Some sort of corn magic, I suppose. She won't let anyone touch it—well, she wouldn't let me touch it, anyway."

"Believe me, maiden, I've no wish to touch any part of her. It may be better to simply put this whole cot in a wagon, rather than trying to disturb her. Know where I might find one?"

She opened her mouth, and realized as she nearly volunteered their own, that it was missing from the smithy yard. Of course, Griffin must've taken it. "I'm sure…there's a lot of things lying around, that belonged to the people who are—the people who are gone."

"Well, I'm sure we'll find one. Thank you for the shovels." His eyes were kind, but impersonal, and she knew that he considered this part of the hard business of war. He turned and ducked his head beneath the lintel and she followed him, hurrying after him through the kitchen into the forge beyond.

"Wait!" she cried. "Did the Duke say nothing about my father?"

He turned, just inside the outside door. "Maiden Nessa." He looked as if he wished he were anywhere but there. "You said it yourself. There're a lot of people gone. I know it's hard, but I think you must accept it—it's clear your father was the first one taken. I spoke to Eban, the man your people sent to the Duke. And when I rode up and saw what happened here.... Well, I think it's clear, that's all." He turned as if to go, but she laid a hand on his forearm. It was covered in blue and red swirls, the clan tattoos of his warrior class. "Lass—"

"I know my father's alive."

"And he is," Kian said swiftly, covering her hand in his. "He's alive in the Summerlands."

She shook off his hand impatiently. She didn't want the sympathy of this dark-eyed warrior who clearly had other things to do. "But—"

"Lass, don't you see?" Kian swung around on her so quickly she took a step backward. "My men and I, we came here hoping to find you and the wicce-woman, too. But it's not our main purpose. We must rally the clans as quickly as we can. And as for me—well, I'll see you and the granny safely to Killcarrick. But to look for your father—it's time we just don't have to spare." He broke off, then patted her shoulder awkwardly, and she saw that despite his matter-of-fact demeanor, it distressed him to refuse her. "I'm sorry."

She met his eyes and knew at once to say more was futile. Her intuition told her that Dougal was alive, in the OtherWorld. To ask these men to search would only delay them from their purpose. And besides, she thought, glancing over her shoulder to where Granny Wren lay, the old woman needed the sort of help which was only to be found at Killcarrick. "I understand."

"I hope you do, lass." He took another quick glance around the forge. "I've got to get to work. If there's anything you'd like to take to Killcarrick, I suggest you get it all together."

With the presence of the five Duke's knights, at high noon, she felt safe enough to go to the well behind the house, and draw two buckets of fresh water; safe enough to creep up to her bedroom and sponge off the worst of the last two days—or however many days it'd been. She laced on a clean tunic over clean underlinen, and fingered Arti-mour's ring, making sure that it was turned so that the red stone faced her palm. Somehow she'd contrive to come back. She'd be able to count on Griffin to help her in any way he could. But did she want Griffin to meet Artimour? She did not think Griffin, loyal as he was, would be pleased to meet the tall, dark half-blooded sidhe. Nor to know about the feelings he'd roused in her. *It wasn't him,* she reminded herself, fingering the tiny twists and knobs and braids of the ring's intricate setting. It was the enchantment of the OtherWorld—the way it all had looked and sounded and felt and smelled. Her bone-melting attraction to Artimour was an effect of the OtherWorld and belonged there, like this ring, she tried to tell herself. She doubted there was even a goldsmith with the skill to make such a ring here in Brynhyvar. The ring wasn't a part of any reality she wanted to know about. And yet… A ray of sun fell across her hand and the stone blazed a red not known in this world, and she realized she'd better wrap a bit of rag around her finger and pretend it was bandaged. She thought once more of marriage to Griffin. It was a match to which her father would probably give his approval. He liked Griffin. It would please him to think her settled here at the forge, with safe, steady Griffin by her side. The thought lay as heavy on her mind as the weight of the rag-wrapped ring on her finger. The bulky bandage teased her, for it was evidence that what she had experienced on the other side of that elusive border was every bit as real as that which she knew here. Which meant that what she'd felt for Artimour was as real as what she felt for Griffin. *Which is?* mocked the small voice of her heart. There was more than simply just that dizzying attraction, she thought. There was a sense of kinship, of connectedness. *I'd bet Papa's biggest hammer that his father was Bran Brownbeard.* But even that didn't seem enough to explain it, and there wasn't time to consider it further. It was better she forgot she'd ever walked into the OtherWorld while she was with the Duke's men. She forced all thoughts of Griffin, Artimour, and rings out of her head, and finished dressing.

In the sky, the sun had turned the corner, as her father liked to say, and there were maybe five or six hours of daylight left. If Kian intended to make a start to Killcarrick today, they'd better be on the road soon. She stuffed her two other clean tunics, all her underlinen, her two kirtles, and her brush into a leather pack, then looked around, wondering what else to take. Her pillow and blanket, she supposed. She grabbed them both and turned to go, when she heard heavy footsteps below.

"Nessa?"

She climbed down the narrow steps to find Kian and Uwen looking down at Granny Wren. The men were muddy and sweaty, plaids long discarded, linen shirtsleeves rolled above their elbows. "How long's she been like this?" Kian asked.

Nessa shrugged. "Since yesterday at least. She's just about how I found her. When I got her on the bed, she said a few things, that didn't really make much sense…." Her voice trailed off. Had Granny Wren referred to Griffin? Surely she'd misunderstood.

Kian sighed. "All right. There's no help for it but to take her in a cart. The others finish burying the remains?"

Uwen nodded, wiping the back of his hand across his forehead. "Aye. I'll have the lads help with the cot, and then be on their way?"

Kian nodded. "And you, maiden. Gather up what you wish to take. I'm not sure how much room there'll be with this cot—but we'll take as much as we can for you."

She looked around, hugging her bundle. "I'm not sure…." After all, she intended to come back. But she couldn't let him know. "I'll get what I can together."

"All right then." Again, that quick pat of reassurance on her shoulder, as he passed her. She peered down at Granny Wren, bending closer to listen to the old woman's breathing. It was steady, deep and even. It sounded as if the old woman was in a deep, healing sleep. She couldn't imagine there was much else to be done. As she straightened up, she heard a muffled curse.

"—to the Summerlands!" was all she caught, as she dashed past Kian. She saw Uwen glaring in dismay at the ground, as he held the reins of his horse. "Curse it to the Summerlands." He looked up when he saw her standing in the door.

"What's wrong?" Kian spoke from inside the forge. He paused beside the table.

"It's Buttercup, chief," Uwen spoke over her head to Kian.

Buttercup? Uwen's horse's named Buttercup? She nearly laughed out loud, but his distress was so obvious, she bit her lip.

"See here, she's lost a shoe. Now what are we going to do? All the blacksmithing tools in the world, and naught to do about it."

"Oh," said Nessa. "I can shoe a horse. 'Twas the first thing my father taught me when I was old enough to use a hammer."

"Really?" asked Uwen. He stared at her as if she'd suddenly grown another head. Or maybe a pair of wings.

She felt rather than saw, Kian come up behind her. "Well, isn't that a stroke of luck for all of us. Including Buttercup." He lowered his open palm, and on it, she saw the three gold coins Cadwyr had left. "And maybe then you'll tell me how three of the Duke of Allovale's coins came to be sitting on your father's table, neat as you please?"

* * *

"What I still want to know, Chief," said Uwen, as he took a slow drag on his long clay pipe, "is what Cadwyr's doing with a sidhe." It was much, much later, and Killcairn lay at least ten or twelve leagues behind them. They'd made camp in the middle of a small clearing. Cadwyr's gold hung in a pouch from Kian's belt. It eased Nessa's mind that it should be in Kian's charge. He'd explained the Sheriff's treasurer would give her the value of it in smaller gold and silver coin, coin she could actually spend, while he took the medallions Cadwyr had given her to show the Duke of Gar.

Now the firelight flickered across Kian's face as he slowly chewed a hunk of the week-old oatcake soaked in honey. It was a treat Dougal had made after Griffin raided a hive on a dare the day before this whole nightmare began, the last day of what Nessa was starting to think of as "before." The rest of the meal came from what they'd scavenged from the village larders. "Cadwyr," Kian murmured, as if to himself. He poked the long stick he held deeper into the flames, turning it over and over in his hand like the name he turned over on his tongue. "Cadwyr."

"You think Cadwyr's got some mischief plotted, Chief?"

Kian shrugged, his expression unreadable. "I'm thinking I need to get back to Gar. Speak to Donnor—make him listen to me even if—" He broke off. "For what I want to know is, in what way does a silver dagger guarantee the throne of Brynhyvar?" He shook his head again.

"You don't trust this Cadwyr?" asked Nessa. She shifted her position on the other side of the fire. She didn't much care to be out in the middle of the woods in the middle of the night, not with goblins lurking. Kian and Uwen had assured her they'd seen no signs of goblins, anywhere on the entire road from Killcarrick to Killcairn. But she felt better, tucked between the fire and the wheel, the cart a solid bulk beside a broad branched oak, Granny Wren's soft snores steady and soothing. With each passing hour the old woman's breathing sounded better. Maybe by the time they got to Killcarrick, she would be completely recovered.

"No," Kian said, looking into the fire. "You're right, maiden. I don't."

Uwen scratched his head, then his ear. "You better watch that sort of talk around the old lion, Chief. Lion don't care for those who don't care for his cub."

Kian's reply was only a dark look.

Nessa hugged her knees close beneath her chin and gathered the edges of her plaid closer. The autumn night was chilly and the twilight had long since deepened into night. The silver-edged ax was on the ground beside her, ready to be grabbed at a moment's notice. "Are you sure we're safe here?"

"As sure as I can be about anything in this topsy-turvy world we've come to, maiden." Kian looked up and around. The firelight carved dark canyons of shadow across his face as he turned his head. "The wicce-women at Killcarrick had some advice for us—'tis why we stopped here for the night, beneath this stand of oaks. They told us this was once a sacred grove, that we'd be safer here from the goblins than in any other place. As for human enemies.... Uwen and I will take turns at the watch." He shrugged. "These are unsettled times."

"Ah, I nearly forgot, Chief." Uwen stood up and loped over to the wagon—the one cart in all of Killcairn that wasn't stained by blood or gore—unhitched the backboard and rummaged in and through the various bundles. He turned with a leather pack, from which emanated a strong, although not altogether unpleasant, aroma. "I got this from Granny Molly—you remember, the wicce-woman from Killcrag. Did you know goblins're repelled by the smell of garlic?"

"Get along with you, Uwen." Kian waved his arm, and the multicolored swirls on his forearm flashed in the fire. "No one believes that. The only things that repel them are sunlight and silver."

"Suit yourself, Chief." He winked at Nessa. "I'm wearing my necklace tonight. If you had any sense, you'd wear yourn."

"If I'd had any sense, I'd've sent Maddig and Tuavhal back to Killcarrick."

"Ah, but I'm the only one who took the time to talk to the lad and the wicce-women. You'd've been lost on this trip without me." He settled back down beside the fire and picked up a long, sharpened stick and stuck a hunk of bread on it. "I won't mind telling you, Chief, I'm disappointed. There's nothing like a coney caught in the wild cooked over a flame with fresh green herbs—even this time of year. Week-old bread and month-old cheese just doesn't sit the same way, you know?"

Kian only poked at the fire with another stick.

"We should've set a trap for one," said Nessa, for the thought of stew made her mouth water. They certainly had plenty of garlic with which to flavor it. "I saw wild carrots just over there."

"Haven't you noticed, lass?" Uwen inspected his toast. "There're no coneys to be trapped. None to be found the whole length between Killcairn and Killcarrick and it may go even farther for all I know. Something's scared them all—scared them so badly they've gone burrowing down into the earth so deep they may never find their way back up. And what a fine thing that would be for the rest of us, now, wouldn't it?" He smiled lazily and blew on the hot bread.

"Go on with you, Uwen, you should've been a bard." Kian poked him, and Uwen threw an acorn at him. Kian held up one hand in mock surrender, and turned back to Nessa. "Speaking of bards, lass, this coming Samhain, you might find one at Killcarrick and see if he can call up your father for you, from the Summerlands. I've seen it happen—it happened to me."

Uwen nudged him. "Tell her what you saw, Chief. Tell her what happened." He winked at Nessa. "If you remember, that is?"

"If I don't, I'm sure you do." Uwen threw another acorn at Kian. This one bounced off his nose. Kian turned to Nessa with a grin that didn't reach his eyes, and it faded altogether as he spoke. "It was the Samhain Donnor made me his First Knight—two years ago now it was." Kian looked into the flames, and Nessa knew he saw far beyond the shower of sparks which rose as a flaming log snapped and broke. "It was at the invocation of the Dead. Toward the end, I thought I could hear his laugh—my father's laugh—and then I heard his voice calling my name, all the way from the plains of the Summerlands. And I looked up, and I saw my father coming through the doors, though they were shut against the night, riding a red stallion. He rode right up to the table where I sat at Donnor's right hand and tossed me his spear. None marked his presence but me, though when I came to myself, I saw I was indeed holding a spear—Donnor's spear—and that I had won the title of First Knight. But I've always been sure it was my father that saw it came to me." He looked across the flames to Nessa, where she sat with the silver-edged ax beside her on the ground. "You might think of seeking your father in the Summerlands at Samhain, maiden. 'Twill help to know he's there."

She knew he meant to comfort her. She knew he felt terrible at having to suggest that her father was dead. But so certain was she that Dougal was alive, only missing, she could not control the words that burst from her lips. "But I know he's not!" she cried.

Uwen took a swig from his flask, and Kian looked up from tending the fire. "Tell me then, maiden." His voice was low and gentle, soft and wooing as if she were a wild filly to be tamed. His dark eyes pinned her to the wagon wheel. She had sensed this was coming. He'd been edging up to it ever since he'd met her, dancing delicately until he had an excuse to probe deeper. He knew she was hiding something from him. "Tell me why you're so sure your father's not dead back there in Killcairn."

"Because the last we saw of my father, he was carrying a bundle down to the lake. He had a silver dagger with him—or at least the blade, for I saw him make it the night before. Cadwyr and the sidhe with him expected the dagger to be finished when they showed up last night—my father wasn't in the same hurry to make it, as I was. And someone, somehow, killed the goblin that washed up on the shore. Don't you see it's possible he might have slain the goblin himself and somehow fallen into the OtherWorld and survives, maybe injured, just across the border? In the OtherWorld?"

"TirNa'lugh," breathed Uwen. "Now there's one for the bards."

Kian cocked his head and opened his mouth to speak just as Granny Wren gave a long, low moan.

"What's wrong with her?" Uwen asked. There was a long silence, and Granny moaned again. "Well?" he demanded, and Nessa realized he was speaking to her.

"Why do you think I have any idea what's wrong with her?" she asked. "I told you, this is how I found her. She was in some sort of trance when I found her, and she's been asleep like this ever since I put her in the bed. She's not moved or said a coherent word since that I've heard."

"You must have some idea," Uwen said. "You're a woman."

Nessa cocked her head. The idea that as a woman she should have some innate knowledge of a matter such as healing had never occurred to her. "I'm a black—" she started to say. But then a wisp of a breeze brought an unmistakable odor to her nostrils and her head shot up, as her body froze. She drew a quick, quiet breath and held up her hand, eyes darting around the perimeter of trees, beyond the circle of firelight. She let the air out of her lungs silently, and drew another cautious breath and knew, this time, that there was no mistaking what she smelled. The blood drained from her face, her bladder nearly spilled on the spot. She fumbled for the ax, even as the men on the other side of the fire reacted by whipping out their swords as they unfolded themselves into a fighting crouch. Nessa saw the edges of their weapons shine silver.

"'Twas a good thing we listened to that young lad at Killcarrick, wasn't it, Chief?" Uwen swung his blade up and around, and Nessa backed up against the wagon, fumbling for her ax. The stench was even worse now, unmistakable, overpowering the strong scent of garlic. Behind her, Granny Wren moaned.

Uwen shot her a look and Nessa shrugged silently. But Kian was nodding at the wagon, a finger held against his lips, indicating that she should check the old woman. She stood reluctantly, and a twig broke under her foot. Both men frowned. Gripping the ax securely, Nessa peered up and over the wagon. The old woman lay curled in a tight knot, quivering. "Gran—" she began.

The goblin popped up on the opposite side of the wagon with a roar and a swipe of vicious claws. Nessa screamed, dodged, and whipped the ax up and around. The silver edge bit hard into the goblin's skull, searing through the bone with a sound like molten iron dipped into water. She spun around, to see Kian and Uwen back to back, broadswords up, engaged in fighting three more goblins, who, unarmed, grabbed and rushed at them with teeth, claws and tails. But armed with the silver-edged weapons, it was clear that, in this contest at least, the mortal warriors would prevail, and she saw to her complete relief that soon all four goblins lay sprawled just inside the perimeter of oaks.

"Well, that answers that question," said Uwen, when at last they stood, back to back, breathing hard, sweat gleaming on their faces and arms in the yellow firelight.

"Which question?" Kian wiped goblin blood off his face with a disgusted look.

"Whether or not the garlic repels them. So now what, Chief? There could be more of these things out there."

Kian snorted. "You mean you don't remember?"

Uwen opened his mouth, then shut it. Nessa eased away from the protection of the wagon. She gestured to the goblin carcasses with her ax, biting back the nausea that roiled in her stomach from the stink. "We have to cut off their heads," she whispered, even as she glanced back over her shoulder into the blackness beyond the clearing.

"What?" Uwen whipped around.

"We have to cut off their heads. Or they'll come back. I think that's what happened to these. Look." She pointed to a raw looking wound that showed through the tattered strips of leather armor on the chest of the one lying at her feet. The wound appeared as if it had just begun to heal. "I think they somehow got left here—maybe Griffin or some other villager thought they'd killed them. But they weren't dead. They aren't really dead until we chop off their heads." She wasn't sure if it applied to goblins slain by silver weapons, but there was no point in taking chances.

"How do you know that?" Kian was looking at her as if she'd suddenly sprung two heads and a tail herself.

She gulped, covering her mouth and nose with the rag-wrapped hand that wore Artimour's ring. "Something the granny told me had to be done."

"I thought you said she wasn't able to tell—" Uwen narrowed his eyes, but broke off as Nessa swung the ax over her shoulder.

She saw immediately the difference in the way the silver-edged blade bit more deeply into the leathery flesh, encountering far less resistance than when she'd used the other to cut the head off the first goblin what seemed an eternity ago. The ax seared through the bone with a hiss. She tugged with both hands to get it out, then kicked the head away from the body with the tip of her boot. "There."

The men exchanged a glance.

Nessa marched over to the next goblin and silently swung the ax.

"I see you may not know much about healing, maiden, but you know a fair amount about killing goblins." Uwen spoke with a degree of awe, as she toed the head away from the torso. Kian nudged him. Across the firelight, Uwen grinned at her, and suddenly she understood. He was teasing her out, as they said. It was a game none but Griffin had ever attempted to play with her. Suddenly she blushed and, to hide it, immediately turned to the fourth and last goblin. She straightened up, planted her feet, held the ax poised to fall, and in that moment,the goblin's eyes opened, and one arm came up and reached for her throat with a snarl and a swipe. She dodged instinctively, and the curved claw caught in the baggy linen of her tunic. She heard, rather than felt, the skin between her breasts tear open, and saw a long line of red blossom through her tunic.

With a cry, Uwen reacted, sweeping his silvered sword in a broad arc that sliced through the goblin's chest as its tail whipped her legs out from under her. Nessa fell onto her knees, the front of her tunic blooming dark scarlet in the firelight. "Doesn't hurt," she breathed.

"Not yet." Uwen caught her as she keeled over, and those were the last words she remembered hearing before the world went dark.

On the other side of the river, Artimour stood on the bank, Nessa's boots in one hand, her plaid across his arm, watching as she dove beneath the surface, then reappeared, all strong legs and arms stroking hard across the water. *The Faerie Queen shall bless thee—no goblin claw shall rend thee.* He muttered the little incantation as the white foam peaks raised by her kicks gradually disappeared into slow swirling eddies in the sluggish water. Part of him wanted to plunge after her, to throw himself into the saddle and follow her into the river across the border into the Shadowlands. She was nothing like anyone he'd ever met in his life. No story, no song, no poem could have ever prepared him for the siren call of her mortal blood.

And part of him wanted to return to the barracks and order a bath and the very clothes he wore burned. He felt tainted, dirty, soiled to his bones. No wonder his human blood was a source of vague shame. It wasn't just the filth and the sweat and the smell which hung about her like a cloud. She was like a puppy, passionate and impulsive and utterly and entirely unpredictable, her emotions dragging him up and down a dizzying trajectory from exhilaration to despair. She put him in mind of a spinning compass, no more stable than the gravel that broke now beneath his boots in a little shower of sand. If the sidhe regarded humans as little more than tempting playthings and dangerous pets, he could well understand why. The energy of mortals was chaotic and churning, neither easily contained nor controlled.

When he could not see her in the water anymore, he turned away, noticing how her bare footprints strode so surely, so firmly to the water's edge. She had only turned back once to wave, before she'd walked into the water with such sure and purposeful intent he'd had no doubt she would find her way back to the Shadowlands. He was forced to acknowledge her courage, and the intelligence, as well as the intuition that led her to not only chop off the goblin's head, but to bring it to the attention of the sidhe as well. That's what made her so unsettling and so dangerous. She was not someone easily dismissed. He hoped he would be lucky enough to find some evidence to convince her to give up the search for her father.

But unexpectedly, he felt a little pang of sympathy for her plight. As much as he wished she would abandon her search, some other deeper part of him hoped the mortal was in fact alive somewhere. It bothered Artimour to think of her left to face her world alone. It was never easy to be an outsider, as he was learning, as he thought of his own demotion. And an oath was an oath, and he did owe her a three-fold debt. With a sigh, he knotted her boots around her plaid, noting the worn laces. They would need replacing soon, he thought. It was a wonder they hadn't disintegrated long before this. He examined the dark brown leather, the stitching which was more finely done than he'd have expected. On impulse he put his hand inside the boot. It was still warm from her foot.

The sole was ridged with planes and valleys, a perfect contour of her broad foot. She was like a tree, he thought, with feet that gripped the earth like roots. He pictured her standing over a blacksmith's anvil, braced against the hammer's recoil. There was a strength and a solidity to the humble boots, a solidity that at once intrigued and repelled him.

His mother had tried to incorporate some recognition of his mortal heritage by creating the title "Master of the Royal Smiths" for him. It was a title he still carried of course, a title he was dismally unqualified to hold. He remembered, to his everlasting mortification, his pathetic attempts to use the tools his father had left behind. Too crude to work the finer ores of Faerie, they finally disappeared one day, and he had never questioned where they'd gone. Into the keeping of some sympathetic Lorespinner, he assumed. And yet, even a maid like Nessa was able to follow in *her* father's footsteps. Of course, her father was by her side, teaching her, guiding her. She had not been left to reconstruct his craft from discarded tools.

Enough wondering about the mortal. He quickly tied the bundle to the back of his saddle, remounted and spurred the horse on, following the path which led down along the River Afon, the great river which had its counterpart both in Shadow and the Wastelands, as well. It was a dangerous road, this, for unless one was quite certain of one's destination, it was possible to end up in almost any of the three realities. At least, for a sidhe it was possible. The power of the Caul kept the goblins out of Shadow, and the power of the Queen held them captive within the Wastelands. The humans were supposed to be safe within their world by the working of the Caul on the amulets they all wore. Now it seemed as if both Caul and Queen were weakening to the breaking point.

He hoped it wasn't too late already. So he rode hard, heading toward Alemandine's palace with grim intent. Along the way, he kept his mind from turning to Nessa by considering the pieces of information she had brought over in his mind, as if, like crystals, their essential structure might only be revealed when viewed from certain angles.

A goblin had gotten into the Shadowlands—that meant the Caul was either failing or had failed. There was no question in his mind about that. An unknown, nameless sidhe had come to her father's forge late in the night, accompanied by a mortal, seeking something only a mortal smith could make. And this mortal, he mused, according to Nessa had the bearing of not just any mortal—he was a noble of some sort, someone whose status appeared to correlate to the level of a Queen's Councilor. Now he'd discovered that something had sealed the border into the Shadowlands, from within the Shadowlands. Not completely, because Nessa had clearly been able to return. But who in the mortal world could work that kind of magic—whatever kind of magic it was?

He rode on. At a ford in the river, he paused, perplexed by what he saw. The road which ran along the river was churned to mud by what could have only been the passing of a great host. The marks of thousands of hooves, of hundreds of booted footsteps, were clear enough for anyone to read. But they led straight down into the water, marching with as much apparent purpose as Nessa's prints. An army had been here, he thought, an army easily the size of the one he was expecting. An army that had marched deliberately into the water. He peered across the water at the opposite shore, but the light and the shadows made it impossible to say whether or not they'd emerged on the other side. But why? And if these were the reinforcements, they were much closer than Finuviel's dispatch had led him to believe. Where were they going and where were they now?

Artimour slid off the saddle beside the river, and paused on the shore, examining the unmistakable prints left by both sidhe and horse. As the horse bent its head to drink, he saw a flash beneath the water. He looked again, and saw a definite shimmer in the air above the object. He splashed through the shallows to the submerged rock on which the object lay. It was a round flat disk, an encircled five-pointed star, on a dark cord. Gray in the clear water, it seemed to waver as the water bubbled over it, as if it gave off some sort of heat. He knew intuitively what it was. It was an amulet, the sort of amulet the mortals wore, the sort Nessa admitted she'd removed in order to ensure that she could cross into Faerie.

It lay beneath the water, silent as a snare. It could be Dougal's, he thought. At least he had something to show Nessa. And certainly, now he had hard evidence to show Alemandine and her Council just how dire the situation was. There was far more silver in the amulet than the Caul should ever have let pass through.

He nudged it out of the water with a piece of driftwood. It dangled off the end of the stick by its leather cord, deceptively innocent. Now what? he wondered. What would contain the silver, so that its harmful effects could be minimized as much as possible? Only something of the mortal world could safely contain silver. He looked back at the horse, and saw the answer to his problem knotted behind his saddle. Nessa's boots—well, one of them. He untied one from the bundle, dropped the amulet into it, and knotted the cord in the laces. He compressed the boot as much as he could, then tucked it into his doublet, where it nestled just beneath the curve of his ribs. The hard wedge of the heel pressed hard against his heart.

He reached up, to ensure that the pack was still securely fastened to his saddle, and saw, to his surprise, Finuviel himself, walking along the riverbank, leading the milk-white stallion he rode in battle. Artimour blinked. Finuviel was the last person he expected to see. What could he be doing here? Where were the reinforcements? According to his own dispatch, Finuviel, like the army, was still at least a six day march away. He narrowed his eyes, noticing that Finu-viel was garbed not in the uniform of the Commander-in-Chief of the Queen's Army, but in a dark gray doublet and hose so unornamented as to look unfinished, and over it, a plain black cloak. Artimour patted the black rump of his own horse and stepped around the animal. "Finuviel? Cousin? Where are the reinforcements? What are you doing here alone?"

"One might ask you the same question, Cousin." Against the bluish-white flanks of the stallion, he stood in vivid contrast, the cloak falling off his shoulders as fluid as the wind. His black curls were loose and long, held off his face in a careless braid. Even in the plain, unadorned costume, he was the very embodiment of a prince of the sidhe from the tips of his boots to the tassel hanging off the tip of the hood on his black velvet cloak, and suddenly Artimour understood something of what Nessa, or any other mortal for that matter, must feel upon standing in the presence of such a being. But there was something different about him, Arti-mour thought, for he had the look of a person waking from a deep sleep. Or a dream. His lips were flushed, his color high. And there was no welcome in his eyes.

"I don't understand, my lord." Suddenly a chill ran through him, a feeling that something was very wrong and it seemed politic to fall into the most clearly defined relationship they had—commander and subordinate—much as it galled him. "I received your dispatch not ten hours ago, and in it, you clearly told me you were some six or seven days out. Where are the troops? They are most desperately needed."

Finuviel had dropped the reins, and was approaching, hands appearing to rest casually on his sword belt. "Some six or seven days out, I'd presume. You only assumed I was with them. But what, pray tell, are *you* doing here? This is somewhat out of your riding, isn't it?"

"It is, my lord, but things have not gone well since you left .The goblin horde presses ever harder and the wards are weakening. We lost Lothalian to the true death last night. He died before my eyes."

Not even a ghost of a response flickered across Finuviel's impassive face. "But that still doesn't explain what you're doing here."

"I carry news of such urgency I thought it best to bring it to the Queen myself. A goblin was found in Shadow, a mortal smith is missing—" Artimour paused, because there was something in Finuviel's expression—or rather, absence of expression—that concerned him. He gestured toward Nessa's boot tied to the back of his saddle. "A mortal maid brought the most extraordinary news, Finuviel." In an attempt to penetrate the dark green veil that had fallen over Finuviel's eyes, he slipped back into a more familiar form of address. He leaned forward, anxious to impress upon Finu-viel the urgency of what might have happened. "The Caul has somehow failed, and one of our own—a sidhe—is involved with a mortal blacksmith. I don't know if the two are connected but—"

Finuviel stepped forward. The blow took Artimour completely by surprise. As the bolt of fire punched up and through him, searing all the way to his heart, he crumpled in shock. His eyes widened and he gasped. Instinctively he fumbled with the handle of the dagger, trying to pry away Finuviel's grip, even as Finuviel pushed it ever deeper. Artimour grunted, as pain, so bright it blinded him, surged through his chest. He went rigid for a few seconds, then collapsed into a heap facedown at the water's edge.

Finuviel withdrew the bloody dagger, mouth compressed in a grim line. Artimour's blood was as crimson as any mortal's. He grimaced, for it had not been his intention to kill Artimour. But once he recognized Artimour's ring on the girl's finger, he'd known Artimour was a problem that would have to be eliminated most likely sooner rather than later. There was too much at stake to hesitate when necessity demanded action. He was learning that very quickly by watching the actions—or rather, inactions—of the Queen's Council. And his mother insisted Artimour would die anyway, in the UnMaking of the Caul.

Now he rinsed Artimour's blood off the blade and resheathed the dagger, tucking it back beneath his doublet, where it lay, smoldering like a live coal against the thin linen of his shirt. There was a potency about the silver even through the thick mortal leather of the scabbard that made his skin tingle. No wonder Gloriana and Timias and the rest had been tempted to try and harness it.

Finuviel walked back to Artimour's limp body, and toed it carefully. He lay facedown, not moving. Dark scarlet blood leaked out from under him, flowing out like locks of long curling hair in the water. If he wasn't dead, he would be soon.

Finuviel weighted the body down with stones, then dragged it out as far into the river as he could. Artimour sank beneath the surface, lips already gray, the gaping hole in his doublet seared around the edges as if he'd been stabbed by a burning brand.

Finuviel waded to the riverbank. Artimour's horse eyed him dubiously, for the smell of Artimour's blood was strong on him, and it was skittish, shy. He reached for the reins, but the black warhorse reared back and wheeled. It galloped off into the forest. He bit his lip in vexation. This was a minor complication he had not foreseen. He looked up at the sky. The sun was already falling down to dusk. The appointed hour had passed and his mother was nowhere to be seen. Fortunately they had a contingency plan in case their sense of time became distorted because of Finuviel's travel in the mortal world. He walked up to the spreading branches of a great oak that grew along the bank. There was a hollow within the oak. He tucked the dagger within its leather covering within it, wrapping it in his cloak. Vinaver would know to look there first. He took a last look around the scene. The river was lapping at the little blood left on the sand, washing it off the pebbles, only a few traces of palest pink still swirling through the water. A few curious fish swam here and there. No one would ever know he'd met Artimour. They might find the horse, but it wouldn't talk. He put the spurs to his own mount, and dove straight into the deepest part of the water.

10

"Is it true you mean to ride to battle without Kian or the rest of the Company?"

Donnor looked up from unlacing his tunic. It was the second time in less than a sennight that Cecily had come to his rooms—something that had not happened in a very long time. Now she stood just over the threshold, her blond hair swept under her white kerchief, most of her simple blue gown covered by a voluminous apron stained in so many places that one could read the entire roster of her day. Her face was drawn, her eyes hooded with shadows, and it struck him that she was much closer to thirty than twenty. "And since when do you involve yourself in the business of war, my lady?"

"Are not more than half the men who march beneath your banner, warriors who owe allegiance to my own house?"

Donnor jerked around as if she'd slapped him, and even the manservant turned to gape at her. Never once before had he ever heard her claim her share of the warriors who marched beneath his standard. Her dark eyes flashed and on her face he read the proud stamp of the blood of warrior kings. He looked at her with new eyes and suddenly it occurred to him that Kian's first allegiance, first loyalty was to Cecily. A cold chill went through him at the realization that perhaps the two of them were plotting against him politically as well. He shot a glance at old Ban, and waved him away with a gruff, "Leave us." He waited until they were alone, then said, "You take an uncommon interest all of a sudden in these warriors of your house, as you call them, my lady."

To his surprise, Cecily took a single step into the room. "I'm neither a child nor a fool, Donnor. Why do you not wait for the knights of the Company to return? They'll come back as soon as the word has reached the clans. The clans are not even rallied—"

"Why, my dear? Does this upset some plan of yours?" He took a single step toward her, wary as a wolf on a scent.

"What are you suggesting, Donnor?"

He raised one eyebrow and shrugged, spreading his hands wide. "Well, I don't know, my lady. But the First Knight of my Company has taken himself off to parts unknown, and now my wife comes to me, alarmed that I would ride out without him. What should I make of this, my lady? What should I think of this, my wife?" There was a bitter edge to the question.

"I've done nothing to shame myself, my lord. Nor has Kian." She crossed her arms over her breasts and raised her chin, and he recognized the challenge in her eyes. It was a challenge he'd never seen there before. The rebellion itself was changing her, awakening instincts in her he'd never thought existed. She was changing right before his eyes.

He hated her suddenly, with a blind and bitter passion. His affront had nothing to do with how she behaved. He had lost her heart despite all he'd done to so carefully cultivate it, hoping that in time, it would someday belong to him as surely as the herds of sheep and cattle, the fertile fields and rolling forests, the chests of gold and jewels that were her dowry were all his to command. Yet after years of his care, she'd given it so easily, so carelessly to one of his own knights—to the very knight who'd sworn to protect Donnor's life with his own if necessary, the knight who must ride into battle at his right hand, the knight who shared his cup at every feast. He took a deep breath and wished he dared to pull the tunic over his head and stand before her naked, virile and strong as he'd been before too many years and too many battles followed by too much feasting had twisted and scarred and padded him forever into a misshapen semblance of the warrior he'd once been.

"So you both say, my lady." The words were bitter as aloe in his mouth. All their denials counted for nothing because he'd seen for himself how they looked at each other when they thought he wasn't watching. It was a longing that neither could deny. It was for that Donnor hated them both: Cecily that she could give to Kian what she'd never given to him; and Kian for accepting something that so rightfully should have been his. Donnor turned away from her, but she continued, pressing on with an intensity that startled him out of his anger.

"I've come to you because I have a bad feeling about this, my lord, and I can keep it to myself no longer. For despite what you may choose to believe, I am fully aware of who I am and where my fortunes lie. So I believe it does concern me when I hear that you intend to ride out and engage the enemy beneath his very gates, without the most trusted of your guard around you. Why do you not wait for your knights?"

"You take an uncommon interest in my knights, my lady." In front of the hearth, a tray set on a low stool before the fire held a flagon, a goblet and a basket of burnished red apples. He poured the wine, then held the goblet out to her. "Wine? An apple? No? I thought not." He drank deeply and swallowed hard, jealousy acid on his tongue. "Maybe you better tell me what sort of game are you and my First Knight playing?"

"Kian is as loyal to you as I've been," she answered, cold and unflinching in the face of his scorn. "He's gone to rally the Clans to your cause—"

"Aye, in *your* name. Think you that bit of detail would not find its way to me, my lady?"

"There's nothing wrong in that. The Clans of Mochmorna and Pentland are my blood kin and I've every right to raise my own standard in your cause. I've done nothing to betray you, and neither's Kian. We're as true to the vows we swore to you as ever. I think you must look closer than the two of us if you would find the one who would betray you." She broke off.

"Who are you talking about?" he demanded. His face was

getting warm and he could feel the drops of sweat forming on the back of his neck.

"Has it not occurred to you that Cadwyr could be leading you into a trap?"

She was serious, and it bothered him for some reason he could not immediately identify. So he dismissed it, as he did so many misgivings lately, and laughed out loud. "What are you saying, woman? Has the smell of blood addled your brains? The heat stewed your reason? Cadwyr—"

"If that's true, then why this uncommon haste? How many knights of the Company are here? Four? Five? Surely not enough to buffer you in battle. And you've yet to answer me."

"You should be glad I mean to go without your light-headed lover." Images of Kian and Cecily entwined were rising before his mind's eye thick and fast to taunt him, brief flashes of naked limbs, hard muscle against round curves, her head bent back in his embrace, mouth open to his kiss. He imagined how the masses of their hair must've tangled together, Kian's palest blond mixing with Cecily's lightest of ash-brown. The wine curdled in his mouth and he spat it in the hearth. "Mayhap a chant or two to that goddess of yours and I'll come home on my shield."

As if he had suddenly doused her with the wine, she looked stunned. She replied with such quiet dignity he was immediately ashamed. "I've done nothing to deserve that. Why have you told the clans to rally at Killcarrick, when you intend to ride to Ardagh?"

Behind him the fire snapped and hissed as a knot within a log burst. For a long moment he stared at her. The blood receded from his vision only slightly. He would be glad to ride to war. It would feel good to spend the rage he felt right now in legitimate killing. "An opportunity has arisen. An opportunity to trade for hostages too advantageous not to seize. We intend to tempt them out under cover of parley. Then we'll strike when they least expect it. The clans will gather at Killcarrick and await what happens next. One bold stroke on our part, and we nip this foreign infection before it has a chance to fester and infect the land. So you see I've not the time to wait for Kian and the rest."

"I don't think you should trust Cadwyr." She stepped farther into the room and lowered her voice. "I know he was here that night less than a sennight past. And now he's induced you to ride out to battle without those sworn to protect you. How can you not see that it could be a trap?"

"He came to tell me of this opportunity—this chance to end it all immediately and secure my place—our place upon the throne of Brynhyvar. So what can you tell me, lady, that Cadwyr has done that I should not trust my sister's own flesh and blood?"

The question hung in the air. There was a long silence and then she raised her head and met his eyes. A light brown tendril had escaped her coif. It curled against her cheek, just below her jawline, but her voice held no hint of tenderness. "Tell me that you trust him implicitly, that you believe in him with all your heart, that there is not one tiny seed of doubt in your mind that Cadwyr would ever betray you, that he is utterly loyal to you and you alone, and I shall never question Cadwyr's honor again."

It was his turn to feel pinned. A small white worm of

doubt squirmed briefly in his gut and he squelched it. Cadwyr merely believed that all means were justified by the end. When Donnor was King, and she was Queen, she would have reason to thank Cadwyr. He was about to speak, when someone knocked on the open door. "Enter!"

A young page stuck his head around the door. "The Duke of Allovale has arrived, my lord Duke. And a messenger from Killcarrick for you, my lady."

There was only one person at Killcarrick who would send a message to Cecily. His vision clouded. "Send Cadwyr to me." Donnor looked at Cecily as he spoke, his eyes hooded and grim. But he tried to keep his face otherwise neutral.

"My sister lives near Killcarrick," she said, and he knew she hoped he might believe that the message had come from her sister. But he knew it hadn't.

It hadn't, but at least it diverted her off the tricky subject of Cadwyr. *Let her go back to her own rooms and drown in her dreams.* "Then you'd better see to it posthaste, my lady." He raised the goblet. "Send her my very best wishes for her continuing good health." He was glad when she silently turned and left the room, head high, back rigid. It would be better to put Cecily and Kian completely out of his mind. Contrary to what he told her, he was glad that Kian had taken it upon himself to rally the clans. He would rather his First Knight be a hundred leagues or more away. In the heat of battle, it would be too tempting to turn in the saddle and swipe his broadsword around in one unthinking arc.

He doesn't trust me. The stupidity of her lie made her furious, for she and Kian were innocent. They'd done nothing to warrant the need for either denial or shame, nothing but to respond to the call of the god and the goddess. Donnor knew they'd done nothing wrong. When Kian had offered to resign his position as First Knight, Donnor refused to accept it. Twice. And since then, though it broke her heart, they'd both kept a safe distance from each other. *But it's not my body Donnor grudges Kian.* Suddenly she understood the reason for her flimsy lie. If Donnor condemned her for giving her heart to Kian, well—she had. No wonder he was able to make her feel guilty enough to lie.

She went back to her solar, and sighed as soon as she saw the waiting mounds of clean linen to sort and fold piled in baskets. Eofe was doubtlessly rounding up what help she could corral from kitchen and nursing duty. But then a scent caught her nose, a scent at once sweeter and more pungent than that which rose from the sun-dried laundry. She frowned slightly, trying to recognize the scent. It was sweet as a pale shade of pink, clean as flowing water, delicately crisp as the first crust of newfallen snow. It was as if someone had distilled some purest essence and released it into the air, one thin drop at a time. She looked around, searching for the source.

The rose lay on her chair before the fire, placed diagonally on the cushion on a piece of the sheerest white silk she'd ever seen. It was just beyond the bud stage, each petal stained darkest crimson on the tips, then fading to a rich velvety red. Even the stem and leaves were lush and green. It was the most perfect rose she'd ever seen, and she touched it gingerly with one outstretched fingertip, just to ascertain that it was real.

"Oh, it's real, all right." As if he'd read her mind, Cadwyr spoke from the threshold of her bedroom, where he leaned against the door frame, his long body relaxed and as much at ease as if it were his right to visit her chambers unchaperoned.

She startled back with a little scream. "What are you doing here? Where's Eofe?"

"Well, now, I don't know where your waiting woman's disappeared to, lady-aunt. Servants are always off on business of their own, it seems to me. Especially when you need them most. But as for why I'm here… Why, surely, Aunt, you've heard. Donnor and I ride out at dawn, and I but thought to come and beg a blessing. After all, tomorrow, or the next day or the day after that may find me feasting in the Summerlands." He crossed his arms over his chest, legs crossed at the feet, and she had the impression that he held himself back only with some effort. He wasn't armed but he was no less intimidating, dressed all in some black fabric that draped as fluidly as water. "Surely you're not afraid of me, my lady-aunt?"

"Have I anything to fear?" She wiped her fingers on her skirt as surreptitiously as she could, sensing it unwise to show any sign of alarm at all. He frightened her far more than she wanted to admit, for he looked at her with a feverish hunger.

"Why, of course not, my lady-aunt." He put an especial emphasis on the last word. Cecily was younger than Cadwyr by at least five years if not more. "You must believe me, Cecily. I hold you in the highest esteem. What do you think of my rose?"

She swallowed hard, remembering a laundry maid who'd

claimed Cadwyr raped her, overpowering her as she bent over the scrub basins. Cadwyr denied the charge, and there were no witnesses, but Cecily believed the girl. He had, after all, agreed to pay a fine, even though he made it clear it was under protest and in no way an admission of guilt. "It's beautiful, but I can't imagine where you found such a thing this time of year. Surely there aren't roses blooming even in the south?"

"But aren't I always full of surprises? Isn't that part of my charm?" He but seemed to shift his stance, and suddenly, he was beside her, moving with that lightning efficiency that made him a terror on the battlefield and assured him a place in the songs of the bards. She instinctively took a step back. He picked up the rose, and, dropping down on one knee, offered it to her, with an expression of what appeared to be genuine humility coupled with reverence. Skeptically she accepted it, twirling it in her fingers to inspect its uncanny perfection, and he rose in one smooth motion, to overshadow her with the breadth of his shoulders, the sweep of his dark cloak. "Cecily. Surely you've guessed? Surely you know how I feel about you?"

She blinked, but stood her ground. Cadwyr of all people was declaring some sort of feelings for her? "How you've felt? About what?"

He loomed over her, but did not touch her, and some hastily suppressed emotion flickered across his face. When he finally spoke, it was slowly and deliberately, as if he held some tremendous force in check. "By the great horned god, you're not my aunt. You no more than I should be married to that mangy old lion."

She placed the rose deliberately down on the mantel and

took another step back. "I think you overstep yourself, Cadwyr." If he took one more step toward her, she was going to scream. Where was Eofe?

But he stayed where he was and spoke with a desperate urgency, which held her riveted despite her fear. "How could it be possible you do not know? From the day that I first saw you, I wanted you for mine. And from the day that Donnor stole you from me, I've watched and waited for the time to win you back. Do you know how it was that Donnor came to steal you? Aye, he stole you from me, Cecily, for I was the one who noticed you first, that Beltane you'd just turned fifteen. You were like a peach just rounding into ripeness, and I was stupid enough to mention to my uncle Donnor the tasty fruit I'd seen, so close to picking. It was under the pretense of representing me that he offered to visit your parents—pretending he'd present me as a suitor when in reality the moment they filled his goblet, he offered himself. He stole you and I never had a chance to even present myself to your parents." His mouth twisted again. "After all, what father would not prefer the mighty Duke of Gar over humble Allo-vale for his daughter, especially one as winsome and as rich as Lady Cecily, the Fair Maid of Mochmorna?"

She stared at him, horrified. Humble Allovale, indeed. There was nothing humble about Cadwyr, and never had been. But how was it possible she'd missed his feelings for her, all these years, if what he said had any truth to it at all? She thought back, thinking hard, remembering glances, glimpses, fleeting impressions, eyes that sometimes lingered a moment or two too long, inscrutable expressions, unreadable looks. She was under no illusions. She knew full well what had attracted both Donnor and Cadwyr. It was her lands that stretched from the rich fertile lowlands of the Uishlian Valley to the forests beyond Pentland, her gold, her cattle and the warriors of her clans that made her such a desirable prize. Her body was almost an afterthought. If Cadwyr cared for her at all, it was the sort of love best expressed in stacks of gold and silver coin. *But why now? Why does he declare himself now? Donnor's not dead.* A cold wave swept over and through her and suddenly she realized that Donnor was the one sure thing that stood between her and this man who looked at her with ravenous eyes.

He picked up the rose and once more, extended it to her. "Will you not accept my gift?"

She gathered the fabric of her skirts in her hands to dry her palms and spoke coldly enough, she hoped, to penetrate his feverish brain. "I am Donnor's wife and you compromise me by coming to me in my private rooms, alone and uninvited. Whatever your feelings may be for me, my lord Cadwyr of Allovale, I've done nothing and will do nothing to encour—"

Cadwyr smiled, but there was a hint of menace in his eyes that made her wary. "So does that mean you won't even give me your blessing, lady-aunt? After all, I ride at dawn to Ardagh. You may never see me again." But the look on his face told her he'd no intention of dying in battle.

I shall not be so lucky. The thought ran unbidden through her mind, but some instinct of self-preservation kept it from leaping off her lips. Instead she lifted her chin and took advantage of the opportunity. "Why such haste?" she asked. "Who are these hostages who must be ransomed so quickly?

Why aren't you and Donnor waiting for the rest of the Company to return?"

"Because we don't have to." He sniffed the rose and replaced it deliberately on the mantel, then smiled as if he was privy to some delightful secret. "But believe me when I tell you to be ready to greet the new King of Brynhyvar when we come marching home, my lady aunt. My lady Duchess. My lady Duchess, who will be Queen." He held her eyes for a long moment. "And remember then what I've told you now." He bowed then left the room, leaving her staring after him in dismayed bewilderment.

Cadwyr's declaration was so unexpected she felt shocked and numb. She understood all too clearly his unspoken message. As Donnor's heir, Cadwyr considered Cecily part of Donnor's estate. He intended—*expected*—to marry her himself if anything happened to Donnor. Suddenly she felt cold all over, even while another part of her wanted to strip to the skin, and order the clothes she'd been wearing burned. She wiped her hands on her apron, and took it off, throwing it over her chair. There was something about Cadwyr's visit that left her feeling dirty, violated. She picked up her shawl from the back of the chair and wrapped it around her shoulders, and noticed the wisp of silk on which the rose was lying when she'd first spotted it. It was so light and airy it actually floated, wafting in a slow drift to the floor, trailing ribbons of the rose's scent.

Without warning the door opened, and Eofe stepped inside, leading a muddied messenger. "Word from Killcarrick has come for you, my lady." The messenger halted just inside the door, and bowed.

"What news?" asked Cecily, noting his stubbled cheeks and dark circled eyes.

The messenger sketched another awkward bow and cleared his throat. "Lord Kian said to tell you he reached Killcarrick in safety and that as I left, he was headed off first to Killcairn, and then most likely into the hills above Pentland to rally the clans. He hopes to see you within a fortnight, and asked that you commend him to the Duke."

Cecily stared at the man. "That's all? He doesn't intend to get here any sooner?"

The messenger nodded. "Those were the words I was bid to say, my lady. He bade me repeat it five times to be sure I got it right."

"No other message? No note? Or letter?"

"No, my lady." The messenger's eyes were gentle. And she realized that despite all the differences between them, he was a man who understood the hopes and fears and longings of a woman left at home.

She drew herself up. Pride refused to allow her to appear as anything less than in complete control of her emotions. "Have you a message for the Duke?"

"No, my lady." Again their eyes met in wordless communion.

"Will you return to Killcarrick?"

"If that is your command, my lady. Otherwise I am to ride on into Far Nearing."

"With what orders?"

"The lords of Far Nearing are called to Killcarrick like all the rest, my lady."

She frowned. So Donnor was riding to Ardagh, without

his full company of knights, without even the lords of Far Nearing, who were the closest of all their combined kinsmen to Ardagh. How was it possible that he intended to challenge the bulk of the Queen's supporters with only the few battleworthy of his own garrison here, and Cadwyr's men? Who else was there? No matter the opportunity, the advantage, surely it was plain to anyone involved that Donnor was seriously undermanned, underreinforced and it did not take a military strategist to see that Donnor was potentially riding right into some sort of trap. But the question was—who intended to spring it?

"On whose orders?" she asked. "Kian's?"

"No, my lady. An order came in, right behind the First Knight. From the Duke himself. Pentland is the first expected."

She stared at the messenger, uncertain she had heard correctly. That Donnor would build his force over the winter and prepare to face the King's in the spring made sense. That Donnor would attempt to draw as many of the clans together and strike a decisive first blow made sense. But to ride to Ardagh to challenge the enemy under the cover of a proposed hostage exchange without sufficient reserves sounded like suicide. She knew Kian knew nothing of this, and a dark foreboding folded around her like a shroud. She didn't trust Cadwyr. Suddenly the sweet scent of the rose was cloying, overpowering to the point of sickening. Donnor never went into battle without a full complement of his knights, and never, ever, without his First Knight by his side. And how could he not believe this opportunity that Cadwyr had somehow fortuitously presented was not a trap? "You must go back to Killcarrick, messenger. Have them give you a strong, fresh horse in the stables and a token to exchange it for another at the garrison on the Daraghduin. You must find Lord Kian. And tell him to get back here as quickly as possible. Donnor and Cadwyr are riding to Ardagh, to exchange hostages, they say. But I think it's a trap."

The messenger stared at her.

"Will you remember?"

"But my lady, the orders from the Duke—"

"Find another messenger to do the Duke's bidding. I need you to go back to Kian, for you've just been over that terrain and you'll find him more quickly. Please. This is a matter of the utmost urgency. Kian must be told what his lord is planning. He could be held responsible for the blood fine, you know."

Whether this was strictly true or not, Cecily wasn't really sure, but it seemed to convince the messenger. For a moment more he hesitated, then finally nodded. "All right. I'm to tell him that Gar and Allovale are riding to Ardagh to exchange hostages. But it's a trap."

"Kian will know something's wrong."

The messenger tugged at his forelock and was gone in a muddy swirl.

Cecily stared at Eofe, unseeing. She felt as if she stood on the edge of a great swirling void, a void that would suck her and everything around her into it, including the stones of this castle, no matter how solid and substantial they seemed. She wrapped her arms around herself, and murmured, "I feel a great blackness, Eofe. A great blackness drawing near."

Without another word, the woman crossed the room and folded Cecily in her embrace. "There, there, my lady, there, there. You're exhausting yourself. Wearing yourself thin with all the cooking and serving and nursing. The winter's coming on, soon there'll be more time to rest."

"I'm doing no more than anyone else. We're all tired." But she clung to the older woman. Something wasn't right—from the goblin, to Cadwyr, to Donnor's sudden urge for battle. Her head ached, but the unearthly aroma of the rose was permeating the room. She took a deep breath, inhaling its scent and miraculously, the worst of her headache eased.

"What's that I smell, my lady?" asked Eofe, drawing back, and sniffing. "That wonderful scent?"

"It's that rose, there on the mantel," said Cecily. "Cadwyr brought it. He said he wanted my blessing. He was in here, Eofe, in these very rooms, waiting for me."

Eofe blanched white. "He would not dare!"

"But he did." *The question was, what else would Cadwyr dare?* Cecily picked up the rose and startled as a surprisingly thick thorn pierced the skin of her thumb. It tumbled to the ground as she sucked the scarlet drop that oozed from the punctured pore. "Take it away, Eofe. Take it to Mag. Tell her to wring it of every ounce of essence, but be careful—it's got very sharp thorns." *Just like Cadwyr—fair to look at, dangerous to touch.* And as Eofe bore it from the room, Cecily saw a flash of herself pouring rose-scented water into a basin beside Donnor's lifeless body, and she knew as surely as the blood in her veins knew the path to her heart that Donnor's day upon the battlefield would be his last. Was there even a chance that he would listen to her, if she went to him once more and told him what she'd seen, what Cadwyr had brought her, and told her? *Not one blessed hope.* Donnor's jealousy blinded and deafened him to all but what he wanted to see and hear. He'd insist Cadwyr be present when she spoke against him—and she could well imagine the lies Cadwyr would tell to twist her words against her. With a sigh, she picked up a bandage from the pile and slowly wrapped it around her thumb, squeezing a few extra drops on the white linen. *Great Marrihugh, accept my blood in token of his. Great Goddess, heed my plea.* But even as she sent the silent prayer out, she felt the sting of a hunger long held in check newly released, and she knew the warrior goddess now marching across the land in her crow-feathered boots would not be so easily satisfied.

With Vinaver's departure, Alemandine took to her bed, refusing entirely the company of her Consort or Councilors. They clustered at the doors of her reception chamber, looking puzzled, almost lost, nearly comical. Of them all, Hudibras looked most disconsolate. He turned away, grumbling, shaking his head, and Delphinea felt a pang of genuine pity. It was clear that difficult and demanding as Alemandine often was, her Consort bore some authentic feeling for the condition of both the Queen and his child. Gorlias threw an arm around his brother's neck and drew him away from the rest, leaving Delphinea, Berillian, and Philomemnon standing before the great doors, which were closed for the first time since Delphinea had come to Court. And judging by the stricken look on Hudibras's face, this was the first time in a very long time.

Philomemnon nudged Berillian, who as usual, was staring at Delphinea's bosom. "Such deliciousness begs to be savored." Berillian simpered with a wink and a quirk of his brow. "So *utterly* beautiful."

"Where's Lord Timias?" blurted Delphinea, without thinking as usual. Her palm itched to slap the arch expression off Berillian's face. How could he engage in such puerile punning when the Queen's well-being—indeed the existence of all Faerie—was jeopardized so profoundly?

At that Philomemnon looked at her sharply. "That's a very good question, my dear."

"One might even wonder why you ask it." Berillian was looking at her just as sharply beneath lids tinged the subtlest shade of violet to match exactly his entire ensemble. The overriding concern for such triviality as the tint of one's eyelids when the world itself was in danger of disintegrating disgusted her.

She glanced from one cold pointed face to the other, and drew herself up. It was immediately obvious that she'd unwittingly allied herself too openly with whatever opposing faction Timias represented. "It only seems a notable absence," she answered just as distantly, refusing to acknowledge the jab, brow raised at the same angle as Berillian's.

Philomemnon's eyes softened just an iota and the ghost of a smile might have flickered across his face. He nudged Berillian once more. "It does, indeed, my dear. Come, Berillian. Good day, my lady. I shall look for you at the Cotillion later on." It was one step above a cut. He took Berillian's upper arm and firmly eased him away.

Delphinea stared after them, feeling at once miserably

lost and alone and seething with a rage such as she'd never felt before. This was what it must feel like to be mortal, she thought, trapped into inaction both by her conflicting feelings and her uncertainty at how to navigate the treacherous waters of the Court. Neither one of them had been willing to listen to her pleas regarding the Caul, and now both condemned her for taking action by seeking out someone who was willing to help her. But what sort of interCouncil struggle had she unwittingly stumbled into? If only she'd paid closer attention to her mother's list of warnings. She made her way to the feasting hall with half-remembered admonitions echoing maddeningly in her head.

But they were all forgotten when she heard the first whispered rumor of a missing gremlin as she stepped across the threshold into the great hall where breakfast was laid every morning by a gremlin army clad in costumes which varied in color and ornamentation in accordance to the seasons. This morning, they were dressed in Samhain's rich, dark purple trimmed with black braid. And there was undeniably a surly, restless edge to their behavior. They slipped in and out of the growing throng with a furtive air, and more than once Delphinea spotted them make a gesture for which she knew no word. Given what Petri had told her, she could understand why Timias believed they were plotting some mischief.

The first real rumor began as no more than a fragment of an overheard question, but was spread so rapidly that by dinner time, everyone knew that a gremlin named Khouri from the kitchens was missing, and that Timias alone had been admitted shortly after dawn to the Queen's presence.

The whispers swirled and circulated, fragmentary as autumn leaves, punctuating every conversation with speculative silences and arch looks. Laughter, high and nervous, rose in fits and starts, and for the first time, the music sounded tinny and slightly off-key, the intricate dances but mechanized gyrations, devoid of life or meaning. Feeling isolated, adrift in a sea of friendless faces, Delphinea watched from the corners, dragged unwilling onto the floor once or twice by Berillian and Gorlias—or was it Hudibras? Did it even matter?

For the first time in her life, she was conscious of the weight of each passing minute, of the long slow ponderous drag of every hour. Each grain of sand within the glass looked not like a tiny particle capable of trickling through the precisely measured opening, but a boulder that must negotiate a narrow bottleneck before falling in excruciating slow motion to the chasm below. Just an hour's worth of sand looked impossibly high piled in the glass, and the idea that thirteen full turns of that glass were required to complete a whole day made her head ache.

She found herself holding her breath as she wandered alone through the crowded halls where the courtiers held a nearly continuous revel, presided over by the Court Master of Ceremonies with a surreal intensity of color and sound and form and taste and texture.

The following morning, a small contingent of messengers rode out, fanning across the land in all directions, and word spread through the palace like fire through meadow grass in late summer: the Queen had called a Convening of her Council. At last.

"So there will be some action, finally." Philomemnon's murmur startled her as he slipped beside her within one of the deep recesses of the wide window seats, as she watched that evening's mandatory revel. The dancers spun and dipped and whirled, reflected in the great mirror hanging opposite.

Within its polished surface, in the golden cast of the candles that shone from the gold and crystal chandeliers, the shining-faced sidhe gleamed translucent, so that for a moment, by a trick of the light, she thought they appeared to be gorgeously gowned skeletons, topped by perfectly topped skulls with hollow eyes and death's head grins. She gave a little gasp, and turned to find Philomemnon leaning in uncomfortably close, startling her even more.

Philomemnon drew back, frowning down at her suspiciously. "What's amiss, my lady?"

"Tell me what isn't," she spat, discomfited that he should take her so completely by surprise.

His smile took her aback. "So the kitten has claws. Come with me, if you will, my lady?" He drew back and extended his hand.

The invitation was open and unmistakable. She saw the immediate glances, nods, shrugs and raised brows and knew that the gesture had been duly noted and passed on. The fact that Philomemnon approached her so openly was extremely significant, and her response was critical. But what had she to lose? She put her hand in his and knew that before they reached the edge of the dance floor, Petri would've heard the first whisper as he stirred her posset deep within the bowels of the kitchens.

But Philomemnon did not lead her on to the dance floor. Instead he drew her away from the entire company, out onto one of the broad terraces that sloped so gracefully down to the broad swath of lawn. He led her to the very edge of the top step and wrapped his arms around her, drawing her up and into him in a most intimate embrace. Momentarily too stunned to react, she smelled the apple-sweetness of his breath, felt the velvet texture of his moss-green tunic, and was shocked nearly speechless by his question. "Can you kiss me?"

"What?" She stiffened in his embrace, pulled back, not at all sure she'd understood.

"Can you kiss me, lady? If I told you the fate of Faerie itself depended upon it, could you kiss me?" Their eyes met and for a heartbeat, she thought he might in fact, press his mouth on hers. She stared at him, totally confused when he just as suddenly released her. He retreated a few steps, then turned back. "It is no simple thing, you see, to surrender even the smallest part of yourself to someone else, even for the greatest of causes. Remember that in days to come."

"I don't understand what you mean."

He glanced around. In the silvery light, his green tunic had faded to gray and her violet gown darkened to black, but his pale hair shone with a gleam that made it easy to spot them. The terrace was deserted, the music muted, and the torches burned upright. The night was very still, and there was no question that sound would carry. He knelt with the grace of a lover, and picked up her hand, drawing her closer, and when he spoke, his voice was so muted, she had to bend low to hear him. To any who might watch, they appeared to be a courting couple. But the grave expression on his face had nothing to do with courtship of any sort. "The timing of all this is most unfortunate, for I told Vinaver you were a force to be reckoned with." Startled, she blinked, but before she could ask anything, he touched one fingertip lightly to her lips. "All in time, little one. You must be patient yet a while longer. A greater working than you realize is in the works."

"But what about the Caul? How can it be destroyed if we can't find it?"

"Hush, I say!" He grabbed her upper arm and pulled her so close their faces nearly touched. "Think of what it is you're saying." He glanced around once more, rose, and dragged her a few steps down, and off the marble stairs, until they stood on the damp grass. The first dew had fallen and the tiny droplets twinkled in the light of the bone-white sickle moon. Like jewels, thought Delphinea. Or drops of blood.

Philomemnon drew her close once more, and they might have been two black shadows that merged and pooled on the grass. "Destroy the Caul, you say. Openly and to all. But Alemandine is linked to the land and the land is linked to the Caul—destroy the Caul and you run a very great risk of killing the Queen." She gasped, and stared at him in shock, until he nodded with grim satisfaction. "Now do you see? You're not the only one. There're those of us indeed who've reached the very conclusion you've come to. But we're not so eager to advertise our plans—"

"You mean to kill the Queen?" The words escaped in one long breath of disbelief.

"Come now, little lamb. Don't raise those great blue eyes to me. Vinaver said she would speak to you. Did she not?"

"She warned me to stay away from Timias. She didn't say she intended to kill the Queen."

"Well, then, my dear young innocent lady. Let me explain it to you. That's what's at stake here. To save Faerie, the Queen must die. The Queen lives, and Faerie crumbles. Take your pick. Which side will you give your loyalty to?"

Shocked to her core by the enormity of what he told her, she could only blurt, "So you would make Vinaver queen—"

"No!" He cut her off with a savage shake and released her arm. "*I* will not Make—or UnMake, for that matter—anything or anyone. Plain-spoken as one of your own cows, aren't you? You've no idea what sort of things you go about blurting. The one thing Vinaver didn't tell you was to stop asking questions. They've been noted. If you want answers, you'll have to bide 'til Samhain. Just two nights more—can you do that?"

"But who's to rule?" she whispered.

In the shadows his face suddenly loomed very close. He bent and whispered directly into her ear, in a voice that shivered through her body to her bones. "Think about it. Can't you guess? Close your eyes, my dear little Delphinea. You're of the land. What name does your blood give you?"

Finuviel. The word rose unbidden from the deepest recesses of her knowing, plucked with absolute certainty from among every other possibility, directly to her lips, so that she whispered it without truly being aware she did so. Finuviel. The soft consonants rolled on the wind, the liquid vowels rippled like the notes of a song. The ground itself seemed to rise and roll beneath her feet, moving like a restless sleeper. Flashes of images from her dreams burst through her awareness and she knew that when she saw him, she would know his face. Finuviel. Beltane-born of Herne himself if what Vinaver said was true. But—and she wrinkled her brow—but the sidhe had been ruled by Queens for as long as any could remember. Why now, a King? So many questions tumbled one upon the other. "But—"

But Philomemnon shook his head and refused to say more. "Two more nights, my lady. If we survive 'til Samhain, my lady, your questions will all be answered then."

"What do you mean 'if we survive'?"

But Philomemnon never answered, for three guards marched up. They saluted Philomemnon and bowed to Delphinea. Then the center one stepped forward. "Lord Philomemnon?"

"You know who I am." Philomemnon stepped a pace or two back, hands on his hips.

"If it would please you to come with us?"

"Where?"

"To the Queen, my lord. She has some questions for you."

Delphinea turned to the guards. "But, Captain, at this hour? Surely—"

"This does not concern you, my lady." The guard turned back to Philomemnon. "Well, my lord? Will you come?"

"Or will you have to drag me there?" Philomemnon said with a sardonic smirk. "So it begins, my lady. The lines are being drawn. Watch out which side you fall on—wittingly or unwittingly."

She watched in silence as they marched him away.

That night she tossed and turned, and even the perfumed linens that smelled of night jasmine could not soothe her. Try as she might to sleep, her thoughts tangled up with snippets of conversations, both recalled and overheard, echoing soundlessly, keeping her from rest.

At last she gave up the pretense of sleep. She dragged herself from the bed, and belted on her periwinkle robe. She nestled in her favorite spot on the window seat once more and, tucking her knees up and under her chin, she gazed out across the twilit landscape. The waning moon shed a purplish light across the blackened gardens, the ghostly white turrets, the inky black depths of the interior courtyards and private gardens. The dreams, Alemandine, Finuviel and the Caul, the whole strange tangle she'd found herself caught in didn't matter. For somewhere to the east, according to Vinaver, her mother was dying.

Surely it was only logical that all who were bound to the land were subject to the poison of the Caul. True death—the cessation of all life, the disintegration of the body—was an unfamiliar concept among the sidhe, and Delphinea could not ever remembering hearing of even one who'd fallen victim to that most unfortunate of fates. It was one of the main ways that the sidhe were different from the mortals. But if the Caul was not destroyed, the sidhe were about to experience the true death in greater numbers than they'd ever imagined. She imagined her mother, alone in her mountain keep. Was she sick? Like the calves? The foals? An image of her mother, covered in weeping sores, flashed before her eyes and she turned away with a little audible cry. She had assumed the reason she hadn't heard from Eponea was that her mother was too busy tending the herds. But had she only been deluding herself, refusing to see what was really only self-evident? *And would Mother even admit the truth?* If Delphinea sent a messenger from the Court, it was unlikely Eponea would send any upsetting message back.

With a sigh, Delphinea pushed thoughts of her mother away. Her mother had charged her with a duty, and it was up to her to discharge it as best she could. But what sort of plot had she stumbled into? It seemed clear both from the way Vinaver had behaved and from what Philomemnon had admitted, that Vinaver was in some way responsible for the removal of the Caul. Was that what Alemandine wanted to question Philomemnon about?

Which meant that Timias was utterly wrong about the gremlins. But who should she believe? Her mother told her to trust Timias—but somehow she doubted her mother had all the information. Philomemnon had hinted that the plot involved nothing less than a complete overthrow of the established order. Would her mother condone such a coup? Could she understand if Delphinea did?

What would her mother tell her to do? she wondered. Confront Timias—but he was first of all closeted with the Queen, and secondly, how could she betray Petri? Even if she didn't believe all the details, there was something in the little gremlin's story that rang with truth. It was enough to make her doubt Timias. What if Faerie could be saved without Alemandine's death? Surely that was the most preferable outcome of all. And yet, she remembered how Finuviel's name had leapt to her lips, how his face had simply appeared in her mind's eye, how it seemed the name itself carried a sort of recognition in her bones, in her blood. The wind had lifted each separate syllable as delicately as a kiss. Was this what her dreams meant? Were they clues to the part Vinaver foresaw for her? And was it true that it put her life in danger?

She pressed her fingers to her face, wishing more than anything that she could be away from these gaudy, gorgeous crystalline towers that suddenly seemed too flimsy to be real. Oh, to curl her toes in the wild mountain thyme, weaving wildflowers into wreaths for the cattle to wear as they grazed over heathered hills, to drink again the sweet milk still hot from the udder, licking the lacy foam off her fingertips. Oh, to dance and sing and sleep beneath the lowering pines. How simple and how sweet was home. *Until the calves and foals began to die.* She pressed her forehead to the cold glass, pushing away the memories of those ghastly corpses. What was happening here, all around her? The world felt like it was all spinning out of control. She could sense it. It was as if a series of subtle rips and tears even now were snaking like a crackling in glass, across and over and through the fabric of the world that was Faerie. Could it really all come to an end? Suddenly she wanted nothing more than to lay her head on Eponea's copious bosom once more for the fall of just one grain of sand in the glass. *Mother, I don't know what to do.* Loneliness enfolded her like a shroud and her eyes welled up with tears. She must not be so childish, she told herself. She was tired and cold, and she simply did not know what to do. It was a bigger puzzle than she could solve in one night.

She noticed that as usual, Petri had left her nightly posset in its golden cup on the tray beside her window seat. It had long ago cooled, but she picked it up, and, cradling it close, gently called the heat from her hands into the milky drink. Despite her restlessness, she was tired, and that effort exhausted her. She drank the posset, savoring the spicy taste of the rich soothing liquid. How could a world where something as simple as a posset was so perfectly rendered, be in such imminent danger of collapse? She closed her eyes, as her head slumped against the window. She fell into dreams of rotting calves that stumbled in and out of mirrors chased by gremlins wearing silver fishnets over their smooth leathery heads.

It was there that Petri found her, just as the sun had topped the trees. He was gray and grim, even as he placed a soothing pot of tisane, fragrant with chamomile, bracing with rosemary, on the small table, deftly removing the posset cup. It was as if he'd sensed her restless night.

She looked up to see him padding into the room, and saw to her surprise his face was wet with tears. "What is it, Petri?"

His wide mouth worked, and his hands shook so she scarcely understood what he said. *Great evil, great lady, great evil is about, and I fear none of us shall escape its hunger.*

"What are you talking about, Petri?" she asked with narrowed eyes.

They have blamed us for the missing Caul, great lady.

Delphinea sighed. She should've realized that was only inevitable. "All of you? Surely only the missing—"

It is not that simple, my lady. We cannot leave the confines of the palace grounds. If we do so, we die. Therefore they assume that he's but hiding and that we, the rest of us, have helped. So they mean to punish us all.

Delphinea bit her lip. "How?"

His shoulders heaved and his hands shook so much through a complicated series of gestures, that she failed to understand most of it. But the last few she did understand, quite clearly. *I fear we shall be sequestered.*

She frowned. "Who's suggested that?"

It is said by some among the Queen's Council, he replied.

Timias, thought Delphinea. She wondered what had happened to Philomemnon the night before. Could he be part of this? "But Samhain is yet two days off. Are you certain? Already?"

He pulled a crumpled piece of parchment from his pocket. It was bordered in an intricate pattern of colored inks, and a bright blue ribbon, set in place with a large blob of red wax, dangled from it, and he proffered it. She took it from him, and she saw it had been ripped in half. Gently she smoothed it. The script was black and flowing, each letter a work of art. In ornate Court phrasing, it requested that all gremlins report to their dormitories at noon today. It was signed by Timias, over Alemandine's seal. It was truly amazing, not to mention alarming, at how quickly he'd been able to establish himself once more. Almost overnight, he had gone from laughingstock to Most Ancient, Admirable, and Honorable Lord High Councilor. A chill went through her, as she saw that Philomemnon's signature was affixed as a witness. She saw at once how Timias's attention on the gremlins suited his purpose.

He is no friend to anyone in Faerie. Vinaver's words echoed in her mind. Certainly it was true insofar as the gremlins were concerned. Delphinea looked from the parchment to Petri. "When did you receive this?"

This morning, my lady. At breakfast.

She peered at the signature. Three days ago Timias had been laughed at openly. This morning he'd signed a writ over Alemandine's seal. How had it happened? What had he told Alemandine about the gremlins that had so completely convinced her and what part had Philomemnon played? Was there a way to spare these creatures any further agony? Surely he would understand if she went to him, upset about the impending loss of her dear little gremlin. "Petri," she said. "You're free till noon?"

Yes, great lady.

The expression on his face twisted her heart. It would also give her an opportunity to find out what happened last night to Philomemnon. This time, there'd be no sneaking through the mirrors. This time, she'd be no desperate outsider. Timias's sudden elevation gave her an idea. What was it Philomemnon had called her, "a force to be reckoned with"? She was at least a vote on the Council. She'd seen how he'd looked at her, and with quick and sudden insight, knew exactly how he should be approached. "Fetch me a pen and parchment, Petri, and ring for my dressing-dame. I think our

Most Ancient, Admirable, and Honorable Lord High Councilor should dine in company for breakfast, don't you think?"

But to her complete and utter astonishment, her invitation was refused. Wondering if perhaps it had something to do with the fact she'd sent Petri, she took it upon herself, once she was as gorgeously gowned and elaborately coifed as possible, to seek out Timias's chambers. But she was told stiffly by his body-servant, a sidhe nearly as old, though not half so decrepit as Timias himself, that the Most Ancient, Admirable, and Honorable Lord High Councilor was with the Queen.

With the Queen. The words carried the weight of portent, hinting at whatever circumstances Timias had arranged so neatly to his own advantage. Slowly she turned on her slipper. It seemed that nearly everyone else was still abed, sleeping off the effects of the revelry last night. The dreamweed had been particularly potent. She could smell its bitter, burned scent lingering in the air, haunting the corners, wreathing the hangings as she hurried back through the silent, empty halls. As she rounded a corner, she came face-to-face with the image of herself reflected back at her from a huge, wall-size mirror that dominated one side of the corridor. Against the arching marble columns, her pale blue gown shimmered the color of the sky. She glanced back over her shoulder. The bright polished sheen tempted her. She had always been particularly adept at navigating the other side of the looking glass world. It was a talent some shared and others didn't.

But it was one thing to use the mirrors as a shortcut, as

a means to make Court life easier, especially with Alemandine as demanding as she'd become. It was quite another to use the mirrors as a means of spying. She had not yet forgotten the punishment her mother had meted out the first and last time she'd been caught doing such a thing. It was a scurrilous practice, something in which no true lady of the sidhe would ever even think of engaging. It had been her mother's fondest hope to mold Delphinea into a true lady. Delphinea had met her expectations with varying degrees of success.

Forgive me, Mother. The palace was too quiet, the idea too tempting, the information possibly acquired could mean the answer to so many of her questions. Nothing less than the existence of Faerie was at stake. Surely under those circumstances, her mother would understand. She glanced right and left and assessed the situation.

To use this mirror as a portal would be foolish. The internal angle cast by such a huge mirror was too broad—she could be seen by far too many possible viewers on the other side if she attempted to step through there. Better to find a smaller, more discreet avenue. She continued on her way. At the bottom of the spiraling stairs which led up to her tower rooms, there was a slim mirror, just high and wide enough for Delphinea to step within. She took a quick glance up, down, and around, then ducked into the glass.

Sunlight was pouring down and through from a hundred bent and twisted angles, momentarily making her lose her balance as she stood in the gray twilight just on the other side of the glass. She paused to get her bearings and to allow her eyes to adjust to the inside-out world. *Left is right and right is left,* she murmured, setting off, feeling her way by instinct and by hasty glimpses into mirrors as she made her way deeper into the heart of the Palace.

The twilit world was empty. Delphinea edged from light to shadow slowly, holding her voluminous skirts close, pausing at frequent intervals to check her bearings. At a turn, she glanced over her shoulder, then turned back and nearly screamed aloud. An intent female face had appeared in the mirror closest to her elbow. She froze, then scurried past, biting back a curse as her petticoats moved with an audible swish. When she was safely out of range, she paused and kicked off her high-heeled court slippers. Holding them tightly in one hand, she scurried on more quickly, silent as a field mouse trapped within the walls in her stocking feet.

A reverse sense of direction led her deeper into the heart of the palace, while all around her, spears and shafts of bent and twisted light refracted at every angle, and in the gray, imperfect light, she tripped suddenly, stumbling and flailing. As she regained her balance, she froze. Was that the Queen's voice she heard, just on the other side of the mirror opposite? Impatiently, she caught the layers of her petticoats up over her arm and edged as close to the mirror as she dared.

It was a dressing table mirror, she knew at once, by the angle at which it was set, by the size of the opening. She peeked cautiously into the frame and stifled a gasp. Alemandine herself was peering into the glass, so intently Delphinea was sure she'd been seen.

Delphinea backed away and to the side. But Alemandine was too absorbed in her conversation with someone whose replies were muted by the glass and proximity to the mirror.

"...necessary to keep them at all?" Alemandine's voice, high and querulous as ever, was easier to understand.

Delphinea strained as close as she dared, trying to comprehend the indistinct answer, hoping to recognize the muffled voice.

"But, I don't understand, Timias." Alemandine herself answered the first question, and Delphinea allowed herself to relax just a bit. "Whyever would my mother have allowed these creatures so close if they truly are as dangerous as you say?"

"Because—" His voice was suddenly as clear as Alemandine's and Delphinea nearly gasped aloud. "Oh, by Horned Herne, Your Majesty, cover that mirror." She bit down hard on her bottom lip to prevent herself from crying out. She realized he must have come to stand directly in front of the mirror. She sensed movement, and two pieces of heavy green silk fell across the glass, leaving only one thin bright line of light. But the voices were still clear. "As I've explained to you, my Queen, the very nature of the gremlins makes them a very necessary and integral component of the magic of which the Caul itself is only another part. As only a few truly understand, my dear Alemandine." He paused.

Delphinea shuddered at the caressing tone he used, trying to imagine why he might have paused. There was something disturbing in the cadence of his voice, and she had to force herself to listen closely as he continued. "The Caul does not function alone. Those who focus solely on it are blind as mortals, who are prisoners of their own dull senses. The Caul is but a part of the intricate web of energy and polarity, all held in balanced stasis, the axis upon which the great orb that's Faerie spins."

A chill ran up and down her spine, as Delphinea felt herself swayed by the magic of his voice, and she realized the effect must be even double upon the Queen. Timias continued in a mellifluous baritone that rang with the authority of a Lorespinner. "—and thus it is my hope that by concentrating the entire population within the Caul Chamber, the energy raised and contained therein will not only exert an influence upon the Caul itself, thus drawing it back to the moonstone, and that wretched thief out of whatever dim hole he's crawled into, but also acting in something of the same way as the Caul itself. Not perfectly, perhaps, but certainly worth trying." There was a rustle of fabric as if he leaned closer, and then he spoke, in a quiet conspiratorial whisper. "You know, my dear, there was a great deal about all this your mother and I were called upon to improvise. When the goblins stand upon the gates, one does what one must."

Delphinea thought furiously, even more disturbed by the implications of that statement. Clearly Timias and Gloriana had taken a great deal upon themselves. Exactly what had they done in the Making? she wondered. And what had happened to Philomemnon? She looked up and around. From behind the mirrors, the palace seemed constructed of spiderwebs of slanting shafts of light. Exactly what had Timias and Gloriana done that had made all this possible?

The gremlins were indeed bound to the Caul, just as Petri had said. But Timias spoke as if their involvement went deeper than mere payment. No wonder they couldn't leave the palace grounds. Or could they? Was that belief just part of the ensorcellment which held them bound in Faerie in the form of miniature goblins? One thing was very clear—they were far more than the exotic servants bred for amusement that most sidhe believed them to be.

And Petri's fears were quite correct. But the quality of Timias's voice was changing, and she realized he was moving away. She leaned as close to the glass as she dared, so that her cheek nearly touched the surface. In this posture, discovery was certain if they pushed the curtain aside suddenly, but she could hear nearly everything. "We have time, my Queen, a little time to determine what the best course of action is to be—"

"But Samhain approaches, Timias. I hear the whispers. I know what's being said. That the Caul is dangerous, disastrous, that it must be destroyed—"

"Let me tell you it's not that simple." Once again, Delphinea could hear Timias with crystalline clarity and she eased back from the frame. "Yes, it's true that Samhain approaches and the gremlins will go mad. But listen to me, Alemandine, all is not so dire as you might believe. This year Samhain coincides with Samhain in the Shadowlands. Xerruw will never be able to prevent his goblins from rushing across the border into the Shadowlands on the first Hag's hunt his people have known in an age. Let them gorge—it gives us time—"

"But what if the UnMaking of the Caul is the end of—"

"I'm not talking about an UnMaking, Alemandine. I'm talking about a ReMaking. We shall construct another Caul if we must. We shall do it, I tell you. It was done once, and we can do it again. It's always easier to do something the second time."

"But, Timias—" Alemandine's voice was faint, tremulous, and Delphinea truly doubted she had the strength to even contemplate such an undertaking, let alone participate in it. That effort alone might be her undoing. "They say the Caul is poison—"

"The Caul is not poison," he thundered, and Delphinea stepped aside as the mirror shuddered in its frame. "Look in the mirror, Alemandine. Look in the mirro—" The silk parted with a jerk, and Delphinea darted back just in time, flattening herself against the wall. Her heart pounded visibly. But neither had seen her for Timias only continued, "The time has come for you to reach within and summon up the strength of your mother, summon up the strength I know you must possess, and rule this land as Queen and sovereign. And listen not to those who would convince you otherwise. In the Caul is your power, Alemandine. Seize it, use it, know it. Call it back to you. It is your birthright, claim it. Demand that it return to you. It is yours by right."

Overcome by curiosity, Delphinea dared a peek through the thin gap in the curtains. As she expected, Alemandine was at her dressing table, her long, white hair like pure spun sugar around her pale angular face. Above her, looming like a vulture, Timias's own face hung, vulpine and wolfish, a gray replica so like the Queen's, Delphinea had to place a hand on the wall to steady herself. The resemblance was so striking she almost gasped audibly, wondering why she had never noticed it before. She pressed her hand against her mouth, for suddenly it occurred to her that Alemandine and

Vinaver were not at all the twins everyone supposed them to be. Sisters, yes—daughters of the same mother, carried in the same mighty womb at once, perhaps—but not the children of the same father. And she understood why Vinaver hated Timias and Timias, Vinaver, and she realized that no matter how many plots or coups Vinaver attempted to organize, Timias would always retain the upper hand. Ultimately. For he carried more than the force of age and long tradition, a living link to the legends of the past. He was the unacknowledged father of the Queen.

Did he know? Delphinea wondered, as she trembled. Did the Queen? As she watched from the safety of her vantage point, Timias picked up an ivory-handled brush and dragged it slowly through the Queen's hair. Pale and white and luminous as a cloud, it shimmered beneath the wrinkled leather of his hands. Something twisted inside her, something sickened, as Timias leaned over the Queen, crooning gently as she closed her eyes and leaned back against his chest. "There, there, my dearest child," Delphinea heard him murmur, as she tiptoed closer, drawn by his wooing tone. "There, there, my sweetest Queen. Rest. The Faerie Queen shall bless thee, no goblin claw shall rend thee, no harm at dusk befall thee. Let the goblins hunt in Shadow a season if they will. We have till the Darkening Day. After all, it may be the lon-gest night of the year, but every night thereafter is just a tiny bit shorter." He looked up, and meeting Alemandine's eyes, appeared to stare straight into the mirror, and Delphinea started, for she was sure he'd seen her. Stumbling back, she turned, slipped and fell. A shoe tumbled out of her reach, down into one of the long shadowy crevices. She heard footsteps behind her, and abandoning her shoe for the moment, scrambled through the labyrinthine maze with the homing instinct of a salmon, toward the safety of her own turret. It was time to turn to the only one she knew she could trust. She was going to contact her mother if she had to leave the Court herself.

She tumbled out of the glass, breathing hard, heart racing. She had not run so fast in longer than she cared to admit and suddenly she felt a pang of homesickness. She closed her eyes and pressed herself against the wall beside the mirror, willing her heart to slow, her breathing to ease. A sound made her open her eyes into Petri's curious gaze.

The question he gestured did not match the one she read in his deep brown eyes. *The Most Ancient, Admirable, and Honorable Lord High Councilor will be pleased to welcome you at luncheon if you would be so most exquisitely kind as to join him?*

She swallowed hard. She owed it to Petri to find out exactly what Timias had in store for the gremlins, but every instinct protested as she nodded. "Of course, Petri. Convey to Lord Timias my deepest and most sincere thanks and anticipation." He turned to go, and Delphinea watched his small straight back disappear down the branching corridor, thinking as she did so it was the last time she would ever see Petri again.

11

For the rest of her life, Nessa associated the scent of apples with the sound of running water, and the cool touch of a woman's hand on her forehead. When she finally opened her eyes, she realized she had not been dreaming, that she had indeed been staring straight up into the branches of a spreading apple tree. Someone had constructed a surprisingly snug roof by interweaving strips of hide and reeds to form a covering that wove in and out and around the branches. She turned her head and met Granny Molly's dark eyes and kind face. From somewhere close by, she heard the sound of rushing water.

"Awake at last?"

Nessa took a deep breath and tried to speak, but her voice came out in a croak.

Molly smiled. "Take your time. You've been sleeping for the better part of two days."

Nessa coughed to clear her throat. "Two days?" She tried to come upright on one elbow, but the sudden movement sent a stab of pain rippling across her chest and down her arm. She winced and peered down at the thick bandage wrapped around her upper body. "I remember I went to kill the last goblin, but it wasn't really dead. It reached up—" She broke off, remembering the rest of it all too well. Mostly she remembered the look on Uwen's face when he caught her as she fell.

Molly was nodding, obviously pleased that her patient was mending. "Ah, Sir Kian told me what happened. So far, it's healing well. You won't be scarred much, and you need have no fear of not nursing your babbies." Molly ignored the flame of Nessa's blush and continued briskly, "I think you were as much exhausted as anything. Seems you've had quite an ordeal." Molly picked up a pitcher and poured liquid into a clay cup. "Have some water."

Obediently, Nessa drank, remembering snatches of the journey. She remembered all too well the long hours in the bone-jarring cart and their arrival at the Keep. By that time, the wound felt like a burning brand and every bounce and bump over the rough and rutted road drove it deeper into her chest. She touched the thick bandage experimentally. "It hurt so much." She knew what pain was—for no blacksmith escaped the occasional accidental burn, bang, or scrape. But this pain was like nothing she'd ever felt before, a pain that seeped down like molten metal through the layers of skin and muscle and bone.

Molly was watching her closely. She bent and touched Nessa's cheek with the back of her hand. "How do you feel now?"

"Better than I did. How long have I been here?" Nessa lay back against the pillows, feeling suddenly exhausted by the effort of waking up.

"The better part of two days. They brought you in late in the afternoon of the day before yesterday. Do you remember that at all?"

"A little." Nessa wrinkled her forehead. The memories were mostly of a sudden rush of strange faces, and a burst of pain so searing when they'd moved her that she'd fainted. She looked around the snug little shelter. "This is Killcarrick?"

"Aye." Molly followed her glance and smiled. "Well, just outside this tent is Killcarrick. I had them bring you out here with me. The keep itself is overcrowded. There're no quiet corners to be found anywhere. I thought you needed the rest."

Their eyes met and Nessa understood. Out of sight, out of mind and fewer to ask questions she'd rather not answer. "Where's Griffin?"

At that Molly's face darkened. "The Duke's men took him. There's some great doing planned—the Duke called for blacksmiths. They came the day before you did."

"Took him where?"

"To Ardagh, they said."

Nessa drew a deep breath, feeling at once both disappointed and curiously reprieved that her reunion with Griffin was to be delayed. Now she wouldn't have to answer his questions, or make any awkward explanations involving Artimour, the reason he'd given her the ring, and the reasons she felt so drawn to him. And if Griffin were well enough to be taken into the Duke's service, physically, he must be all right, so her worries on that score were eased. "What about Granny Wren? Is she all right?"

Again a shadow passed over Molly's face. "She's the same. No change at all."

"Why? What's wrong with her?"

Molly shrugged. "Well, now. If I knew the answer to that I'd be the High Grand Druid himself. I think if you ask me, it's because she's even more exhausted than you were. She's old and she didn't really have the energy she used to work the spell she cast. It was surely a greater working than anything that's ever been attempted in a long time."

"Maybe she's waiting for Samhain," Nessa whispered, staring up into the low-bending branches of the apple tree. The trunk was near her head, and the wood smelled sweet and clean. A gentle breeze was stirring through the branches, and the little enclosure was heated by a small stone pit. It was her own pillow that was soft beneath her cheek. She took a deep breath experimentally. The wound ached but not terribly. It certainly felt better than she remembered. She glanced at Molly, who was staring at her. "What's wrong?"

"Why'd you say that, child? That she's waiting for Samhain? Who told you that?"

Nessa shrugged, feeling uncomfortable suddenly under the scrutiny. "No one. It just occurred to me, that's all—she's so tired—'twould be easier then, I think, when the doors open of themselves, to step into the Summerlands—" She broke off, for Molly's mouth was open.

"You don't know what you're saying, do you, child?" At Nessa's slow shake of the head, Molly continued, even as Nessa listened in disbelief. "If you're not a Beltane-child, surely I've never met one. It's knowing such as yours—the knowing that comes without being taught—that's one of the surest signs of the Beltane-born." It was Molly's turn to stop speaking abruptly. Exhausted already, Nessa let it go, but resolved to ask Molly more when the opportune moment arose. And since it looked as if Molly had brought her to her own shelter, there would surely be plenty of those. But Molly was continuing, in the same brisk tone her father used when he didn't want to deal with questions. "We'll speak of this all later. Griffin told me, Nessa, where you've been. It was well you thought to cover that ring with a rag. It screams so loudly of the OtherWorld I can hear it whispering even now."

Nessa shrank back against the pillows. "You saw the ring—"

"It looked like a bandage, child. I thought it must cover a wound. Fortunately I was alone and the hour was late, for even by candlelight it shone a color I could not have imagined and the workmanship itself…well. Let's just say you'd not have been left alone for two days if anyone else had seen it. Some great working is afoot. Sir Kian has already left for Gar. The other knight—Uwen—has orders to bring you to the Duke as quickly as you're able to travel."

"To the Duke himself?"

"Aye." Molly leaned forward. "Have you any idea why? Is it because of your father?"

"I don't think so," Nessa replied, with a deep sigh that made the wound ache. Molly's mention of Dougal made her miss her father all over again.

"Then why?"

"Because..." Nessa stared up at the intricate crazy quilt of reeds and hides and branches above the cot. "Of the dagger." She turned her head on the pillow and met Molly's eyes. "The silver dagger I made for the Duke of Allovale and one of the sidhe."

The sun had long since slid behind the trees on the opposite side of the river when Molly made her way from the relative peace of the lean-to nestled beneath the apple tree to the bustle of the castle courtyard. Nessa slept again, the healing sleep of the young. That she'd pushed herself beyond the limits of her endurance was mostly what ailed her. She'd faded in and out all afternoon, but what she'd told Molly had made the wicce-woman reach for her shawl and set a few more squares of peat in the stone fire pit just outside the lean-to long before the autumn sun sank below the tree line. For it seemed that Samhain approached not just in Brynhyvar, but in the OtherWorld as well. She had never heard of such a conjunction happening without the protection of the Caul. What would be the effect of such an event now, when there was nothing to stop the goblins from raiding where they would? Puny corn magic didn't stand a chance against such an onslaught. Even the great stone walls of the keep looked woefully insubstantial. The gash on

Nessa's chest was ugly, and both knights had verified that the girl had been merely scraped. And on Samhain, every human would be vulnerable. Nessa's descriptions of the devastation of Killcairn were enough to sicken her, and to confirm that the unbelievable stories of the refugees who'd swept through Killcrag weren't so unbelievable after all. It made her cold all over whenever she thought of it as she clutched her shawl close to her throat and nodded and smiled greetings as she edged her way through the throng.

She headed into the central court, where the refugees were lined up for their evening rations of soup and bread, and paused when she recognized the Sheriff supervising the loading of long wrapped bundles into a cart. The bundles were being carried out of the now-vacated forge. Surely the blacksmith's equipment wasn't wanted as well? She squinted in the torchlight, trying to see what exactly was going on, when Uwen, the redheaded knight who'd ridden in with Nessa, approached with a wrapped loaf of bread in one hand, and a crock of soup in the other. He waved first one item at her, and then the other. "Granny! Granny Molly, I thought to bring you supper. Any news, any change in the blacksmith maid?"

Molly smiled. It had been apparent from the beginning that this knight was smitten with Nessa. He'd hovered like a mother hen until she'd shooed him away, and yesterday, he'd found three separate excuses to check the girl's progress. "Well, sir knight, your patience is to be rewarded. Nessa woke up this afternoon, and she's well on her way to mending. She needs a few days yet, before she can travel safely, and there're other considerations as well, but you'll be delighted to know you'll be able to present her to your lord in perhaps a fortnight's time."

A light flared then dimmed in his eyes. "A fortnight, you say?" He looked troubled. "That long?"

Molly hesitated. She could not explain where they stood; the crowd was getting deeper by the moment. It would cause a widespread panic if she were overheard. "I'll explain elsewhere, sir knight. It's as well you thought to find me. I'd come to find you, too."

He flashed her one of his crooked smiles and she nodded in the direction of the Sheriff. It was clear that he was overseeing the emptying out of the forge. "What's all that about?"

Uwen looked in the direction at which she nodded. "Ah. That. In truth, I'm not sure. 'Tis Cadwyr's men. They asked about some weapons left in the forge—something to do with the smiths who left the other day—"

"Weapons—" Molly bit her lip. "You don't suppose—" She broke off. Gathering her skirts, she forced her way through the crowds of refugees, Uwen loping along behind, trying not to spill his pot of soup. "Sheriff," she cried. "Lord Sheriff!"

"—sure that that's the last of them," the Sheriff was saying to the belted knight who wore the same plaid as the ones who'd taken Griffin. "One moment, Granny, if you will."

"Lord Sheriff—" At that he looked at her squarely, trying to intimidate her with the full force of his rank. But she would not be dissuaded. Her intuition was seldom far off the mark. "That wagon—what's in that wagon? What are they taking now?"

The knight looked at her from his parchment scroll, lips curving up in an interested leer. "Care to come and have a private look with me, Granny? If you give me just a turn of the glass or two, I'll be glad to show you all the way around the back of it." His men guffawed.

She did not deign to favor any of them with so much as a glance, instead planting herself right in front of the Sheriff with her hands on her hips so that he had no choice but to look at her. "Lord Sheriff?"

The Sheriff sighed with the air of a man defeated by a shrew. "It's nothing but the weapons, Granny. The weapons the young lad from Killcairn suggested that we make—you know, the ones he dipped in silver."

"Silver..." She glanced over her shoulder, beckoning Uwen. He was bobbing on the periphery of the crowd that was rapidly gathering. "Uwen, Sir Knight, please—a word with these men if you will. Do you mean to tell me you're going to allow these men to ride off with all the silvered weapons we've got in this keep, Sheriff?"

The Sheriff stared at her, then glanced up as Uwen shouldered his way through the press to stand beside her. "Such was my intention, aye, Granny. We've got a request from the Duke of Allovale, himself. What of it?"

She swallowed hard, forcing herself to speak as calmly and deliberately as possible. It was obvious he wanted nothing more than a reason to dismiss her as a hysterical woman. And she had to be careful of what she said. "You mustn't send those weapons off. You leave us vulnerable—"

"I have a writ of the Duke," said the knight. He turned back to the Sheriff and would've ignored Molly but Uwen stepped into the circle. He handed the bread and soup pot to Molly.

"Well now, that begs the question, doesn't it?" Uwen spoke softly but looked pointedly at the other knight's plaid. If he was confused about why she was so upset, he didn't show it. "Which Duke?"

The knight paused. He was a stockier man than Uwen, more powerfully built by far in the chest and arms, thighs bowed from a life spent mostly in the saddle. His lip curled in a sneer as he took Uwen's measure. "Duke Cadwyr of Allovale, of course."

"Ah." Uwen scratched his head. "Well now. 'Tis there we have the problem. For there's no of course about that at all. Lord Sheriff, who's the overlord of this keep?"

"Why, Donnor of Gar, of course."

"Ah. Of course. You see, Sir Knight, with all due respect, I think you've interpreted your orders a bit too liberally. You have no right to take these weapons."

"Gar has given us permission to take what we need—"

"Aye, but those weapons aren't just any weapons—they've been tipped with silver. Where'd the silver come from, Lord Sheriff?"

At that the Sheriff started and looked embarrassed. He cleared his throat and looked at his feet. "Well now. It came from the Duke's treasure, of course. I see your point, and it's a good one, Sir Uwen."

"Wait a minute, Sheriff. The weapons belong to Allovale now. You've ceded them over."

"Aye, but not the silver that's on them," Uwen interrupted, smiling apologetically. "In the name of the Duke of Gar—"

"And what gives you the right to speak in his name?" Allovale's knight swaggered forward, hand on his hilt.

But Uwen did not back down. Instead he took a single step forward. "I'm one of the First Company of the Duke's own house. I am well able to speak in his name, especially in a matter of defending his silver. In his name—"

"And in the name of Allovale—"

The knight reached for his sword, but the Sheriff cried, "Hold!" He put a hand on the knight's hilt. "Just a moment now. Sir Uwen's right. You may have the weapons but not the silver, and since there's no way of separating the two, especially now that you took even our 'prentice smiths, I'll have to ask you to unload the weapons. You've not permission from His Grace of Gar to take away his silver. I'll not have steel drawn over this, either. You either put up the sword, and unload the weapons, or I clap you all in the dock. I've more than men enough for that."

The knight opened his mouth, but Uwen forestalled his protests by plucking the parchment out of the Sheriff's hands. "Aye, indeed, here it is plain in black and white. Says weapons made by Griffin of Killcairn, says nothing of silver from the Duke's treasure." Over the knight's sputtering, he turned to the stablehands who'd gathered to watch and waved at them. "All right, now, all of you, let's get to this, shall we? Just put them back where you found them. That'll do for now, won't it, Sheriff?"

The Sheriff responded with a dumbfounded nod. Uwen winked. "All right then." He retrieved the pot of soup and the wrapped bread from Molly and made a little bow. "A very good evening to you, Sir Knight. I bid you try the soup before you leave. It's excellent and I promise you'll find nothing like it on the road."

They did not wait for a reply. Hastening through the crowd, Molly followed in Uwen's wake as he shouldered a way through. When at last they broke free of the main press, he turned to face her. "Now can you explain to me what I just did back there? And why?"

Molly made a little face. "Of course. But let's put the soup down first, shall we?"

With another wry grin he waved her on. "Lead the way, my lady Granny."

She could not help but chuckle, and led him back to her makeshift shelter beneath the apple tree. She took a deep breath as they came over the crest of the hill. The sweet scent of the wood was bracing, the low rush of the river calming. She indicated two short-legged stools beneath the spreading branches on either side of the rock-lined fire pit. She took the soup pot from him and hung it from the hook that hung from the tripod set over the flames. "Come, sit. We'll let it warm. It's beef, you say?"

"Has to be beef—or sheep—or pig. There's no deer for leagues all around." He sank down on one of the stools, the cloth-wrapped bread cradled loosely in his two hands. "And the waterfowl—the ducks and swans and herons, even the gulls—they've all flown off." He gazed up at her with a furrowed brow. "I'm thinking they know something we don't." As the shadows flickered across his face, she realized suddenly that part of his comical appearance was due to the fact that his jaw had once been broken and healed slightly askew. But for all his slight frame, he was the survivor of many battles, and she knew it was as much his wits, as his skill with any weapon that kept him alive. He turned his pale water-colored eyes on her. "But what was all that about, back there, not that I disagree with you. That Sheriff's a nitwit. Imagine letting the Duke's silver out of this castle just because some dunderhead with a writ shows up. But what's this about Samhain?"

Molly sank down on the other stool. She knew in her bones Nessa had not told either of the men who'd brought her here that she had been in the OtherWorld. So she answered carefully, constructing as plausible a lie as she could. "Nessa learned from the sidhe that Samhain approaches in the OtherWorld just as it does in this one. It appears that this year, the two will occur nearly simultaneously."

He blinked, shrugged, then shook his head. "Forgive me, Granny. I don't understand."

She sighed. "You will, soon enough. You know how on Samhain, the veils between the worlds—this world, the OtherWorld, and the Summerlands—all thin?" When he nodded vigorously, she continued. "If there's one thing all the old tales tell us, it's that time runs differently in the OtherWorld from the way it runs in ours. The days, the nights, do not line up—that's why in the stories, when a mortal disappears into TirNa'lugh, if he ever does return, he finds that years and years have passed here, while nothing close has passed for him."

"So what about it?"

"In other words, Samhain comes more frequently here. The years go faster, sir knight. And it comes less frequently in TirNa'lugh. But when the worlds line up—and all the veils and all the doors swing wide all at once—" She leaned across the fire and gripped his forearm. "Don't you see? I'm afraid that come this Samhain, we'll see sights the like of which we've never seen or even heard the tell of."

"And so what you're saying—"

"What I'm saying is that you can't take the chance of being on the road to Gar or anywhere else when Samhain falls. And all of us behind these walls had better burrow hard and burrow deep. And all who can reach a fortress such as this had better find their way to it. And we'd better find all the silver we can get our hands on and melt as much of it down as we can and cover as many weapons as we can find. That's why I wanted those weapons stopped from leaving these walls. They're all that stand between us and a goblin horde bigger than anything we can yet imagine. But I'm afraid we'll be able to soon enough. This year, when the goblins come knocking, the gates on both sides are wide open, and the land is full of fat and happy people who've no idea what's coming for them."

For a long moment, Uwen stared at her. Then he rose to his feet with a bitter curse. In the falling twilight, his shadow was long and skinny on the grass. A cool breeze blew up from the water, and the clouds massed and darkened on the western horizon. Molly pulled her shawl closer. "But Kian's counting on me to get her to Gar—he's afraid the Duke won't listen to him alone. How long till she's fit to travel?"

"A sennight. At least." Molly raised her chin, refusing to compromise.

"A sennight till she's fit to travel—three, four slow days to Gar—" He broke off. "Well." He shook his head and threw his hands up. "We do what we must. For surely I cannot leave these people here defenseless. The Sheriff's a well-intentioned man but it's clear his brain's as full of suet as his gut. Well, then. I guess we better see about hunkering down and seeing what there is to deal with. Kian may disagree, but I've seen what I've seen and I see that all the warm-blooded wild things have fled." He heaved an even deeper sigh, and turned to face her, mouth poised to speak. But whatever he meant to say was lost in the shouts of a gaggle of children, who ran up from the riverbank, pushing and shoving and tumbling over each other in their haste to be the first to bring the news that a dead man with long dark hair and pointed ears had washed up on the water's edge.

"Griffin." Engus nudged him as he burrowed deeper into the straw in the rough shelter that served as their quarters. "Come. Time to eat."

For answer, he only groaned. It had been long past midnight when they'd at last been allowed to sleep and dawn was just a faint sliver in the sky. He could feel it in his tired bones and aching eyes.

"Griffin." The nudge was harder now, more of the same kind of cuff his father used to give him when he was slow to rouse. "Breakfast. You need your strength."

It was the one thing they did for the smiths. Forced them to work till they dropped, perhaps, but fed them well—on eggs and bacon, a thick mush of oats and barley and some bracing tonic that gave them incredible energy and stamina for longer periods than he would have thought possible. But when the effects wore off, there was a general collapse that seemed to grow worse and worse with each successive day.

In a daze he sat up, fumbled around for his boots and realized he was still wearing them. He got to his feet with a stretch and a yawn and another cuff by Engus that was followed with a splash of cold water. He gasped and shook his wet hair back behind his ears. He could hear the guards—which was the only way he could think of them, for the place had the atmosphere of a prison—coming up the row of sleeping men, barking orders.

"Come on, get up, you sleeping beauties. One more day and then you rest—come now, each man to do his duty—there's work to be done for your clan and your Duke—" The harsh voices drew near, and Griffin shook himself awake. He stumbled into line behind Engus. In the gray morning light, he could see huge torches were burning, shedding light on the wagons that were beginning to wind out of the camp, bearing load after load of silver-coated weapons. He watched, puzzled, wondering why the weapons were needed here—if they were preparing for a goblin onslaught, why not send out messengers across the land to prepare the people? Or were they preparing for some sort of invasion?

The question occupied his mind every time it drifted off of Nessa. He took a deep breath and pushed all thoughts of her away. He had rapidly realized he'd get no sympathy from the other smiths and apprentices. They'd all, it seemed, left wives and loves behind. It was better to wonder about what they were doing and why they were doing it in that particular location. Load after load of silver melted down in the great cauldrons, then sword after sword, spear after spear, even shields and mail shirts, helmets and body armor, vambraces, and greaves. And now loaded onto these wagons, and hauled away to only the goddess and the god knew where.

"Where are they taking everything?" he asked Engus, more to show that he was awake, than that he expected the man to have an answer.

"They're headed south," he replied. "South and east is Ardagh. So it's just as they told us, I think. They're laying some trap, but who knows what they're up to?"

"Why do they need the weapons coated in silver?" put in one of the other apprentices from Killcarrick, a dark- haired boy a few years younger than Griffin named Gareth.

Griffin stared at the wagons trundling over the brightening hills. "Samhain's coming. It makes sense, really." *If you'd seen what I've seen.*

But he did not want to call up the horrors of Killcairn, and when Gareth ignored him, and chattered on, Griffin was silent. "And wait till you hear what we're to make today."

Engus shook his head. "You mean we're to do more than dip things in silver?"

"Aye, indeed." He wet his lips and looked around. "I heard the guards talking about it when I passed them on the way to the latrine. They say we're to start making the shackles today."

"Shackles?"

"Aye, and chains and they want a lot and they want them quick. And wait till you hear this—there's to be silver in the mix."

"More silver? Cadwyr going after the Goblin King himself?"

"I don't know. Shall I go back and find out?"

The line moved forward, into the torchlight, and Griffin could see the boy's wide glazed eyes in his pale, tired face. He was in that frantic stage beyond mere fatigue. All around him men in varying degrees of exhaustion shuffled and slumped. All of them were tired, even the strongest, feeling the strain of working day and night for four straight days, fueled by that strange, sweet brew. He would have to pay more attention to it, he thought, for his limbs felt heavy as lead weights, his head as thick as a block of iron. He was reaching the limits of his own endurance. He closed his eyes as a wave of dizziness swept through him and concentrated on Engus's voice.

"No, no, lad, that's all right. Shackles and chains, you say. I suppose we'll find out what it's all about soon enough. How're you holding up, lads?" As if he'd read Griffin's mind, Engus cast an assessing eye on both of them.

"Well enough," he answered, and Gareth echoed him.

"Good lads. We'll get this job done and then we'll go home, eh? And you find about that girl of yourn, Griffin." Engus winked. "And you, young man, you hang close to me, you hear? Your mammy'll hunt us from the Summerlands if she thinks I'm letting her Gareth wander among these ruffians, you hear?"

But Griffin's smile and Gareth's reply were both cut short when another man, just ahead of them in the line to get their bowls of oats and eggs, turned and said, "Oh, no, friends. This job's not the end of it at all. We're on to Allovale next. Haven't you heard? They're meaning to march us from here across two rivers and into the uplands, to the silver mines."

His grim eyes met Engus's, then Gareth's, then finally Griffin's. "I'm sorry to be the bearer of bad news, my friends. But this job is just the first our Duke has set before us."

"But Gar will never let that happen—" Gareth said, his young voice high and piping in the thin morning air.

"Aye," said Engus. "The Duke of Gar's a fair man. He'll not require more of any man than what he's due."

"Aye, but don't you realize? Gar's writ runs not on Allovale's turf. And that's where we happen to be standing. He's got us right where he wants us. And we'll do exactly what he tells us." He paused, to let that sink in, then said, "And if you don't believe me, it's because you don't know Cadwyr."

A guard barked an order and the line lurched forward, even as Griffin considered the implications of that remark. It hurt to think, for his tired brain felt thick as the oats in the steaming bowl someone thrust into his hand. A wooden spoon was slapped into the other. He moved forward, and someone else dropped three boiled eggs, still in their shells, into the middle of the oats. "Thanks," he muttered, more out of habit than gratitude.

A general grumble spread up and down the line, as the rumors ran back and forth. Griffin followed Engus to a space at one of the long rows of tables and accepted a beaker of something that resembled foaming milk but smelled richer and sweeter than a honeycomb. He sniffed it deeply and the stench of burning metal, sweat-damp linen, and unwashed men receded, replaced by the aroma of a summer meadow. All around him, men were eating silently, ravenously, cracking into the eggs, slurping up the oats. Griffin looked around.

Whatever it was, it gave them the energy to do what they must. He wondered if anyone else was giving any thought to why chains and shackles were necessary, and what would be required of them all at the silver mines of Allovale.

Young Gareth leaned forward over his bowl, a milk mustache formed on his upper lip. "Do you think it's all true what they say—?"

"Eat your breakfast." The guard slammed the butt end of a pike down on the table between the two. "Shut your gobbers."

Engus held up his hands for peace and gestured to Gareth. "Just eat now, lad. Go on." He nodded at the guard. "He's not more than a boy, surely you see that. He's curious is all."

"He don't need to be curious to do his work." The guard lowered his pike and stalked away.

Griffin dipped his spoon into his bowl and wondered if the chains and shackles were for themselves.

"I don't believe for a moment they mean to exchange hostages. I don't believe for a moment they intend anything but a trap." Renvahr shook his head and folded his arms with a smirk of disgust. "Why—suddenly—should Gar decide he wants to exchange hostages?"

From her armchair at the other end of the table, Merle met her brother's eyes with an approving nod and caressed the soft caramel ears of her lapdog, while she watched Lord Wellis of Uisna, Commander of the King's forces and grizzled veteran of a hundred cattle raids, look up from his position over the great map beneath its protective glass. "I think it's likely he's received less support from his fellow chieftains than he'd counted on. Gar's lands run long, but he needs his clans to muster an army of any force big enough to challenge what you represent, my lord." He paused and bowed in Merle's direction as well. "The return of certain hostages may in fact even be a requirement of some of the war chiefs before they agree to rally to Gar."

She smiled. Most of the lords of the Uisna lowlands had ties of blood or marriage or both to Humbria, which made them very agreeable. The lapdog sighed beneath her touch and relaxed its small body. On the floor in front of the hearth, Hoell sat cross-legged, a pack of scrying cards spread out before him. He was deliberately and intently gazing into each of them in slow turn. It gave her chills to watch for some reason. She turned her attention back to Renvahr.

"And you are absolutely certain there isn't some possibility that they're trying to draw us out into some sort of trap?"

Wellis shrugged. "Ordinarily I would agree with you, my lord, but the scouts are absolutely certain. There is no army large enough to threaten this castle heading in this direction. It's true, there appears to be some scattered forces dug in amidst the Ardagh uplands. But there's nothing to indicate Donnor's rallying of the clans has been successful so far. The upland clans are notorious for the incessant feuding they do amongst themselves. 'Tis no simple thing to get them to agree to anything. Only Pentland has begun any sort of march, and they're far too far away to be a threat to us."

"Then why is Gar not insisting on the return of Pentland's son? Have you seen who they've asked for? If Pentland is the great ally of Gar that it appears he is, why have they not requested the return of Pentland's son?"

In the long silence, Merle listened to the long spears of rain lash against the windows. The first of the autumn storms had come at last. She turned back to Hoell, who was mesmerized by the leaping flames as he hummed a tuneless little song. He was utterly oblivious that the fate of his kingdom was being discussed just an arm's length from where he sat.

"My lord Protector, I've no answer for that specifically. The young lord of Pentland is not being held here, as you know. Perhaps that had something to do with their list. But the walls of Ardagh have never been breached. It's not my intention to move the main forces of our army out. I'll move small units out into the hills—we'll flank them all the way from the Daraghduin if we must. There's no way Gar can muster anything close to what's needed to truly threaten us."

"What about Allovale? Aren't the uplands riddled with his clan?"

Wellis shrugged and made a small grimace. "I'd scarce say they're riddled with him, my lord. There're a few septs here and there, sprinkled throughout the hills. There're not enough to muster more than maybe two or three hundred mounted men at the most. Nothing that would threaten Ardagh."

Merle thrust the lapdog she held onto the floor and brushed off her skirts as she rose. "I say we've nothing to lose by agreeing to meet with them. Maybe we can put this whole dreadful matter behind us."

Renvahr smiled as if his hose was tied too tightly. "And I will most respectfully remind Your Majesty that I am Lord Protector of this realm and I will thank you to keep your say to yourself until you're asked for it."

If looks could kill, Renvahr would've been in the later stages of rot. She was careful to control the urge to flounce over to the window seat. She picked up her own pack of scrying cards in their green velvet sack while the men went back to dickering. She gazed out into the lowering storm. The clouds were massing from all directions, now, the winds blowing fitfully in great gusts that swept about the towers in flat sheets of icy rain. Winter was coming, the child was growing. She shuffled the cards loosely, only half-aware of them in her hands, and as she did so, one seemed to leap out of the deck. It hit her in the chest, and bounced off to tumble facedown on the floor. She gasped. A card jumping out of the deck usually meant that the card had some particular message.

She bent and turned it over, frowning when she saw it was the Nine of Earth. A well-dressed woman presided over a lush garden, a hawk on her arm. The hawk's eyes seemed to catch Merle's. She placed the rest of the deck down, examining the card carefully. Each time she looked at the hawk, a throb seemed to go through her. She racked her brain, trying to remember exactly what the hawk portended. It was the long view—the overall picture. Suddenly the card seemed to speak directly to her, silently affirming that a reading now could provide crucial information.

With shaking hands, she picked up the rest, and rapidly laid out four cards to depict the current situation. She frowned to see what they were. The Seven of Air. The Tower. The Five of Water. The Two of Air. They were cards of deceit, upheaval, regret, and decision. She bit her lip, trying to decipher some coherent meaning. She drew two more to represent that which opposes. A reversed Queen of Fire and the Solitary Man. She rubbed a thumb over her third eye, hoping to clear her second sight. She had the frustrating feeling she wasn't understanding the message. The reversed Queen suggested some weakness in herself. And the Solitary Man suggested a period of intense inner focus. She drew back, trying to assess all the cards together, wishing she had one of her father's oracles to consult regarding her interpretations. *Go with your instincts.* She remembered the words of her earliest teacher and took a deep breath. She wished she had a better idea of the timing suggested by the cards. Was this a look from this point forward, or the entire situation from the beginning?

The hawk seemed to indicate the long view, she reminded herself, deciding to assume the timing encompassed the entire rebellion. Well then. The opposing cards seemed to suggest that she was going to have to enter a period of intense self-reflection in order to make some decision. Or had the decision already been made? Frustrated, she placed down two more cards, to signify that which supports.

The Eight of Water and Three of Fire lay revealed. The Three was auspicious—it showed a figure standing on a river bank, watching his ships sail in. *Or sail by.* It was the voice of her teacher, and it chilled her to the bone. *No,* she thought immediately. *No, surely not. Every other reading has indicated great success.* But the Eight was less auspicious and it made her pause, even as she heard Renvahr assent to the exchange. A cloaked figure journeyed away from eight bejeweled goblets, into an uncharted wasteland beyond. The question was always, were the goblets empty, or were they full, and if so, full of what? *Blood.* She ignored the inner voice, threw down a final card, then gasped aloud.

Death's white face grinned up at her. *No, surely not. Death never means death. It means change, transformation.* It was the card of ultimate change and transformation, an irrevocable passage from one state to another. As Wellis bowed to Renvahr, to the King, and finally to her, she smiled and stroked the small bulge below her navel. It was surely her imagination that the infant fluttered like one of the butterflies blooming from Death's black robes. What more encouraging card could there be? As the door closed behind Wellis with a little bump, Hoell turned to her, a puzzled look on his face. "Soldiers going soon?"

"Yes, Your Majesty," answered Renvahr with a smirk, before Merle could speak. "Your soldiers go to defend your throne—such as it is."

But Hoell was peering down at the card he held in his hand, his brow furrowed in uncharacteristic discontent.

"What's wrong, Your Majesty?" asked Merle.

For answer he held up the very same Death card. "Card. Not pretty."

Suddenly she was frightened. "Cancel the negotiations, Renvahr. I don't think we should agree to meet."

With a stifled curse, Renvahr stormed toward the door. At the threshold he paused. "I don't run a campaign based on cards, little sister. I told you weeks ago this enterprise was absurd but you made sure Father would hear of it, didn't you?" She opened her mouth to protest, but he cut her off savagely. "So now I've received a directive from our dear father himself, ordering me to bring this rebellion to as quick a conclusion as possible by any means at my disposal. And having been reassured that there is no hint of trap in this, I have no choice but to parley." He turned on his heel and stalked from the room, leaving Merle and Hoell staring at each other in mutual dismay.

The baskets were full of neatly folded bandages, sheets and towels and the candles were burned to stubs when the knock came at the door. Cecily looked up, startled, even as Eofe bolted to her feet. "Who could that be at this hour?"

"We'll see right now, my lady." In three long strides, Eofe was across the room. She seized the door and threw it open, to reveal Donnor himself standing there. He was dressed in his riding clothes, and Cecily knew at once he meant to sleep in them, the sooner to be in the saddle the moment the sun rose.

Cecily stood up unsteadily. She could not remember the last time Donnor had come to her chambers, particularly after dark. "My lord? Is aught amiss?" Eofe glanced back over her shoulder, with a raised brow, but Cecily beckoned. "Please—please come in."

Donnor nodded to Eofe. "I—" He broke off, and cleared his throat. "I wondered if I might have a word with you. My lady."

Cecily nodded, mystified. "Of course, my lord. Eofe, if you'd excuse us?"

"At once, my lady." The older woman dropped an immediate curtsy and vanished, drawing the door shut behind her. Cecily wondered how close to the keyhole Eofe'd crouched.

Donnor was standing just inside the door. He looked awkward and uncomfortable, and she pitied him. Perhaps this was a chance to finally make him listen to her sense about Cadwyr. But his first words forestalled that. "I—" Again he stopped to clear his throat. "I wanted to come and tell you that I realize that when you came to me before, you were only motivated out of concern for me. I ride out at first light, lady. I would not part with you on unpleasant terms."

"Where are you going, Donnor?"

He took a breath, then hesitated. "I'm sorry, Cecily. I can't tell you. It's better that you don't know. I'll explain it all to you when I come back. But I have to ask you to trust me now."

What if you don't come back? The question burned in her mind, but he gave her no chance to ask it. He held out his hand awkwardly as a page to his first infatuation. "I—" Again he paused with pained hesitation. Then he said, "But I hoped—"

He broke off and looked so miserable, she was moved to prompt, "Hoped?"

"I hoped that when I return we might begin again, Cecily. Things will be—different—very different from the way they are now, and I promise I will explain it all to you. You must trust that I believe that. When I return, everything will be very, very different."

Because you're going to your death and Cadwyr's lead-

ing the way. She wanted to scream the warning. It angered her that he was so set in what he was willing to hear. But she only said, "Are you truly sure this is the right course of action, Donnor? It's not just your future at stake, after all. I need to believe that the men who march with you will not shed their blood in vain."

He jerked his head back as if she slapped him. His eyes hardened and she knew at once she'd said the wrong thing. "Fear not, my lady, I've called up none of your kin for this endeavor. You may sleep easy this night, and every other, for I've asked nothing of your blood."

"You misunderstand me, Donnor." She shook her head and sadness swept over her. What had gone wrong between them had not begun at Beltane. "You came to me this night in peace. In peace I bid you go."

"Is that the best you have for me, Cecily?"

A wave of complex emotions enveloped her, thickening her throat, blurring her vision. As he turned to go, she found her voice at last. She darted across the room, caught up his age-spotted hand and pressed it to her cheek. "I beg you, my lord, on our unborn children, to listen to me." He was staring at her as if she'd suddenly gone mad, but she didn't care. She was going to speak her piece if it was the last thing she did. "I have a bad, bad feeling about this. I don't trust Cadwyr—I think he's leading you into some sort of trap. Why can't you at least wait for more of your Company to come back?"

"Because." His eyes held hers. "I can't tell you anything more than that." For a moment, she thought he might say something else, but then he only bent and kissed her cheek awkwardly. "I appreciate your concern, my dear. Rest well. I'll be gone by the time you rise."

He didn't want to hear what she had to say. There was nothing else to do but let him go. She watched the door close with a little knock of finality and hoped this was not the last time she would ever see Donnor alive.

Cadwyr did not need to look up to know that Finuviel had come into the room. It was in the way the candles flared and spluttered, in the way a log split in the center of the fire, and broke apart in a shower of twinkling sparks. A brush of air swirled past his cheek, carrying on it the scent of water. The shadows intensified, and the walls seemed to swell, to thicken, as if the very stones and mortar expanded. The room felt suddenly smaller, even as the barest ghost of a breeze tickled his face once more. He shifted in the fur-lined armchair as his pulse gave a little hiccup, and his palms grew ever so slightly moist. "Is everything ready?"

Finuviel stood just inside the door, tall and silent and still, poised as a spear. So perfectly did his black garb blend into the shadows, that his face, glowing with some internal incandescence, appeared to float, just below the lintel. He smiled, drawing back his lips, even as he shook the hood off his head, so that his black curls spilled like gleaming raven feathers over his shoulders and chest. He whipped off his gloves, his long hands graceful in the flickering light, then bowed. "Indeed, my lord Duke. The host but awaits my order. And the hours pass so quickly here—'twill seem that hardly any time at all has gone by since last they saw me." He unhooked his cloak, and it cascaded off his shoulders.

He threw it over the table, then turned to Cadwyr, still wearing that inscrutable smile. "Shall we drink to the success of our enterprise?"

So mesmerized by Finuviel's actions, so enchanted by the rise and fall of his voice, Cadwyr came to himself with a start, alarmed to have to shake himself from a reverie into which he'd been so easily lulled. He cleared his throat, assessing the sidhe. Finuviel's color was high, his eyes were bright. He was looking at Cadwyr with the intensity of—of a what, wondered Cadwyr. He nodded at the table to cover his confusion. "There's wine in that flagon—or I can call for honey mead."

But Finuviel silenced him with a wave of his hand. "Forgive me, my friend, I can't drink the stuff you mortals call wine. And so great an undertaking as ours deserves some special recognition. So let us drink the wine of Faerie—we'll use your cups of mortal make." From inside his doublet, he withdrew a small gold flask and held it up. In the reddish firelight, it glowed as if it contained a fire itself.

Cadwyr inhaled sharply. The wine of Faerie—the wine of the sidhe—was said to be the most potent in all the worlds and a single goblet all that was required to render a grown man stewed in drunken bliss. He smiled, feeling uncustomarily off balance. The room was growing warm. He could feel the drops of sweat beginning to trickle down his neck. "We ride at crack of dawn tomorrow, my lord Prince. Surely we should not be profligate in our pleasures tonight?"

Finuviel glanced at the flask, then back at Cadwyr. "Just a taste. Just a toast. Surely, you—we deserve it." Their eyes met and Cadwyr flushed as he felt his body stir in response to the unmistakable invitation in the sidhe's eyes.

The discipline of years kept Cadwyr steady on his feet as he rose, feeling suddenly pinned between the chair, the fire and the table. Finuviel stood between him and the door, though why should that matter, he wondered. He felt trapped, and it was not a feeling he was accustomed to. And why should he? He was the one who had the Caul, the one thing Finuviel needed to claim the throne of the Other-World. The Caul hung from a leather cord, a reassuring bulge over his heart, secure in its leather pouch. Finuviel was not the predator here. That thought steadied Cadwyr even more, and he nodded as Finuviel reached across the table for the two goblets which stood side by side beside the flagon of mortal wine, then uncorked the Faerie flask.

The dark purple scent of the wine bloomed like some exotic flower. He breathed deeply, involuntarily, the scent alone so intoxicating he felt as if he'd already downed a full goblet. He met Finuviel's eyes squarely as he accepted one of the goblets, then raised it. "To success."

Finuviel nodded, moving as if to music. He raised his own goblet in return, and Cadwyr was struck by how thick and crude the stem looked between Finuviel's slim fingers. Finu-viel touched the lip of the cup gently to the lip of Cadwyr's in a gesture so intimate, Cadwyr felt a pang of lust so heady it was like another draught of wine. "To success," echoed Finuviel. His tone harmonized with Cadwyr's, so that the simple phrase sounded like a song.

With difficulty, Cadwyr shook off the powerful attraction. He'd felt the lure of the sidhe every time he was in Finuviel's presence, but this was like nothing he'd ever felt before. It was a need so great he wasn't certain he wanted to control it. The aroma rising from the burgundy liquid in the goblet tantalized and teased him like a wanton woman, tempting him to open every sense, surrender all control, and give himself over to the exhilaration of the sidhe.

He looked down and saw his hand tremble visibly. He wanted to roll a mouthful of the wine around on his tongue to see if it stung his mouth with its promised delight. And it took all his self-control not to tip his head all the way back, and pour the wine down his throat, draining the goblet to its dregs, licking the inside dry. He could suddenly imagine the rough scrape of the clay on his tongue. Involuntarily he licked his lips and saw Finuviel watching.

He took a deep breath to steady himself and inhaled another whiff of wine. It swirled around inside his head, tangling up his thoughts like long skeins of red and purple silk. He raised the goblet and touched the surface of the wine with the tip of his tongue.

The taste that exploded in his mouth reduced every other wine he'd ever tasted, even the finest Lacquilean vintages, to vinegar. He could taste each component individually and as part of a bouquet more complex than anything he'd ever imagined—pulpy grape, burning sun, acrid soil, drenching rain.

He took another sip and noticed that Finuviel's mouth was red, his lips swollen. They gleamed in the candlelight, wet from the wine. And suddenly Cadwyr knew exactly how he wanted to taste the Faerie wine. He wanted to lean over and lick it from Finuviel's lips.

He drew back, breathing hard. Finuviel was very still, watching him from the depths of those glittering eyes. Eyes like emeralds, Cadwyr thought, or eyes like the dappled green of the forest floor on a summer's day at high noon. Eyes you'd see in a stag, glimpsed elusively through the trees on the hunt. Yes, that was it. That's what Finuviel reminded him of. A stag. As he stared, Finuviel himself seemed to change, the angles of his face lifting, the planes of his shoulders and chest broadening, deepening, rounding until the creature who stood before him seemed some hybrid of man and stag—powerful and strong, vitally, vigorously, and wholly male. His clothes seemed utterly superfluous, and in that moment, so did Cadwyr's. He wanted to rip and tear their clothes away to feel Finuviel's satin nakedness against his own rougher hide.

Cadwyr seized the goblet, quaffing back a long drink. He set it down, hand trembling as if he'd been drinking all night, head beginning to spin in slow circles, body swelling, his heart beating like a drum pounding out the strokes of galley-slaves. *Strokes,* he thought. Unconsciously he tightened the muscles of his buttocks.

Finuviel raised his own goblet, took another drink, deeper this time, head thrown back, the cords of his neck working as the liquid moved down his throat. *Down his throat,* thought Cadwyr, *into that hot, hard belly.*

But I will be no slave. He reached across the space that separated them and grabbed for Finuviel, a wolf leaping for a stag, but Finuviel caught him, held him, pressed Cadwyr's long length to his so that they stood chest to chest, groin to groin. Finuviel's nostrils flared like a stallion's, but his voice was even and firm, cutting through the rampant tide of rut like a sword. "Are you sure you want this as well, mortal?"

Cadwyr hesitated a moment, intent only on the residue of wine that glistened in the wavering light as Finuviel's mouth moved. Finuviel's skin was smooth as honey mixed with butter, and suddenly Cadwyr wanted to taste that, too. For answer, he pressed his mouth on Finuviel's, licking in slow deliberate swirls, until the sidhe gasped and parted his lips, his head turning and falling back against Cadwyr's shoulder, the feathery tips of his coal-black curls tickling Cadwyr's cheek.

Cadwyr chuckled, low in his throat, then plunged his tongue deeper, working at the sweet, soft mouth like a suckling child or a drought-parched man, until Finuviel's knees buckled and he moaned as he collapsed into Cadwyr's embrace.

It was late, very late—so late it was early, to use one of Dougal's favorite phrases—when Nessa awoke, teased out of sleep by the demands of an overfull bladder. She lay a moment, blinking up at the shadowy crazy quilt above her head. It was very still. She could hear Molly's soft breathing, punctuated by louder and longer snores. *Uwen,* she thought. He'd been there when she'd woken up to eat.

With a sigh she swung her legs over the side of the cot, and saw that she was alone in the little shelter. Through the gaps in the rugs that formed the lean-to walls, she saw both Molly and Uwen sleeping on straw pallets beneath the stars on either side of the fire pit. The air was cool but the interior of the little shelter was warm. She fumbled under the cot for the chamberpot. As she squatted over it, sighing with relief, she noticed through one gap, a dark object dangling from a limb. It swayed gently back and forth in the breeze. From her perch on the pot, she couldn't quite see what it was. She covered the pot quickly as soon as she finished, shoved it back under the cot, then cautiously got to her feet. A wave of dizziness swept over her, but she persevered, creeping first in a low crouch, holding onto the low stool. Then she reached up, grasped a low-hanging branch, and stood as upright as the shelter would allow.

She pushed aside the rough hide that served as a crude door, and squinted up. Against the dark gray sky of first light, she saw that the object looked like a boot dangling on the end of the branch. She staggered closer, holding on to her branch, straining her eyes in the dawn's gray twilight, scarcely daring to believe what she saw. For unless she was dreaming, she was quite sure that the boot that hung so tantalizingly out of her reach was impossibly, unbelievably, her very own work boot.

12

The news that Kian had been spotted on the river road reached Cecily in the stillroom, where she worked with Mag and half a dozen maidservants, overseeing the distillation of the Samhain herbs. The old moon was waning, the hours of daylight were dwindling, and there was much to be done with Samhain fast approaching. Preparations had been sorely neglected this year. Mag stood with pursed lips, frowning as she consulted her master-list and ticked items off her inventory.

"What's wrong?" asked Cecily.

"That hot wet snap we had, my lady, set a mold among my drying herbs, and now—"

But Cecily was not really listening as Mag continued, gesturing here and there, holding up a leaf or two for her inspection. Normally she loved working in the stillroom, with its fragrant decoctions and infusions gently bubbling on the hearth, the bunches of drying herbs spaced regularly across the wooden ceiling beams, the little pots and pestles and mortars and tiny knives, each with their own special function. She was lucky to have such an accomplished herbalist as Mag as stillwife. But Cecily knew she'd been little help all day, her thoughts divided between Donnor, Cadwyr, and Kian. It disturbed her to think that Donnor's jealousy blinded him to the fact that the man he trusted with everything he had was not so much loyal to Donnor, himself, as to Donnor's possessions. Possessions which in Cadwyr's mind included her, possessions to which he felt entitled. And it frightened her to think of Donnor out there on the fog-bound roads, without even a quarter of the full company of the men who were sworn to protect him. Cadwyr had never taken such an oath, for all that he was Donnor's heir, for he had never ridden in the company of Donnor's knights. And why was that? she wondered, suddenly struck once more by the break in custom. She had always assumed that Cadwyr had been fostered in Donnor's house and had been surprised to find out a year ago that that had not been so. When she asked Donnor, his answer had been brief, noncommittal and dismissive. But it meant that Cadwyr had never sworn the oath that all the other young knights of the household were required to take.

She knew with granite certainty that Cadwyr would fall on her like a summer storm were Donnor to die. And that brought her thoughts round to Kian, for she would need him more than ever. But he was still at least three or four nights away, according to his message.

Where was he? she wondered, and, as if in response to her thoughts, one of the sharp-eyed boys who served as lookout in the topmost towers burst into the stillroom. "My lady—my lady Duchess—I seen him, m'self—Kian. I mean, Lord Kian—Lord Kian is coming—riding up the river road like the Black Hag herself is after him!"

"You hush that talk of Herself so near Samhain, boy." Mag frowned.

But even as Cecily's heart leapt with joy at the unexpected news, stabs of doubt and worry and a dark foreboding went through her. Why was he here already? What had happened to make him hasten back so quickly? She turned to Mag, and gripped the older woman's arm. "Something must've happened. The last message I had from Kian said not to expect him for a sennight."

Mag cocked her head, shrewd eyes bright in her flushed face. Like Cecily, her sleeves were rolled up to her stout elbows, her once-white apron splotched with oils and decoctions and greenish smears, and round rings of sweat stained the armpits of her worsted gown. There'd be no time to change, thought Cecily, as Mag said, "Then I suppose we'll find out soon enough what it is. Will he be riding out directly, do you think, after His Grace?"

Force of habit brought an instant assent to her lips, but for some reason, Cecily hesitated. "I don't know, Mag. With Donnor gone already—" She paused, wondering if Donnor even wanted Kian there. Was it possible he was involved in something he didn't want his First Knight to know?

The older woman raised one eyebrow and Cecily knew what she was thinking. The entire castle knew exactly what had happened at Beltane. Since then, Cecily and Kian had never been alone—that is, without Donnor—under the same roof. But would it be wise to send Kian out after Donnor? Cecily raised her head. They'd never done anything to merit the taint of Donnor's suspicions. And if her own suspicions about Cadwyr were correct, if Kian were at Donnor's side, Cadwyr would have to kill Kian to get to Donnor. And she desperately did not want Kian to die. Without Donnor, without Kian, she would truly be at Cadwyr's mercy. Cadwyr would force her to marry him before she'd ever have a chance to object.

Kian had already begun to raise the clans, including her own kinsmen. Perhaps there was some way for both of them to get to Killcarrick. No matter what happened, she had an instinctive feeling that she would be safer at Killcarrick, surrounded by a muster of men, most of whom would share her blood. She shook herself out of her reverie. "I suppose we'll see soon enough." She smiled her thanks to the young lookout. "Run down to the guardhouse, and ask the guards at the gates to send Lord Kian to me at once. And thank you for your trouble, young man. Tell the steward I said you were to have a honey cake." She turned back to Mag, all business, and nodded at the list in the woman's broad hands. "Let's get back to this." She was careful to keep her tone neutral. Better that her mind be full of nightshade, sage, and wormwood than the memories of Beltane which flitted about her mind unbidden as butterflies at this unexpected news of Kian's imminent arrival. And surely no better way to allay any latent suspicions that might be flitting about in anyone else's mind than to appear so absorbed in the Samhain preparations that she could not be bothered to change her gown.

He came directly from the saddle, ripe from the road. That alone disturbed her, for it told her that his news was truly urgent. He had not come merely in answer to her summons. He sought her out because the news—whatever news it was—was bad.

His cloak shed crumpled leaves and bits of bramble, and his boots were covered with mud. His face was haggard and drawn, and she wondered how long he'd been in the saddle and how fast he'd ridden to arrive so quickly. But it was the flat, dark look in his eyes and the grim downward set of his mouth that told her her feelings of foreboding were correct. He smelled strongly of horse. The maids paused and nudged each other, a tide of whispers and giggles rippling around the room.

But he caught her eyes as soon as he entered, and with only the briefest of bows, he gestured to the door. "Your Grace. I need a word with you at once. And you, too, Stillwife, if you'd be so kind as to come with us?"

Mag looked up from her mortar and pestle. "Me?"

"Aye." He turned on his heel and left the room.

Cecily glanced at Mag, alarmed. Both women doffed their aprons, and followed Kian, leaving the maids' speculative chorus to rise unchecked. He led them down the corridors and up the stairs and across the hall to Donnor's Council room. Both women glanced at each other as they followed his tall back. When at last they all stood within the confines of the quiet Council room, Kian turned to both of them. "Where's Donnor? At the guardhouse they tell me he's gone with Cadwyr to parley with Longborth and the Queen. Is that true?"

Both women nodded, and Cecily answered, "He left this morning. What's happened?"

He dropped into one of the chairs, elbow on the table, and rested his forehead in his open palm before answering. Exhaustion was etched in every line of his body, in the harsh canyons of shadow beneath his eyes. He looked up at them with gaunt eyes. "I have to make Donnor listen to me. There's more going on than Donnor knows. Do you have any idea where Cadwyr is?"

"He left with Donnor this morning at crack of dawn." Cecily's flat voice cut through the torrent of words. "What happened at Killcarrick?"

He shook his head again, gesturing to the chairs. "Sit. Stillwife, would you be kind enough to call for something to eat?"

Startled, Cecily realized she'd not even thought once about Kian's comfort, but Mag was at the door before he finished the sentence. "I'll be right back, my lord, my lady."

As the door shut behind her, he leaned forward and covered her hand with his. The palm was smooth and callused, the nails crusted with dirt. But she twined her own herb-stained fingers around his, glad he'd bought them a few moments alone. "You're very clever."

For answer, he grinned and drew the tip of one finger genty down the side of her cheek, tracing the line of her face. His eyes found hers and his expression was soft. "How are you?"

"Scared." She tightened her hand on Kian's. "I'm glad you've come back. I must tell you about Cadwyr—"

"Cadwyr?" Immediately his expression hardened. "He's in league with the sidhe—oh, yes, my sweet, sweet Cecily." He slumped back in his chair, shaking his head, as she stared at him in astonishment. "Wait till I tell you—" He broke off and rose as the door opened and closed, and Mag stepped in with a tray, on which was a loaf and a crock of soft cheese, as well as a goblet that foamed a rich brown. Kian's eyes lit up when he saw it and he said, "Ah, bless you, Stillwife."

"The first of the season's honey mead, my lord," Mag answered, dimpling like a maid. "We broke it open yesterday to see the Duke off proper."

Kian had the trick of making people like him, Cecily thought, as she watched Mag serve him. He was a natural leader, one who somehow made people want to follow him. Even into battle. But against Cadwyr? Cadwyr, who was in league with the sidhe? Was that really what she'd heard Kian say?

He took a long drink, then pulled off the heel of the bread and dipped it into the soft cheese. But between bites, he motioned to them. He sat down, still chewing, swallowed hard and took another bite.

"Take your time," Cecily murmured, for he ate with the air of a starving man.

"Forgive me, I'm famished," he said at last. "I forgot to ask for food at the Daraghduin when I changed horses. Stillwife, what can you tell us of corn magic?"

Startled, Cecily blinked as Mag frowned, clearly as taken aback as Cecily. She shrugged. "Corn magic? What of it?"

But Kian leaned forward and gripped the stillwife's arm. "Stillwife, I know you for a wicce-woman. We don't have time for secrets. I've seen things, Stillwife. I've seen goblins. I've seen what goblins do. I've seen how dead goblins walk if you don't behead them first. And Samhain's coming. At Killcarrick, I spoke to another granny who told me what that might mean, if the goblins are able to cross the border while all the doors and veils between the worlds are open."

Mag was staring at him, her bright eyes like iron nuggets in her wrinkled face. She glanced at Cecily, then sat back. "What are you talking about? Goblins?"

"A goblin was found dead in a little village north of Killcarrick, floating in the lake," Cecily explained. "That's why Kian went himself to rally the clans."

"Truly a goblin?" Mag whispered. Her expression was a mixture of disbelief, horror, and fascination.

"Truly." Kian nodded. Briefly he explained his journey. "It's true isn't it, that when Samhain comes, the doors open, and the goblins will hunt—"

"But—" Mag shook her head. "The druids say the border was sealed against the goblin horde with the Making of the Silver Caul of Bran Brownbeard. Such things have not happened—"

"You're right," said Kian. "Such things haven't happened, in an age or more. But the Caul doesn't seem to be working anymore for some reason. At least it stopped working long enough for a hunting party to carry off more than half a village. Now one of the wicce-women up there, one of the grannies, was able to work some sort of magic that seemed to hold them back. Can you—is there something you can do? Something to hold them back, come Samhain? She said that if the Caul wasn't working properly on Samhain, we'd all be in very big trouble. And she said she knew of nothing, but I thought perhaps her being only a simple country granny—perhaps you with your greater learning—"

But Mag was shaking her head, staring at Kian with a look that wavered between shock and dismay. She glanced at Cecily, then addressed Kian. "My lord, forgive me for speaking out so plain. It's only that what you say seems so impossible—I scarce know what to think, let alone how to stop anything—"

Kian patted her arm, eyes steady in his serious face. "I know that, Granny. But I'm afraid come Samhain, if something's not done, a lot of very innocent people and soldiers we can't afford to lose, will die more terrible deaths than you can imagine. I've seen what they do. I've seen what they leave behind."

Mag shook her head one final time, then sat back with crossed arms. "Those country grannies are the best of us, my lord. I may know my herbs and simples, but they're the ones who have the most knowledge of that which can't be taught."

"Then how do they learn it, if it can't be taught?"

She smiled, a little bitterly, thought Cecily, her eyes cast down. "It can't be taught, because it must be remembered. It's a knowing, a knowing that feels like a memory as it rises up from somewhere deep inside. And when the memory comes to you, you must be able to act upon it—it's an act of courage like none other, I can tell you. Some of us remember better than others, you see." She paused, and Cecily wondered what Mag herself was remembering. Then she went on, more briskly, the wistful note gone. "I wish I could tell you what you want to hear, my lord Knight. But on Samhain night, when the boundaries between the worlds dissolve, I know right now there's no corn magic that can hold those doors closed." She glanced at Cecily. "But perhaps there're other things that can be done. The druids should be consulted. They're the ones with goblin lore. Shall I see if I can find one, my lady? My lord?"

Cecily nodded without glancing at Kian. She could feel the tension rising off him and she was desperate to know more about Cadwyr's association with the sidhe. "Please, Mag. And then you'd better get back to the stillroom. I'll join you as soon as I can."

The older woman rose and curtsied, and it was clear that the magnitude of the impending disaster had banished any speculation about what might take place between the two of them in her absence. When they were alone again, Kian threw himself into the chair beside her, and took both her hands in his. "Tell me again where Donnor's gone."

"He's gone with Cadwyr to Ardagh. They've gone to great lengths to set up this parley very quickly—releasing hostages and such. But there's something else going on—"

"Cadwyr's in league with the sidhe, Cecily. That's what else is going on. There's more to this than you or I or Donnor, I'm quite sure, knows."

"I think Donnor does know." Cecily met Kian's eyes. "I think he does. I confronted him about Cadwyr, and he wouldn't admit anything. But he didn't deny anything, either."

"What did you tell him about Cadwyr?"

"I told him I didn't trust Cadwyr."

"Why? What reason did you give?"

She shrugged. "That was the awful part. I didn't have a reason—I didn't have a reason I could tell him. You see last night, Cadwyr came to me, in my private rooms. He was waiting for me, alone. He brought me a rose. He told me he'd always wanted me—that Donnor had stolen me from him. And he told me to be ready to greet the next King of Brynhyvar in five days' time—which is just enough time to go from here to Ardagh and back."

"Quickly though." Kian frowned. "Whatever they have planned, they're not expecting it to take very long. Did you know Cadwyr sent a writ around calling up all the smiths?" When Cecily shook her head, he went on. "Aye. Even from as far away as Killcarrick. Sent a troop around to bring them from all the villages and keeps. This is no parley they've got planned—this is a trap. The question is, which side gets to spring it?"

Kian released her hands and stalked to the hearth, holding the mug. He leaned on the mantel, looking into the dark hearth, and she realized there was a bone-chilling cold in the air. "By the Great Mother," he whispered.

"What is it, Kian?"

"I think I see. Donnor needs to move quickly, to strike a decisive blow before the Queen calls her Humbrian army across the water. But the clans are slow to rally. So he's found another ally—an ally the Humbrian Queen will never expect. I think I see it now. This is a trap indeed."

"What are you talking about?"

"I could be wrong about this, Cecily." He gazed into the cold hearth once again, his brow knit. He shook his head. "I think the sooner I leave—"

"Kian, I don't want you to leave. I want you to stay here, with me. I begged Donnor to wait for you—for any of the knights of the Company. And he refused. He said they'd a brief opportunity and he couldn't wait. I don't think he wants you there."

"A brief opportunity to do what?"

"He wouldn't say."

"Then, Cecily, I've a duty—"

"You've a duty to me, too. You're here because of me—you're one of my kin. I have a bad feeling about this parley, or whatever it's to be, Kian. Donnor wouldn't listen to me because I didn't dare to tell him that Cadwyr came to me, and declared his—his intentions toward me, saying Donnor stole me from him—that when Donnor approached my parents for my hand, it was supposed to be on behalf of Cadwyr. But when Donnor saw me, and realized the size of my dower portion, and all the allegiances I bring, he was quick to snatch me for himself. At least, that's how Cadwyr put it."

Kian slowly straightened. "I see." A light burned in the depths of those hollow, exhausted eyes.

"And he made it very clear that he considered me one of Donnor's possessions."

"One that he'd inherit?"

"That's the feeling he gave me." She gripped the arms of the chair to keep herself from throwing herself at him. "If he does intend to kill Donnor, as I've thought all along, I don't want you there. You'll make him kill you. Donnor went willingly, though I begged him not to, without you. If the worst happens, and Donnor dies, by Cadwyr's hand or any other, I want you here. Maybe we should even go to Killcarrick—is that not where the clans are to rally?"

From the expression on his face, she saw that her words made sense. "But I am sworn..." His voice trailed off, as he struggled with the tug of dual allegiances. "Cecily, is it possible you may have misunderstood Cadwyr when he came to you? It's not uncommon for a man about to ride to battle to declare—"

"By the Hag, Kian, will you not listen to me? Aye, Cadwyr spoke like a man about to ride to battle—a man about to ride to battle who fully intends to come back and claim what he thinks should rightfully be his."

"Then if there's a chance that Donnor's life's in danger, I am bound—"

"There is something more than a word of honor between us, Kian," Cecily said.

His head jerked up as if she'd slapped him. "You don't need to remind me of that."

"If you're right about Samhain—that the goblins will attack—is that not a good reason to stay back? You'd leave us vulnerable?"

Kian took a deep breath. "If Donnor dies, and I make no attempt to go to him—now—when I know he's about to be endangered, they could charge me with the blood fine. Do you see, Cecily?"

With a cry of frustration, she rose from her seat and pounded on the table. "Kian of Garn, you said I'd a better claim to the throne of Brynhyvar than Donnor. Well, then, by the goddess, as she who would be your Queen, I demand you stay here and protect me. From Cadwyr, from the goblins, from Donnor himself if that's my wish. We'll go before the Fining Court together if we must. I've a right to choose a champion, a protector, in the absence of my husband, and so, Kian of Garn, I choose you."

His head reared back, his nostrils flared, and in the long silence that followed, she thought he might refuse. Finally he nodded. "All right. I'll accept that. I can even produce a witness who saw Cadwyr in the company of a sidhe. I can even produce evidence Cadwyr was there."

"What evidence? To prove that he was where?"

"Cadwyr never went to Far Nearing. He went instead to Killcairn—aye, where the dead goblin was found, to Dougal, the smith who's dead it would seem."

"But why? What did he want of Dougal? And why go all the way to him?"

"Dougal of Killcairn was known for three things—the quality of his work, the strength of his mead, and the tightness of his mouth. If I wanted someone to make me a silver dagger so that I could give it to a sidhe, Dougal'd be at the top of my list."

"And how do you know for sure Cadwyr was there if Dougal's now dead?"

"Because even though Dougal wasn't there when Cadwyr came back for the dagger, his daughter was."

"And she gave them this dagger?"

"She made them the dagger." He shook his head shortly, hands on his hips. "You don't see her like too often. We don't have much time, Cecily. What shall we tell the druid?"

Cecily took a deep breath and rubbed her temples. The sun was slanting through the western windows, the afternoon was fading into dusk. "I say we tell him all of it. After all, who knows what Cadwyr intends to lead home from the battle?"

The slant of the bright afternoon sun roused Nessa from a sleep every bit as deep as the one that had lasted two days, and for a long moment she lay, wondering how long she'd slept this time. Then she bolted upright, as she remembered the boot she was sure she'd seen last night. She hauled herself out of bed, heedless of the rush of dizziness and nearly fell as she stumbled outside. The boot was gone. She looked around. Granny Molly wasn't anywhere to be found, either. Could she have been dreaming? She sank down onto one of Molly's short three-legged stools. No, she thought, wrapping her arms around herself. The afternoon sun was warm, but the air off the river was chilly. In the days since she'd been hurt, autumn had fallen like an ax. She looked around, wondering if she had strength enough to seek out Molly. A light sweat broke out on her forehead and she knew instinctively it wasn't the best idea. And yet, she was so sure, so certain it had been one of the ones she'd given to Artimour. She waited a few moments, then decided.

She managed to nearly finish dressing when Molly returned from whatever errand had called her away. "What do you think you're doing, my girl?"

Nessa jumped, startled. "I thought to come looking for you."

"What on earth for? You need to be resting—if you want

to sit outside in this fine sun, certainly, but there's no need for you to come traipsing through the castle—"

"But I wanted to ask you—" Nessa sank down onto the cot, overcome with a sudden faintness that weakened her knees and made her pulse flutter. "Wanted to ask you—" she panted, the world slowly closing in around her, reducing itself down to one small pinhole of light in the center of a great blackness.

"Ah, Great Mother, help us." Molly tsk-tsked as she pushed Nessa's head gently down between her knees. "Breathe, girl, breathe. What did you want to ask me?"

"The boot," Nessa murmured. "The boot. Where's that boot that was in the tree? Where'd you find it? Where's it now?" The spinning in her head eased, and the world expanded out to normal vision. She raised her head cautiously to see Molly staring at her in shock. "There was a boot hanging on that branch last night—I saw it when I woke up close to dawn to pizzle. Where is it?"

"What do you know about this boot?" Molly was looking at her with that same close look as when she'd first mentioned the Beltane-born.

"I wasn't dreaming, then? There was a boot?"

"Indeed. It was found within the doublet of a sidhe who washed up beside the river shore last night. I didn't mention it to you last night when you woke for dinner. You've coped with enough for right now, but I wouldn't have held it from you any longer. The entire castle is fair abuzz with it. Now. What about the boot?"

"I think it's mine. And if it is, the sidhe who was found is the sidhe who gave me this." She held out the hand Molly had rebandaged so expertly she knew no one would ever guess it concealed a ring. "Where is he? Can you bring him to me?"

But Molly was looking at her with concern in those dark soft eyes. "You didn't hear me, child. He's close to death. He was stabbed. Someone tried to get him right through the heart. But if it is your boot, it saved him, for there's a long slash, but the leather stopped most of it. He'd be dead already if it weren't for that."

Nessa blinked. "Stabbed?"

Molly nodded, eyes on the river. "It looks like a stab wound. But the edges of the wound are burned, as if the knife was hot when it was put into him and his clothes, too, are singed around the slash."

"And the boot? Is that singed, too?" Nessa asked, as a truly horrific possibility began to dawn.

"The boot's dark brown leather, and it's wet. 'Twould be hard to see if it were burned."

"But not impossible." Nessa swallowed hard. "Not if you look closely enough—in very bright sun." She'd made a silver dagger. The boot that she'd given to Artimour turns up with a long slash in it. What else could she think but that Artimour was the one who'd been stabbed? *But you don't know for sure,* argued the voice of her reason. *You don't even know that it's your boot.*

"Nessa?" Molly asked gently, softly. "What is it? What does it matter whether or not the boot is singed in the same way as the clothes?"

"Because silver wouldn't singe my boot," Nessa said slowly, trying to think as clearly as the sinking sick feeling in the pit of her stomach would let her. "But it would anything of the OtherWorld—clothes, skin, leather." She looked at Granny Molly with absolute misery. "That's why he wanted a silver dagger, you see. He'd have to use a silver dagger so that Artimour would die the true death."

Molly gently pushed an errant strand of hair off Nessa's face. "Who would, child? What are you talking about?"

"I'm talking about the silver dagger I made." She felt dizzy, light-headed, but not in danger of fainting. The monstrous possibility that the silver dagger might be used to kill Artimour had never occurred to her. "I asked why he needed it. Cadwyr said it would purchase the throne of Brynhyvar. But he didn't say how. And I didn't think to ask—I didn't think it could possibly mean murder. It wasn't even a weapon, not really. There'd not been enough time to properly temper the metal—" The nausea was stronger now, a constriction in the back of her throat, convulsing her tongue, so that it was hard to talk. "And there were things I wasn't sure of—" *Sharpen it.* Cadwyr's words echoed through her mind. *Sharpen it.* She remembered the sound of the blade on the whetstone, the blue sparks that flared and snapped in the early-morning gloom. She remembered the intensity in the sidhe's eyes as he'd stared at the dull blade. There'd been no time to polish it. But they hadn't seemed to care.

Molly shot her an assessing look and reached for the waterskin. "Drink some of this, child. Slowly. How could killing a sidhe guarantee the throne of Brynhyvar?"

"Granny Molly, you don't understand," Nessa cried. "What if Cadwyr lied? I made a silver dagger. I gave it to Cadwyr and the sidhe. What if that's what they really wanted it for? To kill Artimour?" And then Molly could only pat her back and murmur as Nessa doubled over and vomited onto the grass.

The cold night air refreshed Cecily like a summer cloudburst as she crept out of the castle. In her simple gray cloak and white veil, any guard who saw her would only think her one of the nurses who tended the recovering wounded in the growing cluster of tents hastily set up just beyond the main gates. She paused within the well of shadow beside the castle walls and took a few long invigorating breaths. How long had it been since she'd stepped outside these walls, she wondered? Between all the additional tasks generated by the nursing of the wounded, Donnor's comings and goings, and the preparations for Samhain, such as they'd been, it had been much too long since she'd even taken a walk by the river.

Much too long, she thought, too long she'd let herself be bound not just by these walls, but by all the restrictions their height and breadth implied. For a split second, she envisioned calling for a horse, not the lady's palfrey that sufficed for her genteel picnics and herb-gatherings, but a real horse, bred for speed and strength and stamina, and taking off, down that straight and narrow road, over the causeway, and disappearing into the mountain glens of her childhood. What would they say—her father, her mother and her brothers—if she simply appeared one day, and announced that she'd had enough of Donnor?

She was a free woman—over twenty-one—and she could divorce Donnor, if she chose, but her dowry was only eight years paid. Each year that went by saw a bigger and bigger portion paid directly to her, until, in the twenty-first year of her marriage, the entire portion would be hers. Thus, it was as much to her material advantage to stay married as it was to Donnor's.

But she was rich enough already to maintain herself in an acceptable state. Perhaps she wouldn't be able to live as lavishly as she'd lived here or beneath her father's roof. She could divorce Donnor, but what would be said of her, divorcing him at such a critical juncture? Such an action on her part would be construed as disapproval of the rebellion, even as support for Hoell. It would set her against her own blood, her own kin. And Kian, too—Kian with his calm and certain sense of honor and of right would see a divorce now as a repudiation of all that he believed. And so she was trapped here, in this castle, by these walls, by the oaths that bound her to Donnor.

But the dark line of trees beckoned, the forest melting into a solid wall of black as far as the eye could see. The Forest of Gar stretched all the way from the mountains of the Killcarrick uplands to the Sea. What she wouldn't give for one fast horse. Restlessly she paced down the road, the measured steps of the sentries on the battlements above reminding her it was foolish to stray too far from the shelter of Gar's great walls.

Here and there, interspersed between the tents, a fire burned brightly and a few hardy souls huddled close together within the periphery of light and warmth. But otherwise the night was quiet, the sky was dark and the silver crescent of the waning moon hung over the trees. She wondered what the people would say if she were to go and sit beside them. Would they know her for the duchess, she wondered? Or would they simply accept her as one of themselves? If her clothes and her hands did not give her away, she knew her speech and her manners would. When had she become such a duchess, she wondered? Not a boy her age had ever beaten her in a race. But something had happened, she thought, in the last eight years. Something had changed her. Something had made her a silent observer to the world around her, silent as that black line of trees and even less a participant. Was it Donnor, who treated her like the child he saw her as? Except in bed, she thought ruefully. But even that had ended. All that was left between them now were the bonds of oath and honor.

The trees stood like sentries, almost as if they were waiting, she thought, as she gathered her cloak more closely around her shoulders. Waiting for the goblin horde the druid, Kestrel, had grudgingly agreed was a possibility come Samhain? Waiting for Donnor to return? Or something else entirely? The too-familiar pang of thwarted need lanced through her with a pain she scarcely felt. The last time she'd gone to walk beneath that canopy, Kian had led her there. Did the trees remember, she wondered, what occurred beneath their branches, beside their trunks, upon their fallen leaves? Time was blunting the memories, wearing them away like coins too frequently fingered. She wondered if their Beltane bed still existed within that thick stand of pines, in the little hollow, if the mound of needles that had formed their couch had grown higher over the summer, or been dispersed by the heavy rains. She remembered the little fire pit he'd made so carefully, so that the little lean-to was lit with a flickering warmth, how it had illuminated the flowers he'd twined about the entrance and woven into the branches that had formed the shelter. She remembered how the heat had kindled the scent, so that the very air was sweet with violet, honeysuckle and rose. In the woods, beneath the sheltering pines, she had felt a part of herself stirring to life by the presence of the goddess, a part of herself that she'd forgotten. A part of herself that was fading into a dim and distant memory, while she became a shadow of what she'd been.

She closed her eyes and suddenly felt as if the great castle was a sleeping monster, squatting in the deep gash of its dungeons and cellars, trapping her within its rock-lined walls, its straight and narrow corridors, its high and rigid towers that rose at stark right angles out of the broad breast of the land.

Through the thin soles of her houseslippers, she felt the hard, compacted earth, the uneven scrape of the thin gravel. It was the same earth that rolled out from beneath these castle walls, down to the river, out to the meadow, into the forest. She opened her eyes and saw an unmistakable flash of light flicker halfway across the meadow. She frowned. Surely she was mistaken. But no, there it was again. From this distance, it was difficult to see exactly who, or what, it was.

She wondered if the sentries above saw it, too. And then she realized it must be someone who'd left the castle, just as she had. They would not raise an alarm over someone leaving. The light bobbed into view once more and she realized it was indeed someone heading into the woods. But who would go there at this hour? One of the grannies who'd come from the nearby hamlets to help nurse? Or Mag herself, intent upon harvesting some herb under a certain moon?

This was the hour when all who could be were long abed, an hour that she hoped saw Kian fast asleep. His face, already drawn with fatigue even before Kestrel had joined them, had grown gray with exhaustion as the afternoon darkened into dusk. Although the druid was even more skeptical than Mag, he had at least agreed with Cecily that in light of the possibility of a goblin attack on Samhain, Kian was needed to direct the defenses of Gar. And he'd agreed to consult with his druid brethren, although he made it clear he did not believe the blacksmith girl had actually seen what she said she'd seen, and Cecily doubted the man even believed that goblins or sidhe existed except in the legends.

He seemed more interested in hearing details of the Samhain feast and was most disappointed when she told him that venison was not on the menu. There'd been no knights to hunt the deer. It was shortly after that, she remembered, that he had agreed, insisted, that Kian should stay at Gar.

Now Samhain was six—no, five nights away. They had not much time to make the preparations. The last thing she'd done before she'd retired was to give the order that a hundredweight of silver was to be released from Donnor's great store beneath the castle. She wondered if Kian had spared a thought for her before he fell asleep.

For she'd certainly had plenty of him. Thoughts of him in his narrow bed within the soldier's billets while she lay sleepless in the great curtained bed made her restless between the linen sheets. Her nightgown bunched and clung to her too-warm body. She tried opening the casement above her bed to relieve the stuffiness, but even that didn't help. The night was too still, she'd told herself, there was no breeze beyond that initial cold blast.

But she couldn't bring herself to remove the nightgown and lie naked. She knew the linen would lie too stiffly over her body. The sheets would brush against her breasts, rub against her nipples as she moved. They would twine between her legs, catch in the crease of her buttocks. No, she did not want to lie naked in her bed. Not alone, anyway. And Kian lay just a few scant paces away, down a few stairs, through a few hallways, across a courtyard or two, while somewhere south of that black mountain mass to the south, Donnor slept beneath the same sickle moon. At least she hoped they both slept. She could not. Out of frustrated need, she donned a loose overdress over her nightgown. She wrapped herself in a cloak and a veil, took a lantern and slipped out, unnoticed, into the dark stillness of the night.

The light flashed again. It was nearly at the tree line now, and as she watched, it disappeared into the trees. It could not be goblins, she thought. It was most likely Mag, she decided. Midnight, under a waning moon, so close to Samhain, would be an ideal time to gather certain herbs—nightshade, perhaps, wormwood and mullein. And this would be an ideal time to talk to Mag, for Mag knew more about herbs and simples than any other granny she'd ever met. If Kian and the country granny were right, it would not hurt to learn as much about corn magic as possible. And it would distract her.

Scarcely daring to believe her boldness, she picked up her lantern and walked down the long avenue which led over the moat, and away from the castle. She turned into the broad meadow, roughly following a track to intercept the bearer of the light. The light flashed again and this time she could see it within the trees for just a few minutes longer. The dew had fallen, and in the starlight, the knee-high grass sparkled as her skirts brushed through it. In the daytime, the meadow was a tangled blaze of red bittersweet berries and feathery goldenrod, but now it was like a gray-black sea that rustled and parted with a sigh. She realized with a start she was heading for the very spot where Kian had made their Beltane bed.

She held her cloak and veil close to her throat twined in one fist and quickened her pace. Her skirts made a soft whisper through the tall grasses, her slippers squeaked and slid on the damp ground. They'd be ruined by the time she got back to the castle. Her lantern creaked gently as it swayed in her hand. She held it as high as she could, peering into the dark night as she approached the grove of tall pines, and paused. The sweet resin was heavier than she expected in the cold night air. It was a scent that always brought her immediately back to Beltane. Her pulse quickened and she felt a rush of desire that nearly made her sob aloud. She closed her eyes with a soft groan that might have been a sob. The snap of a twig made her spin around, to see a tall figure leaning against a tree.

She stepped back, one hand pressed to her mouth, her heart jumping, her veil floating to the ground, forgotten. The lantern blew out as she dropped it. In that moment, every childhood tale of goblins, of sidhe, of maiden warnings came rushing back and she stumbled backward, even as some more rational corner of her brain recognized Kian just as the light winked out. "Great Mother." She was aware this edge of the great forest was considered a border realm, a middle-ground, one of the most dangerous and magical places of all, where things were not quite one thing, and not quite yet another—or not yet anything at all. From very far away, she heard the distant calls of the changing of the watch, and she knew that it was exactly midnight, the mid-point between dusk and dawn. Something seemed to stir, to swell, to waken within the trees.

"Forgive me, Cecily, I didn't mean to frighten you." His voice was like the caress of finest silk against bare skin. In the starlight, his pale hair gleamed white.

"What in the name of the goddess are you doing out here?" she demanded, angry that she should have been so scared. "It's the middle of the night."

"One might ask you the same thing." In the dark, she heard him moving until she felt that he stood less than a handspan from the tips of her breasts. "What are you doing out here in the middle of the night?"

"Me? I followed you. I saw your light—I thought it was Mag." He placed one finger against the gush of words. She gasped and was still. Through the thin soles of her wet slippers, she felt the earth seem to rise beneath her feet, like the gentlest swell of a wave beneath a coracle. As if in unison, the trees seemed to sigh. She felt a shiver tickle down her spine.

"Thought I was Mag?" He laughed, a soft chuckle deep in his throat.

"Why did you come here?"

For answer he picked up her hand. "Come." He led her through the trees and she knew exactly where he led her. In the center of the pine trees, a small fire leapt in the fire pit, and his lantern threw up a gold circle of light that illuminated the lean-to, and she saw that he had bunched up fresh pine needles, and covered the low bed with a cloak. It was exactly as it had been on Beltane, except for the flowers.

She looked up at him, scarcely daring to breathe.

"I wanted to remember, Cecily. I woke up, and I realized I was losing the memory of it." He moved behind her, wrapping his arms around her, and she flattened herself so that through the thick length of his plaid she felt his erection pressing into her back. Reverently he touched her loose braids. "So I came out here to see if being here again made me remember more."

"Oh, Kian," she said with a sob. She let her cloak fall open and she reached behind her to feel the long muscles of his thighs. She took a deep breath and this time the memory was complete, for entwined with the smells of resin and earth, burning wood and midnight air, sweaty wool and damp linen, was the slick salt musk of her arousal.

She knew he could smell it, too, that he could feel the heat that emanated in thick waves from her body in time to the slow drumming of her heart. "Cecily." His breath burned her ear, her name a caress. It was pitch-black all around them, the trees deeper black against black. The circle of light beckoned. "I don't know what games Donnor and Cadwyr are playing, and I don't know what's to come. But I do know I don't want to let you go. I came out here to remember, and here, I find you come to me. I don't think such things happen by accident. I'll let you go now, if you wish, for you are still Donnor's Duchess, and I am still his knight. But I would rather—"

"No," she cried, above the singing in her blood. "No," she said again, afraid that he'd misunderstood. "I don't want you to let me go. Here I won't be Donnor's. Not his Duchess, not his wife, and here I renounce all vows but those I make to you." The flesh between her legs swelled, her nipples knotting into hard buds against the layers of her clothing. "Will you be mine, Kian of Garn?" *For I will be yours.*

But he only turned her to face him with a low groan that might have been a sob, and pulled her mouth up to his with the savagery of passion too long held in check. *Yes and yes and yes.* She felt the words bubble up from somewhere deep inside, as his shining hair tumbled over her shoulders, as he lifted her up against his chest. *Yes and yes and yes,* she thought again. *All I say three times shall be; as I will, so let it be.*

The crying woke her close to dawn. She started up, out of the warm circle of Kian's arms, and listened to the lonely keen as it drifted down the valley. "What's wrong," he asked, pulling her back down beside him, even as the sound raised gooseflesh on her arms.

"I'm not sure," she whispered, as she curled back down beside him. "Sounds like someone mourning for the dead."

"Sounds like a cat howling for its mate." He turned on his side, drawing her into the curve of his belly. "Come now, sweet. Lie down."

She let him comfort her, let him draw her down to lie beneath him, let him wrap herself around him once again until the grayish light made them separate. But that eerie wail remained a part of every memory of that night.

The next time Nessa opened her eyes it was dark. Frustration at her own weakness roiled through her, for time—precious time—was passing while she slept. She could not be weak. If the sidhe who lay within the keep was indeed Artimour, was it possible that he'd been on his way to her with news of Dougal? Her mind churned with hopes and possibilities. Since last night, at least, Artimour had lain not three hundred yards away. *You don't know for sure that it's Artimour. If he's wounded, do you want him to be Artimour?* A pang went through her as she sat up and reached for the freshly laundered clothes Molly had left at the end of the cot.

No, she did not want him to be Artimour. She twisted the ring beneath the bandage, rubbing it like a talisman as if to reassure herself that it could not be Artimour, could not be the half-mortal for whom she'd felt that curious kinship. There was only one way to find out. She would no more allow the goblin wound to deter her now than she'd allowed Griffin to keep her from the OtherWorld. Molly had refused to let her go anywhere when she'd finished vomiting, getting her undressed and back into bed over Nessa's weak protests.

But Nessa was stronger this time. She could feel herself mending. Each time she awakened from one of these prolonged sleeps she was stronger than before, and the ache in the wound was turning into a deep itch somewhere just above her breastbone. Her stomach rumbled and for the first time, she realized she was famished. A cold breeze swirled beneath the hide walls, tickling her toes as she hauled herself out of bed. It carried the strong smell of stew, onions and garlic and beef, or maybe mutton and the burned earthy aroma of roasting turnips and potatoes. She poked her face out of the lean-to and her mouth watered as the scent of baking bread wafted by. Long bands of red and orange striped the western horizon, and above the river, the first stars twinkled in the indigo sky. Molly had most likely gone to fetch their dinner.

She shook out her tunic, amazed at how soft and clean Molly had managed to make it. All the tears had been neatly sewn, the burned spots patched. The pine-green scent of rosemary rose from the folds, and she caught the worn wool up and held it to her nose. Dougal knew how to wash clothes, knew how to get the worst of the dirt and the sweat out of them. But he did not know how to get them as soft and as sweet as this. She thought about that as she managed to dress quickly, then grabbed one of Molly's shawls and wrapped herself in it against the evening's chill. It reminded Nessa of Molly, herself, for the thick wool was dyed a deep purplish-blue, knit in some intricate subtle stitch. It smelled like lavender. She resolved to ask Molly what she did to make the clothes smell so good, and wondered what Dougal would say, if he knew. Would he simply shrug? Or would he scowl the way he did every time she mentioned one of the grannies?

This time, the dizziness did not strike until she was nearly halfway up the newly worn track to the castle. The wave overtook her as she reached the crest of the hill, and forced her to sag against the trunk of a silver birch. She put one palm flat on the papery bark, and closed her eyes, willing herself to breathe deeply into the enveloping black. She sank slowly to her knees, then pressed one cheek to the bark, clinging to the thin trunk with one arm as she collapsed.

The first sensation was so subtle she was quite sure she imagined it, for the tree trunk beneath her face seemed to rise and fall in a slow, rippling wave. But odd as the phenomenon was, she was too weak, too sick, to do anything but cling to the strong, but supple trunk, and crouch, helpless, at its base. Then she realized that the wave seemed to emanate from somewhere beneath her feet, then undulate all the way up the trunk. It was an odd sensation, but strangely comforting, as if she could hear the tree's heartbeat. *Yes,* she thought, in some detached corner of her mind that was completely uninvolved with her physical state. *Of course that's what I feel. It's the great beating heart of the tree.* She found it easy to breathe in time with the tree's steady pulse. Her lungs filled effortlessly with the waxy scent of the leaves, the green smell of the living wood. It seemed natural and right that she should give herself over to the tree's rhythm, so that the tree itself should somehow enter her awareness. She felt herself touched by something fragile and delicate but strong—strong to the depths of its roots that reached into the black earth, all the way to the solid bedrock below the ground, to the underground river that coursed invisibly through caverns a league or more beneath the surface. The tree drew its strength from the rocks, from the water, from the earth. *And so can I. So can I.* The realization startled her so that she opened her eyes and saw she sat in the midst of a yellow carpet of birch leaves, so that she felt as if she sat cradled on a very broad, bright lap. *So can I.* The third time the thought formed in her mind, the wave rolled directly through her and she gasped, as an energy such as she'd never felt before surged up and through her, from the soles of her feet, bringing her up from her crouch to her knees, to her feet, lifting her up so that one arm remained wrapped around the trunk, but the other reached up, up to the branches, to the light, to the air, to what she understood suddenly with shattering clarity as the other fundamental source of all strength. The tree's magic was that it combined dark earth and bright air, hard rock and running water into living energy. *And so can I.* This time she was afraid to think the thought again. She breathed deliberately, in and out, and the feeling continued up into her scalp, tickling the roots of her hair so that she laughed as her dark curls lifted of their own accord, crackling and snapping with sparks. Another wave surged up and she placed both hands on the trunk, feet planted squarely, instinctively allowing it to roll up and over and through her once more. The wound in her chest tingled. This time the wave didn't quite reach her head. It receded gently, as if the tree gathered it back into itself. Nessa was left facing the tree, forehead pressed to the trunk. She felt better than she had in a long time: lighter, stronger, faster. Harder, as if her very essence had somehow absorbed something of the tree's strength.

"Thank you," she whispered, scarcely sure of who or what she addressed. "Thank you very much." She stepped away from the tree, thinking that perhaps she'd only been overcome by the dizziness. She touched the bandage experimentally. The scab was itching terribly. She rubbed it and the itch eased. And there was no pain at all.

She stood a moment, staring up into the branches of the tree. Was it because she'd been to the OtherWorld that her senses seemed different, that she seemed to see things just a little differently from before? She felt comforted and strengthened in a way she'd never felt before. *Thank you,* she thought again. As she stepped away from the tree, she nearly tripped over a fallen branch lying half covered with leaves. Something told her to pick it up, and as she did so, she saw that the branch was long and straight and relatively smooth, the perfect height for a walking stick. The perfect height for her, she thought, and with a little smile, set off for the castle, leaning on the branch, not so much out of weakness but because it felt as good in her palm as the hand of an old friend.

She followed the path down through the center of the refugee camp and entered the keep through the open gates through which streamed a motley assortment of humanity. There was a relaxed, almost holiday air about it all, with men and women of all ages talking in excited groups, as they milled about with loaves of bread and crocks of stew. She caught the words Pentland, Shining One, and OtherWorld. Rumor ran rampant that the Shining Ones themselves would save them from the goblins. Samhain was very close, she thought, just a few days away. No one took much notice of her, as she maneuvered through the crowds, and up the steps into the great hall of the keep. There she paused, looking right and left. She knew that the sidhe lay in the Sheriff's own bed. She just had no idea where that might be. Finally one of the menservants noticed her loitering.

"Refugees outside, maiden." He pointed in the direction of the main doors.

For some reason she held out the birch staff. "Granny Molly—I—"

"Ah, the granny's upstairs." He gestured to the steps which led up off the hall. "With the Sheriff, and giving him a right good runaround from the sounds of it." He beckoned her closer, and looking around the hall, whispered, "Will you ask the corn granny to let you have a look at the sidhe? I want to know if it's true they've got horns like Herne's." He held out a leather cord, a beaded trinket dangling from it. "Well, maiden? Will you?"

"He doesn't have horns," she spat and took off in the direction he pointed, wondering if that was an indication of the sorts of things people said about her. At the top of the steps, she saw two open doors. From one she clearly heard Molly's voice, arguing with the Sheriff's low rumble. She peeked in the other. A great curtained bed stood in the center of the room, and a fire burned in the hearth, over which hung several iron kettles from hooks and trivets. Scarcely daring to breathe, she tightened her grip on the birch and crept into the bedroom.

The white curtains were drawn around three sides of the bed; only the side which faced the hearth were the curtains looped back. She tiptoed into the room, her boots heavy and clumping on the wooden floor, and gasped as she peered around the bedstead.

Surely the figure lying on the bed, beneath the drab linen

sheets, was not Artimour. He could not be Artimour, she thought, for this man—this being—lay so gray and still, she thought he must be dead already. She edged closer, gripping the staff, a hollow feeling in her gut, her throat constricting. The long black curls lay lank against the yellowish pillow, his nose was thin and pinched, his lips blue. But it was Artimour, and a pain went through her own heart. Was this a result of her handiwork?

His chest was bare, and a white bandage covered one side. She gazed at the perfect planes of his muscles beneath the skin as smooth as white satin. The rough covers were drawn up nearly to his shoulders. He looked like a marble statue lying on the bed, his sidhe blood far more obvious than it had been in the OtherWorld. But as she watched, his chest moved in a great sighing heave. He lived, but barely.

A sudden thump from the next room made her jump, and she glanced down to see if Artimour reacted, but he lay silent and still. Her hand hovered over his forehead, just for a second, and then she snatched it back as she heard the Sheriff begin to shout. "—coming here and asking me to melt down silver? Hanging around with that young knight has made you forget yourself and your place, woman."

There was another loud thump and then a muffled curse. Nessa tiptoed back to the door, and strained to hear Molly's low murmur. But the woman's voice was low, quiet and measured, and Nessa only caught the words, "Come Samhain—"

"Bah, woman, enough of your corn—" the rest of the sentence was lost beneath the thump of heavy footfalls, and Nessa dodged back, biting her bottom lip between her teeth as the Sheriff continued "—give no such orders without permission of the Duke himself. 'Tis his silver, after all, and I am charged with its oversight. How shall I explain to him that half his fortune is now coating his armory?"

"If you don't release more of that silver, Sheriff, you won't have the opportunity to explain anything to him."

"So you say, Granny, you won't have to answer to an angry Duke."

The heavy stride halted abruptly and Nessa knew Molly had somehow stopped him from storming past her. Her voice was clear and strong, determined and deliberate. "Doubt me, if you will, Sheriff. But you'd better have it ready, and a hot fire on that blacksmith's forge come Samhain."

With a snort, the Sheriff did indeed storm out, fuming something incomprehensible under his breath as Nessa darted back, just seconds from discovery. She was still breathing heavily when Molly came around the corner.

"You." Molly shook her head, hands on hips. "I should've known." She glanced from Nessa's stricken face to the bed. "It's him?"

Nessa nodded silently, her throat too thick to speak.

"I'm sorry, child." She cast a long appraising look on Nessa. "You're looking better. Much better." She took her by the chin and held her face to the light of the bright burning hearth. "Yes, you've got color back." Nessa's stomach rumbled audibly, and Molly smiled. "And your appetite." She cocked her head and nodded at the staff, for that's how Nessa was beginning to think of the birch branch. "What's this?"

Nessa took a deep breath. "I found it. Under the birch tree—"

"At the crest of the hill beside the path?" Molly was looking at her closely once more. Nessa nodded, and Molly's eyebrows flew up. "Did you now?" She turned away and began to gather up supplies, nodding in the direction of the wooden chair beside the hearth. "As soon as I change the poultice on his wound, I'll fetch our dinner. I'm sure you're glad to be up a bit, aren't you? But tell me, if you can, where was it lying? How'd you come to see it?"

"It was on the ground." Nessa answered uncertainly. Suddenly what she'd experienced under the tree seemed silly, unbelievable. But Molly was looking at her with that same intense look as when she'd spoken of Granny Wren waiting for Samhain.

"I looked for such a staff, and didn't see one. What made you notice it?"

"I started to get dizzy as I came up the hill. I had to rest beside the tree."

"Go on." Molly placed the linen, the pots of salve and basin on the table beside the bed.

"I sat beside the tree and then I felt better. And as I turned to leave, I saw the branch."

Molly nodded, her eyes focused on her work. "I see. Well, would you mind passing me a little of the bark?"

Nessa started. "Oh, certainly." She peeled the fragile white bark off the branch near the base, where the bark was fissured and peeled off in long strips.

"That's good." Molly nodded. "Would you like to see what I'm going to do?"

Nessa nodded, half-afraid to look. But she'd seen her share of nasty cuts and burns, her stomach was strong—certainly strengthened by the sights she'd seen recently. Molly gently stripped away the top bandage, to reveal a wet-looking pad of some yellowish salve. But it was the bottom pad, black and streaked with greenish pus, that made her nose wrinkle and her stomach turn. "What's that black stuff?" she whispered, as Molly dropped it into a waiting basin.

"It's the poison from the wound," Molly answered. "This salve—mostly honey and willow and a few other herbs—is made to draw off poison. That's what I wanted the birch bark for, but there were no branches lying on the ground with bark enough and I'd not had time to ask the tree properly."

She heard you anyway. The thought ran unbidden through Nessa's mind, as she leaned closer, to better inspect the now-exposed wound. She steeled herself. On the broad chest, just above the nipple, a long red line extended in a diagonal. The edges of the wound were black, and the flesh around it was puffy, and streaked with greenish lines beneath the skin. Molly gently dabbed the wound with salt water. Artimour grimaced, his eyelids fluttering, jaw clenching as the salt water seeped into the wound, and Nessa held her breath, half-expecting his eyes to open.

When they didn't, she forced herself to look at the wound again, and from the thin black slash, she was quite sure that whatever had stabbed him had been very, very sharp. Razor sharp, she thought.

"Hand me those strips of bark, girl." Molly wrapped the linen with the rest of the old bandages. She placed another long pad of linen directly over the wound, and then a few strips of birch bark, a few directly on his skin, the rest over the pad. Then she wrung another pad out in water so hot it steamed, and laid the cloth, still steaming, on top of the bark. Then she covered the whole with another bandage. "There now." She rinsed her hands and dried them briskly on her apron, picked up the basket and nodded at the chair. "I'll be back with a bite of supper for us both as soon as I take this to the laundry."

"Will he live?"

Molly shrugged again, and came to stand beside Nessa. "I'm amazed he lives yet, to tell you the truth. I had not thought a sidhe could withstand even the slightest touch of silver."

At that, Nessa looked up at her wonderingly. But Molly had never had the advantage of knowing what a full-blooded sidhe looked like. "He's half-mortal. He's not quite a sidhe."

Molly was silent for a long moment, then adjusted her basket on her hip with a sudden motion. "Well, then. I suppose that does explain that." She nodded at a basket full of apples on the hearth. "There's apples and cheese in that if you're hungry." Then she nodded at the staff, which Nessa leaned against the chair. "And mind you keep that safe. That's no small gift she gave you out there."

"She?" Nessa echoed, but even as Molly began to explain, part of her already understood.

"The tree—the silver birch. She must've liked you quite a lot, to send such a piece of herself out into the world with you." Nessa opened her mouth to question, but Molly held up her hand. "We'll talk more whilst we eat. All right?" She wagged an admonitory finger. "At least now I've both my patients in one place."

As she turned to leave, Nessa cried, "Wait." Molly looked

at her with a raised brow. "May I see his clothes? I'd like to see—I'd like to see how the blade went through the cloth."

For a moment, Nessa thought Molly would refuse her, but she only nodded at a chest on the curtained side of the bed. "They're over there. We'd no idea how to clean them, but they dried well enough before the fire."

Nessa gripped the leather-covered arms of the wooden chair. The cushioned seat was broad and deep. She stared at Artimour's chiseled face, so white against the unbleached linen, as Molly's footsteps faded down the steps. He lay as if he were carved out of stone, or lay upon a funeral bier. Only the occasional flutter of an eyelid or the ghost of a breath betrayed that he yet lived. She gripped the staff, and shut her eyes. *Great Mother, let him live.* What if he had been stabbed by the dagger she'd made? If he lived, what would he do once he found that out?

You don't know that it was your dagger, the little voice of logic whispered. But what else would explain such a wound? It had clearly been made by a very sharp object, slicing like butter through flesh that blackened at the touch. With a sense of resolve, she crossed the room to examine the clothing lying on the chest. Both doublet and linen shirt showed the same singed edges as Artimour's wound. But the boot—she narrowed her eyes, as she saw, sitting on the floor on the far side of the chest, the very boot she remembered so clearly removing from her own foot. She picked it up, and examined the side. There was a wide slash on the one side, another, narrower slash on the opposite. And as she expected, the edges weren't singed at all. So whatever was used to stab Artimour didn't burn leather of mortal make. But it didn't answer the question as to why he had it in his doublet in the first place, or where the other was. She leaned down to replace the boot and was astounded to hear something slide around inside.

She turned it upside down and shook it, then gasped as she recognized the object that came spinning out, leather cord flying, to lie at an angle on the rush-covered floor. With a trembling hand, she picked it up and held it dangling in midair, scarcely daring to believe that what she held was truly Dougal's amulet.

13

The world had stopped spinning. Dougal realized it the moment he opened his eyes to a gold light that streamed through crystal windows above him, bathing the entire room with a steady glow. He was naked, he realized, lying in a vast bed between green silken sheets that smelled of something at once both woodsy and sweet. He drew a deep breath and knew at once that his vision of Vinaver in the forest had been more than a vision.

For he knew this room, he thought, as he turned his head on the pillows, recognizing the round chamber, whose walls were carved out of the round trunk of a great tree. He knew this room, he thought, with a bitter pang so deep it felt like a spear in the pit of his belly. And he knew this bed.

He rolled over restlessly as if turning away from the memories that threatened to overwhelm his defenses like floodwater crashing through a dam, and realized that amazingly, blessedly, there was no more pain. He was weak as a dayold infant, but for the first time in a long time, he knew he would live. He moved his arm experimentally. The goblin had gotten him in the meaty part of his shoulder where the muscles of his chest and upper arm converged, muscles critical to the plying of his trade. A one-armed blacksmith was no use to anyone. It still hurt—whatever cure that wretched sidhe witch had effectuated wasn't quite complete. But he was healing, and he wondered what bargain he'd have to make this time with Vinaver that would allow him to leave.

A door opened and Vinaver herself stepped into the room, carrying a tray and a basket. She paused when she realized he was awake and smiled. "Good morrow, husband."

"I'm not your husband." His voice was a harsh, hoarse growl and he glared at her with all the hatred he could summon. Vinaver was the witch who'd trapped him here that Beltane night he'd lain on the hillside with Essa, his lost beloved. The anguish of that memory made him close his eyes, so he only heard her light tinkle of a laugh.

"'Twas you that called me wife."

"You tricked me, then." He opened his eyes and saw she was standing beside the bed, her pink mouth pursed in a full-lipped pout, her long white fingers clasped loosely over her deep green velvet gown. She'd grown wings, too, thin white arcs of bone that curved delicately overhead and looked completely uncomfortable. "And you won't trick me this time. I want my clothes. And then I'll be going."

She was silent a long moment, her long eyes slanting up

in her pointed face. "I've no need to trick you, master blacksmith. For you'd agree I'm owed something? After all, I saved your life. It would seem payment of some sort is only fair. That's not much of a bargain, is it?"

He drew back, every weak muscle tensing. He was still far too feeble to even consider attempting to throttle her, so he could only stare and hope she saw the hatred burning in his face. Bargains. He knew all about the bargains the sidhe liked to make with moonmazed mortals. It was just such a bargain that had led to Essa being trapped here. He would not be so stupid as to make such a bargain again. "What do you want?"

"The silver dagger—the one you had with you when I found you. It's not finished. I need you to finish it."

"Why?" He had suspected the moment he'd recognized Finuviel at Cadwyr's side that Vinaver was somehow involved.

The corners of her lips lifted higher, but her eyes narrowed and he saw she was less than pleased. "That," she answered slowly, "is none of your concern." For a long moment they stared at each other, old adversaries, and about her, like a palpable force, he felt a restless energy coupled with an iron determination. Surely nothing happened here in the OtherWorld, he thought, that she had not a part in. Her eyes lingered on his chest and shoulders, and he pulled the sheet higher. Under her scrutiny, he felt more naked than ever. "And let me put it this way, my dear sometime-husband. Whatever else might be between us, I've saved your life. You owe me the value of whatever that's worth to you."

"I'll send you a chest of gold."

For a moment he thought she might hit him. She paced the length of the bed, clenching her hands into fists. "I don't want your mortal gold. I have no use for your mortal gold. What I want and what I need is a dagger made of silver—a finished dagger with a hilt. And I need it as quickly as possible. Now tell me what you'll need and I will see it fetched from Shadow."

"I've not agreed to do it. You may keep me here as many years as you please, but anything you want that badly has got to be of no good—"

"You always were too determined to think things through." She leaned over the bed, and he thought he had never seen anyone—human or sidhe—look at him with such pure and naked need. She drew a deep breath, visibly holding herself in check. She was shaking with the effort. "I saved your life. I need you to help me save Faerie. You must do this."

He smiled. Now she knew what it felt like to need something so much you could taste it. "Must?" He adjusted the pillow beneath his head. "Must indeed. Why must I, and what makes you think I will?"

"Because if you don't, mortal, all of this—everything you see around you—is in danger of vanishing."

"Find another smith."

"There's no time," she hissed.

"What's a silver dagger got to do with saving Faerie?"

Her face flushed a dark red, and her cheekbones seemed to stretch and sharpen, so that she reminded him of a fox, or maybe a bat, as her wings fluttered tremulously above her head. "You owe me your life. I don't owe you answers."

Whatever she looked like, it was something dark and

vulpine and predatory, something that fed on the blood of other things. But he wouldn't show her weakness and he wouldn't show her fear. "But what you are telling me, is that if I don't finish that dagger for you in fairly short order, all of this—" he nodded up and around "—just goes away?"

He thought she might leap on him, but she only nodded. "Forever."

There was another long pause, and then he leaned over the side of the bed and spat onto the polished wooden floor. "Fine with me."

Her fingers curled into claws and he half expected her to kill him then. But she only lifted her eyebrow, spearing him against the pillow with a cold emerald stare. "We'll see." Then she swept from the room, her wings furling in her wake, leaving him to calculate the possible cost of his bravado.

The early-morning fog drifted over the forested hills like fingers through a lover's hair, obscuring the landscape. Renvahr stood on the ridge just below the sheer walls of Ar-dagh, his mouth compressed into a thin line as he scanned the other side of the Daraghduin River suspiciously. The thick forest which covered the uplands that had always seemed like the first line of the defenses which made Ardagh so impenetrable, had a different cast today. He now saw that the trees provided a potential shield to conceal the movements of an enemy beneath the noses of the King's own scouts who, according to that weasel Wellis, were now combing every inch of the hill country, watching the passes and the fords, ensuring a constant flow of reassurance that the rebel exchange party contained no more than the number agreed upon, and that there were no large numbers of enemy troops moving into position. It was all going exactly as planned, so perfectly as planned, in fact, that that alone made him wary.

Beside him, his horse pawed the ground impatiently and he patted the white star just above its nose. The hour to exchange the first of the hostages was fast approaching. From this vantage point, he could see increased activity in the enemy camp that was perched on an easily defended outcropping near the top of the highest hill on the opposite shore. Every instinct he possessed screamed that the rebels had some trap, some trick planned. But every one of the scouts patrolling the mountain passes repeatedly swore they saw nothing but the small caravan of hostages moving through the mountains under the white flag of truce. True, the rebels had pitched their camp in the most defensible position in all the surrounding area, but who could blame them for that? And who could blame them for keeping the river between themselves and the vast fortress of Ardagh, which rose out of the swirling mist like a black fist carved out of the rock. He scowled at the small camp. There was just something about the whole affair that seemed questionable, he thought, try as he might to dismiss his misgivings. It made a certain sense, of course, that the Dukes of Gar and Allovale should immediately move to retrieve their hostages especially after the heavy losses suffered in the last encounter. But Gar, known as a shrewd negotiator and as hard a haggler as a Lacquilean merchant, had agreed to every condition they'd demanded. At once. Almost as if it didn't matter. A cold wind blew against his cheek and he felt the sting of the day's first raindrops. Curse the dismal day he'd set foot on this benighted island.

He was still cursing when Wellis trotted up. "Good morrow, my Lord Protector." He swung out of his saddle with the ease of a man half his age and tethered the horse to a low-hanging branch.

He mangled the Humbrian almost beyond recognition, but Renvahr smiled a thin acknowledgment of the attempt. "What's to do about this fog?" He made sure to reply in Brynnish, however, in order to spare his ears further assault.

Wellis shrugged. "The men of these parts are used to such weather, Lord Protector. As I think you'd be, after all the time you've spent here." He nodded pointedly at Renvahr's thick cloak of black Humbrian wolf fur.

But Renvahr met the other man's dark eyes squarely, with a practiced nonchalance that bordered on insolence. Curse his wretched sister and the day she'd thought to marry that mewling pap of a King. If Wellis wanted to run around half naked as any of the other savages of this benighted land, what did he care? He would not spurn what comforts he could command simply because Wellis thought him weak. And no matter how many years he was condemned to spend here, he would never get used to the weather. Never. "Well, are they used to maneuvering blind? Can they find the enemy with their noses?" Which was indeed a distinct possibility, Renvahr thought, now that it had occurred to him. The Brynnish all stank faintly of cow, due to the traces of manure which clung to their boots no matter their rank.

But Wellis only shrugged again, refusing to take the bait.

"It seems to me, Lord Protector, the fog gives us the advantage. Our men know this terrain like they know the furrows of their women. They'll not need to resort to their noses—you can trust me there." He leaned over and patted Renvahr's arm with an avuncular air. "Now don't you fret yourself, lad. The men of Clan Uishnach and its septs are loyal. We'll have all those upland jackals captured in a trice, then gutted and strung upon the walls like the carrion they are."

The vehemence shocked Renvahr only for a moment. Despite his attempts at surface polish, and his wife's Humbrian relations, Wellis was at heart no more civilized than any of those he termed upland jackals.

"And there's a new piece of luck," Wellis was saying, as he stared off, into the distance.

Instantly Renvahr narrowed his eyes. "What's that?" he asked between his teeth, as he gathered his cloak of Humbrian wolf fur closer about his shoulders.

"Allovale and Gar themselves are up there." Wellis nodded in the direction of the enemy camp, where castle-size clouds floated past the drab tents. A tattered white flag of truce was the only banner, flapping on its makeshift pole, flashing white against the grayer white of the mist.

Foreboding gripped his guts like a claw, and Renvahr turned his head slowly. "What did you say?"

"The report just came in." Wellis looked at him with all the glee of a child chosen to lead the Misrule dance. "That's what I came to tell you, my lord."

And in that moment, Renvahr knew with absolute certainty that there was far more to this than just a simple exchange of hostages, that their own plan to recapture the hostages even while freeing their own was a terrible mistake. "Allovale?" He spat the word. "Gar?" His lip curled as if some stench had suddenly sprouted beneath his nose.

This time Wellis did not reply immediately. He shifted uncomfortably on his feet, then quickly remounted. As he swung into his saddle, he seemed to recover. "My Lord Protector, surely you see what a stroke of luck this is."

"Stroke of luck?" Renvahr unleashed his own horse's reins, flinging them like a whip. He nodded at the enemy camp poised so strategically across the river. "Maybe a right fine stroke of luck, Lord Wellis, but for whom?" It was that piece of news alone that convinced him to follow his instincts. Abruptly he wheeled his mount down the hill, shouting for his captains as he rode, Wellis trotting along at his heels. "Order them back," he cried. "Order them back."

"What's the matter with you, man?" Wellis gripped his horse's bridle before Renvahr could bark any further orders for retreat.

"You talk of luck, Lord Wellis," hissed Renvahr as he wheeled his stallion around. "Look up there. They've positioned themselves like generals on that high ground. I don't know if they've got them dug into the ground itself, but something tells me there's more to this than you and your scouts understand."

For a long moment the men stared at each other, even as all around them, captains and sergeants came scrambling to stand, shocked and questioning. Wellis jerked his reins so that they moved off. He put his head close to Renvahr and met his eyes squarely. "I see where they are. We all see where they are. Will you think about what you are saying?"

He reached across the saddle and gripped Renvahr's cloak by the collar. "Are you moonmazed? We've got the two leaders of the whole revolt up there. The upland chiefs are so disorganized they'll collapse and so will the rebellion once we show them the heads of Gar and Allovale on pikes. Listen to yourself, my Lord Protector." He spat the words directly in Renvahr's face. "Listen to yourself."

It was the ring of truth in Wellis's words that stayed Renvahr's hand upon his dagger. *It's this land,* he thought. *This dank, dismal, miserable, foul, dark land.* The damp was moldering his mind, corrupting his reason. He jerked up and back, twisting away from Wellis's grip. "I insist on moving additional troops into reserve."

"Of course." Wellis bowed and sat back, easing his horse a few paces off, contempt plain on his face. "You are the Lord Protector, after all."

I hate them all, he thought, as he watched Wellis gallop off down the hill. *Every last foul one of them.* With a heart made heavy by an impossible task, he beckoned to the captain of his personal guard. "Oriad."

"My lord?"

They had been together since boyhood, Oriad recruited from the ranks of the pages to serve as his sparring partner. They had been equally matched then, they were equally matched now. The one bright spot in all of Brynhyvar, as far as Renvahr was concerned, was that Oriad had accompanied him. He trusted Oriad as he trusted no other and he had made Merle swear that if ever Oriad came to her with orders to go with him, she was to follow without question. "Wellis just told me that Gar and Allovale are in the camp above. And that tells me this is no simple exchange of hostages."

"But you never thought it was." Oriad spoke quickly, in the liquid vowels of fluent Humbrian.

"I want you to go back to the castle. Make sure that should the worst happen, the King and the Queen are brought safely to my father."

"My lord." Oriad frowned, and gestured a question with one gloved hand. "What makes you say this? I've spoken to the scouts myself. There's no sign of any significant force moving anywhere near us. And there's been no time for Gar to summon enough to threaten Ardagh. He took quite a beating in the last engagement."

"So did we." A sudden cloudburst drenched them both, and Renvahr flung his sodden hair back off his face. A sudden vision of Merle with her cards, demanding that he call off the hostage exchange flashed into his mind. "Just go. Do as I ask. Better to be overcautious when dealing with these lightlipped liars. They'll pat your back with one hand and slide a dagger between your ribs with the other. I don't trust Gar, I don't trust Allovale, and I don't even trust the bastards who ride beneath the standard of the King. I'll do my duty to my sister. But not one more drop of Humbrian blood will I shed than is necessary, do you understand me?"

Oriad leaned closer. "Am I to understand that we're not to fight to the last man?"

Renvahr only raised his eyebrows. It was quite possible that the sense of impending disaster now hanging over him like an ax was only a product of long-standing resentment and overwrought nerves. But he could not admit that to

Oriad and there was no one else he trusted to listen and to follow without question. "Your orders are to protect the Princess of Humbria and her Consort. Do I make myself plain?"

And with a low bow, Oriad saluted and rode away, straight-backed, in silence, leaving Renvahr to contemplate the entire plan from start to finish, hoping to identify before it was too late any possible weakness.

He could feel them, Donnor thought. The collective weight of all the eyes that watched within the wood hung around his neck like a noose. Like flies caught within a web—a caul—they were, strung all throughout the forest, within and above and around the thick trunks of the primeval trees. None were so skilled as the hill-folk of Ardagh in the art of disappearing into their surroundings, so that it was said of them that they had stolen shapeshifting from the sidhe. And what else was out there, he wondered, thinking of Finuviel, slim as a wraith, black as a shadow, dangerous as a blade. There was a whole mort of them out there somewhere, he thought. Somewhere out beyond the mist.

The thick fog pressed in all around him, rising up from the great river foaming below their feet, tickling his skin, clinging in tiny droplets to his hair, to his clothing. It tickled his senses, awakening some new awareness of a dimension he'd heretofore successfully ignored. For he had to believe, in his blood, in his bones, that the drifting mist concealed not just human eyes, but the eyes of the creatures of the OtherWorld, the untested, untried ally with whom Cadwyr swore his throne could be won. Because otherwise, it was insanity that he, a man of more than sixty winters, should be out here, in the early-morning fog, watching the decoy party begin its slow descent down the winding trail that led to the one stone causeway that arched over the thundering water.

Donnor felt, rather than saw, Cadwyr come up behind him. He glanced over and there Cadwyr was, hair bright gold against the whitish sky, color high, chest and arms bare but for a leather breastplate and vambraces on his forearms. The broad curves of the muscles of his chest and upper arms were highlighted with swirling tattoos in intricate patterns of bold green and red and blue, and his trews were the familiar rust-red and brown of the Allovale battle-plaid. His cheeks were smeared with omen-signs, and his hair was stuck with crow feathers. He wore a thick band of wool around his head. It made Donnor look down at the woolen strip lying forgotten across his saddle. He was supposed to be wearing it when the sidhe came—to save him from their song, whatever that meant. With a sigh, he lifted the woolen strip and bound it around his head in the same manner as Cadwyr, who grinned back at Donnor with an animal vitality that was almost palpable. As Cadwyr thrust his cloak off his shoulders, Donnor saw that it was lined with some material the color of rust. It gleamed as wetly as blood in the low light. Fresh blood. He stared across the river at the black walls of Ardagh which rose out of the mist like a single fist, upthrust and defiant. No human army had ever taken it. And here he sat, vulnerable, exposed, utterly dependent upon the word of a sidhe. A bird called once, twice and fell silent. The hackles rose on the back of his neck. So it was beginning. "Cadwyr."

"Aye, Uncle?"

What if the sidhe never appeared? The thought entered his head as he saw the great gates of Ardagh begin to open. But he only muttered, "What's going on over there?" beneath his breath as movement on the opposite shore diverted his attention.

Cadwyr squinted into the distance. "It appears that our noble Lord Protector has some suspicion of us, Uncle. He's moving out more troops."

"And what if that sidhe of yours doesn't honor his word, nephew?" Donnor spoke low in his throat. He could see the decoy party, nearly halfway down the winding trail that led to the bridge. Another bird call came, this time from his left. A short trill, a sharp whistle, and another trill. "They're getting ready to attack, nephew."

But Cadwyr only turned to Donnor with that arch grin he was beginning to dislike. "Finuviel will come, Uncle." He patted the breastplate he wore over his chest. "Have no fear. He'll be here. You'd better cover up your ears, Uncle."

In the camp, Donnor could hear the sergeants giving the orders for the few foot soldiers and archers in their company to draw up defensively. Another bird call, this time the shrill, harsh shriek of the crow. Donnor looked up and saw a black winged figure dip and wheel above. A chill went down the back of his spine, and the first volley of arrows fell over the camp. Cadwyr wheeled around with a whoop, drawing his broadsword from the scabbard strapped across his back. "Up Allovale! Up Gar!" He rose in his stirrups as another volley of arrows fell upon the camp.

"Where's that sidhe?" Donnor growled between gritted

teeth. He drew his own sword and gathered up his reins. Below him, at the river's edge, the forest had suddenly bloomed into a lethal hedgerow of spears and swords, glinting in the pale white sun that shone through the fog like a candle behind a cloud.

Cadwyr glanced at him quickly. "He'll be here."

"Are you sure?"

Cadwyr caught Donnor's gaze and smiled broadly. "If he wants this back, he'll be here." Cadwyr patted the front of his breastplate and Donnor remembered that in the last days, Cadwyr had taken to wearing the pouch which held the Caul openly around his neck.

"If he doesn't keep his word, we're done, Cadwyr. You see that, don't you?" Donnor said, looking down, into the valley, where the line of soldiers had begun to creep upwards, even as another arrow volley made them both dodge backward.

"It won't matter to us if he doesn't." Cadwyr laughed and there was a giddy ring that made Donnor pause for just a moment. Cadwyr swung his broadsword up and around in a vicious arc. "Won't matter to us, for we'll all be dead."

For a long moment their eyes held and then Cadwyr raised his sword aloft once more. "Up Allovale! Up Allovale for Brynhyvar!"

For a moment, an overwhelming weariness enveloped Donnor. Just one more battle, he thought. One more battle, and then his old man's bones would rest either by his own fire, or join in the eternal feasting with his ancestors in the halls of the Summerlands. A sudden movement in the river caught his eye and he leaned forward in his saddle, staring at the old woman who bent over her wash. *An old woman—she'll die if she's caught down there.* He was just about to nudge Cadwyr when she straightened and smiled directly up at him.

The moment seemed to slow and stretch. There was no reason for the sudden chill that went down his back as he gazed down at that wide grin. As he stared, transfixed, she bent once more to her bundle and held up a blood-drenched tunic. *Looks like my tunic.* And then he understood that it was his tunic. She was the Washer, the dread aspect of the Marrihugh who washed the blood of the mortally dead from their clothing before they entered the Summerlands. *Looks like my tunic,* he thought again. *Looks like my tunic.* He took a last look around at the dark green hills, a last long breath of the fresh, pine-scented air. It was as good a day to die as any. He shook off the lassitude and, throwing back his cloak, drew his own sword. "For Gar!" he cried. "For Gar and Brynhyvar!"

He flapped his reins and his stallion leapt forward. They were lost, he thought. If he had to die this foolishly, he would at least die fighting. And then he heard the first clear note, rising up through the mist like a spear of pure white light. It echoed above the water, and rang off the walls of Ardagh, growing in strength, rather than diminishing, a note of pure and unadulterated power. It held no joy, it held no fear. It was only strong. The line of weapons faltered momentarily as the sound held every mortal spellbound.

A breeze blew off the river, fresh and moist as the morning, and Donnor took a last deep breath of air still free of the acrid stench of battle. The note began to fade, and, as if released from a spell, the line charged up the hill. But from his vantage point, behind the advancing line, Donnor saw the foaming river begin to boil. There was a great rushing roar, and up and out of the water, pale riders on horses white as foam rose singing, swinging swords of gold the color of Cadwyr's hair. Out of the river, over the banks and up the hills they charged, spilling like floodwater in all directions, and their song was cold as ice, cutting as the wind. Spellbound, Donnor found himself gaping, staring wide-eyed as the sidhe savaged the mortal ranks, winnowing them down like sheaves of corn falling to the sickle's lethal curve. As if in a dream, he saw the ranks begin to break, heard the high cacophony of screams rise. The spears and swords began to crumple, blood began to spurt and bone to shatter with that unmistakable crunch. Cadwyr was right beside him. He opened his mouth to speak, pointing in horror at the slaughter unfolding below, when a flicker of movement caught his peripheral vision. Automatically he looked to see the edge of a blade arcing toward him. He glanced back at Cadwyr, and saw death in Cadwyr's eyes. *Great Mother, Cecily was right all along.*

He put his shield arm up to block the blow too late.

For the rest of her life, Merle heard that music in her nightmares. She heard the first, cold piercing notes just as the weak sun was turning the indigo clouds a lighter shade of gray behind the wet mist. It stopped her in the act of brushing up her hair, made her turn and pause and listen. It was a sound like nothing she had ever heard before. It made her rush to the window, throw open the glass, and lean out across the wide stone casement. The castle servants surged upon the walls, opening the gates, crying and calling out, despite the orders from the captains and the sergeants of the watch. It was a song that made her blood run warm beneath her skin, her bones turn to liquid, her muscles lengthen into lithe, willowy sinews. It awakened every sense, every secret longing, and she closed her eyes against the onslaught of sudden desires so long buried she'd forgotten they'd existed.

A sudden sound behind her startled her, and she turned to see Hoell standing beside the hearth, a little frown on his face. "Merle?" he whispered, his voice hoarse. In the grayish light, she saw his face had changed somehow. He no longer looked at her with such happy, wide-eyed innocence. Even his eyes were older.

"*Matra mea,* my King?" she whispered. "You—you're yourself again?"

He turned his head briefly, looking down and away, then up once more as the breeze bore another snatch of that unearthly melody into the room. "That music—"

She shook her head, scrambling down from her perch, feeling suddenly unbalanced and dizzy. She stumbled slightly, and he caught her up, and she felt the solid weight of his body. He felt strong, muscled, a man once more, and for a moment she closed her eyes and breathed. He looked down at her. "That music," he said again.

"I—I don't know what it is—"

"We have to shut the windows," he said suddenly, thrusting her aside decisively. "We mustn't listen to it—" She drew herself up, shocked, as he drew the windows shut with a firm slam and pulled down the heavy velvet curtains. "Now, we have to warn everyone else."

"How do you know this?" she whispered, still stunned by his sudden metamorphosis.

He was halfway across the room, but turned to reply swiftly, with a harsh tone of command so completely foreign to him, she could only stare openmouthed. "It doesn't matter how I know, Merle. All I can tell you, is it's the most dangerous sound I've ever heard."

But it didn't matter how tightly one bound one's ears against the siren music, for against the unearthly riders heralded by that music there was no real defense. Their preternatural armor protected them from the defenders' puny weapons and even the strongest fell beneath the onslaught. It was a horrible waking nightmare that refused to end no matter how many times Merle shook herself. Surely she only imagined the muffled sounds of the battle that raged first outside, then unthinkably inside the walls of Ardagh, so that she found herself and Hoell barricaded into the hall, by a few of their more fast-thinking guard.

They'd scarcely settled themselves upon the dais when the grim-faced lieutenant who directed them there strode to Hoell, and spoke quickly into the ear of the King. Hoell nodded, and glanced at Merle, who huddled with her ladies, her little dog cowering on her lap, her hands pressed tight against its ears. Hoell spoke to the soldier, adjusted the covering over his ear, and came at once to kneel beside her.

When he raised the thick strip of wool she'd bound over her ears, and spoke, she realized the singing had stopped. "We have to get out, Merle. There's no way to defend

Ardagh against this unnatural attack. Come." He lifted her up with a gentle hand beneath her forearm.

At that moment, Renvahr burst into the room. His armor was covered in blood, and his ears were bound with a makeshift cover that made his head look misshapen. "Bring the King and come with me." He beckoned from the door.

At once the guards moved to obey, the ladies clucking and fluttering like so many hens. "Renvahr, the King—"

"Let's go, Merle." Hoell tugged at her arm. There was no time for explanations.

But at some point, as Renvahr escorted them through the kitchens and down a narrow flight of damp stone stairs, he realized that something had happened to bring Hoell back to himself, and his dark eyes in his narrow face lost some of their grim expression.

"Where are you taking us?" cried Merle. She scraped her fingertips grabbing for the wall as her slippers slid on the damp stone.

"To the only possible hope of escape that you have," Renvahr replied. He did not look back at her, only led the way through the narrow passageway at the bottom of the steps which led to a wide arched cavern where the river flowed beneath the foundations of the palace like a secret artery. "You may not survive the falls, Your Majesty." He addressed the King as they paused beside a row of shallow boats roped to iron hooks set into the stone. "But those things up there will not stop, I think, until all who dwell within Ardagh are dead." The cavern rang faintly with the piercing echoes of the unnatural horn, and Renvahr gestured to the boats. "You must go now."

"What about you?"

"I am the Lord Protector of the Realm." Renvahr met Hoell's eyes directly as Merle realized her brother was about to stay behind.

"Renvahr, you can't stay—"

The horns were louder now, tugging at the edges of her awareness, diverting her attention from the matter at hand, and Renvahr smiled down bitterly into her eyes. "I can hold them back a little. Give you a chance to get away. Get in the boat, little sister, and tell Father when you see him it was Humbrian honor that held me to my duty, not any love for Brynhyvar. Now, go."

As a sudden breeze whipped black smoke from the long orange tails of the flickering torches, Hoell silently took her arm and eased her past Renvahr into the nearest boat. She looked up at her brother, and saw his face was set and grim, his clothes caked with something that wasn't mud. He cocked his head, again, as faint music echoed from the direction they'd come. "Hurry," he whispered.

"But—" Their eyes met and Merle understood the nature of his message. Renvahr would not abandon his post. He despised the Brynnish for turncoat cowards, always ready to play an opportunity to any advantage, and as easily swayed as scarecrows in the wind. But his was the honor of Humbria and he would stand firm.

The screams grew louder, and Hoell hustled her down into the boat, settling quickly beside her. Renvahr looked at them and nodded, as if satisfied. "There's a captain waiting on the other side of the river, if you make it beyond the rapids and over the falls."

"I've done it before," Hoell answered. "I grew up riding these rapids." The men exchanged one final look and then an unearthly horn rang out, clearer now, from the direction of the passage, and Renvahr turned and drew his sword, as the other boats filled with as many who could fit.

As they pushed off, Merle looked back. She saw Renvahr and the rest of the guards brace themselves against an onslaught of tall and terrible beings who shimmered in the orange light, wielding weapons that blazed of golden fire. Then the boats bore them beneath the low stone arch and out of the castle, into the gushing torrent of the river, and she knew her brother was lost to her forever.

At the end of the day, a profound silence permeated the halls and courtyards of Ardagh, the silence of death and disbelief. The last thin sliver of the old moon hung low over the walls, as if, before it waned completely, it would bear witness to the corpses left lying in heaps both before and within the walls. For the sidhe had left no wounded. Those whom they'd spared—the women, the children, the servants, and the remaining few of the garrison who'd surrendered to Cadwyr—stumbled about in a daze, moving like wraiths through the motions of their tasks. It had happened so suddenly, so violently, so quickly, they were all still in shock.

It made it even easier than usual for Finuviel to slip unnoticed into the great castle, to blend into the shadows and move swiftly through the torchlit halls, the sound of his footsteps blotted out beneath the shuffling footfalls and muttered murmurs of the people who milled around him like stunned sheep. The stink of death hung thick in the sodden air. As he approached the doors of the great hall, he smelled the hot grease of roasting meat and recognized the high wailing skirl and the slow steady drumbeat of the barbarous racket with which the mortals ushered their dead into the Summerlands. Cadwyr's men had commandeered the great hall, he thought, toasting themselves for a battle they'd fought without loss, and it surprised him that they should mourn the enemy dead as if for their own.

In the corridor outside the doors, Finuviel stepped out of the shadows. To their credit, the guards Cadwyr had posted at the door reacted with no more than a sudden intake of breath and immediately swung the heavy doors open. He knew they looked at him closely, but he avoided their eyes. He walked up the steps, his dark cloak swinging, his face mostly hidden by his hood. The killing that day had sickened him and he understood for the first time why his kind were warned against too much contact with mortals, no matter how intoxicating they might at first appear. Certain aspects and emotions might indeed be captivating, but there were others such as the ones he'd felt that day—terror and fear and the raw red bloodlust of battle—that left one feeling tainted, as if, when the passion had finally run its course, some poison had been left behind in the blood. He had seen it in the glutted looks of surfeit on the faces of his knights as they'd stumbled back across the border, dazed and drunk as any mortal on Beltane. He knew he wore it now, as he made his way through the crowd of meaty men, beefy as bulls, red-faced and sweating, who understood nothing of what this day had cost. Not even Cadwyr could understand the enormity of the price he, and the other sidhe, had paid.

The mortals paused in their singing and their drinking as he passed. They fell silent and drew back into tight little groups, watching him with oily mouths from behind the wet rims of goblets and dripping hunks of meat. The music faltered at his approach, the pipes squealing to a discordant end. The musicians stared at him and he did not want to stare back. Something had happened to him out there on that battlefield, something that made the hall seem cramped and close, stifling with the odors of stall and privy.

He realized with a faint shock that for the first time, he was impervious to the allure of the mortals. He walked faster, determined to retrieve the Caul from Cadwyr and conclude this business as quickly as possible. Samhain was coming, he could feel it throbbing in the tides of his blood. The doors, the boundaries were all opening, thinning, bringing the most auspicious time of year, according to his mother, to UnMake the Caul. And then there was the problem of the Goblin King.

But as he passed before the dais, he noticed that a body lay on a long wooden bench, covered with several cloaks. A round shield stood against the base at its feet, a sword lay in a worn leather scabbard on its chest. Beside the body, three men clad in differently patterned cloaks from the bulk of the others, wept. Finuviel looked at the nearest warrior. "Who fell?" he asked.

The warrior flushed an ugly red and grabbed the jug his companion proffered. "Donnor of Gar, may he be feasting in the Summerlands this night," he growled as he lifted the jug to his lips.

Before today, Finuviel might have asked more, for he had

been certain that there'd been no losses among Cadwyr's men. But tonight, he had no wish to linger. He doubted he would ever want to linger in mortal company again. He would bid Cadwyr a quick farewell and then he would return to his mother's house. He had allowed himself to waste enough time in the affairs of these mortals.

But the intimate connection he had forged with Cadwyr was intact and it led him to where he intuitively knew Cadwyr would go: the abandoned suite of the King. He heard a woman's high-pitched nervous giggle even before he opened the door. As he stepped into the room, he saw that Cadwyr sat in a wide fabric-covered armchair beside the fire, a blond woman on his lap, and a dark-haired girl curled up on the floor beside him. They looked up with a gasp as Finuviel allowed the door to swing shut with a soft click. He paused just inside the threshold, assessing Cadwyr's disheveled hair, his full red lips and hands that roamed freely across the woman's neck and arms and bosom.

"Donnor's dead?" Finuviel ignored the women and spoke as if they were alone.

Cadwyr looked up. The room reeked of dog and damp wool, and both male and female sweat. He could smell it rising from them all—heavy mortal musk, a distinctive combination of oily salt, acrid wine, and coppery blood. And there was something else—something that rose from all of them like streamers of murky light, but once again, Finuviel realized it held no allure. If anything, he found it slightly choking, as if the air was too thick to breathe.

"Aye, he fell," Cadwyr answered. "Fitting for an old lion like him, don't you think? He's feasting by now in the Summerlands for sure." He raised his goblet in a toast and drained it in one long drink to the dregs.

Finuviel only frowned. Was the man drunk already?

With a lazy smile and a toss of his golden hair, Cadwyr set first the empty goblet, and then set the woman on his lap beside her companion on the floor. "Look what I found to play with. Pretty babbies, aren't they? Show us your paps, loves." He nudged them both with the tip of his boot. They giggled nervously and glanced at each other, at Finu-viel and then back at Cadwyr, as if uncertain if he was serious.

Finuviel's nostrils flared with disgust. There was something odd about this, something off-kilter that set his senses off-balance. He'd had enough of the Shadowlands, he decided, enough of mortals and their wants and their hopes and their dark and hungry desires. He took a single step forward and Cadwyr rose to his feet, sinewy as a cat. *A cat about to pounce.*

He was still dressed for battle, in his leather breastplate, his rust-and-brown trews. Cadwyr even wore his short sword at his hip, and that detail made Finuviel wary. "And how did it happen that he fell?"

"There was one charge upon us. Your timing was just a few minutes off."

Behind the women, the fire hissed and snapped, and Finuviel felt the tension in the room increase. A pulse was pounding visibly in the veins of Cadwyr's throat, and he noticed that Cadwyr wore the pouch which held the Caul around his neck. Enough of these mortal games, he thought. What did it matter to him whether or not an old soldier fell in battle? Finuviel took a single step toward Cadwyr. "Our bargain is fulfilled. You have your victory, I have my dagger. If you'll return the Caul, I'll be on my way."

Cadwyr gestured to a flagon and another goblet set on a tray. "I thought we might first have another drink. And look at these pretty things—show us your paps, sweetlings—come now—" he nudged the closer girl so hard it was nearly a kick, and she gasped. She bent to unlace her bodice, her hair falling in her face. "That's it—" he breathed, as she unthreaded the lacings. "There now, let me see. Ah, here, look, Finuviel, aren't they pretty? Smile for the Prince of the sidhe, sweetling, think of what you'll tell your grandbabbies about this night." The girl hid her face behind her hair, as Cadwyr forced her hands away and spread the edges of her bodice apart, exposing her small round breasts with their tight, brown nipples.

Something twisted inside Finuviel, and he realized that Cadwyr had the girls there, not for his own benefit, but to entice him. Suddenly he could not wait to be out of the Shadowlands and back where he belonged. He took another three steps into the room, hand outstretched. "Give me the Caul, Cadwyr, and I'll leave you to play your games in peace."

Cadwyr was staring at the girl's high breasts and pointed nipples. He looked at Finuviel. "Look at that, now. Just look at that." He reached down and the girl shied from his touch. But he only eased the thin strip of dirty ribbon she wore around her neck up and over her head. From it, dangled a small silver amulet. He held it up, watching the five-pointed star spin a slow spiral on the end of its frayed strip. Finuviel frowned. Was the man mad with his victory? But there was a knowing in Cadwyr's eyes, in the way they narrowed and grew hard when he saw the look on Finuviel's face that told Finuviel that Cadwyr was as stable as the rocks at the base of the walls of Ardagh. "All right, girls, go on inside with you. We'll be in in a bit." The women stumbled to their feet, the one clutching her bodice together. Cadwyr gestured to the goblets. "Shall we not drink to the success of our venture?"

"I've spent enough time here in Shadow, Cadwyr. Both sides of our bargain are met. Just give me the Caul."

Cadwyr took a deep breath, almost a sigh, and tucked his thumbs in his sword belt. "Well, now," he said. "Well, you see, my lord prince sidhe. I don't consider the bargain fulfilled. The Queen—and the King, too, for that matter, escaped, and it's due to the failure of your sidhe to follow—"

"They were last seen going over the Ardagh Falls in a boat." Finuviel could not quite believe what Cadwyr was saying. "If they're not dead and drowned already—"

"Well, you understand my position, my lord prince. I'll be keeping the Caul 'til we're sure." He patted the slight bulge it made beneath his doublet and gestured to the goblets once more. "Drink?"

But Finuviel was staring at him as shocked as any of the inhabitants of Ardagh. "What are you talking about? You cannot keep the Caul. You have your victory. The throne of Brynhyvar is yours for the taking." Suddenly he understood with monstrous clarity that Cadwyr was in some way responsible for his own ally's death, and he knew with absolute certainty that the mortal who could betray one ally could just as easily betray them all. "The Caul has nothing to do with you." He shifted his shoulders so that his cloak fell back off his shoulders, freeing his arms, but even as his left hand groped at his hip for the reassuring hilt of his short sword, he realized he'd already surrendered it to his body servant to take back to Faerie for him. And Cadwyr, he noticed suddenly, wasn't just armed with a short sword, he had a dagger in his hilt and another strapped to each leg, just on the outside of his boots. "You cannot alter our terms so significantly. What is this you mean to do?" He tried to draw a deep breath, but the atmosphere, like his mind, felt muddy and thick, as if the very air was polluted by some gritty mortal residue they exuded from their pores.

"This." With a motion so unexpected, Finuviel didn't see it, Cadwyr bent and threw one of the daggers in his boots directly at Finuviel. It thudded directly into his thigh, and he gasped, as he realized that the thing that seared through his flesh was made of silver. Horrified by the sheer audacity of Cadwyr's actions, he pulled it from his thigh, even as the pain burned through his leg and dragged him down to the floor, where he crouched, breathing hard, the deadly blade just inches from his knee. It was a pain like nothing else, a sharp plunging bolt that snaked like lightning up and down his leg in both directions simultaneously.

"What is this you do, mortal?" He gasped, as the world spun and tilted and he clung to the tufts of the rug beneath his hands lest he spin away.

"It came to me, you see, my lord prince sidhe." Cadwyr removed the other dagger from his boot, and twirled it speculatively. "It came to me one night. With the Caul removed, the way's clear for me to be King of both Brynhyvar and Tir-

Na'lugh. For as you yourself have shown me, there are things in the OtherWorld not seen here. But why should they not be? I've had a taste of your Faerie wine, and worn your Faerie clothes. I've heard your Faerie music and I've walked beneath your Faerie sun. Why should such delights not be mine—not be every mortal's—for the asking? Are we not the masters of the silver, after all? We need not fear the goblin. We need not fear you sidhe." He hurled the other dagger just as Finuviel had gathered himself enough to rise, and it embedded itself in the back of his shoulder, just beside his neck.

With a scream, he reached for the hilt and yanked it away, the stench of his own burned flesh curling up his nose and down his gullet.

"See how easy," muttered Cadwyr, circling like a predator. Something glittered between his hands in the yellow firelight, and through the reddish haze before his eyes, Finuviel saw that Cadwyr held a thin chain. "See how easy to bring the proud sidhe low." With another fast motion, he pulled Finuviel's arms behind him. He pulled two amulets off his own neck and dropped them on Finuviel's face. The metal seared into his check and he screamed, a huge, unearthly sound torn from the pit of his gut. The amulets bounced off him and landed on the floor, where they spun beside his head, as he lay struggling and writhing beneath Cadwyr's weight. The flesh of his wrists was burning as the silver began to eat through the fabric of his doublet and he gritted his teeth, refusing to cry out again. "My knights will come back for me—"

"Oh no, they won't. For mine went after them. With silvered weapons. Just like these. With orders to take them, just before they cross the border. Even now your host's no more." Cadwyr bent over him, grinning, and Finuviel understood the betrayal was complete. His breath stank of mortal wine, and the short bristles of his beard sticking through the pores of his face reminded Finuviel of a wild pig's. Sweat rolled in fat drops down his cheeks. The short sword flashed orange, and instinctively Finuviel shuddered back from its deathly silver sheen. Cadwyr twisted Finuviel's black hair around one hand and yanked his neck back, exposing Finuviel's long white throat. Delicately as a lover, he traced the tip of the blade down the entire length, watching as a thin red line bloomed in its wake.

"You mustn't kill me," Finuviel managed to whisper, glaring at Cadwyr with every ounce of fury he could muster through the blinding veil of pain. "The Caul is poison and it must be destroyed."

"Is that so?" muttered Cadwyr, intent upon the dagger. "I've no intention of letting you live."

"Then there won't be anything for you to rule." Finuviel gasped as Cadwyr lay the blade flat against the flesh of his neck. He gritted his teeth, struggling against the agony that was threatening to overcome him completely. "You need me to destroy the Caul and make it again. It cannot be simply destroyed or melted in any ordinary fire. It has to be UnMade, then Made again. And only—" he paused and fought the spiraling darkness where the grinning goblins were spearing him over and over with silver-tipped needles "—only I can UnMake the Caul. If you do not let me live to do that, you will destroy Faerie, and maybe even Brynhyvar—forever."

Finuviel knew he'd gotten through to Cadwyr for the mortal drew back, rocking back on his haunches, watching him with cold dispassion. At last he said, "I think you're lying to save your miserable hide. But you might be telling me the truth. So I'll keep you alive—for a while at least. And we'll see what plays out with the Caul." He patted the small bulge beneath his leather breastplate and Finuviel knew he wore it next to his skin.

"May you burn in the belly of the Hag, Cadwyr."

Cadwyr grinned and patted the Caul through his breastplate once more and touched the edge of the silver dagger to Finuviel's cheek with the other. The metal met the surface of his skin with a slight hiss and sent another blast of fire into his brain. "I very well may burn in the belly of your hag, my lord prince sidhe, but first, you'll burn in mine. I'm sending you into the silver mines in Allovale. If you're lying, I imagine the very air inside the mines will kill you. But if you're telling the truth, I don't imagine it will kill you all that quickly."

14

The moment Delphinea bent to put on her shoes, she remembered she'd dropped one somewhere behind the mirrors. Immediately she froze. What if she'd been right and Timias had seen her? What if he'd followed her and found her shoe? He'd told her he couldn't use the mirror magic, but why should she believe that? If Timias found her shoe, he had proof she'd been there. Suddenly she wondered just when Timias's invitation had come and what the offer portended. Petri's footsteps had faded, but there was still time, perhaps, to call him back.

She was in her stocking feet, but if she went to find more shoes, she'd never catch him before he reached Timias's suite. With an exasperated sigh, she gathered the frothy skirts of her gown in her hand and dashed after him. But she soon came skidding to a decorous halt as she intersected a dozen or so courtiers twittering down another corridor, in the direction of the breakfast served in the Great Hall. She paused and curtsied, exchanged what she hoped were greetings calculated to the correct degree of formality. They went laughing on their way and she breathed a sigh of short-lived relief. At this late hour, the halls were growing crowded with the usual press of gaily dressed sidhe who converged, laughing and talking, toward the feasting halls. This morning they reminded her of the twittering songbirds within the gilded cage that was the Queen's palace. Sunshine streamed in from every angle, illuminating the colors, the scents, until her head began to ache and she realized it was pointless to continue. She paused and sank, dejected, onto a bench along the great Hall of Mirrors. She'd never find Petri in time. It would never do to come skidding up to Timias's doors in search of her gremlin.

"Good morning, my lady." A tall lord in pale green satin was peering down at her through an emerald-studded lorgnette with the round eyes of an owl. His hair was a huge mass of white ringlets, from which pale green and blue feathers rose in a fan behind his head. *Wonderful,* she thought. Just what she needed. Another suitor to fend off, just when she was feeling so agitated and anxious. She gathered her wits. The complex insignia worked out in tiny seed pearls across the upper arms and shoulders of his doublet indicated some military rank, she thought, and so she stood and bobbed what she hoped was an appropriate curtsy, even as she racked her brain and tried to remember if she was supposed to know who this gentleman was.

But he spared her the embarrassment. "I don't believe

we've ever been introduced so don't fret. It's better that you don't know who I am, in fact. Lord Philomemnon sent me to find you." Up until this point, his tone was light, conversational, a mellifluous ripple of syllables that tripped off his tongue as lightly as a stone skipping over water. He bent over her hand, drawing her closer to him, and looked up at her through those round, owlish eyes. When he spoke next, his voice changed. It was deeper, darker, and so quiet she had to bend nearly to his mouth to hear him. "Leave now. Go to Vinaver's house deep within the Old Forest as quickly as you possibly can." With a soft gasp, she pulled away and opened her mouth, but he continued as they both rose in a rustle of silk and satin. "The Queen needs a scapegoat. Every Councilor here in residence will be named and held responsible."

"But—" she began.

"I shall not answer to any such nonsense!" The shrill voice rang down the corridor. The anonymous courtier released her hand as Delphinea turned to look over her shoulder, in time to see Berillian standing indignantly before a red-coated steward, flanked by two guards.

"Horned Herne," Delphinea murmured. She glanced back at her companion but he had already melted back into the mincing rainbow-clad horde. What did her lunch invitation really portend? She bobbed and dipped a few perfunctory curtsies, realizing from the sidelong glances, forced smiles, and raised brows, she looked every bit as disordered as she felt. But what frightened and alarmed her more than anything was that there was not one friendly face, not one sympathetic smile, in the entire crowd. Even without Philomemnon's warning, maybe it wasn't safe to stay here.

Samhain was tomorrow night. The gremlins were about to go mad, the land itself poisoned. If she left now, was there any possibility she could reach home? She'd no idea where Vinaver's house in the Old Forest was, but she had imagined from her conversation with Vinaver that it was far away. But the fact that Philomemnon's anonymous messenger told her to go there seemed to imply that it was close enough to reach by Samhain, for everyone knew it was tomorrow night. She could hear the word whispered, carried through the crowd on a dark purple tide of fear and suspicion that she saw peering from the corner of everyone's eyes. But, oh, how she would prefer to go home. Home, to her mother's soft bosom, home to her own sweet bed beneath the eaves. But could she ever hope to reach home by Samhain?

She was in the midst of deciding it was impossible, when a small familiar hand reached out of the mirror beside her and tugged at her gown. She gave a startled little gasp.

Forgive me, my lady, Petri's familiar little paw signaled one-handedly. *Come with me if you will.*

It was the most emphatic request the gremlins had in their vocabulary. Immediately she glanced from side to side, and waited until the largest group of sidhe passed in a swirl of silk. Seeing no one else coming, she stepped into the mirror, still in her stocking feet and wondered if it were worth trying to find her shoe. "What is it, Petri?" she whispered. "What are you doing in here? How did you find me?"

He found your shoe. In the gloom his little face was somber but his dark brown eyes were wide and alert. *I don't think you should stay here, lady. They've called for Lord Berillian.*

"Yes, I saw."

Then you must realize—

"I realize I should leave." She touched his cheek. "Come, let's go quickly. I need to change my clothes—find some boots. But we can be out of here within half a turn of the glass if we hurry."

She reached back and firmly gripped his hand, even as he nearly tripped over his tail, trying to scamper along behind her. *You cannot mean to—*

"To take you with me? Well, why not?"

Samhain. He was looking at her as if he feared she had temporarily taken leave of her senses.

Yes, that was a problem. But maybe not as insurmountable as they thought. As they made their way through the mirror world, her mind raced, considering the possibilities one after the other. Vinaver's house must be closer than she'd thought, for Philomemnon would know she would want to be there when the sun set on Samhain. Of course he wouldn't expect her to take a gremlin with her. But home was at least several days' travel away, even under the swiftest of conditions, and those certainly did not include a gremlin who would go mad during the dark hours of Samhain. She wrinkled her forehead as she rejected idea after idea.

The problem preoccupied her as she retired to her dressing room, glad to shed the elaborate puff of court gown and exchange it for a more serviceable dark blue wool riding gown. Was there a way to prevent Petri from going mad? Was there a way to lessen the effect? She realized that she didn't really understand what the effect of Samhain actually was on the gremlins. She pulled on her riding boots and went to find the little gremlin, who was finishing packing a small basket. "Petri." He looked up but did not stop his work. "What happens to you at Samhain?"

At that he looked distressed and shut the basket. *We go mad.*

"But how? What do you mean by go mad? What actually happens? Are you a danger?"

He looked mortified, and his grayish skin flushed a darker gray in the bright morning sun. *Only to ourselves. We must restrain ourselves from dashing out the windows—from throwing ourselves into walls—* He broke off abruptly.

"Well, then," she said briskly, seeing instantly the answer to the problem. "Pack rope."

What? He blinked.

"I'm not going to leave you here. I'll tie you to a tree if I have to, but there's got to be somewhere—someplace between here and home—somewhere we could go to give us shelter for Samhain. Philomemnon said to go to Vinaver's house within the Old Forest, but I don't know where that is, and I don't know—"

Have you forgotten I cannot leave these grounds? He was looking at her with pure and unadulterated misery.

She squatted down on the heels of her boots so that she was eye to eye with the little gremlin and replied in the same swift set of gestures. The misery on his face changed to surprise. *Maybe you are, Petri, and maybe you aren't. You yourself said the enchantment was wearing thinner every year. One of you's gone missing, hasn't he? Everyone thinks he's hiding somewhere, but we don't know that, do we? So we don't know for certain you can't leave until you actually try. And now seems as good a time as any, don't you think?*

I don't want to hurt you on Samhain, lady.

She rose to her feet. *I don't want you to hurt me, either, Petri. So let's make sure we have rope, all right. I think we'll be safer in the greenwood than in this Palace until we figure out what's really going on. We'll make our way to Vinaver's—* She broke off. How she was to accomplish that escaped her at the moment. But she felt compelled, as if she were carried forward by the motion of some great chain of events beyond her immediate comprehension. Every instinct she possessed screamed *Go.* So go she would, even if it meant dragging a Samhain-crazed gremlin along with her. For what she knew with absolute and utter certainty, that much as Timias and the Queen might make the Councilors into scapegoats, the ReMaking of the Caul would require something of the gremlins. Something they might no more be willing to agree to than they had the original transformation that had locked them into Faerie. She had a terrible feeling that to leave Petri behind was to never see him again. So she went on, even as she gathered up her cloak and swung it over her shoulders. *The only way I will leave you here, Petri, is if it should happen you can't leave the grounds. All right? And then we'll decide where to go. Home's too far to reach by Samhain, but maybe—*

There's Vinaver's Forest House. He picked up the basket and nodded decisively, as if that settled the matter.

Delphinea was amazed. *How can you possibly know about her Forest House?*

They both jumped as a sudden knock pounded at the door. "By order of the Queen!" a deep voice bawled. "Lady Delphinea!"

For a split second they stared at each other, frozen, and then they leapt at once through the mirror. Too late Delphinea remembered this particular wall was the other side of the winding staircase. They tumbled, pell-mell, all the way to the bottom, and landed in the grayish light at the bottom of the other side of the staircase. From far above, Delphinea swore she heard the distant tramp of heavy footsteps.

This way to the stables. Petri gestured. She scrambled to her feet and together they dashed through the Palace, hoping against hope that they could somehow reach Vinaver's house by the time Samhain fell.

Vinaver was surprised to see Dougal sitting in one of the two armchairs beside the fire. He was wrapped in a green silk sheet, and he looked equally surprised to see her when she stepped into the room, carrying two foamy possets of herbed and honeyed cream. The bandages she'd wound around his upper arm were white against the blue-veined whiteness of his skin, which was a startling contrast to the darker tan of his forearms and face. He looked much older, of course, since she'd seen him last, and the twenty mortal years hung heavy on his brow and streaked the hair on his head and chest iron gray. But the breadth of his shoulders and the muscled sinews of his chest were those of the young man she'd seduced that Beltane night. She smiled, remembering. He'd looked at her in much the same way as when he'd woken then to find himself in this very room.

"What do you want?" he growled.

She hesitated just inside the door, assessing the best way to approach him. Time was running out. The first night of Samhain was tomorrow, Finuviel would soon arrive. Their plan to store the dagger in the tree must've gone awry somehow, for why else would Dougal have brought it, half-finished, into Faerie himself? But whatever the reason, there were things that must be done and to accomplish all of them, she needed the silver dagger. She had decided she would do whatever she must to get Dougal to help her, including telling the truth. But first, though it galled her, she had to convince him to listen. "I've brought you a posset," she answered, proffering the tray.

"I've had enough of your Faerie swill." He folded his arms across his chest and looked away.

She hated him then, hated that so much now depended on his cooperation. Of all the smiths in the Shadowlands, how had it happened that Finuviel had chosen this one? "This Faerie swill, as you call it—" she walked swiftly to the hearth in a loud swish of skirts and set the tray upon it "—is what's saved your life. You're not out of danger yet, my good master smith."

"And what's the second for?" he asked.

"I thought I'd join you." She lifted one of the steaming cups and sniffed. "The jasmine honey gives it just that right touch. Taste it, and see." She settled herself into the opposite armchair, adjusting the folds of her wings as comfortably as she could. What an idiot she'd been for suggesting such a thing to Alemandine. It had begun as such a charming game, and then Alemandine with characteristic petulance and a desire to prove hers were the biggest, had insisted on growing her wings over her head, thus creating a conundrum for the ladies of the Court of epic proportions. To not follow the Queen's fashion was an unforgivable slight; to maintain one's balance beneath the weight of such unwieldy wings nearly impossible. The game of How to Flatter and Amuse the Queen frequently led to such irreconcilable dilemmas, and only the thought that she would never have to play it again soon made what she was about to do only infinitesimally palatable.

Dougal glared at her with guarded suspicion. "You can strain it with gold for all I care. There's nothing you can say, nothing you can do, to make me agree to finish that dagger for you."

We'll see about that. She raised her glass in a brief toast, then took a long drink, letting the sweet, spiced cream roll down her throat, preparing to bargain for whatever it took. The posset was rich and nourishing, its flavor a blend of honey with the carefully distilled essences of invigorating herbs. She doubted Dougal, or any mortal, possessed senses acute enough to truly appreciate it. "I'll give you back your wife."

At that he raised his head and spat into the fire. "Thanks and no thanks, you wretched witch. Take her home to die, shall I? Take her home to watch her wither away? Fine waste of a woman that would be. Or better yet, shall I stay here with her in Faerie? Will you give us a cottage—a place to live? A house such as this, here in the heart of your greenwood? [illegible] yes, just what your Queen would allow, I warrant—a couple of humans in Faerie, making human babies every year. So how's that to happen, my sweet lady sidhe? You truly think I'm so easily sopped?"

She tightened her hands around the golden cup, feeling the heat of the posset stabilize between her palms. Perhaps she'd underestimated the depth of Dougal's hatred. Again, she wondered why in the name of Herne, out of all the smiths who inhabited the Shadowlands, had Finuviel chosen Dougal. Now everything depended on him. Perhaps not everything. But quite a lot. She should have known when she'd found Dougal lying beneath the tree it would come to this. So much as it galled her that she, the rightful Queen of all the sidhe, should have to stoop so low as to beg this help from a mortal, there was nothing to do but to try and explain to him as much of the truth as she thought he could understand, and maybe even more that he couldn't. The sun fell on Samhain tomorrow. She could feel the boundaries between the worlds fading as the moon darkened and ebbed, and momentarily, she thought of Alemandine. She hoped Alemandine's strength was enough to maintain the borders of the Wastelands as the veil between Faerie and Shadow thinned away to nothingness for the first time in ages, without the Caul's intervention. The Caul had nothing to do with the magic that held the goblins confined to the Wastelands of Faerie, but Vinaver doubted that Alemandine's ability to maintain it would be taxed this Samhain. The goblins were not about to launch an assault against the sidhe. Not yet, not when they had the chance to run rampant in Shadow, set loose upon a hunt as had not been seen in centuries. It was an unfortunate consequence that could not be helped. But mortals were clever. There were always enough who managed to survive. So she dismissed those thoughts and set her cup back on the tray. She cocked her head and looked at him. "Will you promise to hear me out?"

He frowned and she had the distinct impression he would much prefer to throw the posset at her instead.

She narrowed her eyes at such blatant ingratitude. "I've saved your life, Dougal. You've nothing to lose by listening to what I will tell you. Drink the posset and hear me out. You owe me that at least." His nostrils flared at her use of his given name. She pressed on, despising him for every moment that she should be so debased. "I've never lied to you."

He gave a snort. "No, my lady, that's true enough, I suppose. You've never outright lied. But you've never been exactly forthcoming with the truth, either." He reached for the posset and flipped the golden lid off with a careless hand. It landed with a metallic spin and tinny thud on the polished oak floor. "I'll listen. But I've heard your songs before and I swear you can sing from now till the Hag becomes the Maiden, and I'll not do as you ask."

As if he'd doused her with the posset, she could not have been more shocked. *How odd that he should say that,* she thought. The Hag had not been able to make her transformation to the Maiden since the Caul was forged, and that, ultimately, was the reason the Caul had to be destroyed. Perhaps the fact he'd used that phrase meant that there was hope. She settled deeper into the chair, and spoke into the fire, for it was easier if she pretended he wasn't there. "You know my name is Vinaver. But you do not know who I am."

Dougal snorted. "I know well enough what you are."

She only closed her eyes against the jibe. "I am the sister of Alemandine, the Queen of Faerie. The twin sister, everyone believes, for we were born of one mother, carried together in her womb with our half-mortal, half brother, Artimour. We three are the children of Gloriana the Great, she who forged the Silver Caul."

"That would be Bran Brownbeard who actually forged it."

"Yes." She shook her head with a shrug and a tired sigh. "You're right, smith. It was the mortal, Bran Brownbeard, curse him, who forged it. But that's a story for another day. It's Bran that fathered Artimour, even as—" But she broke off, for she could not force herself to say all to this mortal who looked at her with such angry, hungry eyes. "Suffice it to say that another result of the forging of the Caul was that Alemandine and I, as well as our half brother, Artimour, were born: Artimour was the son of Bran, and Alemandine and I were fathered by the Queen's Consort. At least, everyone thinks that's what happened." She broke off and stared into the flames, wondering how to explain to this angry mortal. "I know you find the things I've done unforgivable. I know you hate me, Dougal. You're not the only one. There're some who've hated me from the very moment of my birth. My own father told them to drown me the minute I was born."

She knew the devoted father in Dougal would react to that. Predictably he frowned and shifted in his seat. "That does seem harsh, even for a sidhe."

"Well, there'd never been a twin birth among the sidhe in all of Faerie, you see. No one knew what to think. Alemandine came first, you see, and so to her were automatically accorded all the rights and honors of the heiress of the Faerie

Queen. And Artimour—well, he was accepted as living proof of the magic that had made the Caul. He's half-mortal but that could be overlooked. But then there was me. And no one—not even my mother—knew quite what to make of that."

"So this is all to get back at your father who wanted you drowned?"

"No." She shook her head and made a sound of derision. "My father doesn't even know he is my father. He thinks we were fathered by the Consort, as I said." She paused. That poor hapless dupe's name was scarcely mentioned anymore. "But the trees know. The land knows. The wind knows. I began to hear things—late at night when the wind was sighing in the trees, or whenever I walked beneath the avenues of trees that surround the Palace. I thought perhaps I was a little mad. No one spoke of such things. Oh, I knew that the Queen was bound to the land, but I didn't understand what that meant. No one thought it necessary to explain it to me. And then one day, I happened to hear my mother and Timias—he was her chief Councilor—discussing my sister, which was not so unusual at all, but what was unusual was that my mother was telling Timias that Alemandine was slow to learn to speak to the trees. I went to the Lorespinners then, and I learned that the Queen of the sidhe and her heiress are able to speak to the trees of the land. It was a gift granted in the Goblin Wars, and such a gift can never be revoked."

"You expect me to believe you can talk to the trees?"

She stiffened. "Whether or not you believe I can talk to the trees is one thing. What I expect you to believe is that I am telling you the truth. And yes, I can talk to the trees. And I'm almost the only one left in Faerie who can, since my mother went into the West."

"And your sister can't do this?"

"Not as well as I." It was hard not to allow the small note of self-satisfaction to creep into her voice. "That was the first time Timias arranged to have me banished."

"Who's Timias?"

"My mother's chief Councilor. And my father."

"Why does he hate you so? And why doesn't he know you're his daughter? Is the other one? Almondine? Is she his daughter, too?"

"Alemandine," she corrected gently. "And the answer to that question is both yes and no."

He sat back with a sour look on his face as if the posset had curdled on his tongue. "How can he not know you for his child? How can he not feel it, here?" He put his hand on his heart.

Something turned in Vinaver's gut and the tone of her answer was so bitter, it surprised even herself. "Timias doesn't feel anything, except for himself. Oh, he'll have you believing he's the most loyal sidhe to ever breathe the air of Faerie and perhaps he even believes it himself by now, but you may be as sure of this as the sun will rise in the east tomorrow. If Timias doesn't recognize his children, it's because Timias cares nothing for a world without himself in it."

"I'm not sure I understand that answer," Dougal said. "But my real question is this." He leaned forward and spoke quietly, quickly, with the arch look of a conspirator. "Which one of them do you want to kill—Timias or the Queen? Or is it perhaps both?" He laughed when she gasped in surprise. "Oh, come now, my sweet lady. You don't think I'm stupid, as well as gullible, do you? It's obvious you're in some sort of a hurry to kill someone, for why else would a sidhe want a silver dagger? Why else but to kill another sidhe?"

"Or a goblin," she spat back. Mortals who thought they could think annoyed her. "I never set out to kill anyone and I certainly don't want to kill my sister. She's not to blame for what she is."

"And what's that supposed to mean?"

At least he was talking to her. He might not be able to grasp the real intricacies of the truth, and there wasn't time to tell him all of it. It gave her hope he would consent.

"What do you mean?" he was asking again.

To give voice to such painful memories was so much more difficult than she had convinced herself it would be. She drew a deep breath and stiffened her spine. She had to tell the story as she'd rehearsed it in her mind, for if she didn't, she wouldn't be able to continue. As if they hadn't digressed, she continued. "I began to listen to the trees. I began to pay attention, since I knew I wasn't mad, and I began to understand what they said. And what they had to say frightened me more than anything I could ever have imagined, but I knew what they said was true, for the trees are the first to know everything. The trees carry the deepest knowledge of the land to the surface."

"And what did they tell you?"

"They said that Faerie was dying."

"Why?"

"The trees didn't know. So I went to my mother, and

asked her if that was true. And that time she banished me herself."

"But why? If your sister wasn't meant to be Queen, why not simply admit it? Let you be Queen?"

"I so often forget you mortals can never live long enough to be truly wise. It's not that simple, master smith. You see, what my mother didn't know—never knew—was that my sister is neither sidhe nor mortal, but an abomination formed in my mother's womb, of the dross left from the magic that created not only the Caul, but brought about the near simultaneous conception of myself and Artimour. She's no more truly of Faerie than she is of Shadow, but she doesn't know it." *She doesn't want to know it.* Alemandine knew and understood far more than she admitted, Vinaver was convinced. "But she is bound to the land by virtue of her birth, and I, true Queen that I might be, was shunted aside by the strongest force in all of Faerie—tradition."

"That's stupid."

"Is it?" she asked icily, tired of Dougal's derision. "And aren't all the songs of Shadow—the ones about all that's good and right and true, are they not all about some glorious hero or other of days gone by, long gone to feast in the Summerlands? Tell me that mortals don't live by their traditions and I will agree it's quite stupid. I've had occasion to learn quite a few mortal songs recently."

His lip curled and she knew that any mention of his wife, even one so oblique as that, was to pour salt on a wound. But Dougal was interested enough in what she was saying to ignore the jibe. "But if they knew all this—"

"They didn't know it. Faerie has remained stable for

more than a thousand of your mortal years. There was no reason to believe that anything was wrong. She was so sure that they had acted for the best, my mother ignored the trees, ignored what I told her they told me. And after my mother went into the West, and Alemandine was made Queen, I was expected to take myself away from the Court if I wasn't ready to go into the West. That's what Timias really hoped, you see. But I couldn't leave the trees. Then he expected me to vanish into the hinterlands, but I could not."

"I don't understand," Dougal said, as he lifted the posset to his mouth at last. "Why would anyone care whether you were at the Court or not?"

"The trees in the Sacred Grove would not speak to Alemandine and Timias said it was because of me—that my presence confused them. And finally, though I did not agree with him at all, I agreed to leave the Court. So I came here, to this great tree in the midst of the oldest Forest at the center of Faerie, and at the invitation of the trees themselves, I made myself this place. For Timias forgot one thing. He could banish me from the Court. But he could not forbid the Court from coming to me. And so I called for the Lorespinners, the masters of all the tales, and they came, one by one, and two by two and slowly I learned all that they could teach me. And I listened to the trees, to the voices that spoke to me on the wind, and slowly, I began to understand. Faerie was not dying. Faerie was being poisoned. I finally understood why my mother accused me of lying and ignored the trees. For it was by her hand and by her magic that Faerie was betrayed. And then one Beltane, Herne himself came to me." She drew a deep breath and shot him a steady look.

"You must understand, this is not an easy thing for me to speak of." Their eyes met.

"Beltane's never been one of my favorite holidays, either."

Maybe she deserved that. She kept her eyes steady, refusing to allow him to see he'd struck a nerve. She lifted her chin and tried to hold his eyes but she could not. The memories were coming too quickly, calling her away to that timeless moment when she had danced with the god himself within the hazel grove. "It happened here." How was she to put it into words for this cloddish mortal? "I was alone—I was usually alone in those days, and I found that I liked it. It was easier to speak to the trees. The trees of the forest aren't quite so easy to understand as the trees of the Queen's Grove, but I was learning. That Beltane, I lit two fires just before my door and danced between them to the song of the trees. And I looked up, and he was just there." She fell silent, remembering how the flames had suddenly brightened the face of a creature neither sidhe nor mortal, but something older and darker and greater than anything she'd ever beheld before. He danced through the fire itself, leaping lightly as a stag over the flames, and she had seen at once that he was already naked and erect, the round red head of his phallus jutting out from thighs covered in a soft pelt of tightly curled light brown hair. And from somewhere deep within the earth, she felt a throb beneath her feet. He had lowered his antlered head, capturing her eyes like a stunned doe, drawing her into the hot, bright center of the Beltane fires, coaxing her deeper and deeper into the steps of an ever more intricate dance she somehow seemed to know. Around and through and over the leaping flames he'd led her, all flashing thighs and gleaming eyes, until she'd realized she was naked, too. He'd said nothing, done nothing, but watch her with his bright eyes, unreadable as the fire itself as they'd danced. Those eyes were with her still. *Dark as a cave, but bright in the fire, they were, deep as still water, but clearer than day, older than the earth itself but younger than the newest seedling.* She shook herself as she realized Dougal was waiting for her to continue. "He led me down into a cave I've never been able to find since." She paused again as a tidal wave of memories crashed over her. She had never felt earth so soft, so thick, so spongy. His eyes had glittered green in the reddish light that filtered in from the fire, and the earth gave readily beneath her as he'd laid her down, covering her. There'd been a dark moon that Beltane, too, she remembered suddenly. Herne had come to her under the Hag's moon. Why had she not thought of it before? "It was there we made Finuviel." She looked away and knew she could tell him no more, for the rush of memory sweeping through her was taking her breath away. Dougal was looking at her with a curious sort of sympathy and she realized he thought she was mourning the loss of a lover. So much of human understanding was rooted around what they loved, that she knew at once it was impossible for him to really understand. "It's nothing I've ever looked to happen again. One visit from the god was quite enough." She gave a bitter little laugh. "It didn't make any of them like me any better. I was not allowed to come to Court at all while Finu-viel was a child. But then the time came for Alemandine to bear an heir. But when she'd been on the throne for more than a hundred of your mortal years, and nothing yet had happened, they finally sent for me to come and speak to the trees of the Sacred Grove."

"What'd they tell you?"

Dougal's dark eyes were fastened on her with a dark intensity that reminded her of Herne. He looked a little like Herne, too, sitting there naked in his green silk sheet. "They told me that a great sickness was falling upon the land and that I must go to the Hag."

He made a little sound in his throat, something like disgust or derision. "I thought you sidhe were beyond such corn magic—"

"Corn magic? Is that what you mortals call it now?" She leaned back in her chair and gazed up at the vaulted ceiling, where tendrils of ivy and mistletoe crept around the frames of the crystal-paned windows. "Oh, indeed, master smith. The Hag is real. Great Herne is real. All who doubt it will know for sure this Samhain, when the Wild Hunt rides forth and the goblins raid across the worlds as they have not done in centuries. Why do you think the time of Samhain is so feared? The Hunt is after souls, the goblins after flesh. You may believe me as you like, I suppose; certainly, everyone else thinks I lied. Alemandine refused to listen to what I said and she banished me. And I told myself I didn't care. Why should I care whether or not my sister had an heir? My son was tall and strong and beautiful, and when he came to Court at last, even Alemandine loved him. But when I returned here, even the other trees began to whisper all around me and so at last, I bid my son farewell, took up my staff, and went in search of the Hag."

"Where'd you go?"

"I wandered the length and breadth of Faerie, and finally, I realized that the Hag was not to be found in Faerie, but below, in the caverns, in the caves, in the deep places that the Lorespinners say go down forever into black tunnels of endless nothing. It was there that I decided at last to seek the Hag. But the Lorespinners didn't know everything. They didn't know what half-formed things dwell there, down where neither sidhe, nor mortal, nor even goblin, has ever dared to go. We are all the children of Herne and the Hag, you know, all of us—sidhe, mortal and goblin—but in those dark caverns, there are other children, older children, but even they, foul, twisted, half-formed things, couldn't tell me where the Hag dwelled.

"And so I walked, on and on, until my boots wore away and my feet bled and finally healed, leaving scars so thick I no longer needed boots. And though I searched everywhere, I could not find the Hag. Until at last, one day, I was so tired and so weary. I had been so long beneath the ground. I was starting to forget what sunlight felt like. It had been so long since my bones were warm. I leaned against the wall and I felt the rock speak."

"Did you now?"

She narrowed her eyes. She wanted to scratch the stubborn skepticism off his broad face. With greater self-control than she'd ever thought she possessed, she continued. "It took me what seemed another age or more to learn to understand what the rocks said. Much they told me was useless to me. But at last, I'd learned enough." She broke off and took another breath. "I won't tell you I came to find my way at last, how it happened or who led me to the great black chamber so far below the surface of the world, the light of the sun is not even a legend. The walls are lit by lichen, you know, lichen that glows like stars, millions upon millions of them." She remembered standing on the smooth stone floor, looking up at the vast round dome of the ceiling, studded with pinpoints of white and green and pinkish light. "They looked like little stars," she said aloud, "waiting to be born. The air was so cold. And my guide pointed straight ahead, and I saw we stood upon the edge of an underground sea. Mist was rising off the surface of the water and I looked out, and I saw that there was an island, with a great rock upon it. And my guide gave me to understand that that's where I would find the Hag."

Her voice drifted, and she gazed off, unseeing, beyond Dougal's shoulder. How could she convey to him how it felt to stand within that vaulted space, and gaze out over that silent water. It lapped at the shore in little waves, and blobs of phosphorescent scum floated over its surface, so that it did not look at all like a lake in the world above. She had come so far and walked so long. The water looked cold as death. Her breath hung white as the mist in that frigid air and the last thing she wanted to do was to submerge herself in icy water. But there was no help for it. Her guide insisted that the island in the middle was the place where the Hag could be found. And so she shed as many of her clothes as she could, and waded in.

At first, she'd been pleasantly startled. "I was wrong and I was so surprised. The water wasn't cold at all. It was warm—blood heat, one might say. But the farther on I swam, it thickened into this viscous sort of slime that formed in long tendrils all around me. It began to twine in my hair and wrap around my limbs, and I felt the energy begin to seep from my pores, into that thick hot ooze, and I knew as I swam that it would engulf me if it could, that the water wasn't really water—it was the great primordial sea from which all things come and to which all things must return and it would take me if it could and remake me, reform me, into something else, something new. So I swam. I swam as hard and as fast as I could."

"You found the Hag?"

He was staring at her, and at least she knew she had him riveted. "Yes." She let the word sink in as she remembered how she'd stumbled ashore, covered in thick whitish mucus that slithered and slid and crawled all over her. But the island appeared deserted, with only the great rock in the very center. The place was empty and once again, she'd felt herself frustrated, her purpose thwarted. In frustration, she stamped her foot, hard and found that unlike the opposite shore, this one was comprised of razor-sharp rocks that sliced her feet to ribbons of flesh. Her teeth were beginning to chatter and she doubted she could survive another swim across that slimy sea. She had fallen to her knees, tears spilling down her cheeks, for she knew she was finished. She could go no farther. And through her tears she was amazed to see the great rock unfold itself, revealing the stumpy misshapen form and ghastly face of the Great Hag herself. *A Queen that's ne'er a queen to be; that's who comes to call on me?* The voice had shivered through her mind, reverberating through her very flesh. She could feel the vibration in the stone beneath her feet, in the swells of water that rippled and lapped against the rocks as if in response. And as the creature's rheumy old eyes scanned the twilit darkness,

Vinaver stared in absolute horror at the thing that crouched over her cauldron, a cauldron that was set on what looked like two polished globes of what looked like different sorts of crystal. Where a third should have been, a curious arrangement of makeshift iron legs propped the black cauldron awkwardly over the flames. *A Queen that's ne'er a queen to be; that's who comes to call on me?* The mocking words echoed again over and over in Vinaver's mind.

"Well?" Dougal was half-leaning out of his chair, his eyes fastened on her. "What happened? What did she tell you? What did you learn?"

"Many things. More than I wanted to know." She closed her eyes. Was she going to have relive the whole horrible experience now, here, before his eyes? Was that what it would take to convince this obstinate mortal to help her? It would have been easier by far to have found another smith. But he did remind her of Herne, she saw that now. She was not as immune to mortal charm as she wanted to believe and there was no more time to find another. What in the name of Herne had Finuviel been thinking? The enormity of all that she had set herself to do suddenly seemed overwhelming. Fortunately there wasn't time to tell him everything. "But the most important thing she told me was that the Caul was poisoning Faerie and had to be destroyed."

Her head fell against the back of the chair as if beneath the weight of the images which came swirling up, threatening to overwhelm her. For the Hag's knowledge was imparted not so much in words, but in images, images that roused sounds and smells and feelings, images that pulsed up from the depths of the Hag's cauldron to the same rhythm as the motion of Herne's phallus pumping between her thighs, images to which she clung with desperate hope for they were the only answers she had.

"But I thought the Caul kept the goblins out of Brynhyvar?"

Dougal had been asking her the same question for several moments, she realized with a start. "Yes," she answered. "Yes, it does. But the very silver that it's made of is poison to Faerie, and if it's not destroyed, and made again into something else, very, very soon, Faerie will corrode away to nothingness. It's already beginning to happen."

"But then what's going to protect us?"

"Well," said Vinaver. "There's always corn magic."

"Faugh." He looked disgusted and drained the posset to the dregs, then set the cup back on the tray with a loud bang.

"Don't you understand? Corn magic is mortal magic—magic every bit as potent in its own way as anything wrought by the sidhe. It may have degraded and eroded in the minds of men over the centuries that the Caul has existed, for its power has been usurped and corrupted in the service of the Caul. But it has power enough of its own kind. Believe me, Timias understood that well and made it part of the magic of the Caul, which is why the worlds are bound so closely together. But don't fool yourself into believing that the Caul was created to keep the goblins out of Shadow. That's one reason, of course, but not the only one. And not at all the most important."

"You still haven't explained why you need a silver dagger."

She stopped. This was the most difficult part to remember. "It's part of the bargain I made with the Hag. She hates Timias even more than I do."

"She wants you to kill Timias?" When Vinaver nodded, Dougal leaned forward. "Why? What does she have against him?"

"I told you how the Hag's cauldron rested on two globes, one of bloodstone, for the mortals, and one of obsidian, for the goblins. But the one for the sidhe was missing. It was Timias who stole the moonstone globe from the Hag. You know your legends, you know of the moonstone which lies in the Palace of the Faerie Queen, the one on which the Caul rests? It belongs to the Hag. It's one of the three globes that form her hearth. Timias took it and she wants it back. And she wants him dead. Forever."

"So that's what you have to do to pay the Hag back for what she told you?"

"That's one of the things I must do."

"What's the rest?"

There was a long silence and a sudden gust of wind roared through the branches of the great oak above them. A tide of acorns tumbled across the crystal windowpanes with the sound of thrown dice. "The knowledge of the Hag comes neither cheap nor easy," she answered at last.

"What else does she want of you?"

She wished she could storm from the room, she wished she could lay a web of enchantment on him so thick he'd never find his way through it. But she could not. Such a great working required the will of all who touched it. So all she could do was answer his questions, and hope she could sway him with the truth alone. "There were three things she required of me, and Timias's head is only the third. The second is the return of the moonstone globe, of course. The first thing she took from me as I stood there."

"And what was that?"

She steeled herself, drew herself up and reminded herself that she'd been born the rightful Queen of all Faerie. "She took my womb."

"She did what?" He spoke in a horrified whisper that made her feel like a monster herself.

"You heard me. She took my womb." She paused for just a heartbeat, fighting the agonizing memory of that cold and hungry claw, entering, probing, grasping, ripping. So she went on quickly: "She took from me the very thing that bound me, like all her daughters, most intimately to the land of which we are a part. And so for the answers I sought, for the knowledge of what must be done to save Faerie, she made me pay with the very part of me that binds me to Faerie, thus ensuring I can never be Queen."

"But why?" Dougal whispered. "Doesn't the Hag care if Faerie disappears?"

Vinaver shook her head and shrugged. "The Hag is neither kind nor cruel. Why should she care? In her cauldron, all is made new. Timias and Gloriana interrupted the natural cycle of renewal and restoration. From the Hag's point of view, I suppose one could say, it's as easy to let it all collapse into chaos, and then build it again into something new. Why save the old when it's as easy to make it new?" She paused, letting the information sink in.

"But if you can't be Queen, and your sister isn't supposed to be Queen, who—"

"Well, you see, that's the point of it all. The power of Faerie must shift from the feminine energy to masculine. The time of the Queens has ended. The new ruler must be a King."

He looked confused, and she cast about for a way to explain it to him. She held her hands before her as if cupped around a ball of light, and the air between her palms shimmered. A bright sphere glowed into existence. "This is the energy of Faerie. It is composed of opposites—light and dark, up and down, male and female. For all these ages, the power has been turned this way—" She rolled it between her palms, and a pale pink light appeared in the top half of the globe, and a pale blue in the bottom. "Now, in order for the Hag to be transformed into the Maiden, the power must shift." She rubbed her hands over it again, and the pink and blue flowed into each other, flared a pure, pale violet, then subsided, each to their new halves. "This is the natural ebb and flow of the energy. The Caul has prevented this from happening in its proper time. The Hag must be transformed into the Maiden. But that hasn't happened, and can't, so long as the Caul exists. Now do you understand what I need you to do?"

"So you don't just want me to make this dagger. You need me to destroy the Caul—"

"Destroy and make it into something else." She wiped her hands together and the sphere of light shimmered out.

"So we kill Timias and destroy the Caul. What happens to your sister?"

She met his gaze squarely. "I don't know what will happen to my sister. For when I finally returned to Faerie, I found that Alemandine appeared to be pregnant at last. But I knew what was really happening. The Hag had done me a service, after all."

"And what was that?"

"What is it do you suppose that nourishes Alemandine? Alemandine thinks she's pregnant, but she's not—she's feeding upon the very thing of me that would enable me to be Queen. She has to stay alive long enough for Finuviel and me to accomplish all that must be accomplished. Or Faerie will collapse. So the Hag bought me a little time. We're juggling a very, very delicate balance here."

"What happens to my world if Faerie collapses?"

It would be easy to lie, she thought. Easy to tell him that Shadow, too, would fade away to nothingness. But that was not true, and she had vowed to tell him only the truth. "I don't know," she answered. "I know that the Caul has bound our worlds far closer than they should've been. I know that what happens in Faerie affects and is affected by what happens in Shadow. I can only assume that if the natural order has been interrupted in Faerie, the same has happened in the mortal world as well. The King of your country is mad, is he not? And two of the great Houses have raised their standards against him?"

Dougal's head snapped up. "How do you know that?"

"Let's just say I've paid more attention to what happens in Shadow of late because it has such an effect here. But I don't know what will happen in your world when the Caul's destroyed. I believe that if it's beneficial for Faerie, it will be equally beneficial for Shadow. But I cannot say for certain."

"How do I know you're telling me the truth?"

"Look at my foot." She kicked the slipper with its pointed, curling toes off her left foot and held it up. "Do you see those scars? Do you see those ridges? It would be an easy thing for me to heal those, mortal, to make my foot as soft and smooth and pink as the day I first drew breath. But I can't. For it's when I walk, when I press those thick calluses, when I feel the stab of those old pains, it's then that I remember what she told me. It's then I see again all the things she showed me in her Cauldron, all the things I would forget to all our peril."

He leaned forward and caught her foot in his hand, his callused palm cradling it gently as if she were a filly to be shod for the first time. The sheet shifted lower, and her gaze was drawn to his navel and the vertical line of black hair below. He examined her foot carefully, his eyes tracing every thick scar, every ugly ridge, every twisted bump of misshapen bone. He raised it higher, unsettling her, so that she was forced to grip the arms of her chair to maintain her balance, and she felt his breath on her bare skin. "This must hurt to walk."

She pulled her foot away, as she struggled upright. She shoved it back into its slipper, indignant as an unmounted maiden at his liberties. "I don't want your sympathy." She spoke spitefully to cover her discomfiture. "I want your help."

"I'll think about it."

"Then think about this. I could threaten you, ensorcel you—"

"Well, why don't you? Isn't that what you did the first time?"

"Because this time, I need your full and free consent. I saved your life and gave you the life of your daughter, that she might grow into whatever miserable mortal life awaited her. I ask you now to help me save my son and make him all that he must be. I give you till the sun falls on Samhain tomorrow to tell me yes or no."

"And what happens if I don't?"

"What happens to a mortal who does not pay a debt of honor?" She rose to her feet with all the grace she could muster. She saw something that might be admiration dawn in his eyes and knew he watched her walk out of the room with a new respect that made her believe she might have reason to hope.

The last rays of the afternoon sun were slanting over the hills when the wagons drew up in a close circle beneath a thick stand of trees overlooking the banks of a wide rocky brook. "I'm not going further tonight," the head wagoneer was heard to exclaim. "Samhain or no, I'm more afraid of getting the wagons stuck in that crick than I am of either goblins or the dead. I'm not taking the chance of getting stuck out there as the sun's going down. I'm not that afraid of goblins."

That's because you haven't met one yet, Griffin thought as he tried to shake himself out of the thick drowse into which the lurch and sway of the cart had lulled him. He scrambled out of the wagon after Engus, his limbs like dead weights. *What's wrong with me,* he wondered as his head spun. They'd broken the camp above the Vale of Ardagh just after dawn of the day before yesterday, and headed east, toward Allovale and the silver mines. He stumbled along, listening as if in a daze to the voices which were floating on the gusty breeze which had come up as the sun turned the corner in the sky. The voices didn't make a lot of sense. *What's wrong with me,* he thought again, as he was forced to grab on to the side of the cart as his legs seemed to collapse beneath him.

"Psst, Griffin." Gareth's voice floated up from beneath the wagon. "Psst."

Griffin frowned then slumped to his knees, absurdly grateful for the opportunity to rest once more. His blood felt like sludge. "Gareth? What're you doing under there?"

"Here. C'mere. You look half-mazed. Have a slug of this, 'twill clear your head right up." In the shadows beneath the cart, Gareth crouched, bright-eyed and eager, proffering a leather flask. "C'mon, have some. This'll cure you."

"What is it?" he managed to ask.

"It's the stuff they gave us to drink to get us to work—the stuff that keeps us awake and strong. I snitched myself some when they were loading the barrels up on the carts. I reckoned we'd need it when they didn't give us no more. Here—take some. That's what ails you—when it wears off, you see, you feel like shit. The trick, in my opinion, is to never let it wear off."

Griffin dropped onto all fours and peered more closely at Gareth. What the description lacked in sensitivity it made up for in accuracy. He did feel like shit. He rubbed his head with one hand and tried to think. Tonight was Samhain. They'd stopped to make camp. They were open, vulnerable, and exposed. They had silver bars and silver coins in plenty, but the bulk of the weapons had been shipped off. Only the guards had silvered weapons, and it was clear that the exhausted blacksmiths were in no condition to go anywhere or put up much of a fight. Including against the goblins. He raised his head and stared at Gareth. The younger boy was squatting on his haunches, his bright eyes dancing in his face. He'd pay perhaps, when he eventually ran out of the stuff, whatever it was. But for now, at least Gareth looked capable of outrunning a goblin. Unlike himself, who to a goblin would look like a haunch of easy meat.

With the last ounce of energy he could muster, he grabbed for the flask and downed a great swig. The drink poured down his throat like liquid silk. A warm surge blossomed in his belly, and he felt a wave of strength pulse through his system. He shook himself and squared his shoulders and raised the flask again, only to have Gareth seize it from him before it touched his lips.

"Easy there, Griff. That's got to last us who knows how long."

"Sorry." He rubbed the last bit of sand out of his eyes and looked over his shoulder. From this vantage point, he saw the legs of horses and men milling about between the wagons in all directions as the head wagoneer and the sergeant of the guards bawled out conflicting orders.

"What do you think, Griffin?" Gareth's irrepressible head bobbed up into his line of vision. "Think we'll be safe enough here?"

"Safe enough as any place, I reckon," he answered. *Safe enough as anyplace that doesn't have four high walls around it and a strong roof over it.* Even from here he could hear the loud rush of the broad shallow brook gushing over the uneven rockbed. The long rays of the westering sun were slanting through branches and the air smelled like dusk. He could understand why the wagoneer didn't want to risk trying to cross that brook at sunset. The water looked just deep enough to conceal rocks that would snag a horse's leg, a wagon's wheel. And yet, were they really safe here? Were they really safe anywhere tonight?

He got to his feet, glad to feel life, even if artificially borrowed, returning to his limbs. He reached into the wagon, and sloshed the dregs from the waterskin over his face, just as a guard thrust a shovel in his hands. "Come along with you, boy. No time to dally. Tonight is Samhain."

No need to remind me. Dubiously Griffin followed, watching the rest of the preparations warily over his shoulder, even as he was made to help dig the latrine. Ultimately it was decided to circle the wagons, and to build four large bonfires at the four quarter points. An argument ensued over the directions until someone pointed out that the sun always set in the west. Gareth scampered through the press of men, horses and equipment, spying, snitching food, and generally avoiding the watchful eyes of the impatient guards who shoved and pushed the dazed men through their tasks.

The night came quickly, suddenly, as if eager and aware. Huddled around the campfires, Griffin sat with his back to a wagon wheel, watching the exhausted men gathered around the smaller fires in the center of the circled wagons, waiting for his turn for a bowl of the stew the cook was dishing from his black iron cauldron.

When the signal came from the guard, it was his turn, he

rose to his feet, and paused to help Engus who muttered a low thanks as he staggered to his feet. "Don't quite know what's wrong with me, lad."

I do, thought Griffin. The men around them were mostly silent, either shoveling in the thick stew, or slumped over snoring. *They might as well ring a dinner bell.* He said nothing as he made his way to the cooking tent. But as Griffin received his food, he looked at the cook as he slopped a portion into Griffin's wooden bowl. "What about a drink of that other stuff?" he asked.

The man raised his head and shot him a wary look. "What other stuff?"

"The stuff in those barrels." Griffin nodded to the wagon, where the dark shapes were piled high in the light of the leaping bonfires. "The stuff you gave us to make us work."

The man narrowed his dark eyes and his mouth turned down in an ugly sneer. "Don't know nothing about that."

"Don't you know tonight is Samhain?" Griffin leaned over the cauldron of stew, and one of the guards stepped forward.

"Here, here, you'll not be threatening the cook. What ails you, anyway?" the brawny guard asked, waving his silvered pike before Griffin.

"I want some of that drink, for myself and my friends. For all of us. It's Samhain—if the goblins come for us, we've nothing to defend ourselves with and no chance at all of even running for our lives all dopey as we are."

"Well, you're not exactly dopey, are you?" He stuck his broad face directly into Griffin's and he pulled back at the blast of rotting teeth.

"We're sitting ducks here."

"Aye, he's right," Engus put in, coming up behind him with the others from Killcarrick. "Whatever that stuff that made us work so hard we didn't need sleep—give us a drink of it. My arms are so tired, they're hanging like stumps from my shoulders. If the goblins come on us, we're dead already."

"Get back to your fire," the soldier snarled.

More guards came running up, as the mass of blacksmiths and apprentices pressed in closer, until at last the sergeant of the company pushed his way to the cook station. "What's wrong here? There's plenty to eat."

"Aye, but naught to drink," answered Engus.

"Give us that stuff you got in those barrels," Griffin said. "Just a swig for every man. If the goblins come hunting us, we've no chance at all as we are." The torchlight snapped and flared across the dark and desperate face, and long orange tails whipped sideways in the windy gusts. He looked up and saw black clouds massing over the indigo sky. A chill went down his back. *The veils are parting,* he thought. *The wheel is turning. Samhain comes.* His eyes locked with the sergeant's and he did not look away.

"All right," the sergeant said at last. "They have a point."

"But—" the cook began.

"My orders are to deliver these smiths to the silver mines of Allovale where they're needed in the Duke's service. Now, I'm thinking my orders mean live smiths." He leaned over the cauldron. "I've seen too many strange things these past few weeks. So you break out the mother-loving joy juice. Whatever crosses over this night, these men deserve at least a fighting chance."

Griffin stood silently as he was handed the first mug. He raised it to his lips. "Thank you."

"My mother's a corn granny," the sergeant said.

"Will you share the weapons? They're all coated in silver, I see." Griffin's dark eyes met the sergeant's unflinchingly. Beside him, he heard Engus chuckle softly and a few of the others gasped at his audacity.

The sergeant stared back, eye to eye, shoulder to shoulder. "You're the one from that village, aren't you?" He nodded when Griffin gave a brief nod. "I've heard about you. Heard about what you did there. We've got no druid—no granny. But we'll do what we can. We've got enough silver to plate a keep." Abruptly he spun on his heel and, pushing his way through the crowd, shouted for the soldiers to share what silver-coated weapons there were.

But after that, the hours dragged. The unnatural energy from his second drink burned like a fire in his veins, making him tense and edgy. The wind shifted repeatedly, coming from every direction in unexpected gusts that rustled through the dry leaves left on the branches. Griffin, crouching beside the fire between Gareth and Engus, fingered the silver-coated spear the sergeant had handed him. As the wind blew, Griffin sniffed carefully, alert for the slightest whiff of that unmistakable smell.

Beside him, Gareth bobbed up and down, whistling beneath his breath as he whittled away at something he held closely between his palms. The high, bright color in Gareth's cheeks disturbed Griffin. And when had the younger boy become so thin? The sharp little bones of his wrists stuck through his paperish skin at odd angles, like those of a crippled bird. At last Engus gave him a tap on the head. "Hush that noise, boy. Can't you hear the quiet?"

It was then that Griffin realized that the entire camp had fallen silent, that the only sounds were the wind in the trees, the snap and hiss and crack of the bonfires and the invisible gush of the water just below. He took a deep breath and a whiff of ordure filled his nostrils. "By the Great Mother," he whispered. He reached for the spear and leapt to his feet, sniffing, searching the air, but realized as the other men looked up at him it was only the smell of the latrine.

"What ails you, Griffin?" asked Engus.

"The smell. It's only the latrine. But I thought for a moment—" He sank down into his spot, feeling slightly foolish. Most of the other men, with the sole exception of those who knew him from Killcarrick, and the sergeant, seemed to think him something of a crackpot.

"What smell?" piped up Gareth. "I don't smell anything—" He broke off and took a deep breath. Almost immediately, his face crumpled. "Whew—what is *that?*"

The wind gusted, the branches dipped down and the flames leapt high. Engus bolted upright and Griffin rose slowly to his feet once more, his scalp prickling. "What was what?"

The goblin roared out of the night, a thing twice the size of anything he'd seen in Killcairn. It leapt out of the tree, just as Griffin raised his spear and aimed it directly at the thing's chest. The goblin's claws raked over his head and he felt and smelled its fetid breath on his cheeks. He closed his eyes and stabbed upward with the spear with all his might. Blood flowed into his eyes, falling like a red curtain across his vision. The weight of the dying goblin collapsed directly onto him as the world exploded into fiery showers and the gleaming black blades of the goblin horde that descended out of the dark like the wrath of some unforgiving goddess.

15

From the highest battlements of Killcarrick Keep, Uwen looked out over the dark Samhain landscape. A cold wind gusted around the single tower. It plastered his plaid to his body and whipped long wisps of hair across his face. How different this Samhain was from every other he could remember. Instead of the leaping bonfires dotting the landscape, stretching across the rolling hills as far as the eye could see, the hills were only silent black shapes against the star-studded sky. The torches on the walls flared up in long plumes of blue and orange flame, and belched white smoke high into the air. They cast an uneven light on the crowded inner ward, for the tent city had been abandoned long before sunset. It had made it difficult to finish the preparations, but he could scarcely blame the families who jammed within the keep's sheltering walls. The upper levels of the tower as well as the Hall were packed, and directly below, the men he'd not positioned on the battlements milled, restlessly awaiting orders he hoped he wouldn't have to give. Awaiting silver-coated weapons he hoped they wouldn't have to make. From this vantage point, he could see the double line of archers on the gates, which overlooked the causeway and the meadows, the one most glaring strategic weakness in the otherwise well-situated keep. He had managed to convince the Sheriff to melt down enough silver to coat the arrows, arguing that with enough arrows, they could repel the goblins before they got to the walls.

But it's only a keep, he thought. It was a single tower, surrounded by a double wall. An outpost, really. It wasn't constructed to defend this many people. Here, in the heart of the Killcarrick uplands, the peace of Gar had reigned as long as anyone but the oldest grannies could remember. He looked out over the black and brooding landscape and shivered as the flagpole shuddered and the Duke's standard snapped open in a sudden gust. He clutched his plaid closer about his throat and stared down at the resolute line of men and boys leaning on the walls, laughing and joking, holding their hands out over iron kettles of smoldering coals.

If it were necessary, he was prepared to overcome the Sheriff's protests by force of arms. He thought of the men he'd positioned outside the cavern below the keep where the Duke's silver was kept. Four scullions from the kitchens tended the fire in the forge, a pile of spears and pikes and maces, some rusting with disuse lying beside it. He hoped Nessa would be well enough to agree to come and oversee the melting down of the silver, if it came to that. He didn't expect her to do the work, but he wanted someone in the forge he could trust. For he could feel the hair on the back of his neck standing on end, his muscles tense and ready. Every sense felt preternaturally aware. He'd taken every precaution he could think to take. He glanced down at the swirling tattoos which covered his forearms, tattoos he'd earned, battle by battle, wound by wound. Now he was about to discharge the greatest duty he'd ever undertaken to his Duke and his captain. He squared his shoulders, and glancing up at the sky, whispered a quick plea to the Lords of Light and Thunder to let the challenges he'd faced so far have adequately prepared him to meet this one, and to lead him honorably to the Summerlands if such was to be his fate. Then he took a quick breath and turned around to face the white faces of the stripling lads who'd been chosen to keep the watch. "You know the drill now, lads? There's to be no horsing around up here. Tonight's a sacred night and this is a sacred duty. And if you see anything—and I mean anything—move out there, from any direction at all, including from the water, you set up the loudest cry you're capable of making, you hear me? I mean it."

"Even a crow, Sir Uwen?" piped up a skinny redhead.

The boy was lanky and freckle-faced, and for a moment he reminded Uwen of the younger brother, Grear, he'd lost to the sweating sickness. A flash of memory flared up—the first Samhain after Grear's death, when the boy had come to stand before the entire family at midnight, assuring them all he'd found the Summerlands a pleasant place to play. He'd have no time for visits with the dead this year. *Might be crossing over with them.* He shook that thought away. He had a duty. There'd be no reward in the Summerlands for him if he didn't fulfill it honorably before he died. And that included answering even the silliest questions seriously before a battle. "Don't you know what the crow portends?" he whispered, meeting the boy's eyes solemnly. "The crow's the Hag's bird, the Marrihugh's bird. So, aye, you see a flock of crows land on that causeway, young master, I want to hear of that, too." He paused, waiting to see if any of the others had questions, then nodded shortly. "All right then. To your posts. And remember, this is the most serious work you've ever undertaken. No horsing around. And no sleeping."

He gave a stern look around as they scampered to take up their assigned positions, then pattered down the narrow stone steps of the spiraling staircase. He had one last stop to make before he took his own position on the gates.

But his pace slowed, despite his urgency. It had been a day at least since he'd seen Nessa. She'd been closeted with the sidhe who'd been pulled up from the riverbank ever since she'd risen from her bed, and the few times he'd happened to catch her, running some errand or such for the granny, she'd made it clear she'd no time to spend jawing with him. *Well, so be it,* he thought crossly. She was a country blacksmith's daughter. He was a belted knight. *Perhaps she thinks I only want to bed her. But she doesn't seem to care if that's what she thinks.* The thought popped unbidden into his head as he reached the level of the Sheriff's quarters, where the most vulnerable of all—the wounded, the sick, the pregnant women, and babes-in-arms, had all been moved into the most defensible place within the keep. This was not the time to dwell on such nonsense. He stepped into the thick press of mostly female bodies, looking in vain for either Nessa or Granny Molly.

"Here." A woman thrust a squalling red-faced infant into his arms.

"For the love of the Mother, goodwife," he sputtered, even as he automatically brought the child to his shoulder, and patted its back with a firm and rhythmic hand. "I'm not here to hold your infants. I'm here to find Granny Molly—can you tell me where she is for the love of the goddess? And take this one." He held out the whimpering child in vain.

The woman only shook her head while she crooned over three bare-bottomed babies. Her nimble fingers skipped over each in turn, and in the blink of an eye, it seemed, a bleached linen diaper magically appeared between each set of fat thighs. She gestured for him to hand her the fourth, who'd quieted against Uwen's shoulder and was now chewing its fist contentedly. "You've a way with the babbies, I see, sir," she said, with a twinkle in her eye. "Molly's in there." She nodded toward the Sheriff's bedchamber, as she expertly diapered the baby. "The old granny's not expected to last the night."

"Ah." He hesitated, watching the babies kick and coo and flail on the floor at his feet. A vision of the carnage he'd buried at Killcairn flashed before his eyes, and he pushed it away. Samhain always brought memories, but this Samhain they were only a dangerous distraction.

"Sir?"

"Samhain blessings on you and yourn, goodwife."

He left her looking startled, as he negotiated a way

through the chattering press of female flesh, and pausing only to knock briefly, opened the door and stepped inside. A different atmosphere altogether reigned over the quiet room. A hush hung heavy in the still air. Granny Wren, the old wicce-woman from Killcairn, lay on a low pallet before the fire. The red woolen curtains were looped back around the sheriff's massive wooden bedstead, and on it, the sidhe was lying white as marble against the grayish pillow. Three women bent over Granny Wren, and they all looked up as he stepped into the room. One was Molly. The others he didn't know. "Forgive me, grannies," he said, speaking softly, feeling as if he'd interrupted something sacred and holy. He felt awkward and out of place in his battle dress.

At once, Molly was on her feet. "Sir Uwen." She gathered her skirts and, carefully stepping past the pallet, beckoned him to the far corner of the room. "Is everything ready?"

"I'm still concerned that we don't have enough silver-coated weapons. That's why I come here. I'm looking for Nessa. I need her down in the forge—not to work—" he said swiftly, as Molly opened her mouth, obviously ready to protest "—just to supervise. I've got men in front of the guard-room. If there's even the whiff of a goblin in the air, they've got orders to smash the door down and bring the silver to the forge. I'll answer to the Duke if that suet-headed Sheriff can't. I've got a few scullions stoking up the fire, I just want Nessa there to watch over it all if we need to melt silver in a hurry. Is she up to that, do you think?" Molly hesitated and glanced over her shoulder. Uwen narrowed his eyes and followed her gaze to the sidhe. Not for the first time, he wondered just why Nessa wanted to spend every waking moment here. He looked not much more likely to live through the night as Granny Wren. Did Nessa think he might know something about her father? Was it possible this was the sidhe she'd made the dagger for? "How is Nessa? I've only seen her once or twice in the last few days. But she seems to be up and about and that's why I was thinking—"

Molly started out of her reverie and looked back at him. "No, I think she'll be fine. She went to fetch me a few things from the kitchens. She'll be back in a moment."

He looked down at his boots and a sudden intuition told him to get to his post upon the gates. "I don't have time. Tell her what I said."

Their eyes met and even as she nodded and began to agree, a high note blared through the air, faint but unmistakable. Untamed and unrestrained, the note shivered with such a preternatural clarity, they both knew instinctively that no horn made in Brynhyvar could ever sound it. It woke something deep inside him even as the warrior in him reacted. "Samhain blessings, Granny." He bent awkwardly and kissed her cheek. She smelled like lavender, like pine. Like victory, he decided.

"May the Marrihugh walk before you," she answered, as he bolted from the room, running as fast as he possibly could to his position on the gates.

Nessa nearly collided with Uwen on the stairs as she darted up, nearly dropping her burden of hazelnuts and garlic. "Great Mother!" she cried. She'd known the moment she'd heard those first wild notes that something was happening.

Uwen reached for her, steadied her. "Take Molly what she needs and then, if you think you can, I need you down in the forge. If that's goblins, and I think it is, then we need more silver-coated weapons and I need you to supervise." His hands on her upper arms were firm, his eyes entirely void of their usual teasing light. The memory of those things roaring out of the night made her shudder. "Do you understand me?"

But she understood what he wanted and why he needed her and she could only nod as another trumpeted burst of notes wailed, louder this time. "They're getting closer," she whispered.

"Samhain blessings." He pulled her close and pressed a quick kiss on her lips. And then he vaulted down the steps and was gone, leaving her standing momentarily stunned. Then she shook herself as the sound of that wild horn came again, and a great draft gusted through the cramped hall, swirling down the hearths, raising tunics and plaids, catching in coifs and cloaks. She pressed herself against the steps as a panicked cry went up. "Bolt the doors! Bolt the doors!"

She stumbled back up the steps, certain that she heard Molly calling her, lumbering as ungainly as a cow through the heaps of crying babies and frightened women, and shut the door behind her. Molly and the other grannies were kneeling beside Granny Wren, who was writhing and tossing on the pallet. Her eyes were wide open, but she gazed beyond them all, to the open window where the silvery call blew in on a gust of wind. And Nessa was shocked as she realized that Granny Wren, who'd barely been clinging to life when she'd left was now fighting to rise from the pallet with some supernatural strength.

"Nessa," shouted Molly. "Lock the door and get your staff. Your birch staff. Lay it over her. Quickly now, girl, before she gets away. And you, Morag, when we get the birch on her, shut that blasted window and pull the curtains over it. Now, Nessa—lock the door!"

Galvanized by Molly's unaccustomed bark, Nessa sprang to the far corner of the room, where the long birch branch, the one she was just learning to think of as a staff, leaned. She handed it to Molly, who, with the other grannies, laid it lengthwise over Granny Wren, left shoulder to right foot. The little granny moaned piteously, but quieted, her claw-like hands snagged in the blanket. Nessa stared, held motionless in the grip of horrified curiosity, even as Morag jostled past her to shut and lock the windows. "What ails her?" she whispered.

"The horns," answered Molly, as she exchanged looks with the other grannies. "It's the horn."

"Bethy, come with me," said Morag before Molly could continue. "There's sure to be a panic downstairs if no one goes down to calm them. Are you all right here, Molly?"

"Nessa will help me."

"Uwen wants me to get down to the forge..." She glanced dubiously down at the dying granny. She'd never thought to see such a display of sheer animal strength from a woman all agreed would be dead by morning.

"Stay with me, Nessa. It's not the goblins yet."

Yet? Nessa wondered as she sank down at Wren's feet,

and gripped the birch staff. The wood felt cool and smooth and always somehow welcoming. Maybe it was the width of it, she realized. It was just the right width for her hand. *Odd how that happened.* But so many odd things were happening lately. She watched Molly closely as she smoothed the gray wisps of Wren's hair off a face as wrinkled as a nut. "If that's not goblins, what is it?"

Molly raised her head as the sound came again. It was undeniably closer, and beneath the staff, Wren stirred weakly and moaned. "Those horns—that's Herne's horn, as he summons forth the Wild Hunt. The Great Horned God rides this night, sweeping up the souls bound for the Summerlands. All who waver on the border twixt this world and the Summerlands are vulnerable to his call, just as all the rest of us are prey to the goblins." She paused and pressed her lips together. "I wasn't sure to expect this or not."

"But—but," Nessa began. A flicker of movement caught her eye, and she glanced at the bed as the horns blew again. Artimour twisted his head restlessly on the pillow, his eyes fluttering open briefly. Then he was still. "Molly—" she whispered. "Did you see that?" She nodded in Artimour's direction.

But Molly's head was cocked in the direction of the door, and she appeared to be listening to the rising cries from the frightened women just on the other side. "We can't leave Wren," she muttered. "He's getting closer."

As if on cue, a single blast sounded, and, as if in answer, there was a wild howling and a savage baying, and she heard what sounded like the thunder of the gallop of a thousand horses. And then, as Nessa gasped, and shrank back, through the brick wall, through the locked and bolted window, a huge horned figure mounted on something that looked like a cross between a stag and a stallion came bounding into the room with another clarion call of that unearthly horn.

"Great Mother, protect us all," cried Molly. "Hold the staff against her, Nessa, don't let it slip."

With every ounce of courage she possessed, Nessa raised her head and looked fully at the creature who filled the entire room with his dark and savage presence. He looked like a man, she thought, a big, burly man but for the huge set of shadowy antlers that rose from his brow. It seemed that they should go through the ceiling, she thought, aware that some part of her remained wholly detached from the feelings he was rousing in her. There was fear, but there was something else—exhilaration and a kind of wild beauty of something forever unbound—that held a perilous attraction.

Those who were caught in the Wild Hunt were lost to the Summerlands forever. *But they rode with Herne,* she thought, and suddenly, she could see herself throwing off her mortal body like a worn-out dress and stepping forward to take his hand. But she also knew somehow that he had not come for her.

As if he heard the echo of her thoughts, he looked directly at her, and she saw his eyes flare red, then green as the firelight fell full upon them. She thought he might reach for her then, with one of those huge fists, and she pulled back, so that Molly rose up on her knees, like a hen over her two chicks. Herne pulled up on the reins so that his mount reared up, and fixed Nessa with a smile so gentle and so beguiling, she gasped. "Come now, darling." His voice was as wooing as the waves, as implacable as granite. "Let her come with me, darling. Can't you see it? She wants to come with me. She wants to ride with Herne." It was like a lullaby, she thought, sweeter and lovelier than anything Dougal had ever sung. He reminded her of Dougal, too, and suddenly it seemed he looked at her with her father's eyes, and she gasped again and nearly dropped the staff.

"Nessa!" Molly's sharp voice stabbed into the enchantment. "Don't listen to him, Nessa." She reached over and tapped Nessa lightly on the cheek. "Don't listen to him."

"Well now, maybe you'd rather come dance with me instead?" The rich voice was directed at Molly, and this time, his eyes flickered a merry invitation.

But Molly was not so easily won. She raised her chin and squared her shoulders. "'Tis not my time, Great Lord, and well you know it. And Wren desires to join her mothers in the Summerlands—she wants no part of you. Ride on, I say, ride on."

His laugh was like the peal of a great bell, rolling through the room with the force of a summer storm. Nessa felt it rumble through her body, as the floor beneath her feet shuddered and the very stones of the keep shifted as if in response. On the narrow pallet, Granny Wren moaned and on the bed, Artimour shuddered.

She wanted to leap up and go to him, but she didn't dare leave the shelter of Molly's presence. Herne turned his great antlered head and guided his mount over to the bed. It bent and sniffed Artimour, whined like a hound, and licked his face. Artimour frowned and turned his face away but did not wake. Herne looked at Nessa then back at Artimour. "You win this one, wicce-woman. There're other pickings this night. But both of you—both of you will see me again ere this tale is told." With another peal of laughter, he wheeled the great mount around and with a whinnied shriek, and another unearthly blast of the horn, the great creature leapt through the wall and was gone, even as the baying of invisible hounds rose in a wild frenzy.

Wren collapsed into a limp heap, and Molly slowly relaxed. She moved the birch staff with a sigh. The horns were still calling, blowing in the wind, but they were beginning to fade.

"Why did he say that?" Nessa whispered.

Molly shook her head slowly, staring at the window. The windows were blown open, and the curtains billowed in the cold night air. "I don't know, child. But it seems it's as I've suspected. We're in the midst of some great working, and Herne himself has a hand in it." Her dark eyes pinned Nessa with a sharp look and for a moment she looked as if she considered saying something else. But all she said was, "Will you shut the windows, Nessie?"

Feeling drained, Nessa rose to her feet. Artimour lapsed back into his feverish sleep, but she thought his color had improved. As she leaned out to grasp the latch, she could hear the fading laughter, the furious howls and a last call of that wild horn. With a shudder, she drew the windows together and latched them firmly. When she turned around, she was startled to see Granny Wren standing by the bed, wearing her simple shift, her thin gray braids lying lank on her shoulders, her hands clasped before her. But she was smiling at Nessa and her eyes were kind. "Granny Wren," she blurted. "What are you doing up?"

But the old woman only smiled. In the shadowy light, she wavered slightly. Nessa blinked, perplexed.

"It's all right, Nessa," Molly said, very softly, very gently. "She's just saying goodbye."

Nessa gasped and saw to her astonishment that a crowd of women had suddenly appeared. They were dressed in a motley assortment of fabrics and plaids and clustered around Molly and the low pallet so that the fire and the hearth were completely obscured. She looked back at Granny Wren, and as she watched, the old woman's hair lengthened, thickened and darkened, her skin smoothed, her cheeks plumped and pinkened. Wren smiled once more, and this time her face was as merry and as young as her eyes and she appeared no older than Nessa. She gave a little bow, and walked around to the other side of the bed. She placed her hand directly on Artimour's wound and, looking directly at Nessa, winked. Then she touched Molly's cheek with the tips of her fingers, a caress as fleeting as the brush of a butterfly's wings, and stepped through the locked and bolted door, the other silent, smiling women following in her wake. Nessa shuffled forward as if in a daze, sure that her heartbeat was audible in that hushed and holy quiet. In the firelight, she saw that Molly's cheeks were wet with tears as she watched the company stream past. Each smiled and nodded at both Molly and Nessa, and Nessa could only stand and stare openmouthed at the shadowy but unmistakable procession. And then, one figure stopped and stepped aside, allowing the others to pass.

Molly rose to her feet, and Nessa saw Granny Wren's frail corpse on the pallet, her jaw fallen open in the awful rictus of death. Her body looked like a husk, a shell, and suddenly Nessa understood that it had no longer been capable of containing Wren's bright smiling spirit. She looked up from the body to Molly to the shadowy, still figure. "Ask her to speak to you, Nessa. They can't if you don't ask," Molly said softly.

Wide-eyed, Nessa gulped. There was something familiar about the woman, something that reminded her of herself. "Would—would you like to talk to me, spirit?"

Nessa.

Her name tickled her skin like the barest of summer breezes, warm and sweetly scented. She looked into those bottomless eyes and suddenly knew exactly who the woman was. "Grandmother," she whispered, not understanding how she knew that this was her mother's mother. As if the word called them forth, other shadows coalesced out of the gloom, women with dark hair and dark eyes, stocky frames and strong shoulders. They gathered around the first and smiled at her with loving eyes.

Nessa.

It was a soft harmony this time, a blend of voices that echoed her name over and over, naming her and claiming her as one of their own, and for the first time, Nessa felt connected not only to her mother, but to the great interlocking chain which stretched, down through the ages and across time itself, from mother to daughter, binding past and future into one always and eternal present. For these were the mothers and the grandmothers of not just her own mother and her grandmother, but of every kinswoman she had who still walked with the Summerlands. *One day one of them will choose you for her mother.*

Tears filled her eyes, spilled down her cheeks, as she knew herself a part of the great tide of life flowing like a river in and out of the Summerlands, and she felt not just connected to her past, but anchored in the present, rooted to her people and the land and she was so absurdly happy, she laughed.

The phantoms crowded closer, surrounding her so that she felt uplifted by a wave of loving warmth that yet contained a tinge of some deep sorrow. *One of our own is lost to us, Nessa. Help us, Nessa. Find her, Nessa. Find us our daughter. Find us our sister, our cousin, our own. Help Essa come home.*

Nessa staggered against the wooden bedstead as the ghostly chorus whispered through the silent room. She felt as if she couldn't breathe and even as Molly leapt to her feet with a little cry, vigilant as always, Nessa gripped the bedpost with a newfound resolve. Of course. Why hadn't she thought of it before? Her mother was in Faerie. If she could find Dougal, she could find her mother. The tears flowed down her cheeks and her throat constricted so that she could scarcely speak.

"Nessa, what's wrong?" asked Molly. "What did she tell you?"

"My—my mother," she managed, even as she realized that Molly had not heard, or even saw the shades now clustering and filling the bedroom close. There were men there, too, now, among the women. Some wore familiar clothing, some wore only rough furs clumsily bound around their loins. And a few were naked, bright blue streaks of woad their only attire. "They want me to find my mother."

Molly reached for her, and as Nessa let herself be gathered close, the ghosts began to fade before her eyes, flickering out like the flames of dying candles, one by one, until the room was empty but for Nessa, Molly, Artimour and Granny Wren's lifeless body. Molly reached for her, and drew her close. "I never stopped to think," Nessa sobbed. "She was there all the time—I could've—"

"Hush that silliness, girl. You could most surely not have gone over into the OtherWorld. The OtherWorld is a dangerous place—the last thing your mother would want for her daughter was for her to risk her own life—"

"But now I could go—"

"Nessa, you listen to me—"

But Molly's advice was lost beneath Artimour's harsh croak. "Nessa?"

Startled, both women looked up to see Artimour lying on the pillow, eyes wide open. "Artimour?" Nessa whispered.

Their eyes met and she wondered what he would say, what he would think if he knew she was potentially responsible for making the weapon that had nearly killed him. But then there was no more time to wonder anything, for from high atop the tower came the desperate blast of another set of horns, ones all too obviously of mortal make. A great shout went up along the walls, and the horns blew again, harder and longer and Nessa knew immediately what they portended.

Molly gave her a little shake. "You've got to get down to the forge, Nessa."

Nessa stared at Artimour, who was looking around the room, perplexed and confused. "But—"

"Nessa, there's no one in this keep who knows what you do." Molly's eyes were desperate as the horn screamed again.

Nessa glanced at Artimour, then at Molly and then dashed from the room, her mind reeling with the message her grandmothers had left her with. *Help Essa come home.* Their daughter. Her mother.

But she had no time to even think about all she'd seen, for the horns were blowing louder, the men were shouting on the walls, and women and children were screaming aloud to the Great Mother for mercy. But as the cold air hit her face, she knew that unless Herne or the Great Mother herself intervened, there was no mercy in the offing. The unmistakable reek of goblin was on that bitter wind.

The afternoon light was fading and great drops of sweat were beginning to run in great rivulets down Petri's cheeks, past his nose and dripping off his brow like salty rain. But he did not complain, only gripped the pommel of the saddle harder as Delphinea slowed the horse to a walk beneath the overarching branches of the great oaks. The air was very still and she could not shake the feeling that there was something else within the Forest, an oppressive presence that seemed to hang over everything and grew more tangible the deeper that they rode beneath the trees.

Maybe it was only the fear of capture that had worried her since they'd fled the Palace. But there'd been no sign of pursuit, either, and she wasn't sure why. Perhaps Timias didn't consider her important. And after all, she was the one who'd alerted him, she was the one who'd led him right to the Caul Chamber. Perhaps it had been his intention to allow her to escape, although he certainly would not have expected her to take a gremlin with her. Not on Samhain Eve, after all. Perhaps that's what had delayed a pursuit for them. No one had thought they'd run away together and in the general outcry for Petri, she'd been forgotten. Not likely, she decided. Maybe Timias was simply too busy to bother with her.

But it didn't mean she rode with any less determination, and so they'd ridden through the darkening wood, barely pausing to sleep. To her utter surprise, Petri insisted he knew the way, and while Delphinea was doubtful at first, it soon became apparent that, although his kind were supposed to be prevented from leaving the palace grounds, their knowledge of Faerie extended far beyond those borders.

We are not generally thought of as having any consequence. He had gestured when he still could. *And so things are said in front of us as if we're not there.*

A chill had gone through her then, at the thought of the voiceless, invisible existence to which Timias and Gloriana had so thoughtlessly condemned the gremlins. No matter that they'd been thought necessary to work the magic, she thought. She continued to walk the horse as the light began to fade. Another way should've been found. But she had no more time to consider the plight of the gremlins, for the plight of the gremlin before her was beginning to demand her full attention. That and the suffocating feeling which was plaguing her like a veil too tightly pulled across her face. Finally she reined the horse to a full stop, and looked down at Petri. He had dissolved into a miserable, shaking little mass. Maybe this hadn't been such a good idea. But what else could she have done? "I don't think we're going to be able to go much farther. The trees are crowding in so close. The air is thicker here somehow—it's making it hard for me to breathe." She said this last as a wave of dizziness swept over her. "Maybe it's Samhain." She looked around and slid off the saddle before she could fall. "It must be Samhain. It will be completely dark in another half-turn or so of the glass, Petri. I don't think we'll reach Vinaver's house, do you?"

He shook his head, and looked at her with tortured eyes.

Her mare whickered and pawed at the ground. She reached up and pulled Petri off the horse's back, for Delphinea had realized at once that her horse had been none too happy about the gremlin on her back. Petri collapsed down into the thick carpet of crisp russet leaves, wheezing audibly. "Petri, I'm so sorry."

He shook his head and, shaking violently, gestured, *Not to blame. Not to blame.*

She rubbed her eyes. The air had a palpable weight that pressed down on her chest. "I don't think we can stay here. Let me look around a little. I'll see if I can find us somewhere to wait out the night." *How terrible could it be?* she wondered. There had to be a place, perhaps beneath a generous oak or a gentle willow, that would shelter them. She remembered the rope. It would be good to find a place with a soft moss cushion. She wished she could shake the feeling that something was terribly wrong. The air was sodden, thick, and cold. But there was no wind, and all the trees were absolutely still as if they held their breath in anticipation.

Or shock. The uneasy feeling intensified. They were too deep into Faerie for the goblins to be a threat. It's just the time of year, she told herself, just Samhain. Another wave of dizziness overtook her and her vision blurred. The trees seemed to thicken, double, then divide. For a moment it was as if she stared at a double image of two forests, one superimposed over the other, and she realized that the veil between the worlds was lifting. Clearly Petri was beginning to feel the effects of it. She lassoed the reins to a low-lying branch and patted the horse's nose. "Watch out for him, all right?" She met the horse's liquid gaze, and read a dubious assent. "I'll hurry."

She gathered her long riding skirts, and glanced in both directions. The dizziness overtook her once more and she bit the inside of her cheek till the pain cleared her vision. Petri needed her now. She could not give in to whatever strange effect the wood was having on her. She'd brought him into this. She had to get him out of it. She slipped between the trees, and saw, just a few feet ahead, a cluster of slender white birches, with smooth bark. Their trunks formed a sort of cradle. She could line it with the saddle blanket and create a sort of nest, she thought, in which she could tether Petri firmly but not uncomfortably. The thought of having to do so at all sickened her, even as another wave of nausea made her head spin. *What ails me,* she wondered. She crept forward, bent on examining the tree, and realized that a shimmering haze seemed to hang in the air, just a few hands' widths from the ground, just beyond the birch. Puzzled, she took a few more steps forward, paused and looked down. For a split second, she wondered what such a lifelike mannequin was doing lying on its side in full battle dress in the middle of the forest. And then she realized what she was looking at, and the shock that it was no mannequin, but a dead knight, punched the air from her lungs and she was forced to hold on to the nearest tree to keep from sinking to her knees. She looked up and around and realized that the corpse at her feet was one of hundreds of knights and horses all lying dead, piled in great heaps between the trees.

The dead wore golden armor emblazoned with Alemandine's crest. They lay staring up at the purple sky, limbs askew, weapons scattered haphazardly all around. It was impossible to say how many of them there were, but she was suddenly sure it was the entire host. The entire host, she thought, remembering the songs the minstrels were singing about the day they'd ridden out the high white gates.

And suddenly she wasn't so sure that they were too deep into Faerie that the goblins weren't a threat. For what else could have so completely slaughtered such a formidable host?

Spurred back by the terrifying thought that perhaps the goblins had already breached the Wastelands' wards, she stumbled back to Petri and the horse. "Come on, Petri," she panted. "We can't stay here. It's not Samhain—this place is cursed." She unwrapped the reins and somehow got him stuffed back into the saddle. The light was fading but she didn't care. She wasn't about to spend the night in sight or smell of that terrible view.

She flapped the reins and the horse leapt forward, Petri clinging to the pommel with what looked like his last ounce of strength. They cantered beneath the trees, and something shimmered in the violet shadows beneath the trees. The shadows darkened to indigo, and then to black, and thickened into nearly solid forms that dashed in and out between the trees, bellowing ghostly cries as they chased after each other. Her mare whinnied its displeasure at the racing phantoms, and Delphinea gripped the reins more firmly. She leaned forward as far as she could and spoke as close to the horse's ear as she dared. "Easy now, girl, easy. It's only the Wild Hunt—" *And only a piece of it, too, thank the Hag.*

The phantoms were closing in beside them now, moving in from all directions as though they would engulf any who fell into their snare. Delphinea pulled back gently on the reins, trying to slow the frantic mare and allow the Hunt to pass. The mare reared up and around, wheeling so that Delphinea clung to both Petri and the reins with all her might, willing the horse to calm and let the Hunt ride on. As the horse danced beneath her, the riders raced past, uncaring, unnoticing. At last she managed to calm the animal, and realized that she herself was still shaking nearly as much as Petri. They really couldn't go any farther. They had to find some sort of shelter, and burrow down as best they could for the night.

"LADY."

Petri's screech brought her back to the moment. Here they were, all alone, in the middle of the deepest forest in Faerie, on one of the most magic nights of the year, quite possibly within reach of whatever had killed that host. "Petri," she whispered, "please, we mustn't make too much noise. We don't know what killed those knights back there—"

He looked up at her with utter and abject agony, and she broke of,f feeling helpless. *This is my fault,* she thought. *But how could she have left him to whatever fate Timias had in mind?* Without warning, Petri stiffened, put his head back and began to howl uncontrollably. He writhed, his spine stiffening and arching until she thought it might crack, screaming as if the Hag herself were after him. *No,* she thought. *He sounds more like an infant calling for its mother.* It brought all three of them to the ground, forcing even the horse's knees to buckle and crumple beneath the weight of its primal sorrow. Delphinea rolled away from the animal, palms pressed to her ears in a futile effort to block that horrendous, heartbreaking cry.

Vinaver heard the howling in her bower, where she had watched the Wild Hunt pass by. It was the howling of a soul in agony, she thought, in aching, endless torment. It was the howling of a gremlin on Samhain. But they were leagues from the palace. Perhaps it was an echo, dragged up and carried by the Hunt. So she waited a full turn of the glass. But the howling, rather than diminishing, intensified until at last she summoned the knights of her household guard, and sent them out to search.

16

The sound of blowing horns brought Cecily to the battlements. Kian frowned when he saw her, darting amidst the archers and the pikesmen gathered on the walls. The wind was howling in fitful gusts and thick clouds were scudding across the moonless sky. *Samhain weather,* she thought, as Kian pulled her into one of the arrow-slits within the walls. "What're you doing up here?" he demanded, his eyes bright in his stern face. He was painted for battle, his hair pulled back and tightly coiled.

She shook herself free. There was no way she was going to be kept in the dark this night. "I wanted to see for myself what that horn was. The people are panicking. The druids don't seem to know what to do." She peeked through the narrow opening into the bleak night, and scanned the nearly invisible horizon. "Is it the goblins? Are they coming?"

"To arms, to arms!" The shouts went up from every part of the castle, as another wild blast echoed across the skies. But Kian was shaking his head. "I don't think that's the goblins—it doesn't smell the same."

Out of the dark clouds, black shadows swept, coalescing into the rough shapes of wolves and stags and stallions. Hounds danced and capered beside the swift and rushing tide, and as they watched, human shapes took form. The men on the walls cried out, and pointed as a massive shape detached itself, the shape of an enormous horned man riding a stallion that bore the antlers of a stag. "Great Herne," muttered Cecily.

"That's exactly who it is," said Kian. "He's after the dying. Don't you remember? There's supposed to be something we should do to protect—" He broke off and ran down the narrow battlement, shouting for a druid, Cecily held back by the rush of everyone to the battlements to view this living piece of legend.

"What do you mean you don't know what to do? Where's Kestrel?" Kian was shouting directly into the face of a white-robed druid by the time Cecily reached him. The druid was looking pained, and remained silent, as he gripped his eagle-feathered staff with a white-knuckled hand. All around them, people were gasping and pointing up, as the shadowy phantoms swooped low, laughing and calling. From the great hall, where the worst of the wounded still lay, a woman began to scream.

"The dying," Cecily murmured. "He's taking their souls. Druid, we have to do something—" She gathered up her skirts and took off through the crowded courtyard filled with the terror-stricken, who pushed and shoved and trampled in all directions. Kian paused and shouted for the sergeants, but she did not hesitate. She rushed into the Hall, in time to see the black outline of a huge horned man bound into the room, his equally huge horned mount tossing its head and pawing the ground like a bull. "Come dance with me," he roared. "Throw off those broken mortal shells, rise up and dance with me! Be free and dance with me!"

He raised his shining horn to his mouth and gave a high, short blast, and Cecily gripped the door frame, feeling an unexpected call. The druid slammed into her, and she staggered forward, watching in horror as the nearly invisible shades of the dying rose from their bodies, and leapt up, to join the capering phantom throng now streaming into the hall from all directions, dancing and laughing to some inaudible music. Herne threw back his head and laughed again, a booming sound that shook the castle to its foundations and brought her to her knees. "A rich harvest here indeed," he bellowed. His eyes found Cecily's and she found herself transfixed by that burning stare. "Such rich harvest deserves a favor. I owe a favor to you, my lady; you ripened these well for me."

"Druid," Cecily managed, horrified that such a favor should have come at such a price. She elbowed the druid, tugging at his robes, but he only stared, stupefied. The shadowy throng, now larger by at least several dozen, cheered as Herne, with a mighty shout and a single leap, disappeared through the solid wall of the Hall, the prancing phantoms following after in his wake.

But they're not dead, she thought. *It's not the same as if they'd passed to the Summerlands. He's taken those souls and they'll never come back again, never know their families again.* She hauled herself out of her own shock and hurled herself at the druid, wrapping her fists in his robe. "Do something. He's taking their souls—those are warriors who deserve to go to the Summerlands, not dance forever to Herne's horns—"

The druid only moaned.

With a sound of disgust, she released him and turned back to survey the hall. It was only just beginning to occur to everyone else what had happened. She stumbled forward, and kneeling, closed the eyes of a tall blond boy who could not have been more than eighteen summers.

"He went with Herne." The woman beside the bed looked at her with blank eyes. "He went with Herne. He's lost to me forever. I'm his mother—I'll never see him again, not even in the Summerlands. Not ever." She sank down on the pallet beside the stiffening body and buried her face in her hands.

Cecily touched her shoulder, too shocked, too stunned to know what to do or what to say. Kian burst into the hall and, ignoring the dazed druid, was beside her in three quick strides. "What happened?"

She shook her head, spread her hands. "It was just as in the legends. The Wild Hunt rode right through the hall. Herne blew his horn and the dying—they rose up and followed. And he—" she paused and pointed to the druid, who'd collapsed onto a bench. "He did nothing."

"I knew not what to do—"

"You would've if you'd listened to the corn grannies," interrupted Mag. She had come up from somewhere within the hall and now stood staring an accusation at the druid. "I brought you several. You wouldn't even see them."

The druid made a face. "Those women—if that's what they were—smelled like pigs and didn't look as if they could remember their names let alone—"

At that Mag stepped forward and stuck her face in the druid's. "You ignorant druid. It's not what they remember—it's what they know."

The weeping woman looked up, cheeks glistening with tears. "So my son is lost to me, because you were too proud to speak to a corn granny? You sicken me." She rose to her feet and stalked away, bearing her sorrow like a tangible thing in her arms.

The druid opened his mouth, but his protests were drowned by screams—loud and desperate, rising from the eastern walls. "Now what?" muttered Kian, and dashed out, Cecily once again trailing in his wake. He pushed his way through the milling crowd, unaware that she followed and she stayed a few paces behind, lest he notice her and send her away before she'd seen for herself what was causing the disturbance.

Halfway up the steps she knew. The stench the wind was carrying over the walls was worse than the stench of rotting meat, worse than the stench of death with which she'd become all too well-acquainted in the past weeks. She grabbed the stone wall and staggered up, for the smell was so ghastly it made her vision cloud. The men upon the walls had fallen silent. She pushed her way through to Kian's side. "What is it—" she started to say, then stopped and simply looked to where he pointed. Out of the forest, out of the hills, a dark gray shape, like a mass of thousands of rats, crawled inexorably toward Gar. But it wasn't rats, she knew. Those stinking things could only be goblins. "Great Mother," she whispered.

"Get back," he said. "Get back. Bar the Hall—women and children to the topmost towers." He picked up her hand and kissed it. "Now go." He did not wait to see if she obeyed him or not, but spun around and began to bellow orders, as Cecily fled in the face of that huge and hungry horde.

From the relative safety of the forge, Nessa watched the men subdue the Sheriff. It could be, she supposed, construed as the worst sort of mutiny, but under the circumstances, entirely understandable. They wrestled him to his feet, and pushed and pulled him up the narrow steps to the top of the walls, where she watched his expression change from anger to abject terror. And then she wondered just what was out there. "I'll be right back," she said. She saw the scullions glance at each other. Uwen should have warned them she was a girl. But she paid them no more heed as she too scampered up the nearest stairs and slipped unheeded to the forefront of the press of the too-lightly armed men, that crowded at the walls, gazing stone-faced and silent at what they faced.

One look told her all she needed to know. Out of the black well of the night, a deeper black was writhing, as the goblins swarmed down from the hills, out from between the trees, like a flood of insects. The first ranks were already converging on the causeway and she saw at once that they were bigger than the ones she'd faced before. Much bigger.

She bolted down the steps as the captains began shouting for the archers to take their positions.

In the forge, she grabbed the nearest bars of silver, and threw them into the iron cauldron. "They're here," she shouted, pointing at the coal. "You there, start shoveling. We need to get the fire going. And you, come here and work these bellows. And you, start handing me the weapons—we'll start with the pikes and the arrows, and you—you go find whatever you can find that might kill a goblin."

"Like—like what?" he babbled, as he skidded out the door.

"Think if you can," she shot back. "Shovels, picks, axes. Knives, forks. Anything with a blade or an edge." She picked up an iron pike and, dipping it into the cauldron, began to stir. "Come on, those things out there are bigger than anything I've ever seen before."

And fortunately, not one of them noticed her slip.

The walls were breached by midnight. In the press of the battle, Kian paused. There were simply too many goblins, he thought, too many who rushed forward to take the place of those that were felled by the silver-coated weapons. They were an endless river of teeth and claws and snapping tails that whipped a man's legs out from under him. Half were armed with no more than their own teeth and claws, and he realized in some detached corner of his brain that those were the ones designated to drag away as many bodies as possible. *We really are just meat.* This is a hunting party, he realized, not just huge, but well-organized and efficient, no matter how crude or brutal. The only hope the humans had, as far as Kian could see, was to try and hold out until dawn inevitably drove the goblins away. And maybe they'd stay away long enough for them to figure out something to do that was more effective than this. He rose up, holding his sword high. "Fall back," he cried. "Fall back to the second ward!"

A page rushed up, tripping over blood and slime and gore. "Sir Kian—the lady Cecily begs to know the progress—" But a giant goblin claw swiped over the wall and reached down, lifted the boy, still screaming, off his feet, to be silenced by a sickening crunch.

It galvanized Kian so that he swung his sword in a broad arc, loping the silvered edge up and around and the huge goblin head went bouncing down the slick stone steps. *Begs to know the progress,* he thought. *If dawn doesn't come soon, we're done.* Grimfaced, he braced himself, determined to die honorably, and a long red line on the horizon caught his eye. A cheer and a shout went up from the men.

"Dawn!"

"I see the dawn!"

"Dawn!"

The cheers echoed up and down the ragged, bloodied ranks, and Kian looked over the walls. Sure enough, a thin red light was steadily brightening. The worn survivors fought back with renewed vigor. But Kian frowned, for there was something wrong with the light, even as it grew stronger with every passing moment. The nearest knight turned to him with eyes alight. "See, Chief. It's the dawn. We're—"

"No," interrupted Kian, suddenly certain it could not be

the sun. "I don't know what that is, but it's not the dawn. Not unless the sun's rising in the west today."

Then they had no time to consider what it could be, for another goblin attack surged upon the walls, and they were forced to retreat to the relative safety of the second ward. Kian was helping slide the great bolt across the gates, when a pipe's harsh skirl reached their ears, floating up from somewhere beyond the walls. The men looked at each other, breathing hard, tensing as they recognized the steady beat of drums.

"Who's that, Chief?" asked one, staring at him with wide and haunted eyes.

"That's Gar's battle-song I hear," chimed in another before Kian could answer. "Listen—do you no' hear it, soft upon the wind?"

And sure enough, borne upon the breeze, slicing through goblin howls and mortal screams, like the ring of pure silver on steel, the ancient call-to-arms echoed through the wild night, stirring up their blood, rousing up their passions, until as one body, they rushed to the walls, and ignoring the monsters that were scrambling into the dark well of the abandoned ward, peered out, into the warm coppery light that streamed as brightly as a midsummer sun over the western horizon.

The sound of the pipes and drums grew louder and Kian felt the men all around him tense, even as he gripped the jagged stones. Over the western hills, marching in a long, tattered line, a motley array of warriors came striding, some armed with clubs and sticks and slingshots, some mounted and garbed in plaid, some wearing nothing but skins or woad. He could see the bright blue streaks and swirls that marked their cheeks, their arms, their chests, the banners that hung on crude spikes, or whipped in long tails about their heads.

The goblins were filling the first ward now, even as the silent army advanced, bringing that fiery light. And Kian put back his head and laughed, for he knew that this night, on this night alone, perhaps, they would be saved, for the dead themselves were coming to protect the living, to slay with that hot and burning light the goblins that would consume their children's flesh.

"Who are they, Chief?" asked the man at his elbow.

"Don't you know them?" he said, even as he recognized his father's banner. "'Tis Samhain, still. That's not the sunrise. 'Tis the dead. Our dead."

As if he'd given some unspoken signal, the vast host raised their weapons as one and with a mighty yell and a screaming shriek of pipes, they came vaulting upon the goblin horde, and their pipes sang of victory as they slew. Their weapons of reddish light sliced like silver through the goblins, and the tattered, tired survivors crowded at the battlements, watching, as the shining dead fell like a summer storm upon the goblin horde below.

Silver was effective, but there wasn't enough. And from the number of goblins swarming up the causeway, Nessa doubted there was enough silver in all of Brynhyvar. She forced herself to be calm as she heard the goblins' first thunderous attack. It froze her blood and made her pause in the act of dipping a pointed piece of wood into the dregs of the melted silver. The goblins were nearly to the walls, the soldiers said, as they'd come dashing into the forge. And she was nearly out of silver. There was none left in the entire keep, and some of the men had even flung their amulets into the pot. She'd nearly flung her own, but something stopped her. It wasn't her amulet she wore, it was Griffin's. She hoped to return it to him someday, though it was hard to imagine living through this stinking maelstrom, punctuated by agonized screams and inhuman grunts and growls.

She could smell the fear on the four scullions, who dashed to do her bidding as soon as the battle had begun, all possible sulkiness banished. Suddenly everyone was a believer. But this new high-pitched screaming cut through the howls of the dying, the roars of the goblins, and the screams and the sickening thuds of hacked off limbs and falling bodies. The wailing echoed through the keep, bouncing off the walls, off the water, until the air was alive with the high-pitched cries. They made Nessa's hair stand on end and the gooseflesh prickle on her forearms. "What's that noise?" whispered the scullion she thought of as Crooknose, for his nose was bent in the middle. Now the blood drained from his tired, sweat-stained face.

She looked up from trying to scrape the last of the molten silver in the depths of the great iron cauldron. "I don't know but shovel in the last of the coal—come on, do it now. Maybe there's a way to stretch it a little thinner if we heat it higher—"

The weird yells rang out again, louder this time, and a curious silence began to fall. The goblin roars subsided, the sounds of hacking and slicing ceased. The five of them paused and listened. The cries were deafening now, and closer, as if whatever made that inhuman noise was advancing quickly. They all rushed from the forge and dashed up to the walls, where the defenders were staring out at some sight. She glanced around for Uwen, but there was no sign of him at all. She pushed her way through the line of staring men and gazed out, over the ramparts. The hair rose on the back of her neck as she saw the source of those unearthly cries.

There was a long line of naked women running in a flood of reddish light over the western hills, waving their arms above their heads, bellowing what could only be an outraged challenge. As they came closer, Nessa saw some were armed with battle axes and short thick swords, others with clubs and long spears, but many brandished nothing more than teeth and nails. A glowing light surrounded them, and a soft breeze, sweet as summer, wafted over the walls, masking temporarily the sickening goblin stink.

"Great Mother," Nessa whispered. For she knew them, recognized them, felt her own blood stirring in response to the primal anger that carried them forward on a running tide of rage. They were the dead. They were the mothers, the grandmothers, the sisters of all who crowded here within these walls. And they were coming after the goblins.

The goblins were no match for the savagery of the dead. For their flesh was too insubstantial to be ripped, but their weapons of shimmering light were more deadly than even silver. With louder cries than the most ravenous of beasts, the line of naked women fell upon the goblins, leaping fearlessly onto them, biting and tearing the goblins' heads from their shoulders with nothing but their bare hands. They were the mothers and the grandmothers of all who sheltered within the Keep, and they would not let their children die. And so they came on, wave upon wave, line upon line, long hair streaming, high breasts bouncing, arms stained dark purple with goblin blood. They fell like a flock of ravens on the goblins, slashing and ripping, raising entrail-laden arms aloft and dancing on the dark, dismembered corpses. The goblins began to run, and the avenging spirits gave chase, until at last, all that lay before the keep was a causeway heaped with dismembered goblins, the stink rising in a palpable miasma.

A profound silence fell as the first gray light brightened the rim of the eastern sky. Nessa could scarcely believe what she'd witnessed. She pinched her nostrils tight. As a few of the more weak-stomached turned away and began to vomit from the stench, Uwen spoke in her ear. "You think there's any chance of them coming back and helping us clean up that god-awful mess down there?"

The howling was so loud Vinaver did not hear Dougal's first few knocks. She threw back the door and was surprised to see him, dressed like a lord of the sidhe in the rich green robe she'd left for him. His dark chest was revealed, and he looked even more like the forest god, with his black curling hair tumbling in an unruly mass about his shoulders, a short black beard thick on his chin. She smiled, almost called him husband, and thought the better of it. Teasing was not the proper tactic. "Master smith. Have you come to toast the season with me?"

"I've come to ask you what do you suppose that god-awful howling might be and if there's a chance of stopping it?"

She stood back. "Come in. It's a little quieter in here—the curtains block the noise."

He hesitated, then stepped over the threshold, peering around suspiciously as he did so, as if expecting some sort of ambush. "Well?" he asked, as she shut the door, and gestured to a chair. "What is it?"

"I'm not sure what it is," she replied. "But I've sent out a search party."

"It's the worst sound I've ever heard," he said. He sank into the chair, and turned to frown into the fire.

"Like a lost soul," she said.

"Like a child, crying for its mother." He fixed her with a cold stare. "I've come to tell you I've made my decision."

Unconsciously she squared her shoulders, tensed her spine, and she realized she would have to rethink her entire plan if Dougal said no. Well, Finuviel should be here at any time. The thought crossed her mind that she had expected him to be here by now, to add his voice to hers. But she only arched one brow, and drew a deep breath. "Well?"

"I'll help you. But there're three conditions."

"I made no conditions when I saved your life."

"Maybe I misjudge you, sidhe. Maybe I don't trust you. Yes, you saved my life. You saved my life because you needed it. So here are my three conditions. The first condition is you tell me the rest of the truth. If I'm to help you, I want to know exactly what's going on between Cadwyr of Allovale and your son. You tell me where the Caul is and who took it and what's to happen when the Caul's destroyed.

There's already goblins getting into Brynhyvar. And that brings me to my second condition. I don't care how you arrange it, but the goblins must be stopped from crossing the border of this world into ours. I don't care how you do it, but that's what must be done. And the third thing. When we're done, I go home. But before I go, I want my daughter to see her mother. To spend an hour, no, a day—a full day—in her company. Are we agreed?"

She sank onto the window seat, considering. What he asked for—the first and the third conditions—were reasonable enough, the last even sweetly pathetic. It was the second that was the sticking point. "There is already magic in the Shadowlands to keep—"

"What good is it if no one understands how to use it? You have to show it to us, teach it to us—"

"That's not possible." She shook her head impatiently. The presumptuousness of mortals never ceased to astonish her. "I don't know mortal magic—it's not mine to teach."

"Well, then, you'll have to figure something out. Because that's what I want. I can't have those monstrous things rampaging in Brynhyvar at will. I saw what one of them did to a grown man. I don't want to think about what might have happened in Killcairn already." He looked her squarely in the eyes.

Oh, he was proud, this mortal, she granted him that. He stared at her with those intense dark eyes and once more, she thought of Herne. *You need him.* The Hag's harsh rasp echoed from the deep pit of her gut. "All right," Vinaver said. "I don't know how. But I will do it." She hesitated. "You must understand, however, that there may be limits to what

I can do. The Caul was just such an attempt to manipulate the ebb and flow of the worlds. So I can only promise to do all in my power to keep the goblins out of Brynhyvar. Is that sufficient?"

He smiled at her, and for the first time, in all the time she'd known him, it was a genuine smile. It began in his eyes, she saw, a warm kernel of emotion that flowered across his face, lifting up his lips in a crooked curve like a sickle moon. "No one can promise to do more than all in their power. That's all I expect from you."

Their eyes met. In the hearth, the fire snapped and hissed, and a log split, falling in a bright shower of sparks. *I wonder if he remembers how he kissed me.* She certainly did. She felt the color start to rise in her cheeks, and the howling stopped abruptly. Vinaver started and the moment was over. "I wonder if the search party's found whatever that is—"

"Let's hope it's out of its misery at last."

He was a good man, she thought, an honest man who tried to live by the code of honor in which he believed. He had agreed to help her not because he liked her or trusted her or even believed in what she was doing. He had agreed to help her out of his own sense of what was right. Such integrity deserved reward. The silence lengthened, then suddenly Vinaver looked up. "Master smith," she began gently, "would you care to see your wife?"

His reaction surprised her. He was obviously taken aback. But he did not answer immediately. Instead he paused, and stared for what seemed like a long time into the fire and she began to wonder if he had perhaps fallen asleep. "There was a time," he said at last, "when I would've leapt for joy to take an offer like that." He drew a deep breath and let it out in a long sigh, and turned to look at her with unreadable eyes. "I know that's what you expect me to do, I know that's maybe what I should do. But it's taken me a long time to come to the place where I've got her locked up tight here in my heart. I don't expect you to understand, and maybe no other mortal can understand it, either. Maybe it's just my way of making peace with it. In my world, when people are gone, they're gone. Oh, maybe a lucky few see a shadow, a flicker, a bird, and think they've seen their mother from the Summerlands at Samhain time. But I've always thought it had something more to do with the Samhain mead and Samhain fires than any real ghosts. I've got Essa here—" he patted his chest. "And I don't want to let her out. Ever." He gave a short laugh. "I grant you one thing, lady. You've loosened my tongue with your Faerie swill, your Faerie clothes and chairs and crystal windows and such."

They lapsed once more into silence, and Vinaver wondered what it was that might unlock his heart. A crowing cock announced the passage of the night and Dougal looked around with a start. "Morning already?"

She shrugged. This was one night when morning could not have come soon enough. Finuviel's continuing delay was troubling her, niggling at her like a pebble in a boot. Already they were past the first auspicious opportunity to begin. She took a deep breath, struggling to calm herself. They had always understood that since there would be so much back and forth between Faerie and Shadow in the initial stages, the precise timing of when to begin would be difficult to plan. But she'd expected Finuviel long before this.

A frantic pounding on the door brought them both to their feet. The muddied captain of her house-guard stood there, accompanied by the Lady Delphinea, and a small gremlin. The captain stumbled into the room, and Delphinea swayed and looked as if she might faint. Dougal stepped forward and caught her as she fell. The gremlin only quivered.

"What is it?" Vinaver whispered, knowing just by looking at the stained and bedraggled trio that something terrible, something unforeseen had occurred.

"We found these two in the greenwood, my lady. And the Lady Delphinea told us what she'd found—that's why we were delayed in getting back." He paused, as if to gather his wits, and she saw tears start in his eyes and cascade in a flood down his cheeks. "The host—the entire host—that Finuviel led forth—the entire host he took into Shadow—they have been slain. Someone—the mortals—must've pursued them back across the border and slew them all with silver weapons. For they are all dead of the true death."

It was Vinaver's turn to stagger. She took hold of the chair even as the captain caught her arm. Dougal looked up from tending Delphinea. But she couldn't reply, she thought, she couldn't answer. She wasn't quite sure she understood what he'd said. "The entire host?" she repeated, feeling as if someone had thrown a cloak over her senses, so that she felt slow and thick and stupid.

"To be honest, my lady, we could not be sure. It was dark. We only had torches. I will take another company back after sunrise. But that is how it looked to me. The dead lay upon ıe dead. It looked as if they were slaughtered where they tood. Horses—knights—all."

"Finuviel?" she whispered. Her heart began to beat again, ı hard hammering slams against the thin wall of her chest, nd she thought she might burst. "What about Finuviel?"

"We did not see him, lady."

"But that's because it's dark." She drew a deep breath, but ıe spiraling blackness was closing in on her and with a lit-e cry, she crumpled where she stood, feeling, as if from ery far away, her brittle wings buckle and rip, so that as she ainted they fell away, leaving a flowing river of blood cas-ading over her shoulders to mingle with her coppery hair.)own, down she fell, deep into the dark cauldron of her ıemory, until all coherent thoughts dissolved and there was nly peace.

A final hush fell over the grisly field around the Castle Gar, as the warrior dead pursued the goblins back to the Oth-rWorld. Cecily found Kian hanging over the battlements, taring out grimfaced. When he saw her, he looked at her vith stricken eyes and she knew at once that something was erribly wrong. "What is it?" she asked, hastening to his side, tepping over gore and hacked limbs, and pieces of dead oblin and human alike.

But he only pointed with his sword, out over the battle-nents to the field below, where a lone rider picked its way lowly across the field of fallen goblins. A bright line had ppeared in the east, and as he approached, his form faded, ecoming ever more faint. A ghostly skirl of pipes sounded aintly on the wind and the phantom horse pricked up its ears and whinnied. But the rider continued to advance. The morning breeze blew off the mountains, and the standard he carried fluttered open and Cecily gasped, and gripped Kian's arm, then pushed away and leaned out over the battlements. "That cannot—surely that's not Donnor?" She looked back at Kian with questioning eyes and the rider halted directly below the walls.

And there was no doubt that it was Donnor, faint and insubstantial, rapidly fading in the strengthening light of the rising dawn. He looked up at them, and she saw a red line around his neck.

Kian leaned out. "My lord—Donnor—speak—" But Donnor was looking at Cecily. Kian nudged her. "Quickly, ask him before he goes—"

But even as she drew breath, the first rays of the dawn fell directly across him. Before her eyes he dissolved away to nothing, leaving her staring, openmouthed, into space.

Cecily looked at Kian. "Too late. Too late."

He turned his head and did not meet her eyes. "I see that you were right, lady." Exhaustion was smudged below his eyes, in the droop of his mouth. "Your sense that Donnor's life was short was right, lady."

"So you believe me now, that Cadwyr could murder Donnor?"

"I'm not sure it's a question of what we believe, Cecily. It's a question of what we know. We know Donnor walks among the dead. And it appears that Cadwyr does not."

"They came because it was Samhain and they could." Molly threw another handful of sweet herbs on the fire. She

usted off her hands and pulled above her nose the linen strip
hat she, like everyone else in the entire keep, wore to block
he nauseating stench that rose from the remains of the dis-
nembered goblins.

The morning light streamed into the Sheriff's bedcham-
er, through the thin horn panes. The windows themselves
vere bolted and herbs burned on the hearth, but the gentle
moke was no match for the goblin stink, and so they'd all
esorted to linen cloths soaked in peppermint oil. Uwen
ressed his own piece of unbleached linen more closely to
is nostrils and glanced at the sidhe, who lay propped up on
he pillows, looking for the first time as if he'd survive. "So
ou're saying we can't count on that happening again."

"Not until next year." She wiped her hands on her apron
nd shrugged. "Of course the question then becomes can
hey get through in such great numbers when it isn't
amhain?" She shook her head. "This is druid lore. It's be-
ond my knowing."

Uwen shook his head and looked at Nessa. She was sit-
ing in a chair on the opposite side of the fire, wrapped in
ne of Molly's shawls, holding a compress to her nose. Her
yes were on the sleeping sidhe and her face was soft, her
xpression so intent upon him and him alone that suddenly
Jwen understood why Nessa spent so much time here. *She
oves him,* he thought. But how was such a thing possible?
There was a dark look on her brow that told him that Nessa's
eelings ran deeper than mere infatuation with a beautiful
idhe. He wasn't even all that beautiful, Uwen decided, his
ace all harsh angles and stark plains. Suddenly the sidhe
pened his eyes and looked straight at Nessa, who'd leaned

forward the moment he opened his eyes. "Nessa," he murmured.

"Artimour." Inexplicably her eyes filled with tears. "How do you feel?"

He took a deep breath and stretched the arm on his wounded side cautiously. Then he nodded and he smiled and Uwen had to grudgingly admit to himself that this Artimour was beautiful after all. "Well, now. I think I might live."

She smiled and pressed her lips together and Uwen glanced from one to the other. Who was this sidhe, and how was it he had such an effect on Nessa? How had she even happened to come to know him? She'd seemed too levelheaded, too intelligent and sensible to so easily fall prey to the influence of a sidhe.

Molly rose to her feet and approached the bed. "Is there aught you need, sir sidhe?"

"Water." His voice was faint but even Uwen could not deny that there was music in just those two syllables.

He kicked his long legs out restlessly and nearly upended the flagon of water set to warm amidst the ashes.

"Uwen!" Nessa cried.

Suddenly he wanted nothing more than to be away from this hot, close room, where the atmosphere and the stink choked him. The thought of the open road appealed to him, even an open road where the goblins roamed at will. And better a goblin than that soft, hang-puppy look in Nessa's eyes. "Then the problem is we have to get answers. For Gar himself needs to know all these things. How soon, Nessa, can you travel?"

Molly glanced back over her shoulder as she helped Artimour drink. "She could go any time now."

Nessa shot Molly a pure black look.

"I'm sorry, maiden. I've orders from Kian, my own sworn chief, to bring you to Gar. He'll want to hear the story of how you came to make that silver dagger for Cadwyr and that other as soon as poss—"

He broke off, for Artimour was choking, and Molly was patting his back, and rushing to dab the spilled water off the sheets. "What did you say?"

The sidhe was looking directly at Uwen, and he felt the stab of that inhuman gaze. "What do you mean—?"

"What you just said to Nessa—a silver dagger?"

"Aye, isn't that what you told the Chief and me? Back in your village when we found you? That's why you had Cadwyr's gold?" He looked from Artimour to Nessa and saw that they were staring at each other in mutual horror.

"You made what?" Artimour was looking at Nessa as if he'd like to leap from the bed and throttle her, and Molly was beginning to fuss.

But Nessa only leaned forward and looked at him as if they were the only two in the room. "I didn't know—" she whispered, her face stricken and bleak. "I— How could I have known?"

"You didn't think to ask?" The snarl came from deep within, and Nessa leapt to her feet.

"I didn't know," she cried. And then she ran from the room, leaving Uwen staring at Molly in perplexed distress, as Artimour collapsed back onto the bed, eyes shut tightly, mouth rigid.

* * *

"Here's the last one."

"Well, turn it over so I get a clear shot at its neck."

The voice penetrated the thick fog swirling around Griffin's brain, even as a blast of cold fresh air ruffled his hair. The wooden lassitude left by the strange brew made his legs feel as mobile as a tree but he managed to raise his head a few inches, in time to see an ax coming down in his direction. He dodged just in time, and the soldier stumbled back.

"Sweet Mother, what have we here?"

"Me—" Griffin managed. He crawled forward and realized his legs were actually pinned under the goblin who'd fallen on his spear last night at the beginning of the attack. His scalp was caked with dried blood and the memory of what had happened came back to him. He squinted up at the bright blue sky, and realized that he had somehow managed to survive a second goblin attack. He fumbled for Nessa's amulet and pressed it in his fist. *You've brought me luck, Nessa,* he thought. *May mine prove as lucky for you.*

"Lucky lad. Hang on there and we'll have you free in a trice."

The first soldier turned around and shouted over his shoulder for help as the second squatted down beside Griffin. "Steady there, now. You'll be all right—we're the Duke's train. You can come with us. Duke Cadwyr is on his way to Gar to claim his inheritance. Should be grand doings. You just wait and see."

Griffin ran a hand over his eyes, reeling with nausea as he craned around, staring in disbelief at what the bright morning sun revealed. The carnage was even worse than at

Killcairn, for judging by the remains of the goblin he'd managed to kill, these were bigger, stronger, their teeth and claws even more deadly. But there weren't a lot of bodies, he realized. There were a few goblin carcasses, but that was all. Lots of blood. No bodies. "Did anyone else survive?"

The soldier dropped his eyes and Griffin had his answer even before the man silently shook his head.

Like the glazed eye of a dead fish, the thin young moon hung low in the sullen gray sky and in the rock-pools beneath the stony outcroppings which rose like tumbled ruins across the plains of the Wastelands, nothing stirred. But on the faintest breath of wind, Xerruw could smell the coming winter. His tailed twitched as he sniffed the air. The low-lying swamps were still, the marsh gases glowed a cold blue over the silent pools, but for the first time in more years than he could count, he felt alive, sated, his appetite fully satiated. He could feel his strength and his senses expanding. It was the human meat, the human blood. He licked the residue of grease and blood off his maw. Cooked or raw, nothing was so nourishing. He leaned upon the battlements and gazed out to the green line on the distant horizon that marked the elusive border of the Wastelands. It shimmered, beckoning and promising as a jewel. Now he could see the twinkling sparks of power which were strung across and through the green line like shimmering strands of pearls, the magic that held the border against his hordes. Before he'd gorged on human flesh, he'd been blind to its opalescence.

Down below, in the great hall, he could hear the howls and shrieks of the hags as they coupled ravenously with whatever hapless goblins as could be pressed into servicing them. Sexually voracious when fed human meat, the hags were laying eggs at a rate heretofore unheard of for centuries, enormous eggs needing scarcely any incubation at all, from which hatched gobling broods which doubled in size and strength and cunning every day. The caverns below the castle were piled high with leathery gray eggs clustered around fire pits. For no sooner had a hag laid one clutch than she was frantic for another to form within her belly. Hags in heat had been known to kill their partners if not capable of satisfying their urges, and Xerruw had ordered guards posted around the perimeter of the hall, charged with preventing such a murder.

"Great Xerruw." Iruk's voice disturbed his reverie with a grating rasp. "We have captured an intruder in the lowest cellars."

At that he turned, uncertain he'd heard his captain correctly. "An intruder? What sort of an intruder?"

"Not mortal."

That was obvious. Mortals weren't intruders. They were meat. "A sidhe?" Iruk shook his head. He was silent, and Xerruw frowned. It was not like his captain to struggle for words. "What is it?"

"Something you will have to see for yourself, Great Xerruw."

"Is it dangerous?"

Iruk shook his head. "I am not sure what you will make of this—this creature. It tells a most extraordinary tale—it brings a most extraordinary offer."

"An offer of what?"

"You should hear for yourself."

"And where was it found?"

"Crawling up through the lower cellars. It had dug its way. All the way from the palace of the witch of the sidhe."

Their eyes met and Iruk's gleamed, opaque as the dead eyes of the sidhe they'd captured in one of their raids upon the border, and tortured 'til it died. Its head now hung from a stake stuck into a crevice of Xerruw's throne. "Bring it here." Xerruw turned back to the balcony and stared out across the desolate plain. He did not see Iruk's bow, nor hear the tramp of his footsteps as he marched away to do Xerruw's bidding. A creature. An intruder. Who came calling at the Court of the Goblin King? Who—or what—would dare? Neither mortal nor sidhe had ever crossed the threshold on their own two feet. He scanned the horizon, watching how the lights flared and flashed and twinkled, the now-visible manifestations of the magic that held the border. It wavered a little more every night.

At the tramp and click of clawed feet, he turned around. A moment passed and Iruk entered, followed by two goblin guards. Xerruw frowned. Iruk stepped aside, and between the guards, Xerruw saw, to his complete astonishment a creature that resembled nothing so much as a hatchling of perhaps a month out of the egg. But it smelled wrong. He hissed, but before he could speak, the creature stepped forward as boldly as if it matched Xerruw.

"Great Xerruw!"

Its voice was a high-pitched shriek that made him want to cover his ears, but so intrigued was he by the creature's appearance, he only leaned forward, his tail coiling reflexively beneath him.

"I come to offer you an alliance."

Xerruw glanced at the guards, at Iruk, then bent his gaze to the thing which stood before him, stubby tail quivering with suppressed tension, small claws clasped in a tight fist at its waist. In the light of the flickering torches, the thing's face was orange and Xerruw could see more clearly that the thing was not exactly of goblin stock. The maw was not quite the same—it was blunter, the teeth barely insignificant nubs of bone. The ears were longer and set higher on the head, and lacked the distinctive flaps of leathery skin that resembled bats' wings. And the paws ended in fingers—not claws. "What manner of thing are you?" he asked, almost to himself.

"I am one of that most unhappy race of elementals that once roamed the hills and glens of the world you call the Shadowlands. But we were handed over to the sidhe by the humans, betrayed and bound into slavery. I come to you, Great Xerruw, for long years we have worked in silence and in solitude, tunneling down through the lowest reaches and we have reached your realm. We can lead you within the gates of the Faerie Queen herself, and you need never breach the walls."

Astounded, Xerruw stepped back. "So you would betray your masters? And what do you want of us? What would you ask in return?"

"We would destroy the Caul that binds us into these forms, so that we may return to our rightful homes within the Shadowlands."

Xerruw spread his hands and shrugged his shoulders. "Do with that accursed thing what you will. We'd not stop you."

"The Caul's disappeared."

"What?" Again, Xerruw spoke more to himself. He looked up into Iruk's eyes. So that was the answer to the riddle. Something had happened to the Caul. "Where—"

"No one knows. And if one does, no one is saying." The little thing seemed to stretch itself out. "They call me Khouri—it is not my name, but it is our name for our kind and so I accept it. I have come to offer you a treaty between our peoples, Great Xerruw. In exchange for access to the tunnels we have made beneath the caverns of the palace itself, we ask you to help us find the Caul. For it is only in the UnMaking of the Caul our bonds will be loosed forever."

"It stinks of sidhe magic, Great Xerruw," snarled Iruk. "Let me throw it off the battlements."

"No!" Xerruw snarled. He squatted down, so that he was nearly eye level with the creature. He sniffed. It smelled not in the least appetizing and the reek of the magic of the sidhe was strong on it. "How do you propose my warriors get through your tunnels? You're not the size of a hatchling half-grown."

"Are there not smaller ones?"

Xerruw glanced up at Iruk. The eggs now hatching—the clutches now breaking apart in mounds of stinking straw—those hatchlings would be just about this one's size. Right around the Longest Dark, just when the goblin power was at its height. The sidhe would expect an attack. But they would never expect an attack to come from within.

He rocked back on his haunches, eyes fixed on the creature before him. Iruk was right. It did reek of the sidhe. The odor that rose from its garments was nauseating up close.

No wonder it had been brave enough to walk into his hall. But how had it known it would be unappetizing? He put that puzzle aside to solve another day, then nodded, as he uncoiled himself and rose to his full height. "You have a bargain, little gobling. You get my warriors into the palace of the sidhe witch at the Longest Dark, and I will find the Silver Caul for you if I have to personally tear apart every sidhe witch and wizard to do it."

EPILOGUE

There was fire and there was nothing. The very air itself burned like a thousand red-hot needles, a searing agony that blazed through him every time he drew a breath. It boiled in his belly, a seething raging cauldron that bubbled up into a black void that was the only mercy the silver mines of Allovale offered. Lying alone, wrapped only in a mortal blanket that spared his flesh from the touch of that contaminated earth, Finuviel willed himself to stay alive long enough to visit such torment on Cadwyr's flesh and clung to his memories of a time before he'd known it was better to welcome pain, for only a surfeit of it brought relief.

To be continued...

An Interview with Anne Kelleher

Why do you write fantasy?

I write fantasy in the same way other people write poetry or songs—that's what seems to come out. It isn't that I set out to write epic fantasy. It just seems to be what I do best so far. It's not the only thing I see myself writing—and in fact, as you know, I've done four romances. But apart from the fact that I think fantasy is how my particular imagination best expresses itself, I also think that in fantasy, unlike any other type of fiction, one is free to create anything one can imagine. To hold in my hands one of my novels of epic fantasy is quite literally the tangible expression of my belief that all one can imagine, one can be, that all one can dream, one can do. For me as a writer, that translates to what I can imagine, I can write. What I can write, you can read. A fantasy novel is the encapsulation, in paper and ink, of the purest essence of the human imagination spun to its most epic levels.

Do you think fantasy's recent popularity is a reflection of a national mood?

I think that fantasy, like science fiction, provides a way to explore all sorts of what-ifs? What if an asteroid was hurtling toward earth? What if a great evil arose in the East and threatened all the various people around it? What if there really were magical folk among us of one sort or another? I think the current rise in interest in fantasy can at least partly be explained in that there does seem to be a cultural shift going on—a shift away from the old, patriarchal ways of thinking—and fantasy allows us to explore these various alternatives. I think one reason so many women are drawn to fantasy is that right now, against a still largely male dominated über-culture, if you will, it's in fantasy that one can create and explore a matriarchal culture, for example. My current trilogy is heavily drawn from Celtic mythology, which is more female-friendly than the more familiar Greco-Roman, Judeo-Christian mythologies. I don't think the current rise in interest in fantasy is just about escape. I think it's more about exploring alternatives. Fantasy is in some ways the most subversive of all fiction, because it challenges established beliefs. The ideas that drive cultural change can be explored in heroic proportions. I think that's one reason people are more interested in reading fantasy right now—there's a general dissatisfaction with the status quo. The times, as they always do, are changing, and I think one reason to explain fantasy's popularity is that it serves as a kind of sounding board where alternative ideas can be as safely explored and considered as alternative ideas ever can be.

Who are your favorite authors?

J.R.R. Tolkien, Ursula Le Guin, Madeleine L'Engle, C.S. Lewis, Jane Austen, Emily Brontë, Margaret Atwood, Jodi Picoult.